Beyond the

by
Karenne Griffin

To Max

Enjoy!

Best wishes
from Karenne
x

www.publishnation.co.uk

Dedication

In memory of my father, Dr Noel Loveday Sullivan

www.publishnation.co.uk

Chapter 1

It was a warm spring morning in Sydney and the sun glinted fiercely off seemingly millions of panes of glass. A faint grey pall of smog hung over the central business district, surmounted by the clearer blue of the stratosphere. The harbour bridge swept dramatically past, quite close to where Robyn Trescowe sat at her desk on the eleventh floor of one of the office blocks comprising the heart of the city. Her mind drifted from the task in hand. Gee, statistics were boring.

It was only twenty to eleven. Robyn frittered away ten minutes counting the number of Porsches crawling across the chunk of bridge she could see from her window. Three, and two of them were red. To her regret she wasn't close enough to be able to check out the drivers properly. From this distance it was too easy to mistake long-haired women for potentially hunky long-haired surfer-type men. She wondered idly whether Harrier Reynolds would consider moving to an office with a better view of the bridge. Robyn's thoughts drifted towards the weekend, even though it was only Tuesday. She wondered what Delia was planning to wear to Jason's party on Saturday night, and reached for her mobile. But before she was able to call her best buddy the phone on her desk chirruped insistently.

'Robyn, my office. Now,' barked her boss.

'Yes, Nick,' said Robyn brightly into the phone. 'I'll be there right away.'

'Oh, help!' she thought, springing to her feet before she'd put down the phone. As she struggled back into the high-heeled shoes she'd slipped off under her desk she winced from both the tightness of black patent leather and the effort of concocting an excuse, for no doubt Nick was chasing her progress with the statistical exercise. Unless he was completely fed up with waiting and had decided to give her the sack.

At that moment Casey returned from the coffee machine and parked his hefty beige-chino-clad buttocks on the corner of her desk.

'I'll be there right away,' he mimicked in a ridiculous falsetto that sounded nothing like Robyn. 'I'll run up the stairs and come flying to your side. Your wish is my command, O Master! Robyn, you're such an arse licker,' he added in his own lower register.

Robyn balled up a piece of paper and threw it at Casey, grinning all the while. By the time her missile found its target she was already half way across the office. Casey caught a glimpse of her traffic-stopping red dress as it disappeared and reappeared from behind filing cabinets and large potted plants. He shook his head and smiled.

When she had started working at Harrier Reynolds Robyn instantly found a rapport with Casey. His camp sense of humour had her continually in stitches. It was a wonder they ever got any work done. However she still didn't quite know what to make of Nick Robinson. He had been her boss for nearly six months, but she didn't actually see that much of him. He spent a lot of time away at meetings. The consultancy business was like that. The lower orders did all the research and groundwork, and the top dogs took their findings to meetings. Robyn had been thrilled to get a job as a researcher straight out of University. Some of her friends were working in petrol stations and supermarkets, and others were still unemployed. She knew she had much to be thankful for, even on those days when all she did was tot up boring old statistics. At the end of the day surely nobody really cared how long it took a courier to deliver a package?

Robyn was nearing the end of her trial period at Harrier Reynolds. She hoped she had a future with the firm; it was difficult to know what was on Nick's mind. He had never actually offered any praise, and could be quick to lose his temper if he didn't get exactly what he asked for.

Robyn tapped timidly on the bright blue door and entered at Nick's barked acknowledgement.

***

The white Rolls Royce took the hill easily in its stride, and the glittering promise of Mount's Bay came into view. The three Trethewey children on the back seat gasped with delight. George wound down the window and leaned out, shading his eyes as he sought out familiar landmarks. He loved their summer holidays in Cornwall. His sister Josephine crowded his position at the window.

'Oh, look, George! Donkey rides on the beach!' she enthused.

Their younger brother Lucien jigged up and down excitedly. St Michael's Mount stood darkly silhouetted against the shimmering, calm sea. This year George was determined to walk all the way there from Newlyn.

Caroline Trethewey, or Lady Kenner as she preferred to be known, sat bolt upright beside her husband, but turned her head slightly to the right as they passed an imposing house set in beautifully kept gardens. This was Bellerive, summer residence of Hubert and Madeleine St Clair. Apart from being members of Parisian high society they were bohemian, flamboyant, hospitable ... Lady Kenner smiled secretly in anticipation of a wonderful summer.

'George, do sit down!' snapped Charles Trethewey. 'And you too, Josephine. It is hardly becoming for a young lady to lark about like a hooligan.'

George and Josephine did as they were told. George knew that if they toed the line at the start of their holiday any later minor transgressions at least had a chance of passing without comment.

Josephine didn't really care if Father thought she was behaving childishly, but she sat down anyway. The sight of the sea always made her heart leap ridiculously. She longed to scrunch her toes in the warm sand and feel the cool wash of the frothy tide around her ankles. George and Josephine exchanged knowing glances. They had of course noted that, as usual, Lucien had not been reprimanded. At five he was still tediously mollycoddled by their mother, and the little puss could do no wrong as far as either parent was concerned. He had the knack of creating six kinds of mayhem and returning innocently to his seat before their parents came upon the scene of the crime. George and Josephine had lost count of the number of times they had been blamed in error for the misdeeds of their little brother.

Josephine had overheard Flora, her mother's maid, saying to Cook that Lucien was spoiled rotten because of Her Ladyship's inability to have more children. Whether or not this was true, it hardly made preferential treatment fair.

The Rolls Royce purred smoothly and silently along the sea front towards Penzance, attracting curious glances from promenading holidaymakers. Charles Trethewey smiled smugly at his wife and tapped on the glass partition with his cane. 'Straight on to Roskenner please, Carrington,' he instructed.

Caroline caught a glimpse of her husband at her side. Charles Barrington Arbuthnot Montague Trethewey – Lord Kenner. Ugly, piggy little eyes and a fat red nose surmounted his prim mouth. He was opinionated, snobbish, narrow-minded and simply no fun at all. But he was rich. Madame de Crespigny had done her homework before sending her young daughter to

London for the Season, and Lord Kenner had been one of the men she had set her sights on. Caroline knew it was pointless wondering whether she would have been any happier married to any of the other men on *Maman's* list. Someone younger might have been preferable. Still, Charles being more than twenty years her senior made it likely that he would predecease her. Though at sixty he seemed sprightly enough to go on forever. Caroline bit her lip and looked out at the cheerful seaside scene beyond the car window. Hermetically sealed in her cocoon of wealth, Caroline consoled herself with the knowledge that she would never again know the poverty of her early years in Paris, and that she and her children had the best of everything that money could buy ... that Charles's money could buy.

***

'Ah, Robyn. Take a seat,' said Nick Robinson, flashing the smile that helped earn him his nickname: The Shark. No man should have that many sharp, white teeth, thought Robyn as she crossed the pristine navy carpet and perched awkwardly on a stylish chrome and leather chair.

'So, Robyn. How are you finding things at Harrier Reynolds?'

Nick steepled his fingers and her eyes were drawn to their movement. He raised his eyebrows, poised menacingly for her reply.

'The work is, ah, interesting. And challenging. I think I'm picking it up quite well,' she added, hoping this wasn't a step too far.

Nick lowered his gaze and picked an imaginary speck off his sleeve.

'I have a proposition for you,' he said. 'One which I hope you will find interesting.'

At least it didn't sound like she was about to get the sack. So what was the proposition?

Nick moved over to the window and adjusted the blind.

'I understand you have British citizenship as well as Australian.'

'That's right,' said Robyn. 'My parents were born in England.'

'I need to send someone to England for two months on a fact-finding mission for one of our clients. Sending someone with a British passport would save us the bother of having to apply for a visa at short notice. You'd need to leave in about a week. We'd pay you the equivalent of your present salary in Pounds Sterling plus generous living expenses. And a car allowance, of course. How does that sound?' he asked, giving her the full force of his brown eyes.

Robyn felt like a stunned bunny caught in headlights. She thought quickly. Today was Tuesday. There was the party on Saturday night, but she could be ready any time after that ...

'Sounds fine,' she replied with a calmness she certainly wasn't feeling.

As Nick talked through the practicalities Robyn felt her insides dissolve in a huge, fizzy rish of adrenaline like a hangover cure dropped into a glass of water. As she left Nick's office she had to fight the urge to run down the corridor, whooping and turning cartwheels. As she burst into her own office she indulged in a short aeroplane ride to her desk. Casey peered at her over his glasses.

'Someone's in a good mood,' he observed.

'Someone's going on a business trip to England for two months,' she replied with a grin. 'Ah, the sacrifices I make in the line of duty ...'

Casey's eyes widened. 'Wow! Who's a lucky ducky. When?'

'Sir Nicholas will let me know later today, but I expect I'll be leaving in about a week. Celebratory doughnuts are on me. Jam, or chocolate icing?'

'Ooh, both! I told you not to get your knickers in a knot about the trial period, didn't I?' shouted Casey as Robyn disappeared through the door and popped into the lift.

Once at the ground floor she clattered across an expanse of highly polished granite and out into the sunshine, her mind fixed on the forthcoming trip. Her shoulder-length brown hair rippled and glinted in the sun as she trotted along the street in the direction of Doughnut Desire. Robyn sent a silent prayer of thanks to her parents for being born British. They had taken Robyn and her brother to England for a couple of years when Grandma was too old and frail to cope by herself. Robyn had been just five when they returned to Australia after her grandmother's death, but she still remembered the gentle, white-haired woman and her lovely garden. She also remembered getting into trouble for breaking one of her china cups.

Back in the office, having supplied Casey with sufficient doughnuts and coffee to sink a lesser man, Robyn took her coffee out onto the fire escape and used her mobile phone to call her mother.

'Estelle for Hair, how can I help you?' said a cheesy voice at the other end.

'G'day, Stella,' said Robyn. 'Is Mum there, please?'

'Just a moment, chickie.' Stella called everybody chickie, even the health inspector. Robyn could hear her mother's voice coming closer. Rose Trescowe rarely stopped talking; you couldn't even count on silence when she was asleep. Working a hairdressing salon suited her very nicely. She had no qualifications but was happy to sweep the floor, wash clients' hair and do anything else she could to help her friend and neighbour, Stella Papagyrios.

'Hello, Robbie. What a nice surprise to hear your voice,' chortled Rose.

When Rose heard her daughter's good news she was overjoyed. 'You must go and visit Uncle Morvah and Auntie Emily and ...'

'Whoa there, Mum! I'm going over there to work. But I will try to fit in some family visits. I'll be in Hampshire, which probably isn't very far from the rellies. Now I reckon I'd better get back to work or Nick might change his mind. I just wanted to let you know. I'll pop in to see you tonight and we can talk properly then.' Robyn ended her call and took a swig of her coffee. Ugh! Cold.

***

Lord Kenner's Rolls Royce stopped outside an imposing set of gates. Their gardener, Cuthbert, nodded a welcome and stepped forward to open the gates, revealing the grandeur of Roskenner House, the Trethewey family home. Since their marriage eighteen years previously Lord Kenner and his wife had religiously journeyed south-west from London in the last week of June each year, returning to their London residence in the first week of September. Lord Kenner excused himself from the company of his family from time to time in order to return to London for business reasons, but Lady Caroline retreated into her inner circle of local nobility, glad to leave the social hurly-burly of London to its own devices for two months. Despite being a city girl born and bred she liked the clear skies and freedom of summer in Cornwall.

The car motored slowly down an avenue of spruces and scrunched to a sedate halt on the gravel next to a shallow flight of stone steps leading to the front door. Carrington opened the car door for His Lordship, but George wrenched the back door open with impatience and the three children tumbled out, stretching their cramped limbs. It was a long journey, even in a car that was the height of modern technology in 1925. They were greeted by a grey-haired dumpling of a woman in a white apron.

'Why, Miss Josephine, how you've grown! And Master George,' she added as an afterthought, though she knew the poor lamb would be small even as an adult. Polio was a dreadful illness.

'I've grown three inches since last summer,' pouted Lucien, irritated that the stupid woman hadn't appeared to notice him.

6

'Why, so you have, young man,' said Mrs Cuthbert evenly. She had no desire to start off on the wrong foot with Her Ladyship's little pet, a tetchy child at the best of times. 'You're going to be a tall one, and no mistake,' she added for good measure, turning to bob a curtsey to the Lord and his Lady.

'Mawson and his wife, and Flora, will be arriving tomorrow by train,' said Lady Caroline for the benefit of Mrs Cuthbert, wishing to make it plain that she would be expected to cook and generally make do until the full retinue arrived.

Mrs Cuthbert knew that once Carrington had unloaded the luggage and put the car away he wouldn't lift a finger until he was required to resume chauffeur's duties. Carrington considered himself a London gent, just a shade below the status of Lord Kenner, and would not deign to muck in and help.

Josephine lifted her skirts and hurried upstairs to her room. She flung the window wide open, breathing deeply of the warm sea air. The sea itself hung in a bright blue chunk below the horizon, only partly obscured by the woods surrounding Roskenner House.

Josephine flopped onto the window seat, resting her elbows on the warm sandstone sill. She had been born at Roskenner and felt more at home here than in London. She took after her father's side of the family, and they were Cornish through and through. Fortunately she was much better looking than her father.

Her great grandfather had started the tin mine that made the family fortune and enabled him to build Roskenner House in the early 1800s. She marvelled that the house was now over 100 years old. The hall was liberally hung with family portraits, and Josephine knew that with her curly auburn hair and distinctive hazel eyes she carried the family likeness. Her mother's people were descended from French nobility, with pale complexions and straight, dark hair. George took after *Maman*. Lucien was blond and blue-eyed, a bit of a misfit. Maybe his hair would darken as he grew older.

Josephine sighed happily. It was bliss being back at Roskenner, looking out over the sea as it twinkled invitingly in the sun. She longed for lunch to be over so that she could cycle round to Gwennap Head and stare out over the blue vastness of the ocean and feel the breeze pull playfully at her curls. She loved the sea, even on grey days when the wind whipped it to steely peaks that crashed onto the rocks below Gwennap Head, seeming to suck the life of the land back into its depths. Josephine sometimes dreamed of the sea, of falling down, down, down into its depths, but somehow being able to breathe and not feel any fear. In reality she was afraid, knowing that if she did fall from the cliff she would be pounded to a pulp against the rocks. 'Respect the sea, for the sea does not respect you,' was one of her grandfather's favourite sayings. Josephine had loved to listen to her grandfather's tales of his voyages on the tea clipper *Esmeralda*. Grandfather had been the black sheep of his generation, having sidestepped management of the mine. Sadly Grandfather had died a few years earlier.

At first Josephine had thought a tea clipper was some kind of silver instrument, sort of like a candle-snuffer, used for clipping the tender young shoots of tea leaves from the bushes. Luckily she'd leanred the truth before uttering her foolishness for the ridicule of the rest of the family. George was less vindictive now he was fourteen, but up until recently he'd gone to great lengths to score points over his older sister. Josephine knew he resented the heavy iron calliper he was sentenced to wear for the rest of his life, and that he was jealous of her long-limbed freedom to run like the wind.

The relationship between Josephine and George had gradually improved since the arrival of Lucien. Right from the start their mother had favoured the chubby, pink baby to the exclusion of her other children. George and Josephine had a private nickname for the spoiled baby: The Frog. He had resembled a pink frog, lying with legs and arms akimbo in his basket. And now that he was five there was still something decidedly froggy about his prominent eyes and cold, detached stare. He was a calculating child, old beyond his years. Josephine didn't trust him as far as she could throw him, and as he was a plump little boy, that wouldn't be very far. Sometimes when he was being particularly tedious she fantasised about throwing him off Gwennap Head on a stormy day, and watching his blond head disappear below the waves. She knew this was extremely wicked, and asked God to forgive her for thinking such a thing.

Chapter 2

By the end of the day Robyn's flight had been booked for a week Saturday. As she lurched towards Newtown on a crowded bus her mind was far away, already on a plane bound for London.

Robyn shared a flat with Jenna and Tony. The trio lived independently, and sometimes several days could pass before they were all at home at the same time. This was no bad thing considering the size of the flat. It was located in a street mostly comprising modern blocks of flats that looked rather like piles of children's building blocks the way they stacked into the hillside. As the lift ground reluctantly up to the ninth floor, Robyn mulled over the packing list she had composed in her head. Would three jumpers be enough? It was difficult to think about winter clothing on a warm afternoon.

Robyn detoured to the kitchen to fill a glass with iced water from the fridge, slipped one of Tony's questionable heavy metal CDs into the player and stepped out onto the balcony. The faint breeze stirred her hair, and the early evening sun glowed on her olive skin. Robyn did not equate to text-book definitions of beauty (and she hated her long nose and flat chest), but her youth, energy, clear complexion and long legs, not to mention the smile which lit her hazel eyes from within, made the sum of the parts seem more attractive than when analyzed independently.

The insistent ringing of the telephone penetrated the roar of the rush hour and Death Metal in Overdrive, and Robyn slipped back into the living room to retrieve the cordless phone from beneath a cushion. The caller was Delia.

'Deedles! Guess what?' shrieked Robyn. 'I'm going to England for two months! I leave in less than two weeks!'

'WHAT?' screeched Delia in reply.

'You heard me. During the course of the day I've become a jet set businesswoman. Nick the Shark wants me to do some research for him.'

Delia had the hots for Nick Robinson, and Robyn knew Delia would be green with envy to think that her friend had been singled out for special attention.

'Gee, babe, I don't know what to say. Congratulations sounds a bit feeble. Hey, you'll be able to see all the London shows …'

'I won't be staying in London. The company I'll be working for is in Hampshire, some distance south west. But I expect I'll be able to get up to London some weekends.'

'Wow! It's like a dream come true! You'd have to save for ages to do this on your own.'

'Speaking of dreams, Deedles, I had the strangest one last night. I nearly drowned, and I got washed up on a desert island.'

'Sounds like you had too many beers before bedtime. And dreams about water usually have something to do with sex, I believe.'

'You're probably right, as always.'

'Trust me, Robs. I usually am. Hey, I've just had a thought. You'll miss Mad Terry's party next month.'

Robyn's heart sank. Mad Terry's parties were unmissable. But what sort of excuse would that make to forego the trip of a lifetime?

'Sorry, Dee. Terry'll just have to get by without me,' she replied with a sigh and glanced at her watch. 'I'd better go. I'm due at the family mansion for dinner.'

Delia snorted. 'My commiserations. What is it tonight? Cod and cucumber parcels with passionfruit sauce?'

The two friends laughed in unison. They would never forget the torture of Rose's gourmet cookery course.

'Hey, I've just had a thought,' said Robyn. 'Would you like to look after Rover while I'm away? I can put you on the insurance policy.'

Delia was almost speechless with gratitude. She was a small-time actress and couldn't afford a car. 'Robbie, you're the best! I'll take the greatest care of him.'

'You'd better,' added Robyn sternly. 'Anyway, must dash. I'll sort out the details. Seeya later, alligator!'

As Robyn replaced the receiver she wondered why Delia had rung. Conversations with her friend were like that sometimes.

Robyn showered quickly and changed into a little flowery dress that made her look demure and daughterly. Grabbing her handbag she cantered down the staircase to the basement car park where Rover lay in wait. Rover was not a Rover, but an elderly blue Volkswagen Beetle. His engine started obediently, and with Robyn's practised guidance he chugged noisily up the exit ramp.

It was nearly half past seven by the time Robyn brought Rover to a sedate halt outside her parents home in Roseville, one of Sydney's North Shore suburbs. It was only a handful of miles from the Harbour Bridge but a different world altogether from the business district. The setting sun cast a mellow glow over quiet suburbia. Robyn bypassed the stepping-stone path to the front door and entered by the side gate that led to the back door. Her mother was preoccupied with chopping fruit, but looked up when she heard the screen door squeak in protest at being opened.

'Hello Robbie!' said Rose Trescowe with a broad smile. 'I've told your Dad the great news already. He's in the lounge watching the cricket. Did you know he went to the doctor today?'

'No, Mum. Is he all right?'

'He has to have some tests at the hospital, but he says they're just routine. Go on in and say hello, I'm nearly finished here.'

Robyn left the cramped kitchen and walked down the hall to the lounge.

Joseph Trescowe reached for the remote control as soon as he saw his daughter.

'Hello, love. I hear you're off gallivanting.'

Robyn smiled broadly. 'Great news, huh? Anyway, what's this I hear about you seeing the doctor?'

'Probably just a bit of indigestion, love. Dr Wilson has referred me to the hospital for some tests. Don't worry. I'll let you know as soon as I get the results. I'll send you an email.'

Robyn smiled. Despite his manual job and previous lack of interest in modern technology her father had picked up computer skills with ease, and enjoyed surfing the net as much as the average teenager. He often emailed his daughter at work instead of telephoning.

Joseph opened a drawer of the desk in the corner of the room and brought out an envelope.

'Since you're going to England I thought you might be able to do something for me. There are some things that puzzle me about our forebears. I've drawn up the family tree and highlighted the gaps. I've also prepared some helpful information. Addresses of relatives, places to make enquiries and stuff. I know you've got a job to do, but maybe you can find some time ...'

'Sure, Dad. I won't have anything much else to do in my spare time. Two months is a lot of wet weekends.'

Robyn stuffed the envelope in her handbag. Their conversation was cut short by the arrival of Robyn's brother Steve with his wife, Giulietta, and their three year old son Joey. Joey ran to his grandfather and climbed on his lap. Robyn couldn't help noticing that her father winced slightly as he stood up and lifted Joey above his head.

'How's my favourite grandson, then?' he asked with a grin, placing the small boy gently on the floor.

Giulietta handed Robyn a gift with a smile that brought her serious face to life.

'Jules, what's this?' asked Robyn.

'Just a little something for your trip.'

Robyn eased off the wrapping paper. It was a travel diary.

'You can write about the places you visit, then keep it forever to remind you.'

'Gee, thanks. It's lovely,' replied Robyn, meanwhile thinking that she could write about her travels much more quickly and legibly on the laptop Nick was lending her for the trip. But she had no intention of bursting her sister-in-law's bubble and spoiling the moment. Although they were both twenty-one the two girls were very different. The daughter of Italian immigrants, Giulietta had met Steve at school and they had started dating when she was fourteen. She had been just seventeen when they married, and eighteen when Giuseppe Antonio was born. Giulietta was content as a stay-at-home wife and mother. Robyn, on the other hand, didn't yet know whether she would ever want to marry, let alone have the responsibility of children. For the moment she couldn't think beyond the excitement of her forthcoming trip.

'Dinner's ready!' called Rose from the kitchen. 'Come and help me carry everything out into the garden, it'll be much cooler out there.'

The family trooped obediently towards the kitchen. As she carried the salad bowl out to the table under the colourful bougainvillea vine Robyn wished just for a moment that she didn't have to go to England. Summer was her favourite time of year, and she knew she would miss these family dinners at the long table in the garden. Everyone said that winter in England could be cold, wet and miserable. But then again, she'd only be gone two months. Nick had explained that the extra responsibilities of representing Harrier Reynolds abroad would stand her in good stead for promotion when she returned. Robyn didn't want to spend the rest of her life assessing statistics, after all.

***

The following morning Lady Kenner cast a despairing eye over her daughter.

'Josephine, do sit up properly and eat your porridge,' she said, trying not to betray her growing irritation. One disagreement with Josephine over breakfast was quite enough.

Josephine shot her mother a look of disdain. Josephine was stubborn, like her father. Charles had declined the invitation to join the rest of the family in a visit to Hubert and Madeleine St Clair at their home near Marazion. He said he had already made plans to check on a consignment of tin, but Caroline knew that her husband would probably spend the morning in his study with his pipe and newspaper. She on the other hand couldn't wait to visit her friends, to lapse comfortably into the French language and catch up on the gossip from Paris. Letters from her mother were few and far between. The children were usually happy to play on the beach while the adults sat in the shade of the trees, but it appeared Josephine had other ideas today. She had some wild idea of walking the coastal path, and had been quite short-tempered at the prospect of visiting *chez* St Clair. Caroline put the irritability down to hormones. The girl was sixteen, almost a woman.

George diplomatically broached a more neutral topic.

'I wonder who will win the yacht race this year?' he ventured, chasing the last of his porridge round the bowl. 'I hope it's Josh Polvean. It was such a shame that his boat capsized last year.'

Charles Trethewey regarded his son over the rim of his half-moon spectacles.

'Does this mean you're taking an interest in sailing, George?'

Charles felt a glimmer of hope. His son's physical disability had so far put paid to sporting activities, but perhaps he could manage to sail a small boat.

'I quite enjoy it, Papa,' replied George, his face growing pink. 'Monty let me have a try when I stayed with him at half term.'

'Well, we'll have to see that you get some more experience this summer. Carstairs is coming down soon. I know he has a smart little boat. I'll make some enquiries.'

Charles Trethewey would gladly have rushed out that very morning and bought the finest sailboat that money could buy, but he tried not to favour George over the other children.

'I want to go sailing too!' wailed Lucien, his lower lip jutting forward petulantly.

'First you must learn to swim, dear,' said Caroline.

'I *can* swim!' objected the small boy.

George's eyes twinkled mirthfully. 'Yes, Lucien. Just like a fish. Underwater, blowing bubbles.'

Lucien's face puckered and grew red, denoting impending tears.

'Enough, boys!' said Caroline briskly. 'Now, the three of you may leave the table and gather your beach things. We'll be leaving in half an hour.'

As it was such a pleasant day, Lady Caroline decided that she and her three children would walk to Marazion. She hoped this would partly appease Josephine's desire for a walk by the sea.

As they set off down the drive she marvelled at the way the sun glittered on the calm blue sea, framed by the avenue of tall, dark green spruces. She wished she could stay at Roskenner all year round. As she grew older she realised she was becoming bored with the London social scene, and would ideally like to spend her days walking by the sea and cultivating the garden. She knew *Maman* would be appalled at her daughter living like a peasant!

They walked past Newlyn harbour. George stared wistfully out at two yachts swiftly plying the waves out beyond the calm waters of the bay, and hoped that his father wouldn't forget to speak with Lord Carstairs. He hung back, filling his lungs with salty air, lost in the remembered feeling of the wind in his hair and the water slipping by at close range under the hull of Monty's boat.

'Do come on, George!' called his mother.

'Sorry!' he replied, making an effort to increase his pace and catch up to the others despite the pain in his shin and the weight of the calliper on his left leg. Sometimes he dreamed that he could fly above the earth without even flapping his arms, and he wished dreams could come true.

The sun was high in the sky by the time they reached Bellerive, the St Clair summer residence. Madeleine and Hubert St Clair spent their winters in Paris or Monte Carlo. Sometimes one would go to Monte Carlo and the other would go to Paris, or vice versa, never mind the gossip that ensued.

Bellerive was an imposing sandstone house surrounded by extensive gardens. The four visitors entered an ornate gate and the scent of the roses and lavender in full bloom tantalised Lady Caroline's senses. They followed a long, golden stone path through the gardens to a shallow flight of steps at the front of the house.

The Trethewey party had no need to ring the doorbell. The butler opened the door as they drew near, and ushered them into the cool, dim drawing room. Madeleine St Clair joined them after a short pause.

'My dear Caroline!' she gushed, embracing her friend. 'And *mes enfants*! 'Ow you are growing! Ah, Caroline, you grow more lovely every day!'

Caroline smiled her gracious assent to Madeleine's flattery.

The two women started twittering in French. Josephine was bored already. She couldn't help thinking that it would be peculiar if she and her brothers hadn't grown from one summer to the next. Why did grown-ups always make such a fuss about children growing up? Madeleine St Clair was a stupid, fatuous old fool.

As they chatted, Caroline felt confident of her superiority to the plump, red-faced woman. Madeleine looked like a badly stuffed sofa; she must have gained ten pounds since they had last met. Hubert and Madeleine had no children. They were in their forties, a little older than herself, and Madeleine was a few years older than Hubert. Although Caroline had grown weary of London society she never tired of talk of the Parisian social scene. She loved news of the girls she and Madeleine had known at *Lycee Hermione Armand*, the expensive school upon which Caroline's mother had spent the last of her inheritance in order to give her daughter *entrée* into the most fashionable clique. None of Caroline's old friends bothered to correspond since she had defected to Britain, but she delighted in news of their marriages and affairs – particularly the affairs. Sometimes she felt almost faint with excitement when Madeleine imparted choice details of a dalliance. Caroline often wondered whether Madeleine knew what went on between Hubert and herself when they were able to steal an afternoon alone together. Hubert always maintained polite aloofness in company, giving no clue in public to his physical attraction, but somehow Caroline felt that Madeleine knew everything and that she had unwittingly become part of a dangerous game the couple played. But there was no going back.

Madeleine ushered the party out through the French windows and across the lawn. The gate at the far end of the garden was open, and Caroline could see a shady awning positioned where the lawn gave way to the sands.

'I 'ave everthing in place under the trees,' chortled Madeleine as she trotted behind them. 'Come, sit in the shade.'

They did as they were bidden. As Madeleine poured cool lemon drinks, Caroline noticed Hubert strolling towards them. A thrill shot through the core of her soul. It had been simply months since they had last managed a couple of hours together in London at the home of one of Hubert's associates who was absent on business. She felt her face grow pink at the memory of their antics in front of the drawing room fire.

Hubert beamed, taking in the pleasing sight of Caroline and her offspring assembled under the trees.

'Good afternoon, Lady Caroline,' he said formally without making eye contact, kissing both her cheeks mechanically.

He shook Lucien and George formally by the hand. As he reached to take Josephine's hand Hubert stopped in his tracks.

'And who is this charming young lady? Surely not *la petite* Josephine!'

Caroline suppressed a pang of irritation.

Hubert placed his hands on Josephine's shoulders and kissed each of her fresh, youthful cheeks. Josephine was partly flattered at his recognition of her new-found maturity, and partly repelled by the man. A deep-seated instinct told her not to trust Monsieur St Clair. His wife was a fool, but there was something undeniably not quite right about him.

The children drifted away as soon as the adult conversation began in earnest. They had no interest in tales of people they had never met. They took turns changing in the bathing tent and took their buckets and spades onto the firm, wet sand at the water's edge where they set about building sand castles. The sea was very calm, and only the smallest of waves lapped delicately at the shore. Josephine found that she still enjoyed such childish pastimes, and her irritation at having to join this family outing was soothed by the warmth of the sun beating on her skin despite the thick navy blue swimming costume that modestly covered her body.

Caroline momentarily turned her attention away from details of Marielle Charentaine's liaison with Philippe Leclerc. She could see her three children playing in the sand, seemingly happy in each other's company. She knew that before long Lucien was bound to come running, but for the moment all was well. The gin in the fruit punch induced a sense of summer-time laziness and well-being, and she turned back to Madeleine's ruinous gossip.

'I'm all covered in sand!' protested Lucien, looking down at the greyish sludge that clung to his legs.

'You can wash it off in the water, silly!' said George. He looked down at his own legs that were also covered in wet sand, knowing that there would be trouble later if his calliper became rusty. But for the moment he didn't care. He was happy to sit at the water's edge making sand castles with his brother and sister. The tribulations of living with a malformed leg faded temporarily into insignificance.

'Lucien, don't walk out too far,' cautioned Josephine. But suddenly, with a squeal, Lucien slipped underwater. Josephine hurried to his assistance, but he was some ten yards away and her bathing costume hindered swift movement through the rapidly deepening water.

Lucien surfaced, gasping and spluttering. Josephine glanced back at George, who was pacing fretfully in the shallows.

'Go and get help!' she shouted, waving her arms in the hope that the grown-ups might see.

George turned immediately and hobbled up the beach. Meanwhile Josephine didn't seem to be getting any closer to Lucien. With horror she realised that the current was carrying him out into even deeper water. She could see the line of demarcation between light blue, shallow water and the darker, deep water. Lucien was almost at that point. And his struggles were becoming feeble.

Panic drove her desperately onward. Then she started to swim, striking out towards the little head just visible on the surface. She seemed to be swimming quite fast but getting no closer. Then she realised that she too was caught in the current and it was sweeping them further out into the bay.

Then, without a sound, Lucien's head disappeared beneath the surface of the water. Josephine began to sob, which made swimming more difficult. Reason told her that she had to calm herself and regulate her breathing. She trod water for a moment, turning back to the beach. George had only just managed to alert the adults, and they were running towards the water. Josephine turned back, searching the surface of the water for any indication of Lucien's presence, but he was nowhere to be seen. Panic stabbed her heart. There was no escaping the swift current. She was helpless in its grip, and she knew she couldn't stay afloat much longer.

Chapter 3

As she floated, Josephine realised she was being carried far out to sea by a tremendously strong tide. Swimming being quite pointless, she tried to conserve her energy by breathing evenly and trying not to panic. Surely the tiny figures on the distant beach would somehow send a boat to rescue her?

Then Josephine realised she could hardly see the beach, let alone determine what possible rescue activity was taking place. To her dismay she noticed she had drifted far beyond the reassuring sentinel of St Michael's Mount.

Her swimming costume felt heavy, as though it was trying to drag her under. Cold seeped treacherously into her flesh, threatening to sap her remaining strength. She was terrified by the sheer depth of the sea, and dared not look down into the murky, dark waters. She had no idea how much time had elapsed. Surely a boat would come soon? She clung to the thought of strong arms reaching down to pull her on board, of being taken home and put into a bed with soft, warm, dry blankets. She thought longingly of hot soup and her mother's soothing voice. She also thought miserably of Lucien, and hoped that the grown-ups had managed to pull him out of the water and revive him. Lucien was very annoying, but she would never really have wished death by drowning upon him. She envisaged her mother fussing over Lucien. Perhaps that was why they were so long in coming for her? However a ghostly voice in the back of her mind suggested it was quite possible that Lucien had drowned.

Josephine wanted to believe that death by drowning would be much like falling into an eternal, dreamless sleep. She didn't want to think about the pale, gelatinous, lifeless body of her little brother being tumbled back and forth on the sea bed, nibbled by fish or crawled over by crabs. She put such thoughts as far as possible from consciousness, in the hope that if she did she could ward off the threat of her own death by drowning.

Josephine blinked the salty water from her tired eyes, hardly believing what she had seen. Was it a boat? Something was definitely coming towards her. With a pang of regret she realised that the object was too small to be a boat. It looked rather like a life preserver. It was! As it swirled by, Josephine desperately flung her cold, leaden arm over the hard, white ring and held on for dear life. Written on it in large, black letters were the words *'Queen Maud'*. Josephine wondered what had become of the ship and its passengers. This took her mind off her own plight for a short while.

The rolling swell gathered momentum as Josephine was swept further from the shore. At first she struggled as she and her life preserver were swept up and flung over the crest of a wave, but the movement soon attained a lurching monotony and she surrendered herself to it. The passing of time became a blur of sea and sky. Josephine drifted into a state approaching unconsciousness, numbly cold and by now very, very weary.

George lay alone, panting, on the sand. *Maman* and the St Clairs had reached the edge of the water, and he could hear their cries. He watched as Monsieur St Clair stripped to his underclothing and dived into the sea, swimming powerfully out to the deeper water where he dived repeatedly, searching frantically for Lucien and Josephine. George cradled his head in sand-caked arms and sobbed. He knew in his heart that searching was futile; both his sister and brother had drowned.

Josephine awoke in darkness. She'd been having a terrible nightmare. No nightmare had ever seemed so real. Gradually her foggy sensibilities focused on the realisation that this was no nightmare. All that existed was cold darkness, the surge of the tide, and her cramped arms clutching the life preserver. She slipped back into drifting semi-consciousness. The pain of extreme cold that had stabbed into her very soul was now receding. All she could feel was a dull ache, and that was lessening as she slipped further away. Then, with a jolt, she realised that something had touched her left foot. She jerked her foot away, panic snapping her back into consciousness. Was it a shark? Or some other horror of the deep, waiting to rip off her legs as they dangled from the surface. She thrashed and struggled, and the pain of extreme cold returned with a vengeance. Josephine had resigned herself to slipping gradually into an endless sleep, but now it seemed that a more gruesome death awaited her.

***

As she prepared for bed, Robyn flipped through the folder of papers on her bedside table. Her itinerary, insurance documents, and the airline tickets for her departure on October 21st. Tomorrow. Well, today, actually. It was

19

just past midnight. How could she possibly sleep? Nick had called her for a final briefing just before six p.m. All afternoon various colleagues had been dropping by, expressing a mixture of good wishes and envy. After the meeting with Nick she had felt like a school kid on the last day of term as she hurried back to her office and grabbed her handbag before Casey swept her off to a lively tapas bar for a riotous session. Despite having drunk rather a lot of tequila, Robyn was still wide awake.

Shortly after seven a.m. Robyn surfaced from a restless sleep. She encountered Jenna outside the bathroom.

'Hi! Heavy night?' enquired Jenna.

'Gee, do I look that rough?' Robyn replied, running a hand through her tangled hair.

'Nah. What time do you leave?'

'Delia's coming to get me at nine. The flight leaves at twenty past one.'

'Loads of time, if Tony ever comes out of the bathroom. What on earth can he be doing?'

'I'm putting on my make-up,' replied a falsetto trill from behind the bathroom door. 'If that excuse works for you two girls there must be some mileage in it for me,' Tony added in his normal voice.

Jenna pulled a face.

'Gee, I'm going to miss you guys!' said Robyn with a sigh.

'But you won't miss queueing for the bathroom,' said Jenna.

'You never know, I may have to share my next bathroom with more than two.'

'Gawd! I hope not.'

Robyn eventually claimed the bathroom for long enough to take a reviving shower, and she was dressed and ready by the time Delia arrived.

'Nervous, babe?' enquired Delia as she helped Robyn into the lift with her luggage.

'Nah. Flying's a piece of cake.'

'Flying to London is a bit more serious than a weekend jaunt to Surfer's Paradise. Hope you've got a good book.'

'Three, actually,' said Robyn, displaying the contents of her handbag.

'Trust you!' Delia aimed a friendly punch at Robyn's shoulder. 'I'm really gonna miss you, y'know.'

'Ditto. At least you'll have Rover to remind you of me.'

'Yeah, I can't thank you enough for that.'

'Better than leaving him rusting away down below in Cockroach City.'

'Ugh! Don't even mention cockroaches!'

'Do you want to drive?' said Robyn, brandishing the keys.

'Ooh, yes please!'

'Remember we're collecting Mum and Dad on the way. You won't mind dropping them home afterwards, will you?'

'What do you reckon, I'm gonna leave them to make their own way back on the bus?'

The two girls laughed and joked as Delia carefully backed Rover out of the underground car park commonly known as Cockroach City. The alien-like insects bred prolifically anywhere that was dark, and were a problem in Sydney's warm climate.

Robyn had to bite her tongue several times on the journey to the Trescowe home. She could only hope that Delia's driving would improve as she became more familiar with Rover.

Her parents were already waiting on the front step when they pulled up with a jolt. Robyn could tell that her mother was already quite flustered.

'Now, Robbie. Have you got everything? Tickets? Passport?' she fussed, trying to connect her seat belt the wrong way round.

'Yes, Mum,' said Robyn patiently, untangling the straps in her mother's lap. 'If I've forgotten anything it's bound to be trivial.'

Rose drew in a sharp breath, frowned anxiously and opened her mouth to speak. Robyn pressed her fingers to her mother's lips with a smile. 'It's all right, Mum. I'm only joking. I've double-checked everything several times over. Okay, Dee, let's go! We've got plenty of time, even if the traffic on the expressway is bad.'

'Roger, wilco,' said Delia with a grin and a clumsy gear change.

'You're quiet, Dad,' said Robyn, glancing back at her father.

'How can I get a word in edgeways with all you women?' he retorted.

'Your Dad had his tests yesterday,' said Rose. 'They told him to ring in a week for the results.'

'I'll email you as soon as I arrive, Dad,' said Robyn. 'Nick's lent me this lovely laptop,' she added, patting the slim bag resting on her lap.

'That's good,' said Joseph. 'We'll be able to keep in touch regularly without running up a tremendous phone bill. Not that I would begrudge you, girl.'

'Gee, Dad, I'm very impressed with your computer skills.'

'I don't know what all the fuss is about, love. It's easy, really.'

All the same, Robyn was proud of her father. He'd done manual work for a timber merchant for as long as she could remember, but had taught himself quite a lot about computers from a selection of books and was now in the process of building one.

Delia piloted Rover to the airport without incident, and soon they were inside the terminal. Casey was there already.

'Robyn!' he bellowed, rushing to greet her. 'I didn't think you'd ever get here!'

'What's the panic, Case? Plenty of time,' she said, submitting to his exuberant hug.

Casey glanced at his watch. 'So there is. Sorry. Just being a drama queen as usual. Hello, folks,' he said, acknowledging Delia, Rose and Joseph.

Delia and Rose were accustomed to Casey, but Joseph flinched slightly at the large man's crimson shirt and effusive handshake.

The time before Robyn's flight soon ran out. Robyn extricated herself from a final round of hugs and kisses, and made her way into the No Man's Land designated for passengers only, still waving as she walked through the door which marked the point of no return. The silence that marked the absence of her parents, Delia and Casey was like a vacuum. Little did she know that her life was about to change irreparably.

However with no sense of foreboding Robyn followed the signs pointing to Gate Lounge 23, marvelling how quickly the series of travelators carried her along the vast length of corridor.

Robyn was impatient to make a start on her journey, but soon became absorbed in the activities of her fellow passengers. She watched two grey-haired ladies in jeans and t-shirts who looked like seasoned travellers. A couple who seemed hardly older than herself struggled to keep their three young children under control. Robyn hoped she wouldn't be seated anywhere near the three squealing, squirming kids, the youngest of whom had already managed to spill a carton of chocolate milk down the front of her dress. Robyn was so distracted she didn't hear the announcement that the flight was boarding. Then she noticed the surge of people moving towards the departure gate, and hurried to join them.

Luckily Robyn was seated well away from any junior passengers. She had the two older ladies on one side and a shy Chinese lad in his teens on the other. The two ladies were indeed seasoned travellers and very chatty.

'I wish I'd been able to start travelling as young as you, dear,' said the one who had introduced herself as Mavis. 'But when I was twenty I had a husband and a young son, and twins on the way. Now that Fran and I are both widows and the children are all grown up we've plenty of time on our hands. In the past few years we've spent very little time at home. We started gradually, first with a coach tour of eastern Australia right up to Cairns. Then we bought a camper van and spent nearly a year going right round Australia. Then we went to Europe and America. This time we're starting in Singapore and going all over the Far East. We're planning to spend millennium eve in Tokyo.'

'Gee, I haven't really thought that far ahead,' mused Robyn. It was difficult to think beyond whatever the next week would entail.

Robyn caught her first glimpse of Singapore as the plane dipped below the clouds in preparation for landing. Thankfully the first eight hours of her journey had passed quite rapidly.

Robyn had a two hour wait in Singapore before joining her flight to London. She joined Fran and Mavis for a farewell Singapore Sling in one of the airport's luxurious bars before they gathered up their back packs and departed on their next adventure. The drink was stronger than it looked, and Robyn felt a little giddy as she wished the ladies *bon voyage*.

Robyn suspected she would fall asleep if she sat down to read, so she decided to explore her surroundings. The airport complex was beautifully decorated with displays of tropical flowers. It was a treasure trove of shops. She treated herself to a pair of exotic gold earrings in the shape of orchids. A hundred and ten Singapore dollars sounded expensive, but her credit card took care of it. She was starting to feel like a wealthy jet-setter, and wondered what else she might buy. Perhaps some shoes and a matching bag? Then she noticed that her flight was boarding at gate number eight. Robyn congratulated herself on the ease with which she was circumnavigating the globe, hopping off one flight and onto the next. Heavens, navigating around Sydney's western suburbs was more difficult than this!

The next leg of her journey would take nearly thirteen hours. She was sitting by the window, with a businessman on her left, probably in his forties. Still feeling light-headed with gin and duty-free shopping, Robyn flashed him what she thought was a winning smile.

'G'day. Do you come here often?' The words sounded lame before they were out of her mouth.

'Too often,' he replied stiffly, returning his attention to his newspaper.

Rebuffed, Robyn decided to amuse herself with the in-flight entertainment. She flipped through the guide on the screen set into the back of the seat in front. The movie about to start was one she'd seen two weeks earlier, but she watched it anyway.

After nearly four hours Robyn became restless. She wondered how people in years gone by had managed sea voyages of six weeks or more between Britain and Australia. And they'd had no padded seats, air conditioning or movies. But at least they'd been able to walk on deck. A stroll was just what she needed, culminating in a visit to the loo. But she didn't dare disturb Executive Man, who was now dozing behind his eye mask. The couple beyond him were also sleeping. Robyn tried to ignore the twinges of her bladder, meanwhile sending her neighbours subconscious messages to wake up soon. She wished she hadn't drunk the fruit juice and wine served with dinner.

Time had no meaning. Their journey was a line of red dots on a map on the screen in front of her. Robyn willed the little red plane to hurry along the dotted line to London. She feared that even when the little plane reached their destination she and her full bladder would still be suspended in the air. She couldn't concentrate on her book; the voice of the woman behind kept penetrating her consciousness. And still Executive Man and his two companions slept on.

***

Josephine drifted into semi-consciousness. Whatever it was that had touched her foot must have gone away. Had there ever been a time when she wasn't chilled to the marrow? At least the sea is calm, she thought vaguely, her grasp on the life preserver growing weaker as she slipped further towards certain death.

Chapter 4

Josephine didn't drown. At least she didn't think so, unless she was dreaming she was being carried in someone's arms. Her entire body ached. Then she heard voices.

'Hey, James. I think she's waking up,' said a boyish voice.

'Not far now,' said the young man who was carrying her. Then he stopped and laid her carefully on the sand.

Josephine groaned and raised a hand to brush her wet, sandy hair out of her eyes. She could see they'd stopped in front of an opening in the rocks. Her rescuer entered the opening and called out to someone.

A woman emerged into the daylight. Her clothes were ragged and scrappy, and her dark hair hung in tangles. She knelt beside Josephine, taking her wrist and feeling for her pulse.

'Where did you come from, my beauty?' asked the woman gently in a voice with foreign intonations.

'We found her on the beach,' said the younger boy. His dark eyes were wide with excitement. Josephine focused her attention on him briefly, her mind wandering inanely in her exhausted state. His skin was very brown, more than the other boy who was just bronzed by the sun like the gardeners at Roskenner House. The only other truly brown boy Josephine had ever seen had been dressed up in a fancy brocade suit, working as a bell-boy at one of London's fine hotels. Her father said he'd come from Africa.

'Am I in Africa?' asked Josephine feebly.

The young, dark skinned boy laughed.

'Shut up, Sol!' snapped the older boy. 'She must have fallen off a ship,' he added, addressing the woman.

'She's very cold and weak,' said the woman, frowning. 'What's your name, my dear?'

Josephine forced her dry lips to move. 'Josephine Trethewey.'

'I'm Luisa,' replied the woman, stroking the sand from Josephine's cheek. 'These two rogues are James and Solomon. Now relax, I'll soon have you warm and dry. You must be thirsty and hungry, too. Bring her into the cave, boys.'

As soon as they laid Josephine on a rug in the darkness of the cave, the woman pressed a bottle to her lips. The liquid with its strange taste quenched her terrible, salty thirst, but very soon she drifted once more into unconsciousness.

Josephine regained her senses to the sound of a babble of voices outside the cave. She tried to sit up, but her back ached terribly. While she tried to summon the strength for further movement, she cast her eyes over her immediate surroundings. She had no idea of the time of day for the interior of the cave was quite dark, but the opening showed a slash of light. The embers of a small fire glowed nearby, giving enough light for Josephine to make out a shabby, Oriental-patterned carpet. She smiled at this whimsical touch. She half expected to see antique furniture and heavy curtains, but all she could make out was a large wooden trunk and a tumbled heap of blankets that looked like someone's recently vacated bed. Josephine realised she was dressed in a soft, white cotton nightgown, and that she was wrapped in a large eiderdown which made a comfortable bed on the carpet. It felt as though the carpet was laid directly over the sand, as it gave gently with her movements. The cave smelled faintly of woodsmoke and dried herbs.

Josephine was more successful on her second attempt at rising from her bed. She staggered a few steps towards the mouth of the cave and leaned against the wall to regain her bearings. The woman named Luisa appeared, silhouetted in bright sunlight.

'Ah! So you are awake!' she said with a smile, moving forward to steady Josephine. 'Do you feel ready to come and meet the rest of our little group?'

'I'd like to wash my face and brush my hair first,' said Josephine, running her fingers through the salty tangles of her hair.

'Of course, my dear,' said Luisa, moving further into the cave. Josephine followed her. Luisa took an enamelled basin and a battered saucepan from the top of a rickety dresser that looked as though it had been constructed from odd pieces of wood. From a barrel in the shadows she scooped the saucepan full of water, stoked the embers of the fire into life and placed the saucepan on an iron stand over the coals. She passed Josephine a wide-toothed comb.

'Perhaps you can try to comb the tangles from your hair while the water becomes warm,' she suggested.

Josephine smiled. 'Will you stay with me? I don't feel very strong yet.'

'Of course I'll stay. Now tell me, do you remember what happened?'

Josephine found that concentrating on combing her hair helped her to tell her tale of woe without bursting into tears. Luisa sat on the carpet beside her and laid her hand soothingly on Josephine's shoulder when she got to the part about the likelihood of her little brother having drowned.

'You are a very lucky girl. You know you could easily have drowned. And there are sharks out there.'

'It was truly horrible,' said Josephine with a shudder. 'I've never been so cold in my life. But tell me, Luisa, where am I?'

'This is called Hogshead Island. It lies off the coast of Cornwall, south of the Lizard.'

'How did you get here? And the others? How many of you are there?'

Luisa muttered names under her breath, counting on her fingers.

'We are eight. The youngest, Thomas, is six years old. I am the eldest, aged thirty-one, and I have a daughter, Marielena, aged fourteen. The others are James, Solomon, Lucy, Simon and Roberto. Most of us came from the workhouse in Truro. We narrowly escaped death when it burned down, and I decided to take care of some other children as well as Marielena. That was nearly three years ago. At first we lived rough in Cornwall. It was summer and we slept in barns and on beaches, foraging for food wherever we could. Then we met James. He knew of this island, as his father had been a fisherman. He knew we could live here undetected as it was far enough from the coast. This island apparently has a reputation for being haunted, and fishermen keep well clear. The only other member of our little tribe who didn't come from the workhouse is Roberto. He is a Spanish boy who was lost from a fishing boat that blew off course in a terrible storm. We found him like you, nearly drowned on the beach near Porthleven. He still doesn't speak much English, but as I was born in Spain we are able to speak in Spanish. Of course my daughter speaks Spanish, and some of the others have learned a little. So we get along just fine.'

Luisa finished her short history of their occupation of the island with a broad smile that showed her lovely white teeth. Despite her tattered clothes and unruly hair Josephine decided she was really rather pretty. Luisa turned her attention to the water in the saucepan, lifting it from the fire and pouring it into the basin. She added a little cold water from the barrel and pronounced it suitable for Josephine to commence washing. She opened the wooden trunk and produced a bar of pleasant-smelling soap.

'Would you like me to wash your hair? It's a sunny day, it'll dry in no time.'

'Oh, that would be wonderful!' replied Josephine. 'It feels like straw!'

They laughed together as Josephine quickly washed her face and bent forward for Luisa to pour the warm water over her head.

Before long Josephine emerged from the cave, blinking in the bright sunlight. As well as washing her face and hair she had managed a discreet sponge bath in the basin, and felt very much refreshed although still rather stiff and sore. Luisa had lent her one of her dresses, which was only a little bit loose.

The assembled group fell silent. They stared at Josephine, and she stared at them.

Luisa broke the silence. 'So, my friends, this is Josephine. And Josephine, may I introduce my daughter Marielena. And the rest in turn are Lucy, Roberto, Simon, James, Solomon and Thomas.'

They mumbled a chorus of greetings, and most smiled.

Josephine glanced shyly from one to the other. 'Forgive me if I don't remember all your names straight away.'

'We understand,' said Lucy solemnly. 'We have only one name to learn whereas you have eight.'

'Here's your life preserver,' said Thomas, handing over the battered article.

Josephine felt slightly ridiculous accepting it. Roberto said something in Spanish to Luisa, who replied to him at length.

Luisa turned to Josephine. 'Roberto asked if you had fallen from a ship named the Queen Maud, but I explained that you had been carried out to sea while swimming.'

'Golly, is that true?' asked Thomas, his brown eyes large and round in his chubby brown face. 'You must be a real champion swimmer to have swum this far.'

Josephine grinned. 'I just floated, really. I found the life preserver purely by chance, and it stopped me from sinking. The sea did all the work. I was incredibly lucky to be washed up here. If I'd stayed in the water much longer, or if you two hadn't found me when you did, I would surely have died.'

'You talk very posh,' said Thomas. Are you a princess?'

Josephine blushed. 'Goodness, no. I had elocution lessons at school, but I've never even met a princess. Or any member of the royal family.'

Thomas screwed up his face. 'What's lercution lessons?'

28

'Elocution,' corrected Josephine. 'It's learning to talk posh.'

They all laughed, including Josephine.

'Do you feel well enough to take a walk?' asked James. 'We'd like to show you around our island.'

'That would be fun. Just as long as you don't go too fast. I'm not very strong yet.'

'You'd better have something to eat first, Josephine,' admonished Luisa.

'Oh, yes please! I'm absolutely famished! But I'm also eager to explore.'

A compromise was easily reached. Josephine set out along the beach with her new friends. In her hand she had a large slab of bread liberally topped with jam. The texture of the bread was rather coarse but it tasted like manna from heaven, and the sweetness of the jam masked the metallic taste of salt water that still lingered in her mouth.

James led the way, talking over his shoulder as he strode ahead. Josephine followed next, with Luisa and Marielena by her side. The others followed behind.

'Cornish fishermen call this Hogshead Island because a load of barrels of ale – hogsheads – got washed up here from a shipwreck,' explained James. 'It don't warrant a name on the map, just shows up as a tiny dot. I first thought of coming here because seafaring folk avoid it. They think it's haunted, and anyway there's no water, no spring or anything.'

'Why do they think it's haunted?' asked Josephine between mouthfuls of bread.

'My father, who worked on a fishing boat, told me that a boat came out here after the shipwreck to pick up the ale barrels. The crew thought they could drink their fill and then make a pretty penny selling the rest. Just after the shipwreck the skipper had seen the barrels all over the beach, but when he got here with his crew they were all gone.'

'Maybe someone else had taken them,' suggested Josephine. 'Or else they'd been washed away on the tide.'

James shook his head. 'There's more to it than that. The skipper and his men heard noises, moaning and suchlike. They couldn't find anything, but when they wanted to return to their fishing boat they found their dinghy had been cast adrift. Yet there was no sign of anyone on the island. It put the wind up them something terrible. Fishing folk are superstitious. The story travelled by word of mouth, and everyone still avoids the place.'

'You must have been truly desperate to come here,' said Josephine.

'You might say that,' replied James, a guarded expression stealing across his face. 'Anyway I met this lot on the mainland,' he added, glancing around at his companions, the tension on his face lifting. 'This place had been on my mind, and when I mentioned it to Luisa she jumped at the idea. Convinced me it would be the best thing we could do, like. I wasn't so keen to come here on my own, better with some company. So that was that. Anyway, two of these little tinkers turned out to be expert boat thieves.'

Simon and Solomon grinned. Simon bowed comically, and everyone laughed.

'We waited for a calm spell of weather, pinched a boat and made the journey by night. My dad taught me to navigate by the stars, and I kept the charts he gave me. We pulled our boat up onto the beach, buried it in sand and covered our tracks. We found the cave that first day, and laid low for weeks, not daring to light a fire. But like I said, folk steer clear of this place. I guess Jed Trevarthen decided to write off the loss of his boat. He had three altogether and we took the smallest. Some compensation for the way he treated my dad,' he added softly, eyes downcast.

In the awkward silence that followed, Josephine looked back along the stretch of golden beach. The sea lapped benignly at its edge, hardly the terrifying force that had almost swallowed her in its depths. Turning, she saw that the beach gave way to a rocky headland. James led them along the beach and up through the dry, yellow grass onto the rocks at its base. Josephine struggled to keep up, and Lucy took her arm.

'You must be very tired still,' she said. 'Don't worry, we can catch up with them.'

Luisa clapped her hands. 'Slow down, boys!' she called ahead. James and the others came to a halt on a large, flat rock near the summit of the headland. Lucy took Josephine's hand and helped her up the steep track that soon became little more than a series of footholds between large boulders. They stopped a couple of times for Josephine to catch her breath, but before long scrambled up to join the others where they were sitting in the sun. Young Thomas sat on the very edge of the flat rock, dangling his little brown legs in mid air. Josephine thought that he and Solomon must be brothers; with their dark skin and fuzzy black hair they looked very much alike.

Luisa turned and smiled. 'Just look at that view!' she cried.

Josephine had to admit that the view was indeed breathtaking, similar to that from familiar haunts on the Cornish mainland. Below, the turquoise sea frothed into white lace where it surged up onto the rocks. The sun glittered on the calm water, and the sky was a clear blue without a single cloud. The sea stretched as far as Josephine could see, uninterrupted by any discernible land mass.

'You get a better view of the whole island from the top,' explained Solomon. 'It's not far now.'

'Can I get my breath back first, please?' panted Josephine. Unaccustomed to walking without shoes, her feet were tender from clambering over the rocks. She glanced enviously at the hardened feet of her companions.

'There's no hurry,' said Luisa in her pleasant, warm voice.

'Which part of Spain did you come from?' asked Josephine, plucking a strand of grass from a crevice in the rocks. She noticed pretty little purple flowers sprouting from another crevice.

'I was born near San Sebastian,' replied Luisa.

'Oh, really? My father has business dealings with a Senor Vasquez in San Sebastian.'

'What is your father's business?'

'Tin mining. His firm exports tin to lots of countries, including Spain.'

'Your family must be very wealthy,' said Marielena wistfully.

'Yes, I suppose we are. We have a house in London as well as Roskenner House in Newlyn.'

'Roskenner House?' said James, his eyes widening. 'You must be the daughter of Lord Kenner, then.'

That's right,' said Josephine with a proud jut of her chin.

'How do you know about the likes of the gentry, James?' asked Marielena.

'I just do,' he replied stubbornly, his expression hardening. He rose to his feet with a fluid movement and set off up the slope.

'You've upset him now,' said Marielena accusingly.

Josephine shrugged and stood up, brushing sand from her palms. 'I can't help who I am,' she replied, feeling ridiculously tearful. She realised that she had very little in common with people from the workhouse, people who had stolen a boat and sailed to this island. And who had lived here for years like savages. She wanted to go home.

***

Robyn stretched her cramped limbs as she waited for her luggage to appear on the carousel. Even though she had already paid one visit since disembarking, she needed the loo again.

Executive Man pushed in front of Robyn and whisked a slim, stylish black suitcase off the carousel. She bit back her immediate response to comment that it was rude to push in; life was too short. Then her distinctive green suitcase hove into view. Mum had been right in suggesting she should buy something individual that could be recognised easily among all the other black and navy luggage.

Robyn thought she had been clever buying a suitcase with wheels, but hadn't realised that such small wheels would make it difficult to handle. And now all the luggage trolleys were gone. She was just about exhausted by the time she'd manoeuvred her suitcase and hand luggage through customs and all the way out to the taxi rank. She lost count of the number of toes she'd apologised for crushing en route.

Nick had reserved her a room in the Albany Hotel in London. Robyn had been chanting the address under her breath while waiting for her luggage. A shower and a nap would be very welcome. It was not quite three p.m. but she was already thinking longingly of a soft bed with clean sheets.

She stared through the terminal window, glad to see blue sky and brilliant sunshine. So much for the rumour that it rains constantly in England!

Her spirits were soon damepened by the queue of people waiting for taxis. A trail of men, women and children of varied ethnic origin, with copious luggage, snaked for hundreds of yards. However Robyn soon realised that the steady flow of cute, chunky black cabs was rapidly absorbing the assembled multitude, and soon it was her turn.

'The Albany Gardens, Sussex Paddington Hotel … er … the Albany …' she faltered.

'Blimey, darlin'!' chirped the taxi driver in his finest Cockney accent, his eyes popping as he hefted her suitcase into the boot. 'Yer didn't 'ave ter bring yer rock collection wiv yer, we got plenty of rocks 'ere. Now where was it yer wanted to go?'

Having given her destination more clearly, Robyn perched upright on her seat, not wanting to miss anything. She noted the different style of suburban housing, more compact and multi-storeyed than the sprawling, ranch-style houses in the modern outer suburbs of Sydney, but similar to the Victorian houses in the older, inner suburbs. The taxi sped along, and Robyn's excitement grew upon seeing a sign for Central London. The driver chattered away, but she found it difficult to get the gist of what he was saying. He shot words rapidly out of his mouth like gunfire. She hoped she was saying yes and no in the right places.

The Albany Hotel presented its modest frontage for Robyn's inspection, but she was more concerned with finding the right notes to pay her driver. British money seemed rather drab compared with the bright Australian notes. She contorted her weary brain to calculate a tip. The taxi fare seemed quite reasonable until she converted it to dollars. Robyn realised that with the unfavourable exchange rate she would be taking very few taxis.

'Fanks, luv!' said the driver with a cheery salute. ''Ope you enjoy your stay!'

Robyn smiled, looking hopefully for a doorman. But no, she had to perform a complicated three-way tango to get her luggage through the revolving doors.

Although her room was small and basic, it seemed like heaven after the confines of the plane. The window offered a soulless view of the back of a drab, grey building, probably another hotel. However the exciting bustle of London noise penetrated the glass. As Robyn made a cup of coffee she planned a quick shower and recce of her immediate surroundings, but closing her eyes for five minutes put paid to that. She fell into a deep sleep, the imitation cream curdling in her cold, untouched coffee.

It was almost seven in the evening when she awoke. It was dark, and for a moment Robyn wondered where she was. Then she realised with a start that she had meant to telephone her new, albeit temporary boss, Paul Sinclair at Waldron Technical, before six. Luckily she also had his home number.

'Yes?' answered a male voice with a touch of arrogance.

'Er, g'day. I'm Robyn Trescowe, from Australia. Is that Paul Sinclair?'

'Speaking. Ah yes, the girl from the Antipodes.'

'Can you tell me how to get to Eastleigh please? By train.'

'Bear with me a moment while I consult the timetable. I believe I have one here somewhere.'

Maybe it was just the accent, but Robyn thought he sounded a bit frosty. Perhaps she'd interrupted his dinner.

'Right,' said Paul, back on the line. 'There are trains leaving London Waterloo station on weekday mornings at seventeen and thirty-seven minutes past the hour. Are you travelling tomorrow?'

'Er, Monday. Is it Saturday or Sunday today?'

'Sunday,' he replied with a touch of impatience. 'Give me a call at the office when you reach Eastleigh and I'll send someone to fetch you.'

With that he rang off. Definitely a man of few words, thought Robyn. She looked at her watch. Seven fifteen. That meant it was already Monday morning in Sydney, but too early to phone her parents. So she reached for her laptop and plugged in, ready to send an email.

Hello folks, she typed. *Well I'm here. In London. Haven't seen much of it yet but the night is young. Seriously, I'll probably be asleep in a couple of hours. Hope you are both OK and not missing me too much. Any news from the hospital yet Dad? Love you both lots and lots, Robyn.*

Ah, Sunday night in London. Robyn couldn't help feeling a tingle of excitement despite her jetlag. She pulled out her map, intent upon finding Waterloo Station in readiness for the morning. Luckily it was clearly marked.

She felt a bit lost and alone, thinking of her friends and family back in Sydney. Still, she realised, there was nothing to be gained by wishing she was where she wasn't. Most of her friends had expressed serious amounts of envy upon hearing of her forthcoming trip. Some had already done the working holiday thing, temping in London and taking boozy trips around Europe. However being alone in a very average hotel in an unknown city rated much lower on the scale of fun things to do. After a shower, which was thankfully hot and strong, and a cup of coffee much the same, Robyn decided to explore a little. She gathered her coat, handbag and doorkey.

Having noted the time on her watch, Robyn walked the short distance to Marble Arch underground station and went down the stairs. After a confusing conversation with the Asian gentleman in the ticket office she bought a ticket and followed the signs to the platform for Eastbound Central Line. A distant rumble was followed by a rush of warm air emanating from the black hole of the tunnel, then Robyn saw the headlight of the approaching train. There were few fellow passengers, and in less than ten minutes she had travelled the three stops to Tottenham Court Road. Here she alighted and followed the signs for Southbound Northern Line. After about ten minutes a train pulled in to the platform, and it was only four stops to Waterloo. Having found the main line station Robyn noted how long the journey had taken her, and then retraced her journey to Tottenham Court Road.

After leaving the Underground Robyn decided to check out the famous Oxford Street. It was a pity that all the major department stores were closed. The only shops open at this hour on a Sunday were those selling tacky souvenirs. She knew even Casey would be disgusted with a t-shirt with a picture of a red London bus.

Next she bought a postcard to send to her flatmates. It was a relief for her bank balance that all the top stores were closed, and she had to content herself with browsing in their windows.

Robyn stepped into a doorway to consult her map, just to make sure she knew exactly where she was. She was startled by a voice, its origin a mystery at first.

'Do you mind?' it said, polite but a bit muffled. 'You're standing on my bed.'

Robyn froze in her tracks and glanced at the ground. Sure enough, her left foot was standing on a ragged piece of cloth. A tousled grey head, sex indeterminate, popped out of the other end of the cloth. Shrivelled eyes sent a menacing stare down a patrician nose.

'S-sorry,' mumbled Robyn, hurrying off down the street. Gee, even the beggars in London sounded posh.

Robyn became aware that a number of shop doorways contained street dwellers, some in makeshift cardboard coffin-like structures and others bundled up in grubby sleeping bags or blankets. The evidence of such poverty rather took the shine off Robyn's window shopping excursion.

Suddenly she was back at Marble Arch underground station. And just round the corner she found Edgware Road exactly where it was supposed to be.

Robyn hadn't realised there were so many Middle Eastern people in London. Many shops had signs in that interesting writing that looked like shorthand gone wrong. The street she was walking down had numerous cafes and restaurants, and they were surprisingly busy. Even in the chill of the evening, people in exotic, flowing clothes were seated at tables on the pavement, and Robyn was fascinated by a man smoking an enormous hookah that looked like her Auntie Lil's standard lamp. She didn't dare look too closely, but wondered whether the substance he was smoking was entirely legal.

Her original plan had been to find a café for a simple meal. Feeling weary, she walked into a nearby McDonalds. A quick burger suddenly seemed very appealing. Robyn was starting to feel quite fuzzy-headed and knew it was time for sleep. She had planned to email Nick, Casey and Delia before hitting the pillow, but couldn't manage to gather her thoughts. It would have to wait until tomorrow. Having eaten she retraced her steps. Luckily the hotel was right where she'd left it, and she dragged her weary bones up to her room. As she slipped into bed, Robyn realised with a start that she didn't know where she'd be spending the following night. Paul Sinclair hardly sounded like the sort of man who would welcome her with open arms and make his spare room available. Oh well, Eastleigh was bound to have at least one hotel, she mused as sleep laid its claim on her overtired brain.

Chapter 5

The awkwardness between herself and James detracted from Josephine's enjoyment of the rest of her guided tour of the island. The view from the top of the rocky crag at the summit of the headland gave her a perspective of the whole island, such as it was. There seemed to be little vegetation, mostly scrubby grass and a few spindly, windswept trees. Literally the desert island that children fantasised about after reading Robert Louis Stevenson's *Treasure Island*. The reality was a sobering matter.

Josephine caught up with Lucy. 'What on earth do you find to eat here?' she asked anxiously.

Lucy smiled. 'Oh, we eat all sorts of things. Luisa is a very inventive cook, and we all help as much as we can. Simon is hopeless, but Roberto definitely has the knack. We catch, fish, birds and small animals. We eat birds' eggs. We find shellfish on the rocks. We pick leaves and pull up roots. And we go across to the mainland in our boat every now and then for basic supplies like flour, sugar and tea, but we have to ration those things strictly.'

Lucy twirled and flung her arms in the air. The sea breeze caught her long, fair hair. 'We certainly don't go hungry!' she called, laughing. 'And Luisa knows how to make medicines from plants. She keeps a store of dried leaves and things in the cave. So if you get a sore throat or a boil or whatever she makes up a potion.'

Josephine smiled weakly. She thought it sounded pretty disgusting. Just the thought of eating birds and small animals turned her stomach over. And as for grubbing around in search of roots …

Josephine looked out across the calm sea. It shimmered menacingly in the midday sun. There was nothing as far as the eye could see. No land, no ships. Josephine looked down over the island. From this height no signs of human occupation were visible. She stared intently in the direction of the cave. Nothing. Even the footprints they'd left on the beach less than an hour before had been washed away by the incoming tide.

Josephine turned to Lucy. 'Didn't James say there was no spring or well? How do you get water?'

'When it rains we put out our barrels and collect the rainwater. These are the barrels that used to contain ale. The Man hid them in the cave. It rains qute a lot, you know. We get a bit low on water sometimes in the summer, but we just don't wash until the supply builds up again. Marielena is our Water Monitor, that's her job. She makes sure we have enough and that we're not using more than we should. We all have jobs. I'm the Chief Wood Collector. You'd be surprised how much gets washed up on the beach. All sorts of stuff that we use for our fire. Thomas helps me. There aren't very many trees growing here, so we don't cut them down. Sometimes branches fall, and we burn them, but we've made a rule not to harm the trees.'

'You all seem very well organised.'

'It was difficult at first, but we learned by our mistakes. We find it's best for everyone to have a responsibility. We'll have to think of something for you to do,' added Lucy.

She meant it kindly, but Josephine felt a rush of panic. The thought of being trapped here without clean clothes, a proper bed or hot bath, designated Chief Seagull Plucker or something equally repulsive for the rest of her life made tears well up in her eyes. Josephine turned into the wind, determined not to let Lucy see her distress. She had to be strong. She had to talk to Luisa. Luisa would be sure to understand and let her go home. After all, Lucy had said they went back to the mainland occasionally for supplies. Josephine determined to get Luisa on her own as soon as possible and present her case. She took a deep breath. Soon she would be on her way home, back to Roskenner. Never again would she take her privileged life for granted.

***

Robyn took a deep breath as the train gathered momentum. The southern suburbs of London drifted by, grey and damp in the autumn morning. Many of the trees beside the track were bare already, but some still retained the remnants of golden and amber glory. To her surprise and delight she saw a fox standing like a statue in the long grass on a sloping embankment. She almost expected him to raise a paw and wave at the train.

The train called at all stations, and Robyn plotted her progress on the map given to her by the patient gentleman at the ticket office. At each station the loudspeaker rattled off the list of delightfully English-sounding stations at which the train would call. Finally the next stop was Eastleigh. With a surge of adrenalin Robyn rose from her seat and wrestled her suitcase from the luggage rack. She could see the reflection of her pale face and wayward hair in the window opposite. Oh hell, she thought. I look a total mess, and this coat is a disgrace! With the English winter on its way Robyn knew it was time to look out for something more flattering. It was a pity there'd been no time for shopping in London.

'Can I 'elp yer with yer case?' enquired a voice which made Robyn jump. She hadn't noticed the skinny youth in railway staff uniform approaching. He hardly looked strong enough to cope with her massive suitcase. The train's wheels shrieked in protest against the rails as it came to a halt alongside the platform. Before she had time to say anything, the lad whisked her case out of the door and onto the platform.

'Thanks,' she said with a grin.

''S all right,' he mumbled, stuffing his hands into his trouser pockets as he ambled off along the platform.

Robyn bullied her wayward suitcase through the exit, pausing in the car park to find her mobile phone. Thankfully Nick had suggested she have her mobile converted for international use. Phone boxes were few and far between in England as well as Australia these days, it seemed.

A bored-sounding receptionist answered and transferred Robyn wordlessly on to Paul Sinclair's extension.

'Hello, Mr Sinclair. It's Robyn Trescowe. I'm at Eastleigh station,' she said, feeling awkward.

'Oh … right. I'll see who I can find to collect you. Someone will be there soon.'

'How will I know …?' said Robyn, but Mr Sinclair had already rung off.

At least she seemed to be the only person waiting. She hoped there wouldn't be any complications as the battery in her phone was almost dead.

Robyn amused herself by watching three little sparrows dipping in a puddle. Then it started to rain, so she pulled the hood of her unflattering coat over her head.

After about ten minutes a red Mini skidded to a halt outside the station, and a blonde woman emerged, unfolding her long legs and drawing herself up to a height approaching six feet. Robyn wondered why a lot of tall people seemed to drive small cars.

The blonde woman approached and smiled. 'Hello! I'm Lori. You must be Robyn Trescowe.'

That's right. Thanks for coming to get me. Gee, I hope my case will fit in your car.'

Lori opened the boot. 'You'd be surprised how much I can get in here,' she replied, shoving the case in with gusto. 'Your carriage awaits, milady!'

Robyn had already decided she liked this friendly, easy-going girl who looked like she was a similar age to herself.

During the short drive across town Lori kept up a humorously deprecating commentary on the delights of Eastleigh. 'Seriously, it's not such a bad place. There are plenty worse.'

'Were you born here?'

'Not far away. Southampton. Ma and Pa still live there, but I've been renting a little flat in Eastleigh for the past couple of years since I've been working for Waldron. I got used to my independence at university, and anyway if I'd gone back home Ma's cooking would have soon put back on the weight I lost when I escaped for three years.'

They both laughed.

'But you're as skinny as a rake!' chuckled Robyn. 'I don't believe you've ever been fat.'

'I could show you photos ... anyway, here we are. Waldron Technical.'

Lori guided the Mini into the car park beside a low, modern building. The rain had stopped, so Robyn removed her coat.

'Leave your case in the car, it'll be all right,' said Lori.

'Gee, that reminds me. I need to sort out a hotel for tonight.'

'Hasn't Paul arranged accommodation for you?'

'Not that I know of. I don't really like to ask.'

'You're welcome to bunk down on the sofa bed at my place if nothing's been sorted out. I share the flat with a mad architect named Colin, but he won't mind.'

'That's very kind of you. I'll see whether Mr Sinclair says anything and let you know.'

They entered the building through a plate glass door that led to a spacious, grey-marble-floored reception area. The receptionist sat at an impressive white console. She looked as bored as she'd sounded on the phone.

'Robyn, this is Julie,' said Lori. 'Julie, Robyn is here from Australia.'

Julie showed a momentary spark of interest. 'Oh yes. Mr Sinclair told me about you. Welcome to England.'

'Thanks,' replied Robyn, turning to follow Lori down an empty white corridor.

'Gee, this place is so modern!' she commented.

'Great, isn't it. White throughout with touches of green. I'd love to do my flat like this.'

Robyn smiled non-committally. She thought it looked like a psychiatric institution.

Lori came to a halt outside a white door, barely noticeable in the expanse of wall. 'This is Paul's office,' she said, tapping on the door.

'Come!' barked a voice within.

Paul Sinclair looked just as stern as he'd sounded on the phone. Probably around fifty but well-preserved. He had steely grey eyes, and his grey hair was slicked back neatly. He stood up and formally extended his hand, which Robyn shook. She was surprised that he wasn't much taller than herself.

'Welcome to England, and Waldron Technical, Robyn. I hope you had a pleasant flight, and that our railway system hasn't been up to its usual tricks.'

'Tricks?' queried Robyn, alarmed.

'Delays, cancellations, leaves on the line, wrong kind of snow, that sort of thing,' elaborated Paul Sinclair.

Robyn looked relieved. 'Oh, no. The train was on time. No problems at all.'

Sinclair shot a snowy cuff and consulted his expensive-looking watch. 'I'm afraid I've got a meeting in five minutes. I'm sure Lori won't mind showing you around. Then perhaps we can have a get-together at, say, two p.m.?'

'Fine,' said Robyn.

Lori showed Robyn around the rest of the building, including a cubbyhole in the large, open-plan office which had been allocated to Robyn.

'Where's your desk?' asked Robyn.

'I'm in the next office with the CAD computers.'

'Is that what you do, design?'

''Fraid so. Do you know what you'll be doing? It seems unusal for someone to come over from Australia.'

Robyn stifled a yawn. She still felt a bit jet-lagged.

'My employers, Harrier Reynolds, are going to be overseeing some changes to the computerised accounting procedures. The Australian parent company wants to see if they can improve on methods with the subsidiaries here and in South Africa. I'm just here to gather information and report back to my boss.'

'Will they send you to South Africa as well?'

'Gee, I don't know. Nick didn't mention it, so I expect someone else will get that one.

Lori fiddled with her flaxen hair. 'Is Nick your boss?'

'That's right. We call him Nick the Shark. Dangerous as a hungry Great White. You have to be careful to keep on the right side of him. He doesn't suffer fools gladly. Bit of a cold fish.'

'No chance of an office romance, then?' asked Lori with a mischievous grin.

'Gawd, no! He's very good looking, way out of my league. I saw him once in Donizetti's, that's a fancy restaurant in Sydney, with a girl who looked like a supermodel. Anyway, your Mr Sinclair was a bit of a surprise. I'd imagined someone younger. He didn't sound very friendly on the phone, but he seems quite nice really.'

'I know what you mean. I've heard him on the phone to some of our suppliers. Frosty as a winter's morning. But he's a pussycat really. Probably just suffers from Small Man Syndrome.'

'Huh?'

'The theory is that small men tend to be bossy in order to compensate for their lack of height.'

'Oh, I thought you meant something else,' said Robyn, relieved.

'Really, Robyn!' said Lori, blushing. 'I don't know him that well. He's old enough to be my father, and anyway I believe he's married. So his physical attributes are none of my business. Anyway, what about you? Have you left a loved one yearning for your return?'

'No such luck,' said Robyn ruefully. 'And you?'

'A maiden alone, since parting with Andrew nearly a year ago. I've taken a vow of celibacy. Anyway, how about a coffee?'

After a quick pick-me-up Lori went back to her design work. Robyn seated herself at her new desk. There was nobody much around, just a couple of men talking on phones over by the window. She switched on the computer and logged onto the internet in preparation to send Nick an email. Then she remembered his insistence that she contact him solely using the laptop. Puzzling, but it wasn't her business to wonder why.

Robyn took paper and pen to her meeting with Paul Sinclair, and made notes on the functions of the various departments and their personnel. Paul made no mention of accommodation, so she was determined not to raise the subject.

When the briefing session ended Robyn went in search of Lori, who was engrossed in something complicated on her computer. A convolution of geometric shapes filled the oversized screen.

'I'd like to take you up on your offer of a sofa bed,' said Robyn.

Lori smiled. 'Fine. Perhaps after you're settled we can go out for a drink tonight. I'll introduce you to the watering holes of Eastleigh.'

'Sounds good to me. What time do you finish work?'

'It'll only take me a couple of hours to sort this out. Meet me in reception at five?'

'Sure thing! And thanks.'

***

Maybe it was because she'd worked up quite an appetite on her tour of the island, but Josephine was surprised to find the evening meal remarkably palatable. It was some kind of stew. She had no desire to find out what had gone into it. They sat in a circle around the fire, talking as they ate, twilight gradually darkening the summer sky.

Marielena and Solomon had cooked the meal, which was served later than usual due to the lengthy walk they had taken. Josephine offered to join the washing-up brigade.

'Roberto and I are on washing up this week,' said Lucy. 'But you're welcome to join us.'

Josephine decided she liked Lucy best of them all. Luisa was nice too, but more in a motherly way. There was something a bit spiteful about her daughter, Marielena, that she didn't care for. James was OK, but a bit moody. Thomas was sweet in a little-boy sort of way, and the others were, well, just boys.

Josephine watched Simon take a second helping from the pot. Dare she do likewise? She was simply ravenous.

Luisa must have seen her looking longingly at the food. 'Would you like some more, Josephine?' she asked gently.

'Perhaps just a little, thank you,' said Josephine, scrambling to her feet.

Having filled her bowl, she turned to gaze at the sunset that seemed all-encompassing from her vantage point on the tiny pinprick of an island.

'It's beautiful, isn't it,' said Luisa.

Josephine nodded. She looked around. The others appeared engrossed in their own conversations. She took a deep breath and plunged ahead.

'Luisa, thank you very much for taking me in and looking after me. However I'd really like to go home as soon as possible.'

'I understand, my dear. I'll talk to the boys. They should be taking a trip to the mainland soon.'

'How soon?'

Luisa's face clouded. 'That I do not know. But soon. Be patient, *carita*.'

42

'I'll try,' said Josephine forlornly. She sat down next to Lucy, who was attempting a conversation with Roberto in a mixture of Spanish and English. Her stew had become cold while talking to Luisa, and was not as appetising as the first helping.

Roberto noticed that Josephine wasn't eating her food, and said something to Lucy.

Lucy turned to Josephine. 'Roberto says he'll eat it if you don't want it.'

Josephine smiled and handed her bowl to the hungry lad.

'*Gracias,*' he said, tipping her a small salute.

While he ate, Josephine turned to Lucy. 'You said something earlier about a man hiding barrels in the cave. Was this man previously part of your group? What became of him?'

Lucy shook her head. 'No, the man was here when we arrived. He must have been responsible for taking the barrels off the beach when they were washed up in the shipwreck. He must have hidden them in the cave, and set the fishermen's dinghy adrift, causing them to think the island was haunted.'

'Where did he come from?'

'We don't know. He was already dead when we arrived. Perhaps he starved, or drank himself to death on the ale. We found his body in the cave beside the barrels, just a load of bones inside some clothes.'

'Ugh! How awful! I'm not going into that cave ever again.'

'Don't be silly, Josephine. We took his bones out of the cave and buried them round the other side of the island. We marked the spot with a large rock. That was three years ago. We've been sleeping in the cave ever since. Even little Thomas isn't afraid, and he was the one who found the man's bones. Don't be such a baby. Surely you don't believe in ghosts?'

'Of course not!' protested Josephine. 'It's just … not very nice sleeping where someone has died.'

'Surely people have died in your big, fancy house?' reasoned Lucy.

'I suppose so, but not in my bedroom.'

'Ah, but can you be sure?'

'Well, no.'

Lucy scrambled to her feet. 'Come on, it's getting cold. Time we were settling down for the night.'

'Just promise me you won't show me where Thomas found the bones.'

'Of course not. Anyway it was right at the back, nowhere near where we sleep.'

Luisa was already in the cave, settling young Thomas into his quilt and telling him a bedtime story. 'Hello, girls. Are you coming to bed now?'

'Lucy's been telling me about the man,' said Josephine.

'What man? Oh, you mean … well, never mind. We gave him a proper burial. He rests in peace. The dead can do you no harm,' said Luisa, her voice soothing as the distant lapping of the waves.

'I suppose not,' said Josephine reluctantly. She was so tired she felt as though she could sleep anywhere.

Luisa opened the battered trunk and handed Josephine the nightdress she'd been wearing when she awoke that morning.

'May I wash my face and clean my teeth?' she asked.

'We don't usually wash before bed, but you may as a special treat. We have to be careful to conserve water, particularly in summer. Having enough water to drink is more important than being clean. Here's the toothbrush, we all share it.'

Josephine felt quite ill at the thought of sharing a toothbrush with a host of strangers, so she pretended to use it and instead scrubbed her teeth with her fingers. Of course there was no tooth cleaning powder.

As she emptied her basin of water outside the cave she wondered about toilet facilities. Earlier in the day she'd popped behind a bush when needing to pass water, but nobody had as yet mentioned the delicate subject.

Lucy must have read Josephine's mind. 'In case you're wondering, we have a trench over there which we use as a latrine. It's behind that brushwood screen. We add sand after each use, if you see what I mean. Then after a while we fill it in completely and dig another trench. But if you need to go in the night there's a chamber pot behind a screen at the side of the cave.'

Josephine knew she would have to be very desperate to suffer the humiliation of urinating within earshot of her companions.

Josephine fell asleep long before she had a chance to dwell on thoughts of home. The others didn't disturb her as they prepared for bed by candlelight.

***

The red Mini screeched to a halt at an imposing gateway. It hadn't taken Robyn long to realise that Lori was a much more impetuous driver even than dear Delia. Lori proceeded more slowly down the gravel driveway beyond the gate, and brought the car to a halt outside a charming, white-painted house.

Robyn's eyes widened. 'Gee, Lori! Don't tell me you live here! Wow, it's massive!'

Lori grinned. 'It's not all mine, just one of the ground floor flats. The owner, Lady Wetherby, lives upstairs. Posh, but penniless. She lets out four flats on the ground floor.'

Lori helped Robyn with her suitcase. They struggled along a narrow path leading around the side of the building, pushing through overhanging foliage like a pair of explorers.

Lori stopped outside a door inlaid with stained glass panes, and thrust a key into the lock. 'In you go,' she urged Robyn. 'I'll leave your suitcase in the hall for now. Kitchen's on the right.'

Robyn looked around. 'Wow! It's really nice. Very olde-worldy.'

The hallway was spacious, with a high ceiling rising into a dome set with more stained glass panes. The effect was only slightly marred by the surfboard propped against the wall.

'I'm afraid the hot water and central heating are a bit old-fashioned and temperamental, but we manage,' said Lori, filling the kettle. 'While this boils I'll show you the sitting room which will be your bedroom.'

The room was huge, with a bay window overlooking the garden.

'Lovely!' exclaimed Robyn. 'And the garden's like something out of a glossy magazine.'

'One of the lodgers looks after the garden in exchange for free rent. Roger. He's a funny bloke, a few sandwiches short of a picnic. But totally dedicated to the garden. I've seen him out there in the pouring rain pruning and planting things.'

'Who lives in the other flats?' asked Robyn, dumping her handbag on the sofa.

'Jason and Matthew live next door. Roger lives alone in the flat round the back, and Josie and Niall share the front flat with their baby, Skye.'

'Is that a boy or a girl?'

'She's a girl. But you never hear her crying. The walls are very thick. This place was built to last.'

'I'll say,' said Robyn, running her hand over the cast-iron radiator that squatted against the wall like an outsize mutant caterpillar. 'This water-filled central heating is something you don't see in Australia. You get underfloor heating in fancy new houses, but the rest of us make do with portable electric radiators when the weather turns cold.'

'I don't suppose it gets very cold in Sydney,' said Lori.

'Rarely below ten degrees in winter.'

'I could get used to that! In winter it regularly gets down below zero here.'

'Does it snow much?' asked Robyn, eagerly imagining the rolling green lawns blanketed in white.

'We usually get a couple of decent falls each winter. Sometimes more.'

'I'll look forward to that,' said Robyn, rubbing her hands together with glee. Then a guilty expression crossed her face. 'I don't want you to think I'm planning to impose on you permanently.'

'Don't worry. Stay as long as you want. But you'll probably need to get a car. Buses are few and far between.'

'Nick is allowing me to hire a car and charge it to the company. I'd better look into that soon. I don't expect you to keep running me backwards and forwards to work.'

'I know of one car hire place in town, and there are bound to be more. Maybe we can drop by there tomorrow. But be warned – the price of petrol here is extortionate!'

Robyn grinned. 'Something else I'll have to charge to the company.'

'Well if that's the case perhaps you can submit a bill for the petrol I've used running you around today,' said Lori with a mischievous grin. 'I'd rather spend my money on alcohol than petrol. Spaghetti Bolognese OK for dinner?'

'Depends what it's going to cost me.'

'Oh, no more than a round of drinks later at the Blind Vicar.'

'The Blind Vicar? Gee, that's another thing. The funny names you English people give your pubs. I heard about one in London called the Rat and Handbag.'

'Well, what do you call your pubs in Australia?'

'Oh, boring things like The Barn and Sundowners. But my favourite haunt is a new place called Long Tall Sally's,' said Robyn wistfully. It would be a while before she'd be sharing a jug of Fluffy Flamingo in Sally's with Delia.

'Well, pubs with funny names are part of our charm,' said Lori.

Further comparison of the two countries was temporarily suspended by the arrival of Colin, heralded by a loud tapping at the sitting room window.

'Can't find my keys!' he called through the window.

Robyn immediately liked the look of the lanky fellow with long, unruly brown hair. The navy velvet jacket worn with a blue t-shirt and jeans gave him the look of a rock star, not movie-idol handsome but interesting. Robyn followed Lori to the door.

'Hi, Col. This is Robyn. She'll be staying awhile. Robyn, this is Colin, my flatmate and chief spider catcher.'

Robyn felt her cheeks grow pink as Colin kissed one of them.

'What's this about catching spiders?'

Colin grinned. 'Lori's terrified of spiders. Whenever she sees one she screams and I come running. It's part of the deal. I catch spiders, she sews on buttons.'

'Sounds like a good deal, just as long as you don't lose too many buttons.'

'That's just the trouble. I lose all sorts of things, including my keys,' he said, patting his pockets and springing open the well-worn leather briefcase at his feet.

'Aha! There you are, you buggers!' he cried, pulling the offending keys out from under some papers.

'Sorry, Robyn. I haven't even made you a cup of tea yet,' said Lori, heading for the kitchen.

'I'm surprised you're not already on the G and T. Lori is a terrible old soak.'

'That's so unfair, Col!' protested Lori. 'You know very well how hopeless I am. Two drinks and I'm gone. But you're welcome to a glass of wine if you'd prefer, Robyn.'

Robyn nodded enthusiastically, wondering whether Colin was gay. If not, she didn't know how Lori managed to live under the same roof as such an attractive man without throwing herself at his feet. Or into his bed. She knew she'd have to be careful not to make an idiot of herself.

Robyn sat at the kitchen table drinking her wine, watching Colin and Lori getting under each other's feet and creating general havoc while they prepared the evening meal.

'Do you two always cook together?' she asked, trying to gauge the level of their intimacy.

'Good lord, no!' snorted Colin. 'If we did this too often we'd end up killing each other!' He turned to Lori. 'Now, what have you done with the tomato paste, you silly old tart?'

After a surprisingly tasty meal, Robyn insisted on washing the dishes.

'The iron and ironing board are in the cupboard in the hall in case you need to press anything before we go out,' said Lori from the doorway.

'Thanks,' replied Robyn, elbow deep in bubbles.

'Where are you off to?' asked Colin.

'Just a swift half at the Blind Vicar. Care to join us?'

Colin shook his head, and Robyn paused in her labours to admire the way his brown curls caught the light.

'Sorry, girls. I'd love to, but I'm already promised to the lovely Virginia this evening. We're going to the cinema.' Colin consulted his watch. 'Gosh, I'd better get a move on.'

A short while later Lori and Robyn set off on foot down the quiet lane, Lori being mindful of the drink-driving laws. Robyn had put on her coat; even though it looked dreadful she didn't want to get cold. After all, she could take it off once they reached their destination.

Robyn hesitantly phrased a question. 'This Virginia, is she Colin's girlfriend?'

Lori smiled. 'Why do you ask? Do you fancy him?'

'I thought he might be gay. He seems a bit … you know.'

'I know what you mean,' chuckled Lori. 'He can sound rather camp. But seriously, he's as heterosexual as …' she searched for an appropriate simile.

'As a mallee bull?' suggested Robyn.

Lori laughed. 'Whatever that is. Really, I think you do fancy him.'

Robyn felt her cheeks colouring, and was glad they were walking in darkness. 'Well, maybe a bit. He's definitely got something.'

'That's just the trouble,' sighed Lori. 'Half the British female population seems to think old Colin's got something. Take Virginia, for example. She works with Colin, and she used the old ploy to get him to go with her to the cinema.'

'What old ploy is that?'

'She said she'd won two tickets in a radio phone-in.'

'I see.'

'Take my advice, Robyn. Leave well alone. He's broken more hearts than Casanova. He gets through girlfriends at the rate of roughly one a month. He says it's not his fault he has a short attention span, but that sounds like a poor excuse to me. Admire from a distance, but don't get involved.'

'Why, have you got a crush on him?'

'Good lord, no! Heavens, I've known him since we were toddlers. His parents are my parents' closest friends. He's like a brother or a favourite teddy bear. I know him far too well for any romantic interest.'

Robyn still thought Lori had perhaps protested too much.

The lane joined a street with a handful of shops, all closed. A cold wind whipped pages of a discarded newspaper along the pavement. Robyn counted three hairdressing salons in just two blocks.

'Gee, people must have their hair done a lot to keep all these hairdressers in business,' she observed, pulling the collar of her coat closer around her neck.

'I'd never really given it much thought, but you're right. Eastleigh is simply bursting with hairdressing salons. And most of them have really silly names. Just look at that one: *Curl Up and Dye*. We turn left here, and there's the Blind Vicar at the end,' she added, pointing to an attractive old building.

By the time they reached the pub door Robyn and Lori had invented a selection of even sillier names for hairdressing salons. Once inside, Robyn shrugged off her coat. There were few patrons, and they found a table by the fire without difficulty.

'Enough about hairdressers,' said Lori. 'Name your poison.'

'Um, Bacardi and Coke, please,' replied Robyn, taking in her surroundings. The lounge had a low ceiling crossed with wooden beams, and the floor was carpeted in luridly patterned red. Comfortable sofas and chairs were arranged around an assortment of well-worn, wooden tables. There were two older men chatting quietly at the bar, an elderly couple occupying a table at the window, and a young lad who looked barely old enough to enter a pub legally playing on a pinball machine. Its pinging punctuated the silence.

Lori returned with their drinks. 'So. First impressions of Waldron?'

Robyn paused, chasing the ice around her glass with her straw. 'It's a bit soon to get a real idea of the place. It's smaller and quieter than Harrier Reynolds, but I think I'll get on OK. Do you like working there?'

'It's not madly exciting, but it's a job,' replied Lori, smoothing her hair behind her ears. 'I'm saving, making plans to travel. Maybe South America, or Australia.'

'Sounds like a good idea. Gee, I must check my emails when we get back to your place.'

'Sorry, my computer's out of action.'

'It's okay, I've got a laptop.'

'Lucky you!'

'Well, it's not really mine,' confessed Robyn. 'My boss lent it to me.'

Robyn soon felt tired. The warmth of the room made her eyes fel heavy, and the second drink made her stomach feel bloated.

'Would you mind if we went soon?' she asked, feeling guilty at being such a party-pooper.

'Of course not. I must say you do look rather tired. Must be jet-lag.'

The return journey seemed mercifully shorter. Having declined a mug of hot chocolate, Robyn prepared for bed. Lori had shown her how to pull out the sofa bed. Once in her comfortable winter nightie she pulled the laptop out of its case and logged onto the internet. There were six emails. The first was from Casey.

Hi there jetsetter. No news from you yet??? Hope you haven't been hijacked. Though if you had, maybe Nick would have said something. Or maybe not. Anyway, I digress. They've got this gorgeous blond bloke in as a temp while you're away. He's got a lovely little cupcake bum. Don't know yet whether he bats for my team, but time will tell. Meanwhile I'm having to show him the ropes. Oh, my dear! The sacrifices I have to make in the line of duty! Email me soonest, you old bag. Love you to bits, missing you loads, Casey xxx

Robyn smiled as she recognised her father's email address directly below.

Hello, my girl. Good to hear you made it to Blighty without difficulty. Have you started work yet? Now for our news. It's not good, I'm afraid. The tests show that I have cancer of the oesophagus. Don't worry, dear. All is not lost. I start chemotherapy in a week, and Dr Wilson says I've got a good chance of recovery. Rose is a tower of strength, she fusses too much but I'm grateful really. Despite my troubles I don't feel too bad. It helps to know why I've been feeling tired and out of sorts. I'm thinking of you, and hoping that you won't find this too much of a shock. Please don't come rushing home. I'm getting the best medical care available, and I know I'll get better. Lots of love from us both, Mother and Dad xxx

Chapter 6

Josephine drifted back to consciousness after a restless sleep. It was still dark, and she could hear someone snoring. The air in the cave smelled dank. She sat up. A tangle of quilts and blankets covered the square of carpet on which she had slept. In the darkness she could just about make out the humps formed by her companions, still asleep. She could see a few arms and legs that had crept from beneath their blankets, and a couple of dark, tousled heads.

It seemed very strange to be sleeping in close proximity to a group of near strangers. Very different from waking in her light and airy bedroom at Roskenner House, or her stylish bedroom in London. Josephine knew it would take some getting used to.

The snoring stopped suddenly. At least she hoped it was someone snoring, and not noises made by the ghost of the dead man. Josephine regretted that thought as soon as it surfaced in her mind. She tried instead to think of pleasant things, of Christmas morning at home, of walking along the beach at Newlyn. But thoughts of the beach led back to that nightmare day when she had watched Lucien slip out of sight beneath the surface of the sea, followed by her still not quite believable journey to the island.

Sleep would not return. Josephine lay on her back, folded her hands across her chest, and tried to count her blessings. She was alive, apparently unharmed by her lengthy immersion in the sea. It was a miracle that she hadn't expired from pneumonia or been torn to pieces by sharks. She had been found by kind people who had taken her in and given her food and water. And she would, before long, be returning to her family, and to the comfort and luxury of Roskenner House.

By the time Josephine's thoughts had wandered along the path through Roskenner Woods she noticed daylight was beginning to show at the mouth of the cave. She wriggled out of her quilt and padded across the sand, eager to visit the latrine while she was the only one awake. She walked to the left of the cave and stepped behind the screen that thankfully offered some privacy. Straddling the trench, she realised to her disgust that she had no paper. She looked around helplessly for a solution to her problem. Just a few yards further down the beach the waves lapped gently against the wet sand. The water was cold against her feet, but she waded out a short distance, lifted her nightdress discreetly and washed as thoroughly as she was able. She did not want to get back into bed with a wet body and sandy feet so she sat on a rock, shivering while she watched the sun rise.

After a while two of the boys emerged from the cave.

'Good morning,' she called.

'Oh, 'ello,' replied Simon with a smile.

'What you doin' up so early?' asked Solomon.

'I couldn't sleep.'

'Well, you can 'elp us gather wood for the fire,' said Simon brusquely.

'Shouldn't I put some clothes on first?' asked Josephine, brushing sand from the back of her nightdress.

'Don't matter. Come on,' replied Simon.

She followed the boys along the beach. They seemed to walk terribly fast. At least she was warming up a bit trying to keep up with them. Solomon already had his arms full of short pieces of driftwood, and Simon was dragging a large branch. Josephine felt a complete novice; she had collected just one small stick. Then she saw a large, well-weathered branch high up on the beach and detoured to claim it for her own, pleased that the boys had missed it. To her horror, the underside of the branch was crawling with small crabs. Josephine only just stifled the scream that was her initial reaction and, holding her breath, managed to scrape off the crabs using her stick. She stood up and noticed that the boys had turned back.

'Hey, well done!' called Simon. 'That's a good big 'un.'

Josephine grinned proudly, brushed the sand off her hands and set off in the direction of the cave, towing the branch behind her. It was not as big as the one Simon had found, but she felt it was a passable effort for a beginner.

Back at the cave, the others were awake and dressed. Josephine left her branch beside the remains of yesterday's fire and entered the cave. All evidence of bedding had been cleared off the carpet, but on top of the chest she found the dress and knickers she'd been wearing the day before and slipped into them. She remembered Luisa's admonition about the use of water; if nobody else had washed their face surely it didn't matter that much. But wearing the same knickers two days running did not please Josephine, and she knew she must talk to Luisa about the possibility of some more clothes. She shook the sand out of her nightdress, folded it and popped it into the trunk. Glancing towards the back of the cave she gave barely a thought to the man who had died there.

Out in the sunshine the fire was blazing and breakfast preparations were under way.

'Good morning!' called Luisa. She was spreading jam on lumpy doorsteps of home made bread. 'You were the early bird?'

'Yes, I did wake rather early,' replied Josephine, digging her bare feet into the cool sand. 'When Solomon and Simon woke up I went with them to gather wood.'

'Well done! Now, we must think of a special task for you. I know! You can take over the keeping of our diary. Would you like that, Josephine? With your good education I'm sure you write better than my poor Mari.'

Josephine nodded and smiled. She felt a little alarmed at being offered a job implying permanence, but was pleased to have avoided anything to do with the killing and preparation of animals for the cooking pot.

'That will be your special job,' said Luisa. 'And when we sit down on Sunday night to work out the rota of general chores for the coming week, we will include you.'

Josephine felt the smile fade from her face. It seemed she hadn't escaped the nastier aspects of island life that easily.

'I'll get you the diary after breakfast and you can make a start,' said Luisa.

'Thank you. I always had good marks for my essays, you know. Luisa, are there any spare clothes I could borrow? In particular, underwear,' Josephine added in a whisper.

'Of course, my dear. I'll look in the trunk. I'm sure there'll be something. Now, we each have a wooden box where we keep our clothes and personal possessions. James is our chief carpenter. I'll ask him to make one for you.'

'Thank you, Luisa,' said Josephine, accepting the slice of bread offered. She was uneasy about putting James to the trouble of making a box if she wasn't staying long. And she hoped he was in a better mood today. She looked around and saw him sitting on a rock, eating his bread and staring out to sea.

Luisa walked over to James with a mug of tea, and paused to talk with him. Josephine watched them discreetly, aware that she could just about hear what they were saying. She saw James nod. Then Luisa said something that Josephine failed to catch, but she felt a stab of alarm as she heard James's angry reply. He said that she must not be allowed to go home.

In her shock and confusion, Josephine missed the remainder of the conversation between James and Luisa. She saw Luisa walk away and busy herself with the cauldron of tea, ladling it into a motley assortment of tin and earthenware mugs. Josephine fought to keep her tears at bay, concentrating on sifting the sand between her fingers, sensing rather than seeing Luisa approach.

Luisa squatted down beside Josephine and handed her a mug of tea. Josephine forced herself to smile and took a sip. She winced. It had a peculiar taste.

'We have no milk, I'm afraid,' explained Luisa.

'I don't think milk would help very much,' said Josephine, having bravely swallowed the first mouthful of bitter liquid.

'The taste is strange, but you'll soon get used to it. It's a special blend of herbs that help to keep us healthy. We get them from a wise woman when we go ashore. We have just one cupful each day.'

Josephine nodded, relieved that she would not have to endure the disgusting taste more often. She plucked up the courage to voice her concerns: it was now or never.

'Luisa, I heard what James said to you just now.'

'And what was that?' replied Luisa, her dark eyes suddenly hard.

'He said I must not be allowed to go home,' said Josephine flatly.

'*Carita*, you must understand things from our point of view. If people on the mainland know that we are living here they will come for us.'

'Why?'

Luisa sighed. 'Well, it's mostly James they will come after. He is wanted by the police.'

'Gosh! Whatever did he do?'

'He didn't do anything!' snapped Luisa, fiercely loyal. She brought her emotions under control before speaking further. 'He is suspected of committing a murder, but he didn't do it. He knows he was set up as a scapegoat, but he doesn't know who really killed the woman.' Luisa looked over her shoulder. 'Come with me along the beach, I will tell you the story.'

Josephine walked with Luisa along the high tide mark. When they had distanced themselves sufficiently from the others Luisa continued her explanation.

'James was working on the estate of a Monsieur Roquebrun.'

Josephine gasped. 'My mother knows the Roquebrun family. She is also French.'

Luisa absorbed this piece of information. 'I see. Well, Madame Roquebrun's maid was found dead, brutally beaten. She was found in the stable, next to the room where James slept. For that reason only he was blamed. But he says he didn't do it, and that he heard nothing.'

'Gosh! How awful! When did this happen?'

'In February 1922. Did you not hear news of the incident?'

Josephine searched her memory and shook her head. 'No, not a word. In any case we spend our winters in London. We only come down to Roskenner for the summer.'

Luisa paused and traced a circle in the sand with her bare foot. 'Even so, we cannot allow you to return to your family. Particularly as your mother knows Monsieur and Madame Roquebrun. If you were to tell anyone that this island is occupied ...'

'But I wouldn't!'

'We can't take that risk. You would not want James to go to prison for nothing, would you?'

Josephine shrugged miserably, but knew reluctantly she had to recognise that it would only take a small slip of the tongue on her part to send a search party out to the island. So, her fate was sealed. She was to be stuck here forever. A cloud crossed the sun, matched by a similar cloud crossing her heart. Never again would she sit by the fire with her family, discuss Paris fashions with her mother, help George over the stile in the woods, eat roast beef for dinner, luxuriate in a hot bath, ride in her father's Rolls Royce ... the list of deprivations was endless. Josephine's lips crumpled and tears flowed down her cheeks.

'Don't cry, little one,' soothed Luisa. 'I'll look after you.'

***

Robyn burst into tears, and sat sobbing on the carpet for several minutes before consulting her watch. It was nearly midnight. That meant it was nearly eleven a.m. in Sydney. Surely Mum and Dad wouldn't have gone to work? She dug her mobile out of her handbag. The phone rang emptily at the other end, no matter how much she willed her parents to answer.

Robyn cancelled the call and dialled her brother's number. Giulietta answered.

'Jules, it's Robyn.'

'Hello. How are you?'

'I've just got Dad's email. I know he's got cancer. I've tried ringing them but there's no answer.'

'They must still be at the hospital,' explained Giulietta. 'Your father had an appointment this morning. Please try not to worry, Robyn. Your father is a strong man. The doctors will help him to get better.'

'I know, but I just wish I could be there with them!'

'Be brave. I think that's the best thing you can do for your parents.'

Robyn sighed. 'Thanks, Jules. In case I don't manage to catch them can you let them know I've called?'

'Of course, Robyn. I'll get them to phone you, and Steve too. What time is it now in England?'

'Just after midnight. But they can phone any time. I'll leave my mobile on.'

Robyn checked the battery level on her phone as soon as she hung up. Three quarters full. Nevertheless she put her battery on charge before lying down on the sofa bed. The alarm on her phone was set for half past seven, but she hardly expected to sleep.

Robyn felt like a zombie when she hauled herself out of bed later that morning. Added to the turmoil in her mind, the sofa bed was less than comfortable. It squeaked every time she moved, and seemed constantly on the verge of folding her up in a flimsy metal and fabric sandwich. A hot bath helped to some extent, and by the time Robyn reached the kitchen Lori had appeared.

Lori's face registered concern as soon as she laid eyes on Robyn. 'Goodness, you look dreadful! Sorry, that was a bit tactless.'

Robyn attempted a smile. 'It's okay. I've had some bad news. I had an email from my father. He's got cancer.'

'Oh, Robyn!' groaned Lori. 'Goodness, you mustn't even think of coming to work today. I expect you want to make arrangements to fly home as soon as possible.'

Robyn gratefully took the mug of coffee offered by Lori. 'Dad says he doesn't want me to rush back home. He says he's getting first-rate treatment and is determined to beat it. So I've decided to stay for the moment. Anyway, I've been sent here to do a job. I don't want to let Nick down. Gee, that reminds me. I haven't emailed Nick yet to let him know I've arrived. I'll just go and do that before we head off to work.'

Lori shook her head. 'I still think you should stay in bed today.'

'Nah. Bed is for wussies. Besides, I need something to take my mind off Dad.'

'I see what you mean,' said Lori, reaching up on top of the cupboard for a box of bran flakes. 'I'll get us some breakfast while you email your boss. Cereal, toast or both?'

Robyn smiled. 'Thanks, Lori. Just cereal for me, please. I'll be back in five.'

As soon as she booted up the laptop a message from Nick popped up on the screen.

Hello, Robyn. Hope you had a pleasant flight. Have you made contact with Waldron Technical yet? There are some things you need to know, strictly confidential. Couldn't tell you earlier because I didn't have all the facts, but I do now. Our client wants you to keep a close watch on Paul Sinclair. They think he's cooking the books, raking money off into an offshore account of his own. Don't put yourself at risk, but keep your eyes and ears open. Let me know if you find anything untoward. Above all, don't tell a soul what you're doing. Please delete this message, your reply, and any further correspondence between us.

The plot thickens, thought Robyn, stunned by Nick's message. A quick look at her watch galvanised her into action.

I'll do my best, she replied. *I'm in Eastleigh at the moment, staying with one of the employees, Lori Edwards. I've spent one day at Waldron. Not aware of anything suspicious, but I only spent a few minutes with Sinclair. I'll update you regularly and will of course delete all messages. Regards, Robyn.*

Robyn felt guilty sitting at the breakfast table with Lori. Here she was, accepting her hospitality while planning to spy on her boss. She also felt very much out of her depth. If Paul Sinclair was up to no good surely he'd cover his tracks. Particularly with a stranger around. Then she had a glimmering of an idea. Perhaps one way she could gain information would be to play dumb, pretend to know very little about the accounting system and lure him into a false sense of security. It was the only approach she could stretch her weary brain towards at this stage.

***

Josephine dried her tears, finished her tea and helped the others clear up after breakfast. As she wiped the sticky edge of the jam pot she looked into its depths, unable to make out what sort of fruit it contained. It was dark and unusual tasting, but quite palatable. She looked up from her musings straight into James's face. How had she not previously noticed the jagged scar across his forehead?

His grey eyes were serious. 'So,' he said, taking the jam pot from Josephine's hands. 'Luisa told you why we can't let you go back.'

Josephine nodded, fighting to quell the tears welling up in her eyes.

'I just wanted to tell you I'm sorry,' he added quietly. 'This morning I'll make you a nice box to keep your things in.'

This was just too much. Josephine's temper flared hotly. 'Do you really think a box made out of assorted bits of driftwood will make up for you ruining the rest of my life? Don't bother. I'll build my own box!'

Josephine ran off along the beach, but found it difficult to maintain her dignity while wallowing along in soft sand. She made her way down to the firmer wet sand. She walked down to the water's edge and looked out over the rippling sea, breathing deeply, trying to calm herself. She tried to stop the tears that threatened to overflow yet again. She could hear the younger children playing a ball game on the sand behind her.

Determined to commence her first attempt at carpentry, Josephine walked back to the cave. She had noticed some pieces of wood stacked against the wall. She assessed Marielena's box of possessions, roughly noting the size of the pieces of timber she'd need. There was a small store of tools in an open chest, and Josephine selected a saw. She carried the saw and some pieces of wood outside, and set to work away from prying eyes behind a large rock.

However using the saw was more difficult than it had seemed when watching Mawson making a dog kennel at Roskenner. No matter how hard she pushed and pulled, the teeth barely bit into the wood. After five minutes her arm was aching, and she'd hardly scratched the surface. She took the saw back to the toolbox to see if there was anything else that she might use. James was there, cleaning the blade of a larger saw with an oily rag.

'How's the box going?' he asked with a grin.

'Just fine, thank you!' she blustered. 'Perhaps you would kindly show me where the nails are kept.'

'Certainly, madam,' said James with mock humility. 'Here are the large ones, or perhaps madam would prefer a smaller size?'

She snatched the oilcloth containing the nails from his hand, whereupon the cloth unravelled, spilling the nails into the sand.

'You did that on purpose!' she snapped, dropping to her knees to retrieve the nails.

'My, you've got a temper like a cat!' marvelled James, chuckling with amusement. 'Let's hope you ain't got the claws too.'

'You are simply the most irritating person I have ever met!' raged Josephine, rising to her feet with her fist full of nails.

James followed her out of the cave and round to where her pieces of wood lay. 'Not much sign of any carpentry going on,' he mocked, picking up the piece of wood she'd attempted to saw. 'It's a good thing I've already made a start on something better for you.'

Josephine seethed with fury. 'I've a good mind to slap your face! Or scratch it so hard that you'll have another scar to match the one on your forehead!'

'Now that's not nice.'

'I don't care!' stormed Josephine, squaring up to her tormentor.

'No, I don't believe you do. We should have left you to die where we found you washed up on the beach, except you would have rotted and made a dreadful smell.'

'Would not!'

'I suppose you think your shit don't stink either!'

'There's no need to be downright crude,' said Josephine, trying to suppress her laughter. She'd never heard such a comical expression.

'Yes, miss high and mighty. That's me. Crude and common, and a murderer into the bargain. Or so they say,' added James with a grin, doffing his cap.

'Then why don't you just murder yourself,' hissed Josephine. 'Then I'll make a box to bury you in!' She picked up the piece of wood she'd tried to saw and flung it in the air. It landed a few feet away.

'It would take you quite a while the way you were going. By the time you finished I'd probably have rotted away to just bones. If you like I could give you a lesson in carpentry.'

'Oh, all right,' sighed Josephine. 'You never know, I might have been holding the saw upside down.'

'There's every possibility,' said James drily, picking up her piece of wood.

He showed her the pieces of wood he'd already sawed. It took him just a few minutes to saw the last piece, and she marvelled at his accuracy.

'If you hold these two pieces together I'll knock in the nails,' said James.

Josephine did as he asked. James took the hammer in his strong, weathered hands and swiftly joined the two pieces of timber.

'Now it's your turn. I'll hold the wood.'

Josephine picked up the hammer and aimed it at the nail, but the nail skewed off to one side.

59

'It takes practice. Try again.'

This time she managed to drive the nail straight into the wood, and sat back to admire her handiwork.'

'That's better.'

She tapped in a couple more nails where James showed her. Before long they'd nailed the sides together and attached the base. James smoothed the rough edges with a file.

'Now all it needs is a lid.'

With that in place the box was complete.

'You've got the makings of a carpenter, lady,' said James.

'It's not that difficult. I might just build my own boat and sail back to my home.'

'Now that I would like to see!' he chuckled.

'You've told me your father was a fisherman. Is he still alive?' said Josephine, gathering up the tools.

James shrugged. 'I dunno. How would I know, living out here? I hope he is.'

'What about your mother?'

James pursed his lips. 'She died giving birth to her fourth child. A boy; he died too. My Dad went to pieces, started drinking heavily, so his sister, my Aunt Flo, took charge of my younger brother and sister. And I went to work for the Roquebruns.'

'I'm sorry to hear that.' Josephine glanced at his forehead, eager to change the subject. 'Do you mind me asking how you got that scar?'

'I know you won't give up until I do tell you, Empress Josephine. My father sometimes used to let me go out on the fishing boat with him and the other men. One day we got caught in a storm. Part of the boat's railing came away and hit me in the head. My father said it served me right for not staying below like he'd told me.'

'Seems you're just as stubborn as me.'

'Not a chance! You invented stubborn. I bet your parents could tell a tale or two. And now we're stuck with you. Now all this box needs is your name on it. Empress Josephine.'

Josephine found she was enjoying their banter. And she liked being called an empress.

'You never know, I may be related to the real Empress Josephine. My mother is from a French titled family. She's taught me to speak fluent French.'

'Well, la-de-da. A fat lot of good that's going to do you here on Hogshead Island.'

Josephine burst into tears.

James tentatively put his arm around her shoulders. 'I'm sorry, Josephine,' he said, smoothing her curly hair. 'That was cruel of me. You were very brave to hang onto that life preserver and float all the way here. And Luisa told me about your brother. I'm sorry. I know it's going to be difficult for you, and I promise I won't make fun of you again.'

'P-please take me back to Newlyn,' blubbered Josephine.

'I'm sorry, I can't do that,' said James, his thoughts far away as he held the sobbing girl in his arms.

***

Robyn took her mobile out into the sunshine during her morning coffee break. After only a couple of rings her father answered.

'Oh, Dad!' she said, feeling tears welling up. She did her best to put on a brave front, but was totally overcome with emotion.

'Now, now, m'girl. No need for such a carry-on. I'm going to be all right, don't you worry.'

'But Dad, you've got cancer!'

'So have plenty of other people, but they survive. They have a good success rate with these modern treatments, you know.'

'I really want to be there with you.'

'There's nothing you can do, love. It's all in the hands of the doctors now. What with Rose and Steve and Giulietta fussing around me, I don't get a minute's peace. So don't go adding to my troubles, please,' he said firmly.

'How's Mum?' asked Robyn, blowing her nose.

'She's all right. She said to me earlier that it's a relief, really, to know what's been troubling me these past few months.'

'Months?' said Robyn with a gasp of surprise.

''Fraid so,' admitted Joseph sheepishly.

'Gee, Dad. Why didn't you go to the doctor sooner?'

'Don't you start, Robyn. I've had all that from your mother. Anyway, this call must be costing you a fortune.'

'You're worth every cent, Dad. Now hurry up and get well. I suppose I'd better get back to work.'

'I wouldn't want them to think you're slacking off.'

'We do get a coffee break every now and then, Dad. Anyway, promise me you'll keep me up to date with what's happening, do you hear?'

'Yes, love. I'll keep the satellites running hot with my emails. And when you get a chance, get in touch with that brother of mine.'

'Of course I will, Dad. Love you lots. 'Bye!'

Robyn felt another lump constrict her throat, but she willed the tears not to spill over. She stopped off in the ladies' loo on the way back to her desk. Her nose was red and blotchy, and her eyes looked a bit puffy. She envied girls who cried prettily.

Robyn sighed. She had to admit she felt a bit better having spoken to her father. From twelve thousand miles away it was all too easy to imagine the worst, but hearing him sounding quite normal was balm to her unease. As she walked back to her desk she paused by the glass partition to signal a thumbs-up to Lori. Lori smiled and mouthed 'see you at lunchtime.'

Chapter 7

It was the dreaded sofa bed that acted as the major catalyst in prompting Robyn to look for alternative accommodation, but her guilt at spying on Lori's boss gave her another reason to move on. There was also her attraction to Lori's flatmate Colin.

Now that she had a car she felt more independent. She and Lori had gone out in their lunch break and arranged the hire of a smart, dark green Renault Clio, which Robyn very originally christened 'Clio'.

The following day Robyn bought the local paper and a street map. Armed with these items after returning from work she settled herself in the sitting room at Lori's flat. Lori had gone to the gym after work. Robyn didn't want to broach the subject of moving out with Lori as yet, feeling it would be better to present her with the done deed and a thank you gift when she managed to find somewhere new.

Before long Robyn had devoured the 'rooms to let' section of the paper, tracked down two possibilities that were within striking distance, and arranged to view both that evening. As she was preparing to leave she heard the front door slam.

'That you, Lori?' she called.

'No, it's me,' replied Colin.

'Oh, hello,' said Robyn, crossing the hall and pulling a coat off the bank of hooks by the door.

'I think you'll find that's my coat,' said Colin, unwinding a colourful striped scarf from around his neck.

'Gee, I'm sorry,' replied Robyn. 'One black coat looks pretty much like the next.'

'I don't usually have this effect on women, you know,' said Colin with a mischievous twinkle in his green eyes.

'Huh?' Robyn gulped, blushing, thinking he'd picked up on her attraction to him.

'Women don't usually leave as soon as I arrive.'

'Oh, I see. It's not like that, really. I've arranged to meet someone.'

Robyn had by this time found her own coat. Colin moved round behind her and helped her into it, and she caught a tantalising hint of his aftershave.

Colin smiled. 'Well, I suppose I'll have to let you off on this occasion. Is Lori out?'

'Yes, she's gone to the gym. She should be back soon,' said Robyn, hoping her cheeks weren't as red as they felt.

'Will you be back for dinner? I've made one of my curries.'

'I reckon I'll be about an hour. But if you're hungry don't wait on my account.'

'It'll take me at least an hour to cook the rice and prepare the other bits and pieces.'

'Sounds great. Well, I'll see you then.'

Robyn slipped out of the house and crunched along the path to her car. Clio had less character than Rover, but she had to admit a nearly-new car started much more reliably.

The first house seemed a possibility. The room was large, with French windows leading to the garden. The house was owned by Celia, a divorcee with a boy of about six.

'It's quiet here, and close to the shops,' enthused Celia. 'I usually have students from the agricultural college, but you'd be more than welcome.'

Robyn explained that she had another place to look at, but that she'd be in touch. However there was something a bit dreary about Celia that made Robyn think she might become clingy and dependent. And then there was the child to take into consideration. Robyn couldn't imagine what it would be like to live with a six-year-old.

The second house was owned by an older woman named Margaret.

'Please call me Maggie,' she said cheerfully, offering a capable, firm handshake.

Maggie was a widow, apparently quite well off, who liked to travel. She liked to have a lodger to keep an eye on the place while she was away. She was leaving in a few weeks to travel around New Mexico by motorbike with a friend.

The house was quirky and untidy, crammed with artefacts from Maggie's travels. The room to let was small, but Robyn felt more at home than at the previous house. Then something occurred to her.

'I'm only here for two months, Maggie. My employer has sent me over on a short contract. Would that be a problem? How long will you be away?'

Maggie smiled. 'Oh, only a month. I want to be back to celebrate the Millennium with my friends.'

'My flight back to Australia is booked for December 23rd. I'm looking forward to Christmas and the millennium parties at home.'

'The room is yours if you want it,' said Maggie.

'Gee, thanks! Is it okay if I move in at the weekend? I'll pay the rent now, of course.'

'Just the deposit will do for now, you can pay the rest on Saturday.'

Robyn went on her way, pleased with her evening's work. She paused in the car to phone Celia and tell her she'd found other accommodation.

Passing by the shopping centre Robyn stopped at an off licence to buy wine and beer to go with Colin's curry.

'You Australian?' enquired the man behind the counter.

Robyn nodded.

'We beat you at the Oval last week,' he said with a mocking grin. Seeing her blank expression he explained. 'Cricket. Don't tell me you're not a fan. I thought all Aussies were.'

Robyn went on her way, feeling as though it was her fault the Australian team had lost.

Back at Lori's flat a savoury aroma assailed Robyn's nostrils even before she opened the front door. Exotic music warbled from the CD player. The table in the dining room was laid, and Robyn could hear Lori and Colin in the kitchen, presumably putting the finishing touches to the meal.

'Smells wonderful!' she called as she dropped her handbag beside her suitcase in the sitting room.

Lori came through from the kitchen carrying a basket of steaming naan bread.

'Give us a hand bringing things through?'

Within minutes Colin, Lori and Robyn were seated before a feast fit for a maharajah.

'Gee, Colin. Where'd you learn to cook like this?' asked Robyn, savouring her first mouthful.

'Aha! I spent a couple of months last year in India. Goa, actually,' he added, shovelling more rice onto his plate.

Robyn observed Colin intently as he talked about his experiences in India. She found his green eyes quite mesmerising, like deep pools in a woodland stream. She longed to run her fingers through his lovely, floppy hair. She intercepted a glance from Lori and scolded herself for seeming so obvious.

When Colin returned to the kitchen for more poppadums, Robyn jumped at the opportunity to tell Lori of her plans.

'Thanks for letting me stay, but I'm sure you won't want me cluttering up your sitting room forever. I've been out this evening and found a room with a nice old dear called Maggie. She lives in River Lane. She's off to the USA shortly and wants someone around to scare off the burglars.'

Lori smiled. 'It's been lovely having you here, but I suppose you'd like a proper bedroom. And if you keep looking at Colin like you were just now …'

'Gee, is it that obvious? Okay, I admit it. I think he's totally gorgeous. But totally out of my league. So it's best that I move on before I make a fool of myself.'

'You never know …' said Lori.

'You never know what?' asked Colin as he returned, licking his fingers as he placed a sticky dish of chutney on the table next to a stack of freshly-cooked poppadums.

'Robyn's found lodgings in River Lane,' explained Lori, quickly covering for Robyn's embarrassment. 'She thinks she might be lonely while her landlady is away in the USA, but I was on the point of saying you never know, you might like a bit of solitude.'

'I'll come round and keep you company,' said Colin with a cheeky grin.

Robyn blushed. 'That's very nice of you, Colin. I hope you'll come and visit too, Lori.'

'Of course, silly. You won't be lonely at all.'

Having finished their meal, the three heaped their dirty dishes in the kitchen sink and flopped in the sitting room to watch television and recover from their serious bout of overindulgence.

***

Josephine drew back, embarrassed that she had sobbed on James's shoulder like a child. She had even left a damp patch on his faded shirt.

'I'm sorry,' she said, taking a deep breath and wiping her eyes with her fingers. 'I'll stop being such a baby.'

James ran a brown hand through his tousled hair. 'Like I said, you're very brave really. A lot of people would have given up and drowned.'

Josephine managed a watery smile. 'I don't feel very brave.'

'Well, what can we do to cheer you up, Empress Josephine? A bath in asses' milk? A box of exotic sweetmeats? A new dress?'

Josephine laughed at the ridiculousness of his suggestions. 'Ummm, don't make me think of sweets. When *Maman* takes us into Penzance we always to to Mrs Trescothick's shop and she buys us whatever we want. George usually has liquorice. Lucien likes a pink sugar mouse, but I like caramels best.'

James rolled his eyes. 'Cor, it's years since I had a nice square of caramel. And what about Turkish Delight?'

'Oh, yes! We always have that at Christmas, delivered from Fortnum and Mason in a pretty box.'

'I'll have a chat with Luisa. See if we can make some sweets. I dunno how we'd make caramel, let alone Turkish Delight.'

'I don't know anything about cooking,' confessed Josephine.

'Maybe with Luisa's help we can turn out a surprise for the others,' said James, sifting sand through his fingers.

'Why not?' said Josephine, standing up and brushing sand off the back of her dress. 'Thanks for making my box,' she added before picking up James's handiwork and carrying it into the cave. She placed her few possessions in the box: her swimsuit, two pairs of bloomers and two vests, and a nondescript cotton dress that Luisa had given her after assessing what she could spare from her own meagre wardrobe.

James followed her into the cave. 'I meant what I said about writing your name on the box,' he said, sitting cross-legged in the sand at the mouth of the cave. 'Pass it here.'

She did so, and he set to work with a stump of pencil. His tongue crept into the corner of his mouth as he laboriously wrote 'Empress Josephine' in flowing script on the lid, and underlined it with a fancy scroll.

'Very good!' enthused Josephine. 'You should work as sign writer.'

'Not much call for sign writing hereabouts,' he replied with a wry grin.

They heard laughter and splashing, and glanced over to where Marielena, Solomon and Roberto were frolicking in the shallows. Young Thomas sat at the water's edge, playing with a large shell.

'Let's join them,' said James, stripping off his shirt and trousers and running towards the sea.

Josephine turned away, embarrassed, but upon looking back was relieved to see that he was at least wearing long johns. She extracted her swimsuit from her new box and slipped into the shadows at the back of the cave to change, not for a moment thinking of the man who had died there.

Josephine ran down the beach and into the water without hesitation. It would not have been unreasonable to expect that she might feel anxiety at plunging into the sea that had very nearly claimed her life, but she showed no sign of such qualms.

Roberto said something in Spanish as he floated happily in the clear waters, and Josephine turned to Marielena for explanation.

'He's saying the water is warm today,' said the dark-haired girl with a superior smile.

'Do you understand Spanish?' asked Josephine of James.

'I know a bit, but not as good as Mari,' he replied, turning on his back. The sun shone on his brown, well-muscled chest.

Josephine glanced discreetly at her companions. Simon had naturally dark brown skin, but Marielena, James and Roberto were burned almost as dark by the sun. Although *Maman* had admonished Josephine to keep out of the sun in order to keep her skin as fair and aristocratic as possible, she couldn't help thinking that tanned skin looked healthier than pasty paleness. She hoped her own skin would turn a pleasant shade before too long.

A shout rang out from the direction of the cave.

Marielena turned and scowled. 'Mama wants help with the cooking,' she explained. She turned to Josephine. 'Time you got your hands dirty too, miss,' she said with a spiteful glare.

Josephine followed Marielena out of the water, wounded by the girl's sharp tongue. She wondered where Lucy was. Lucy was much nicer.

Luisa was certainly more gracious than her daughter. She patiently taught Josephine how to knead the bread dough and set it to bake on the large, flat stones in the fire.

Before long, James emerged from the water and, true to his word, asked Luisa whether they might make some sweets.

Luisa smiled. 'I think we can spare enough sugar to make some toffee. I'll show you how. This is most unlike you, James, to show an interest in cooking.'

'That's Josephine's fault. She got me thinking about caramel and stuff. How do you make caramel?'

'You start with toffee, but you need to add cream. If we had a cow we could do this, but sadly …' She shrugged expressively. 'Even if we managed to get a cow over here, what would it eat?'

Josephine looked around at the sparse vegetation. She knew that were it not for Luisa's knowledge and ingenuity they would starve.

Josephine spent a restless night, and the following morning woke with a dull ache in her stomach. She was thankful to be first as usual at the latrine, but alarmed to find fresh, red blood trickling down the inside of her leg. She

68

waded into the sea and washed, but by the time she had walked back up the beach she could feel more blood running down the inside of her legs.

She hurried into the cave and shook Luisa awake. 'I'm bleeding from my insides. Quite a lot,' Josephine whispered urgently.

Josephine was surprised to see Luisa smile. Bleeding was no cause for amusement.

'Come outside,' said Luisa, rolling out of her quilt and opening the trunk.

When they emerged into the sunshine Josephine was relieved to see that Luisa had brought a cloth.

'You'll have to let me go home now. I hope I can get to the doctor before I bleed to death. I must have injured my insides by swimming such a long way.'

'Calm yourself, *carita*,' said Luisa, laying a warm hand on the young girl's shoulder. 'To bleed like this is perfectly normal for a girl once she reaches maturity. I bleed like this once each month. So does Lucy, and it will happen to my Mari before long.'

'But that's terrible!'

Luisa shook her head. 'It's part of being a woman. I'm surprised your mother didn't tell you about such things. As I said, you will bleed once every four weeks, give or take a few days. The bleeding lasts for about five days. It does no harm; your body has plenty of blood to spare. Although it looks like a lot compared with a cut on your finger you don't actually lose more than a few spoonfuls. I will give you some cloths to wear inside your underwear. You will need to change the cloth every few hours. And you won't be able to go swimming while you're bleeding.'

'What a nuisance!' sighed Josephine. 'How do you put up with it?'

'Ah, it has its compensations. It shows you are now able to have babies. Walk with me down to the sea, and we will wash that stain from your nightdress.'

Josephine was pensive during breakfast, mulling over the information Luisa had imparted. She shifted position in the sand, feeling the reassuring bulk of the cloth between her legs. She planned to change the cloth as soon as they had cleared away after breakfast. It would not do to embarrass oneself by staining one's clothing.

'You're quiet this morning,' observed Lucy, squatting in the sand beside Josephine. Her fair hair reflected the morning sun like a sheaf of corn.

Josephine nodded gravely. 'I've become a woman.'

'Oh, you mean ...'

Josephine nodded again. 'Yes. Luisa explained everything to me.'

'Welcome to the club,' whispered Lucy with a smile.

A bit of womanly solidarity made the bleeding seem a little less daunting. It was just one more of life's trials to which she must become accustomed. Life seemed to be full of them these days, but on a summer's morning with the sun already beating down on her head and shoulders it was easy enough to ignore the dull ache in her belly.

Chapter 8

It was difficult for Robyn to know how to start spying on Paul Sinclair. During the normal course of her working day she spent very little time in his company. She tried playing dumb, asking him to explain various things about their accounting system, but his visits to her work station were brief and to the point. Paul was largely preoccupied with meetings, it seemed. Clients appeared on a regular basis, and almost every day he could be seen dashing out of the office, briefcase in hand, presumably visiting clients on their own premises. He kept his own diary; his secretary, a snooty-looking woman named Anthea, seemed to spend much of her time tidying her office and fussing with flowers.

Robyn spent her days tinkering about with the computerised accounting package, checking every facet of its operation. She tried cross-referencing the accounts, but was beginning to think that finding any irregularities was going to be harder than trying to find a needle in a haystack.

She reported back to Nick by email on her laptop, alone in the sitting room at the flat after Lori and Colin had gone to bed.

Hello Nick, well, what to tell you? Nothing at present. To tell the truth, I don't really know how to proceed any further without asking Paul Sinclair point blank whether he's on the fiddle. I've been through the records and everything seems to add up. I'd be grateful for your suggestions.

Before Robyn moved into Maggie's house the following Saturday morning she bought half a dozen bottles of wine for Lori and Colin and left them in the kitchen with a thank you note. She arrived in River Lane shortly after eleven. Although Maggie had given her a key, she thought it polite to knock.

Maggie appeared, her grey hair curling up like Medusa's snakes, holding a large wooden parrot in one hand. 'Just sorting out some things in the attic, dear,' she explained. 'Goodness knows how I brought this thing back from Honduras. He can go off to the church jumble, someone might want to give him a home.'

Robyn cast her eye over the varied clutter that wasn't boxed up for the jumble sale, and privately thought there were quite a few other things that were surely surplus to requirements. Still, they gave the house a cosy, lived-in look, and thankfully her own room showed no evidence of totem poles or scary masks.

The bedroom window offered a view of the garden, with the river beyond partly obscured by willow trees. Robyn unpacked her case, hung her meagre collection of clothes in the wardrobe, and sat down on the bed. Maggie's house was very quiet, and she missed Lori and Colin already. She'd grown to like the way Colin crashed about the flat. He never closed a door quietly, and his footsteps seemed to make the whole house shake. It was like sharing a flat with a very large, lively dog. Lori called him The Elephant, and said he should never think of moving to an upstairs flat in case he fell through the floor onto the occupants below.

That afternoon Robyn got around to telephoning her aunt and uncle. Although Maggie had said to feel free to use the phone, Robyn didn't wish to impose so she used her mobile.

A woman answered. Robyn explained who she was, and asked if she was speaking to Mrs Emily Trescowe.

'Yes, speaking. So, you're Joseph's girl. What a surprise!' she said in her warm, countrified voice. Robyn wondered whether everyone in Cornwall spoke like Aunt Emily.

'Just wait till I tell Morvah!' continued Emily. 'He won't believe me! You must come and visit us. Where are you staying?'

'I'm in Eastleigh, Hampshire. I'm here for a couple of months.'

'Heavens, you sound so grown up. The last time we spoke you were just a little thing. Anyway, we live near Truro. Do you have our address?'

Robyn checked her father's information sheet. 'Um, Primrose Cottage, Kershaw's Lane ...'

'That's right,' interrupted her aunt. 'Now, you should be able to get a train from Southampton that will take you to Truro.'

'It's okay, I've got a car.'

'Even better. So, when can you come and stay? How about next weekend?'

'Gee, that'd be great,' said Robyn, hoping she hadn't promised Lori anything. 'I'll set off first thing on Saturday morning, and I'll phone you when I'm near Truro.'

'Oh dear. You might have some trouble finding a phone box. There aren't very many hereabouts.'

'No problem, I've got a mobile phone. I'm talking on it now.'

'I've got one too. Morwenna gave it to me for my birthday last year. I feel ever so fashionable walking round the supermarket talking to Morvah, asking him whether he'd prefer cornflakes or rice crispies. Next thing you know, I'll be surfing that internet.'

'I'll bring my laptop, Aunt Emily. We can do some surfing together,' chuckled Robyn.

'Just wait till I tell my granddaughter. That's Olivia, Morwenna's little girl. She's only two, but bright as ninepence. Her daddy, Colum, has a computer, and Olivia plays games on it already. Where will it all end, I ask myself ...'

'I'd better go, Aunt Emily,' said Robyn, noticing that her battery was running low again. 'See you next Saturday.'

'I'll see if I can get Morwenna and Colum to come for Sunday dinner, and bring Olivia. I'll bake a chocolate layer cake. Do you like chocolate cake, dear?'

Robyn eventually ended the call and smiled to herself as she plugged her phone into the charger. Aunt Emily sounded a bit of a card. Robyn could just imagine her strutting around the supermarket with her phone clamped to her ear. She was looking forward to meeting the family. England seemed more like home already. She booted up the laptop, eager to send a message to her parents with news of her call to the relations.

When she made the internet connection there was a message from Delia, whose typing left much to be desired.

Hello Rob, me here. Justust wanted to tell you ho much I am enjiying Rover. Think e like me too. Mor reiliable than eny boyfiend. Hop all is goin well. Luv, Deedles XX

Of course Robyn had to reply immediately, tactfully reminding her friend to take the greatest care of her precious car. Also time to put on a bit of swank, telling Delia that the firm was paying for her to hire a brand new car, definitely more reliable than any man. A sexy French car, nonetheless. And here she could drive to a workplace with plenty of parking spaces instead of sweating like a sardine on the bus.

Then a quick message to her parents reporting contact with Morvah and Emily, and time for a short nap before thinking about what to have for a late lunch.

***

Josephine looked up from her writing. She had fallen a little behind with her keeping of the diary, and had spent some time at the end of the day recording the events of the past nine days in the damp-stained accounts ledger which they used as a diary. Even though she hadn't been keeping up with the journal Josephine made a point each morning of marking off the previous day in the front of the book. Today was the thirty-first of July. Tomorrow was her brother George's birthday, and she thought of him with a hollow feeling of longing. The shadows cast by the rocks were lengthening. The sand glowed a deep gold in the early evening sun, and the calm sea was suspended from the horizon, a mass of deep blue shot through with gold.

Josephine was growing accustomed to the lack of a wristwatch. All that mattered on the island was day, night and mealtimes. If anyone was missing when food was served, someone banged on the tin bath. That soon brought stragglers running.

Josephine could sense a buzz of excitement at the mouth of the cave. She closed the diary and brushed her wayward hair out of her eyes. Everyone except Thomas and Marielena had gathered by the cave, and they were deep in animated discussion. Josephine rose to her feet and joined them.

'We're planning a voyage to the mainland,' explained Lucy, her blue eyes shining with excitement.

Josephine's heart soared and then sank. So near, yet so far. Knowing that she'd have to stay on the island while some of them journeyed to the mainland deflated her spirits, but she did her best to feign interest.

'Who's going?' she asked. 'And when?'

'James, Mari and Simon. James says the tide will be right in about a week. We need supplies. We try to make a few trips in the summer so that we can stock up for the winter months when the sea becomes too rough to make the crossing.'

Something suddenly occurred to Josephine. 'How do you pay for supplies?'

Lucy grinned. 'I don't think you've seen our treasure trove yet.'

Josephine looked mystified. Treasure trove? Surely not gold doubloons and jewellery?

'We make things to sell, and keep them for our trips to the mainland.' Lucy grasped Josephine's wrist. 'Come with me, I'll show you.'

Josephine followed Lucy into the cave. Lucy dropped to her knees and lifted the lid of yet another trunk. 'It's a bit too dark to see. Help me pull it out into the light,' she said, tugging the handle at one end.

The girls pushed and pulled the trunk out into the fading daylight.

Lucy stood back, hands on hips. 'See, we've carved wooden dolls and dressed them in clothes made from scraps of fabric. And we've also carved pegs from odd bits of twiggy driftwood. That was Roberto's idea. His father taught him woodcarving, and Simon and James have become quite good at it too. Haven't you noticed them working away in the evenings as we sit by the fire?'

'I thought they were just whittling. I didn't realise they were actually making something.'

Lucy smiled. 'Look at these shell necklaces, threaded on fishing line. Luisa and I make them, and she and I, and Mari, make the dolls' clothes. Mari will take a basketload of our handiwork to the market in Helston. She's a good saleswoman. She always comes away with an empty basket and a purse full of coins.'

Josephine looked across to where Marielena and James stood apart from the others. She couldn't help noticing a proprietary gleam in Marielena's eyes as she brushed something from James's cheek. She turned to Lucy.

'Are Mari and James betrothed?'

Lucy shrugged. 'I suppose there's a sort of understanding between them. Mari's only fourteen, but then many girls of her age are ready to settle down and raise a family.'

'My goodness! I'm sixteen, but I have no intention of such things yet.'

'Me neither. And I'm seventeen. Practically an old maid,' added Lucy with a giggle.

'*Maman* was planning to send me on a tour of Europe as soon as I finished my education,' said Josephine wistfully. 'She assured me I'd meet plenty of wealthy young men among the nobility of Europe, suitable husband material. My life will be very different now I'm stuck here.'

'Try not to think of the future. You won't have to stay here forever, I'm sure.'

'What about you?' said Josephine, changing the subject before she became too upset.

'I'm happy enough here. Though I'll probably end up marrying Simon, or perhaps Thomas.'

'That's disgusting! He's not much more than a baby!'

Lucy laughed. 'He won't be a baby forever. One of my aunts was ten years older than her husband. Anyway it's miles better here than in that workhouse,' she added, screwing up her nose with distaste at the memory.

'Do you mind me asking why you ended up in the workhouse? You don't seem like the sort of person who was born in the slums.'

'Oh, all sorts of people end up there. You shouldn't assume we're all guttersnipes. My father was a private tutor, but he died of pneumonia when he was thirty-four, leaving my mother, my sister and me without any income. It was hopeless.'

'So where are your mother and sister?'

Lucy took a deep breath. 'They died in the workhouse fire. Along with the mother of Solomon and Thomas. And she had several other children who also died.'

'Oh, Lucy! I'm so sorry! I'd no idea,' gasped Josephine, putting her arm around Lucy's shoulders.

'You weren't to know,' said Lucy, wiping her eyes surreptitiously. 'Silly me. It's been three years now. You'd think I would have got over it.'

Josephine drew the sobbing girl close. 'There, there. Don't cry, Lucy. Gosh, I don't know what to say. Nothing can make up for your loss, but I want you to know I understand.'

Lucy managed a watery smile. 'Yes, I suppose you do. Luisa told me about your brother.'

'He wasn't the nicest of brothers, but it was still very upsetting. Not knowing whether he drowned is the worst.'

Lucy and Josephine sat together in silence as the last of the daylight disappeared.

***

By the end of her third week at Waldron Robyn was pleased to observe that Paul Sinclair was loosening up a bit, definitely becoming more friendly and chatty. As she drove home through the rain on Friday evening she mused over their conversation that afternoon. She had mentioned that she was heading down near Truro for the weekend to stay with her relations.

Paul had waxed lyrical about Cornwall. 'I spent my childhood there,' he said. 'My parents had a property near St Ives.'

'Gee, I really must buy a map,' said Robyn. 'I meant to get one last Saturday but I forgot.'

Paul slipped into his office and returned with a road atlas.

'You may borrow this. I won't need it at the weekend.'

'Thanks very much. I promise I won't lose it. I love the sound of all these strange place names. Perranzabuloe, for instance. Did I pronounce it right?'

'Pretty much. The Cornish are a different race than the rest of the English. They have their own language.'

'Really? Do you speak it?'

''Fraid not. My mother's people are from Devon, and my father is French in origin. Mother did quite a bit of research into both sides of the family tree. My father's ancestors made lengthy visits to England from the time of the French revolution. They were members of the minor nobility and probably thought it the best way to ensure they kept their heads firmly attached to their bodies. My father's uncle was the one who took up permanent residence in Cornwall, joining the small number of French ex-pats already established in the area around Penzance in the early part of the twentieth century.'

'I'm supposed to be finding out about our family tree for my father while I'm over here. Filling in the gaps.'

'Good luck with that,' said Paul. 'It can be very complicated.'

Robyn pulled into the gravelled drive and brought her car to a halt. Maggie was in the sitting room. She was due to leave for America the following Wednesday, and was busy sorting out her luggage.

'I like to travel light,' she said. Observing the size of the pile of clothing on the sofa next to the dinky red backpack Robyn thought Maggie was going to need a magic wand.

It seemed Maggie could read Robyn's thoughts. 'I won't be taking all this,' she said with a jangle of brass bangles. 'I'm selecting the necessaries from a pile of possibles. I always do it like this. Now what do you think of my leather gear?'

Maggie held up a black leather jacket and trousers. 'I bought these in Southampton today.'

Robyn was stunned. Maggie was older than her mother, and hardly seemed a likely candidate for membership of the Hell's Angels.

Maggie grinned. 'Leather is the best thing to wear on a motorbike. Good protection in case you fall off. But it's such bulky stuff. I think I'm going to have to wear this lot on the plane. Just take a few t-shirts and things in my back pack, maybe one dress,' she mused.

'Can you ride a motorbike?'

'No, dear. I'm going with a friend, Roger. He has a Harley Davidson. But we'll hire a bike once we arrive in Albuquerque. It'd cost a fortune to take his with us.'

'Maggie, you're amazing! My mother would never dream of doing such a thing. Anyway, she's got other things on her mind at the moment. Dad's just been diagnosed with cancer.'

'Oh, my dear. I'm so sorry. I lost my husband to cancer ten years ago. How well I remember the many hours spent at the hospital, all the waiting for results of tests ... sorry, I'm upsetting you. How thoughtless of me.'

Robyn blew her nose on the tissue Maggie offered. 'It's all right, Maggie. I'm okay. But I get a bit teary thinking of Mum going through all that with him. I've got nothing to cry about really.'

'On the contrary, dear. Being so far away you must be feeling quite frustrated, unable to do anything. Except, of course, offer moral support which is important.'

'Yes, I suppose so. I'm sending Dad regular emails.'

'That must be a real tonic for him.'

'Mum and Dad were born in England so they get a kick out of hearing about the places I go. They went to Australia just after they got married.'

'How romantic!'

'I don't think it was really, from what Mum's told me. She said they had the cheapest ticket possible, and the ship's rats had more home comforts. The voyage took about four weeks. Then when they arrived they were put in disused army barracks for a couple of months. Then they went to a horrible little council house. That's where they were living when I was born.'

'True, we all tend to think that what other people do is much more exciting than our own lives. My sister envies me my trips abroad, but she wouldn't be so pea green if she could have seen me in Honduras, knee deep in mud, trying to get out of the hotel before it got carried away in a landslide.'

'Gee, that must have been really scary.'

'Ah well,' said Maggie, ripping the price tag from her new leather jacket. 'It's all part of life's rich tapestry. What doesn't kill us makes us stronger.'

Robyn could only hope that would apply to her father.

***

They all gathered on the beach to wave farewell to James, Simon and Marielena. It was near dusk. The sky was overcast but the sea was calm. Josephine felt downcast but resigned as she watched the rowing boat become a little smudge in the distance and then disappear.

'How long will it take them to reach the mainland?' she asked Solomon.

'Most of the night. They took me with them last time,' he said proudly.

'Tell me all about it,' said Josephine, settling on the sand beside Solomon and hugging her knees to keep warm.

'We took turns rowing. James kept us going in the right direction, he has a compass and charts. We saw land in the distance as the sky grew light. James looked out for Poldhu Point, just to the left of Mullion Island, and we landed in a small cove. We pulled the boat up into the bushes. Simon stayed behind to make sure no-one stole it. Then it was a long, long walk to Helston. I was fair whacked. We went to the market square. There was no market that day, but we found out it was on the next day. Mari nicked some bread off the baker's dray, and we hid in an alley to eat it. It was lovely, all soft and squishy. Not like the stuff Luisa makes. Then I found some money in the street! Someone must have dropped it. James went into an ale house and bought some meat and a jug of beer. We went down by this stream and had us a feast. 'Cept the beer made me feel sick and dizzy. I spewed up all my food! We walked back to the boat after that, and slept the night on the beach. The next day James stayed at the boat. He was a bit scared in case someone recognised him in the town. Pushing his luck to go two days in a row, he said. So Mari, Simon and I went to the market. Mari sold all the things in her basket. We were rich! Then we bought loads of flour and sugar and stuff, and dragged it all back to the boat. That was hard work! Then we had to set off right away to catch the tide. I slept most of the way back. I felt bad, but I felt too tired and sick to do much rowing.'

Solomon grinned. It was almost dark and his teeth glowed white in his brown face.

'What an adventure! Will you go again?'

'Oh yes. We take it in turns. Of course Tom's too little. Three or four of us go each time.'

'Aren't you worried that you might bump into the man whose boat you stole, and that he would recognise the boat?'

'Ah, no. James painted it a different colour with new markings. He's clever like that.'

'That's good to hear,' said Josephine with a shiver. 'I'm going into the cave now, I'm cold. Are you coming?'

'Nah, I'm not cold. I'm going down the beach to catch some crabs.'

Josephine smiled at the retreating figure. She liked Solomon. He was a plucky fellow. She liked most of them, even James now. The only real fly in the ointment was the abrupt, sullen Marielena. But Josephine supposed even Marielena had her redeeming qualities. Particularly her ability to sell a basket of wares and make enough money to keep them in essentials.

***

Late that night Robyn opened the envelope of family tree information her father had given her. Just looking at his angular handwriting made her feel closer to him. She settled on her bed to read his notes.

As you will see, the family tree on my side is more of a small shrub. Despite my best efforts on various websites I haven't been able to trace back any further than my grandparents. The first step is for you to get in touch with other members of the family. The address of my brother Morvah is given below. Morvah is a bit of an old misery, but he may know where you can find the others. In particular our uncle, William Rostrevor. He's my mother's brother.

Success in finding relatives through other relatives depends very much on their interest in such matters. If you draw a blank with Morvah you can always consult the records office in London (address below) or look at parish records in Cornwall. It may help you to practise your methods by retracing the information I've already given you. For example, I was born in Penryn, near Falmouth, on July 4th, 1950. Parish records for Penryn will show my christening when I was around six months old, and will also show my date of birth. Looking ahead to records for 1973 you will see my marriage to your mother, Rose Jarvis, on May 12th. From the family tree you'll see that I've been able to trace your mother's family back to the eighteenth century.

You'll see that my mother, Maud Rostrevor, was born on 4th January 1927. One thing I don't understand is that my mother's name is listed as Maud. My father always called her Nellie, but I suppose that must have been a nickname. What I haven't been able to find is a record of her parents' marriage, which would give me her mother's maiden name. Also, I haven't been able to find any other Rostrevors who seem to be related to them. What you will need to do is search the records for marriages involving any man named Rostrevor during the years when my maternal grandmother would most likely have married, say from 1880 to 1927 when Maud was born. Or maybe anything up to 1932 in case they married after she was born. Some information may have been lost during World War Two, but it's worth a try. I won't be annoyed if you can't find the time to do this, but you may find it interesting. Good luck!

Robyn hadn't expected it would take her quite as long to drive to Truro. It wasn't anything like driving in Australia. There was no direct route, no

80

freeway. At least the road system skirted round most of the major towns, but the Saturday morning traffic was heavy.

It was nearly two in the afternoon before she pulled into a petrol station on the outskirts of Truro. Having filled Clio with petrol and munched on a chocolate bar, Robyn put in a call to her aunt and uncle to apologise for her lateness.

Aunt Emily sounded pretty laid back, saying lunch was merely a pot of soup and some nice home made bread, and would be waiting when she arrived. Robyn checked the last part of her route with her aunt, right down to where she must turn left after the white gate with the sheep's skull nailed to the railings.

It didn't take Robyn long to reach Old Kea. She turned left, following where the signs pointed down a country lane edged with a dense hedge. The hedges were full of pretty, bright red berries. The sky was soft and grey, melting mistily into soft, freshly ploughed brown earth. The ploughed ridges gave perspective to the scene, and the bright berries added a cheerful touch.

Robyn pulled in to the side where the lane widened for vehicles to pass, whipped out her camera and snapped a couple of quick shots. Shortly after she set off again at a cautious pace she saw the white gate with the sheep's skull and turned left. She was thankful for her aunt's directions, as there was no sign to indicate this was Kershaw's Lane. At the end of a gravel driveway stood a pretty cottage painted the palest shade of yellow. Sure enough, this was Primrose Cottage. There was a plaque on the wall with twirly writing and hand-painted primroses. Robyn manoeuvred Clio in beside a little car with a canvas roof.

The front door opened and a slight, grey-haired woman appeared, beaming from ear to ear. She looked like a little pixie. Her hair was short and wispy, and she wore black leggings, trendy black boots and a green velour jumper.

'My, don't you look the image of Joseph!' she cried. 'I'd have known you in a crowd even though you were just a little girl when I last saw you. Oh, my dear, you shouldn't have! Are those for me?'

Robyn handed over the bunch of flowers, Sainsburys' finest, to her aunt.

'Ooh, I just love lilies!' she enthused. 'Do come in and say hello to your uncle. Morwenna's here too, with Colum and little Livvie.'

Robyn followed her aunt into the kitchen. Her uncle was perched on a stool by the kettle, fixing something electrical. He looked up. Robyn was startled by the resemblance between him and her father, and for a horrible moment thought she was going to cry. She realised with a pang that she hadn't told Aunt Emily about her father's illness. Now was not the time, but she knew she'd have to mention it at some stage during the day.

'Hello, girl,' said Morvah softly in his warm Cornish accent. His face was sadder than her father's. Seen together, Joseph and Morvah Trescowe would have been like the theatrical masks of Comedy and Tragedy. Robyn hoped that her uncle's sad face was just a trick of nature and not the result of an unhappy life.

Robyn grasped her uncle's well-weathered hand in both hers and squeezed, unable to trust her voice for a moment.

'Doesn't she look like Joseph!' said Emily. 'It's those lovely eyes.'

Robyn found her voice. 'Gee, I think you look very much like my Dad.'

'Ah, how is the old coot?' asked Morvah, motioning for her to take a seat at the kitchen table. Emily was arranging soup plates on the table.

Robyn realised it was now or never. She had to tell Morvah and Emily that her father had cancer. She felt a shadow pass across her heart.

Chapter 9

The shore party had been absent for four days. Even Luisa looked worried. Then finally, on the fifth morning, they were woken by their return. It was barely daylight. Luisa hugged her daughter and spoke to her passionately in Spanish. Within moments the cave was full of excitement and chatter. Sleep was forgotten. Except for young Thomas, who slept on oblivious of the cacophony.

'We were so worried!' said Lucy, hugging both James and Simon. 'You've never been gone this long before!'

'We had a bit of trouble,' admitted James.

'Not ...?' Lucy's eyes grew wide.

'No, not me and the law. Simon tripped over and knocked himself out cold. Drunk as a skunk, the silly bugger. Just look at the state of his arm!'

Simon gingerly peeled back the ragged sleeve of his jumper to reveal a graze that extended from wrist to elbow. It was as raw as meat on a butcher's slab.

Luisa swung into action, rummaging in her box of potions. 'This is going to sting,' she warned, making ready to pour liquid from a small brown bottle directly onto the wound.

'Yeah, like the salt water didn't sting on the journey back,' said Simon through gritted teeth. He winced as the liquid flowed over his injury, but recovered his composure with a grin.

'Ah, feels better already, Luisa,' he said with a wink to the others.

'Good boy!' she said, eyes bright at the prospect of another successful cure. 'You'll need to keep it clean and dry until it is completely healed,' she admonished. 'And you mustn't get sand in it.'

'Tell us everything!' begged Lucy, dancing about in her nightdress.

'I'll light the fire and put the kettle on,' said Josephine.

'Good idea,' said James. 'I could sell my soul for a hot drink.'

Josephine noticed the dark circles under his eyes. He looked weary and strained.

Before long the fire was blazing merrily and the kettle was in place. Simon and James were warming their hands by the flames, and Marielena was combing and drying her long, bedraggled hair.

James began to recount the tale of their journey.

'We hid the boat in the usual place near Poldhu Point. The market was just getting ready by the time we reached Helston. As usual, Mari sold everything in her basket. We did our shopping and headed back to the cove. But on the way I had a bright idea. We still had some money left. We stopped off at Millstone Farm and I sent Simon in to see if he could buy a goat. A milker.'

'A goat!' cried Luisa.

'Yes, a goat,' repeated James. 'It's tethered over there by the trees. You can go and see it as soon as I've finished my story. Anyway, the farmer kept Simon hanging about, and by the time we got back to the boat the tide had turned. So we had to stay the night on the beach. The three of us and Mildred. That's what we've named the goat. We still had a few pence left, so I stayed to mind the boat and the goat, and Mari and Simon went off to buy some beer. Simon decided he liked the congenial company in the pub, and he had a bit too much to drink.'

Marielena took up the story.

'Some of the men were buying him drinks. He kept saying we'd go in a minute, soon, not long now, but it was past closing time when I managed to pull him out of the place. It was only the threat of the local bobby doing his rounds that got him moving. And he was drunk as a lord! Red in the face, grinning and shouting. Stinking of beer! Then he tripped on the cobbled path and knocked himself out cold. I couldn't wake him, no matter how I tried. So I rolled him into the shadows and went to get James. By the time we got back Simon was starting to come round. He was being sick all over the place. It was disgusting! We tried to pull him to his feet but he started yelling. Then we discovered that he'd hurt his arm.'

'I must've scraped it on the wall as I fell,' added Simon.

'So we dragged him back to the boat,' said James. 'He was a bit of a mess. Had a bad headache the next day as well as a scraped arm, so we missed two more tides.'

'But why did you stay four days?' asked Luisa.

'Ah, that's another story,' said James. 'We were just about to pull the boat out of the bushes when a fishing boat moored in the cove. You guessed it. Jed Trevarthen on the *Blue Daffodil*. He seemed to be doing some sort of repairs to the rigging, and the bugger stayed overnight. I didn't think he'd recognise his old rowing boat but there was a chance he'd recognise me. So we laid low. We were bloody starving! Simon managed to creep off through the bushes after dark, down to the pub for a pasty. That was all we could afford, just one pasty between three of us. We were so weak with hunger we barely had the strength to row all the way back here. Meanwhile we had to do everything we could to keep old Mildred quiet. Trevarthen was quite a way offshore, but he might have come to investigate if the goat had made a racket. Now, who wants to come and see our goat?'

They all set off along the beach, including Thomas who had woken during the telling of the voyagers' tale.

Sure enough, a plump white goat was tethered to one of the windblown trees, munching delicately on the scrubby sea grass that grew in irregular clumps.

'She took the sea voyage in her stride,' said James. 'Good thing, as she's in kid. Farmer said she's due in a week or two. Now I don't think there's enough here to feed more than two goats, so if she has more than one kid we'll have to slaughter the rest. That will mean roast goat! And skin to make shoes and whatever. Then there's all that lovely milk until she weans the kid. And milk means cream, so we can make butter. And caramel,' he added, with a wink to Josephine. 'Let's hope Mildred has a son so we can mate them. Of course too much inbreeding down the generations will lead to problems, but it's worth a try. What do you think?'

Luisa laughed and clapped her hands together with delight. 'I think you've done very well!' she cried. 'The milk of a goat has less fat than that of a cow, but with luck we will get *some* cream. And at least we will now have nice fresh milk.'

'Of course we got all the usual stuff,' said Marielena. 'Flour, sugar, candles … and I got some plums so we can make proper jam. I'm tired of the taste of those berries that grow on the rocks. And I brought you a little present, Mama. Come and see.'

Luisa went with her daughter, back to the cave.

Thomas plucked some leaves from the tree and offered them to the goat. 'I like Mildred,' he said. 'She has pretty yellow eyes.'

'Fancy that,' said Lucy. 'A female goat with a beard.'

'I think all goats of that breed have beards, whether male or female,' said James.

'You seem to know a lot about animals as well as boats and fishing,' said Josephine, twining her hair between her fingers as she observed the confident way James scratched between the goat's horns. She had every intention of keeping well away from the sharp end of the animal.

'Ah well, That's from when I worked for Mister Roquebrun. Or *Monsieur*, as you would call him. He had all sorts of animals, probably still does.'

James turned away from the others who were occupied with petting the goat, and motioned for Josephine to walk with him. They strolled down to the sea. Josephine liked to walk where the waves surged rhythmically up the shore; she liked the tickly sensation of the sea pulling the sand from under the soles of her feet.

James reached into his pocket. 'I brought something for you,' he said shyly.

Josephine took the damp twist of paper from his hand. She pulled it open to reveal a small quantity of caramels. Slightly squashed, but caramels nonetheless.

'Oh, James!' she gasped, her eyes gleaming with pleasure. 'Thank you! But you must share them with me.'

He shook his head firmly. 'No, they're for you. Sweetmeats for an empress. Well they were fit for an empress before they got all squashed in my pocket. Sorry.'

Josephine separated one sweet from the lumpen mass and sank her teeth delicately into it. The rich sweetness flooded her mouth with saliva.

'Mmmmm, tastes simply wonderful! It doesn't matter if they're a bit misshapen.'

She picked up another sweet and reached up to pop it in James's mouth before he had a chance to protest. She felt the warmth of his tongue against her thumb. It reminded her of how she used to give dog biscuits to her favourite spaniel, Ginger, sadly run down by a wagon a couple of years previously. Ginger used to lick her fingers, and *Maman* would scold her unladylike behaviour. Josephine supposed it also wasn't very ladylike for a boy to lick one's fingers.

James grasped her wrist. 'You shouldn't have done that! Now you're really in trouble!'

He chased her along the beach, and they shrieked like a couple of little children. Josephine saw Marielena turn in the direction of the noise and raise her arm to shield the sun from her eyes. She couldn't help noticing the sullen pout or the murderous glare, even from such a distance. Was no-one allowed to act childishly, she wondered. Surely life was not meant to be all work and no play.

Emily was visibly saddened by Robyn's news of her father's illness, but Morvah's expression gave little away.

Any discussion was pre-empted by the arrival of a small girl with a man and a dog in tow.

'Pickles went swimming in the pond!' shrieked the child, her blue eyes shining almost as much as her rosy cheeks.

'Come and meet your auntie, dear,' said Emily, reaching for a cloth to wipe the small girl's muddy hands.

The child turned her attention to Robyn. 'Hello, auntie. Is that your name?'

Robyn smiled. 'Robyn, really. But you can call me auntie if you like.'

'Don't you talk funny,' said Olivia, sidling up to Robyn.

'Don't be rude, Olivia,' chided the man.

Robyn assumed he was Olivia's father. 'Oh, that's okay. She's probably never met an Australian before.'

Olivia's eyes grew round. 'An alien?' she said, stopping in her tracks.

'No, an Australian,' repeated Robyn. 'I come from a place called Australia. It's on the other side of the world.'

The dog, Pickles, sat at Robyn's feet, looking up at her beseechingly. She patted its brown and white head.

'I've been to France,' said Olivia. 'I had Crap Suzie.'

Robyn looked puzzled.

'She means Crepes Suzette,' explained Olivia's father. 'Australia's a lot further away,' he added, turning to Olivia. 'I'm Colum, Olivia's father,' he said, turning back to Robyn and offering his hand.

The kitchen door opened and a slender woman with pale skin and long, straight dark hair drifted into the room.

'Did you enjoy your walk?' she enquired of Colum and Olivia. Then she noticed the stranger in the room. 'Hello, you must be Robyn. I'm Morwenna.' She extended a pale, cool hand.

'Well, that's all the introductions done with,' said Emily, reaching for her oven mitt. 'Who'd like some soup?'

'It better not be affluent soup,' said Olivia, hands firmly on hips. 'I don't like the bits.'

'She means alphabet soup,' explained Morwenna. 'No, dear. It's pea and ham.'

Emily began ladling the thick, savoury smelling soup into bowls.

'Gee, for a minute I thought she meant effluent soup,' said Robyn.

'We don't have none of that round here,' said Morvah with a dour expression.

''Course you do, Dad,' said Morwenna, lifting Olivia into her high chair. 'Every farm has effluent of some sort. Your pigs aren't any different from anyone else's. They don't pee perfume.'

'No need to be crude, girl.'

'I was only joking.'

Robyn was mortified that she'd unwittingly sparked off a conflict between father and daughter.

'Don't take any notice of those two,' said Emily as she took a tray of bread from the oven. 'If one says something's black, the other says it's white. They've been like that ever since Morwenna learned to talk. Well, probably before that. Now sit down everyone, and tuck in.'

They did as she asked, any further conversation being temporarily halted by the serious business of lunch.

Robyn found she was very hungry, and was sure that she'd never tasted such delicious soup. She emptied her bowl.

'Have some more, dear,' urged Emily, bringing the saucepan to the table. 'I do like to see a girl with a healthy appetite.'

'I didn't realise how hungry I was,' said Robyn, feeling gauche and greedy next to Morwenna, who was still delicately dipping into a nearly full bowl.

Colum interpreted Robyn's expression. 'Don't take any notice of my wife. She eats practically nothing. I have to watch her like a hawk or else she'd fade away to a skeleton.'

'I don't do it on purpose,' pouted Morwenna.

Colum reached over and ruffled her hair. ''Course you don't, my little sprite. Picky eating is just part of your charm.'

Pacified, Morwenna relaxed. She extracted a tissue from her pocket and reached over to wipe her daughter's face. 'You're meant to eat it, you little muppet, not paint your face.'

'I like painting,' said Olivia proudly. 'And I do drawings too.'

'Perhaps you'd like to do a drawing for Auntie Robyn after lunch,' suggested Emily.

Olivia wriggled in her seat, clearly wishing to leave the table.

'After lunch,' reiterated her grandmother firmly. 'I want to see a clean plate before you get down.'

Robyn decided this was a good time to broach the subject of her ancestral investigations.

'My Dad is trying to put together our family tree,' she announced. 'Are you in contact with William? That is, if he's still alive. What about any other family?' she said, her eyes resting on Morvah.

Help came from an unexpected direction.

'Great Uncle William is indeed alive,' said Morwenna, putting down her spoon. 'I can give you his address if you like. He doesn't live far from here. His wife, Annie, died last year, but William is still going strong. He's too obsessed with the war to even think about dying. Did you bring the family tree with you? I'd love to have a look at it.'

'It's in my bag,' said Robyn.

'Mummy, why does auntie have a tree in her bag?' said Olivia.

Everyone laughed, and any remnants of formality dispersed. Robyn felt accepted into the family. As her father had said, Morvah was a bit of a dry old stick. Emily was a sweetie, a sort of modern twist on the traditional farmer's wife. Olivia was a cute little thing, bright as a button. Robyn's first impression of Morwenna had been of a rather precious, delicate princess, but it seemed they had a common interest. Family history. Although Morwenna looked fit to grace the pages of glossy magazines she still seemed to have a strong sense of tradition, of her family's continuity through the generations. And Colum … Robyn sighed. Did Morwenna know how lucky she was to have such a thoughtful, good-looking man, clearly devoted to her? Seeing such an attractive couple with a lovely child gave her a pang of longing to settle down and play house with the man of her dreams. Her thoughts lingered momentarily on Colin. Was he the one?

After they'd washed the dishes, Morwenna made tea and took the tray into the sunny conservatory at the back of the house where Emily and Morvah were already relaxing in their comfortable chairs. Olivia crouched over the small table, already intent upon her artwork.

Morwenna put the tray down on a larger table. 'I'll just get my address book,' she said, glancing at Robyn.

'Oh, right. I'll get the family tree.'

Robyn retraced her steps to the sitting room where she had left her handbag. She cast her eyes around the cosy, homely room, taking in the family photographs on the side table and the portrait of Emily as a younger woman, smiling winsomely from the chimney breast. Robyn could see Emily's resemblance to her beautiful daughter. She peered into the mirror before leaving the room, and frowned at her reflection. Clearly their beauty came from a different branch of the family. And her hair was a total fright. Snatching a comb from her bag she did what she could before returning to the family gathering.

She spread her father's papers out on the tablecloth.

'As you can see, Dad managed to find out quite a lot about Mum's side, the Jarvises. But he's drawn a blank with anything further back beyond his grandparents, Josephine and James Rostrevor. He doesn't know her maiden name or when they married. Do you think Uncle William would know anything?'

Morwenna shrugged. 'It's possible. I'll write down his address and phone number for you. But he's away this weekend, gone up to London to stay with his grandson, Gerald.'

'That's a pity,' said Robyn, disappointed that she couldn't get going immediately on the task in hand.

'You're welcome to come back any time,' said Emily. 'We're usually here.'

'Can't afford to go anywhere much,' grumbled Morvah.

'Farming's not what it used to be,' explained Emily with a sigh. 'We've had to sell a lot of our land to pay off debts. We only have a couple of fields now. We grow a few potatoes and turnips, and there are a handful of sheep and pigs, and some chickens. Money is tight, but we get by.'

'What do you and Colum do?' asked Robyn of Morwenna.

'Colum's a graphic designer, he works for a printing firm in St Austell. We live in Tresillian, just the other side of Truro. I work from home. I illustrate children's books.'

'Yes, you look like an artist. Or a model.'

Morwenna smiled. 'Funny you should say that. I did a bit of photographic modelling to help pay my way through college.'

'I'm going to be a artist when I grow up,' said Olivia, reaching for a different coloured crayon.

'Coming from such artistic parents I wouldn't be surprised,' said Robyn. 'Is that me?'

'Yes, auntie.'

Olivia had given her a fantastic pair of breasts, nothing like the reality of her modest endowment.

'Here's William's address. He lives over in Sithney, just outside Helston. Some of his family also live round there. His daughter, Catherine, is in Sithney, but her children have moved further afield. Her daughter Moira lives in Dorset, and her son, Gerald, lives in London. That's the one

William is staying with at present. Gerald's boyfriend is an interior designer, and they live in Fulham. Very trendy. Uncle is a bit old-fashioned, but funnily enough he doesn't seem bothered that his grandson is gay. I suppose it helps that Gerald's a nice fellow. So's his boyfriend, Martin. Uncle goes to stay with them every now and then so he can catch up with some of his old army pals. Gerald and Martin usually take him to some sort of gallery opening or celebrity function which he pretends he doesn't enjoy but he does really. 'Specially meeting famous people. After meeting Elton John at a charity concert he didn't shut up about it for weeks. I can give you Catherine and Moira and Gerald's addresses too if you like.'

'Gee, thanks. That'd be great. This is such a beautiful part of the country. I'll enjoy coming here again. And I expect I'll spend some time in London.'

Olivia clambered to her feet. 'I've finished my picture of you, Auntie Robyn.'

She held out her piece of paper for Robyn to inspect.

'What are those things sticking out of my head?'

'Those are your alien things. They go with your alien armour,' she added, pointing to the chest.

'Oh, that's my armour, is it?' said Robyn. Her hopes for a large bosom were dashed.

'Can we go for a walk now, Mummy?'

'If you pick up all your crayons. Fancy a walk, Robyn? We can go down by the estuary. Even though it's nearly winter there are still plenty of birds about.'

'Sounds good to me. Everyone coming?'

'I'll give it a miss if you young folk don't mind,' said Emily. 'My hip is playing me up today. But you'll go with them, won't you Morvah?'

Morvah nodded resignedly and rose to his feet.

'Mum's on the waiting list for a hip replacement,' explained Morwenna. 'We hope she'll be able to get it done some time next year. She's been waiting over a year already. Lucky she's pretty fit otherwise, but she has her bad days.'

'Gee, I'm sorry to hear that,' said Robyn. 'It's a long time to wait for an operation.'

Emily shrugged. 'They class it as non-urgent. Only the life-threatening things get operated on quickly. That's the National Health Service for you, but at least it won't cost us anything.'

'You're lucky. In Australia we have to pay or else join a health insurance scheme, and you can still expect to wait a while for an operation. I suppose it's a blessing Dad's cancer is being treated as an urgent case. Things got going right after he was diagnosed.'

'He'll get better,' said Morvah gruffly. 'My brother Joe will be back here one of these days to bore us with his latest obsession, you mark my words!'

'Morvah! That's a terrible thing to say about Robyn's father! Sometimes I could slap you! Now apologise, you old fool!'

Robyn forced a smile. 'Don't worry, Uncle Morvah. I know what you mean. Dad's latest obsession is his computer. He's done really well, learning things that a lot of people half his age can't get to grips with. He runs rings around me with his talk of processors and disk drives. But I agree, he's definitely a founder member of the team that bores for Australia, much as I love him. And well I remember when he was into photography. He drove us all crazy using the kitchen as a darkroom. Just 'cos Dad's ill we shouldn't make him out to be a saint. That always drives me mad, when someone dies and everyone says oh, he was an angel, the perfect father or brother or whatever. That's rubbish. No-one's perfect, especially my Dad. Poor Mum has a lot to put up with, but then he has to put up with her funny ways. I love them both, but they're enough to drive anyone to drink!' Robyn glanced around the family group. 'I'm sorry. I'll get off my soap box now.'

'No, you're right, lass. People do come out with a load of insincere nonsense when someone dies. But we won't have to worry about that just yet. Joe's going to pull through.'

Morvah got to his feet and gathered up their coffee mugs.

'Shall we go for that walk, folks?' said Morwenna. 'There should still be some ospreys down by the river. With global warming the seasons have all gone to pot.'

The walk was bracing, and when they returned to the warmth of the kitchen Robyn could feel her cheeks glowing. Emily had tea ready. Robyn quite liked this life of regular meals punctuated with a small amount of activity, but knew that if it became a regular habit she'd soon put on weight. It was with the knowledge that she'd soon be returning to her own rather spartan cooking that she could justify helping herself to a second slice of thickly buttered date loaf.

After tea Morwenna took Olivia upstairs to the spare bedroom. Morvah had settled in his armchair to read his newspaper, and Colum was watching cricket on TV with the volume turned down. Emily had said she'd be back in a minute, she was just dropping some eggs over to an elderly neighbour. Robyn popped out to her car to get her laptop. She paused to revel in the silence. Although it wasn't quite seven o'clock the sky was pitch dark due to cloud cover. All she could see was the occasional pinprick of light from neighbouring farms. Compared with Eastleigh, the small hamlet of Old Kea was definitely out in the sticks.

Emily returned from her visit.

Morvah peered over the top of his newspaper. 'Ah, like father, like daughter,' he said with a wry smile.

'Not really. I'm no techno-bore. Aunt Emily said she was interested in learning how to surf the internet.'

'Whatever that might be,' said Morvah, disappearing once more behind several square feet of newsprint.

Emily came through from the kitchen. 'What a dear little computer!' she exclaimed. 'I remember when they were gigantic things that took up a whole room. I worked for a big company back in the seventies, so I know. They didn't let us mere mortals get near them.'

'Things have certainly changed,' agreed Robyn. 'Now, let me show you how to search for information.'

The next hour simply disappeared while she showed her aunt how to do her supermarket shopping on line and look up the opening hours of a garden centre she wanted to visit. They had personalised a greeting card and sent it to Colum's email address so that Olivia would be able to view it when she returned home.

'She'll love that,' said Emily. ''Specially as it plays a tune.'

Morwenna had returned from reading Olivia a bedtime story, and settled on the sofa next to her husband. She looked on in amusement as her mother peered at the computer screen through her spectacles, poking timidly at the keyboard.

'You're becoming quite the whiz kid, Mother,' she teased.

'There's life in the old girl yet,' replied Emily, her eyes still glued to the screen. 'Do you have any games on your computer, Robyn? Olivia let me have a go at Sonic the Hedgehog recently, but I kept dropping him in the water.'

A short while later Morvah folded his newspaper and dropped it on the table. 'Well, I dunno about the rest of you, but I think I'll turn in,' he said, scratching his neck.

Colum and Morwenna looked at each other. 'Us too,' said Morwenna.

'Well I'm not going anywhere until I've got this pesky little ant through to the next level,' said Emily, stabbing at the keyboard.

'Just don't keep Robyn up all night,' chided Morvah as he headed for the door.

Robyn grinned at her uncle. 'No chance of that, Unc. The battery's only got about another half hour of life, and I forgot to bring the mains cable.'

'Thank goodness for small mercies,' he said, closing the door behind him.

'That man has no soul,' sighed Emily. 'Now, where was I?'

Chapter 10

Three days later, Mildred the goat gave birth to three kids. Two were stillborn, and the third lived only a short while. It appeared that the sea voyage may have had a detrimental effect on Mildred after all.

The mood of the island's inhabitants was sombre. They had all hoped they would be able to raise at least one of Mildred's offspring.

Josephine could not bring herself to try the meat of the poor, wizened little goats. Nor could Lucy or James. The others ate their fill, and Luisa prepared the remainder with salt and herbs and packed it into a small barrel that she stored at the back of the cave.

Josephine was relieved that her squeamishness did not extend to the animals' skins, and she helped Luisa cure and stretch them. They were looking forward to some new moccasins; footwear was in short supply.

James sought out Josephine's company often during the long, hot weeks of August. Most evenings, unless it was raining heavily, they made a circuit of the island, searching the beaches for shells and useful bits of flotsam as they walked. Sometimes they talked, and other times they kept a companionable silence.

Lucy explained to Josephine why Marielena was being so moody. 'You've stolen her boyfriend from right under her nose. She feels she's lost face. She's jealous of your pretty, curly hair and fancy education, in fact everything about you. So her defence is to criticise you and try to pick fights. She can't seem to see that by doing so she's alienating James even further.'

Josephine nodded, deep in thought. 'Gosh, I didn't realise she thought James and I were that close. We're just friends. He's teaching me so much about nature on our walks.'

'I think that's just what Mari is worried about. She thinks he definitely fancies you.'

'This is silly. Why can't we all be friends?'

'I think the best thing you can do is spend less time alone with James, and keep out of Mari's way. And that's not going to be easy on such a small island.'

The following morning Josephine woke early. It was a glorious day. She lit the fire and put the kettle on to heat the water for tea, and sat on the rocks near the cave to catch up on her diary keeping.

After a while Luisa emerged. 'Good morning, *carita*,' she said, stifling a yawn. 'You are a good girl, getting things ready for breakfast.'

Josephine was thankful that Luisa remained pleasant and impartial despite the situation between the newcomer and her daughter. To lose Luisa as a friend would be more than she could bear.

After breakfast Luisa suggested an attempt at making caramel while Mildred was still giving milk. Josephine, Lucy and Simon expressed interest in the project, but Mari drifted away with the rest of the boys.

'See how the sugar and water have melted together,' demonstrated Luisa as she stirred the clear syrup. 'Josephine, put another log on the fire, please. We need to keep the heat up.'

After a few minutes of stirring the syrup became drier and grainy.

'Look!' said Luisa. 'Now the grains are melting again. Soon it will begin to turn golden.'

Sure enough, after a few more minutes of persistent stirring, the syrup darkened through yellow to the deep brown of tea without milk.

'Now I will take the syrup off the heat as I don't want it to burn any darker. Lucy, will you please add a few drops of cream. Just a little, now.'

The cream hissed and spluttered as it met the molten toffee syrup, but with Luisa's expert attention with the wooden spoon the mixture soon formed a glutinous, caramel-coloured mass.

'Now we leave it to cool,' said Luisa with a satisfied smile.

Josephine helped clear away after their sweet-making session, then went back to the cave to put on her swimming costume. Luisa had suggested shellfish for the evening meal, so she took a small bag knitted from fishing line out of one of the trunks and made her way down to the rocks.

She could see Mari, Lucy, Luisa and Roberto sitting in the shade of the trees. Poor Mildred stood nearby, munching placidly on some grass. The others were nowhere to be seen.

Josephine worked her way around the rocks to the far side of the island. She collected quite a number of edible shellfish in her bag. The sun was hot on her head so she put her catch in a rock pool and weighted the opening of the bag with a rock to stop the creatures escaping.

She waded out to where the water became deeper and plunged her head under the surface, coming up again only when her lungs were bursting. She didn't see or hear James approaching, and was startled when his brown face appeared over the edge of the rocky outcrop.

'Don't creep up on me like that!' she scolded, splashing water at him. 'You nearly gave me a heart attack!'

James jumped off the rocks into the sea, landing with a massive splash. He surfaced and rubbed the water from his eyes.

'Sorry, Empress. I didn't mean to scare you.'

'I was off in my own little world, that's all, and I wasn't expecting anyone.'

'What you thinking about, then?'

'Nothing much, really. I was enjoying the moment. You know, the heat of the sun, the nice cool water.'

'Life's not all bad, is it?'

She shot him a grin. 'Not all bad, I agree. Being able to bathe in the sea whenever I want certainly beats getting measured for next year's school clothes, which is what I'd normally be doing round about now. Being stuck with pins and having my feet squeezed into shoes.'

'Don't sound like fun at all.'

Josephine nodded absently. 'I'm going to get out of the water now and lie on that nice flat rock until I'm dry. Then when I'm all hot and bothered I might just jump in the water again.'

James clambered up the rocks in Josephine's wake and they settled together in a niche in the rocks. Volcanic activity had no doubt caused the reef of rocks to jut up from the sea bed and form the platform where they lay, hidden from view. In the heat of the late morning sun Josephine and James fell asleep like a pair of basking seals.

When Josephine stirred she felt James stroking her shoulder.

'You're getting brown,' he said. 'Almost as brown as me.'

He moved closer so that their shoulders touched. His skin was warm and firm, and she liked the way it felt next to her own.

James sat up a little and began delicately untangling her hair with his fingers. 'You've got seaweed in your curls,' he murmured. 'And you look like a mermaid spread out like that on the rocks.'

'Ah, but I have legs instead of a fishy tail.'

'Very nice legs,' he replied, placing a hand on her firm, brown thigh.

The touch of his hand filled her stomach with tiny butterflies. She stared up into his grey eyes, and time stood still.

James moved closer and kissed her gently on the lips. Josephine lay still, floating in a haze of warmth and pleasure. She didn't stop to realise this was her first kiss. She didn't have time, because James quickly followed it with a second, longer kiss. It felt good, so Josephine kissed him back. Her blood was fizzing and her heart beat rapidly. All she could think about was the unexpected wonder that kissing could bring so much pleasure.

His tongue flickered between her teeth like a little fish, and her stomach lurched wildly. She slipped her tongue into his mouth, hoping he liked it as much as she did.

He slipped her swimsuit off one shoulder and worked his hand under the still damp fabric, reaching for her breast. His finger circled the nipple, and she squirmed with enjoyment.

'Do you like that?' he whispered.

'Ummm.'

He slipped the other strap and slowly pulled her swimsuit down, exposing her breasts to the warm sun. Josephine lay shamelessly on her back. James kissed each nipple in turn, then sucked gently on them. Josephine moaned with delight. Never had she felt such utter pleasure. She looked down and noticed that her nipples were standing erect and swollen like raspberries.

Before she knew what was happening James had peeled her swimsuit completely off her body and she lay naked on the rock.

'You're so beautiful,' he murmured, his voice deep with desire.

His hand gently stroked the inside of her thigh, and his tongue probed deep into her mouth. His fingers hovered over her pubic hair and probed gently into the moistness between her legs.

Josephine felt she was sure to faint with delight. The blood in her ears rushed in harmony with the steady stroking of James's fingers. She felt him move above her, and felt something much larger pushing into her, gaining entry to her body. There was a sudden burst of pain, then she rode the pleasure with him, meeting his thrusts with cries of delight.

Then she felt James tense. He cried out her name then lay still.

'Are you all right?' she whispered, concerned that he may have passed out.

'Never better,' he groaned, rolling off her.

Her eyes widened in alarm at the size of his penis. Was that what he had thrust into her?

James caressed her face. 'I'm sorry if I hurt you. It only hurts the first time. Next time will be better for you.'

Josephine sighed. 'If it gets any better than this I shall simply explode!'

James took up the challenge and they made love a second time, savouring the rapture of their bodies joining together. Eventually James quivered as though having a mild fit, and lay still once more.

'Why do you do that?' she asked when he opened his eyes.

He cradled her head in his hands. 'You're such an innocent, my little Empress. When I go like that it's because my sperm is shooting out. My sperm is what meets with a woman's eggs and makes a baby, if the time is right. Didn't they teach you about babies at that fancy school of yours?'

'Gosh, no. Nor did *Maman*. Luisa told me a little when I started the bleeding, but she didn't go into detail. She didn't tell me that making babies happened like this, and was such fun!'

James laughed softly and held her close. 'Oh Josephine, Josephine. I'm going to have to teach you everything about lovemaking. Believe me, it will get better and better as we get to know each other. But we'll have to be careful. I didn't realise you'd started your monthly bleeding. I don't think we want a baby just yet, do you?'

'Oh, no. I just want to enjoy being with you. I don't want anything getting in the way of our fun.'

James found Josephine irresistible. He'd never met a girl who took so naturally to physical pleasure. So they made love yet again. Josephine smiled her newfound understanding when James withdrew before ejaculating. They lay back on the rocks, exhausted, their naked bodies beaded with sweat.

'Time for a swim,' said Josephine, sitting up, feeling the welcome breeze cooling her skin. She moved low on the rocks in order to conceal her nakedness. She worked her way to the water's edge and slid into the cool sea, sighing blissfully.

'That's three things I've done for the first time, all in one day. Swimming naked, kissing a man, and making love.'

James slipped into the water beside her. 'Ah, my Empress!' he murmured, laughing softly as he cradled her in his arms. They sank below the surface. Josephine felt her lungs bursting for air but had no fear that she would drown. She felt she could trust James with her very life.

They made love again, clinging together in the bright water. The world suddenly seemed perfect to Josephine, as though a new dimension had been added.

They hauled their weary bodies back onto their rocky ledge. Josephine shook her long, curly hair like a spaniel.

'Have you made love to many girls before?' she asked with a teasing glint in her eyes.

James stared out to sea. 'Not many.'

'Have you made love with Mari?'

'Certainly not! She's a strict Catholic. No sex before marriage.'

'So you tried?'

James blushed. 'Just once. She got really upset. Anyway, Mari's in the past. It's you I want to be with. You're the finest, most exciting woman in the whole world.'

'No-one's ever called me a woman before. Let's see,' said Josephine coquettishly. 'Am I better than the other girls, or women, you've made love with?'

'Oh, miles better. You're not going to let it rest, are you? Well, I'll tell you. My first time was behind the dairy with a girl at the Roquebrun farm. I did it three times altogether with her, but she was dirty and I caught lice. I had to paint myself with stuff to get rid of them. So I went off the idea and didn't do it again for a long time. The next time was with an older woman. She was rich and lived in a big house near Penzance. She got me back to her house by asking me to carry a heavy parcel from the Roquebruns'. She locked the door and forced me to do it with her. She was fat and ugly but she knew a thing or two. She was French. Mrs St Clair was her name.'

Josephine burst out laughing. 'Oh, my! Madeleine St Clair! Why, I know her! She's my mother's friend. But she's hideously fat, and old. Ugh! How could you make love with her?'

James looked despondent. 'She didn't give me much choice. Anyway I was curious.'

Josephine seemed far away. 'We were visiting the St Clairs they day Lucien and I were swept out to sea. It seems so strange to know that she had already done these things with you. Amost as though I was destined to meet you.'

'Don't talk daft. Penzance is a small place,' said James with a shrug. 'Anyway, she tired of me after a matter of weeks, and I was relieved. She was totally obsessed with sex. It was flattering at first to be desired by a rich woman, but some of the things she wanted to do were downright dirty. I was glad when it was over. Things were getting out of hand, and I was scared her husband would catch us at it.'

Josephine frowned. 'I never liked him. Sinister.'

James sat up, his feet trailing in the water, and stared into the distance.

'I agree. I met him a couple of times when I was working as a beater with the hunt. I remember him because he always spoke in French to Roquebrun. He had a terrible temper, kicked one of the dogs almost to death.'

'Yes, I could certainly believe that of him.'

Josephine moved over to sit beside James on the rocky ledge.

'Well, it's all in the past,' he said. 'I doubt I will ever cross paths with the St Clairs again. She was a randy old cow, wore me out completely.'

'I would never do such a thing to you,' said Josephine suggestively, whispering in his ear and encircling him with her arms.

'Get off, woman! I haven't got the strength to do it again!'

'What, never again?' Josephine pouted with disappointment.

'Of course I want to make love to you again and again for the rest of my days. But for now I need a rest. You've drained me.'

'And you've got a sunburned bottom, too,' said Josephine. 'That's going to be sore tonight.'

'Not the only thing that's going to be sore tonight,' said James with a scowl, pulling on his shabby, cut-off trousers. 'Now get your swimsuit on before you tempt me again. If I have to see to you any more today I won't have the strength to walk back to the cave.'

***

Robyn had plenty to mull over as she drove back to Eastleigh late on Sunday night. She had only vague memories from her childhood of Aunt Emily and Uncle Morvah. It had been great getting to know them again. She'd enjoyed showing Emily how to send an email to her brother-in-law in Sydney. Dad must have been at his computer first thing in the morning, and Emily's delight at getting a speedy reply had been heartwarming. Even Uncle Morvah had seemed enthusiastic at Emily having made electronic contact with his brother.

Morwenna, Colum and Olivia had headed off home early in the evening. Olivia had a bit of a tantrum after tea: too much excitement for one day.

Emily had pleaded with Robyn to stay longer, suggesting she bunk off work the following day. But Robyn had stood firm. After all, her boss knew where she'd gone for the weekend. Only by promising to return in two weeks' time had she been able to leave with her aunt's blessing and a large jar of damson jam.

Robyn felt at peace with the world. They were good people, and she knew she would enjoy getting to know them better. She reminded herself to write to Great Uncle William without delay in the hope of arranging to visit him.

Her eyes felt tired and gritty and she was having difficulty concentrating on the road ahead, so she stopped at the next roadside services for a cup of coffee. Even near midnight there were signs of life in the shop. The coffee was hot and strong. Next to the till was a revolving stand holding postcards. Even though she was now almost back in Hampshire there were cards showing scenes of Devon and Cornwall, so she bought one of Cornish beaches and scribbled a message to her parents. Robyn hoped she'd remember to take it to the post office.

Feeling more alert, Robyn pulled out of the services and rejoined the A303. As her uncle had said, the inland route was much more direct. Once she reached the M3 and headed south it seemed only a matter of minutes before she was pulling into the drive at the side of Maggie's house.

The house was dark and empty, and Robyn shivered. Maggie had been gone only a short while but Robyn had already decided she didn't like living alone. Tired but keyed-up after the long drive she plugged in her laptop. No new messages, so she bashed out a quick email to Casey and another to Delia. She missed their company.

Robyn sought out Lori for coffee and a chat the following morning.

'My, you do look tired!' tutted Lori, heaping sugar into her cup.

'I was pretty late leaving the rellies last night. Then when I got home I was too hyped up and it took me ages to get to sleep.'

'So what are they like, these relatives of yours?'

'Oh, great.' Robyn sank her teeth into a piece of flapjack, disappointed that it tasted like mashed cardboard. 'We got on like a house on fire. I'm going back again the weekend after next. Fancy coming with me?'

Lori looked dubious. 'I wouldn't want to intrude ...'

'They're very laid-back and welcoming. Aunt Emily is like a little pixie. Uncle Morvah is a genuine sort of bloke. Their daughter Morwenna is very nice even though she looks like a supermodel. She's married to Colum, who's a total hunk, and they have a funny little daughter called Olivia. She thinks I'm an alien, not an Australian.'

Lori laughed. 'Oh, all right then. As long as you're sure I'd be welcome.'

Robyn dropped the rest of her flapjack in the bin and wiped her fingers.

'Aunt Emily actually asked me if I'd like to bring a friend. Hey, changing the subject, how would you like to come round for dinner on Saturday night? And bring Colin too, if he's free.'

'Thanks. I'd like that. I'll ask Colin next time I see him.'

'The house seems empty now Maggie's away. I need to fill it with people.'

'Shall I ask Colin if he wants to bring Virginia?'

'Steady on. Three's company, four's a crowd. Is he serious about her, then?'

'Not as far as I know. I think he's only been out with her once or twice. You fancy him, don't you?'

'You've got to admit he's a bit of a sex god.'

'Ugh. I don't see him that way at all. To me, Colin is just Colin. Heavy on the feet, eats all the peanut butter.'

'He can come and eat my peanut butter any day.'

'Don't be smutty. Anyway, this dinner on Saturday night. Can I bring anything?'

'Just Colin. And perhaps a bottle of wine. I'll check out Maggie's cook books and come up with something to dazzle your taste buds.'

'I'll try to catch Colin tonight. I'll let you know ASAP whether he can make it.'

'Gee, thanks.'

As Robyn made her way back to her desk she started thinking about what to wear in order to grab Colin's attention. Maybe a shopping trip was on the agenda.

**

That night after they'd eated a dinner of boiled shellfish and fresh bread, Luisa brought out the tray of caramel.

'It's set quite well,' she said, cutting it into squares. 'Next I will try making butter if I can get enough cream from Mildred's milk.'

There were mixed reactions as the assembled company tried the caramel. Solomon thought it too sweet, but most thought it was pretty good. Josephine, however, was disappointed that it was nowhere near as tasty as the caramels James had brought her from the mainland. She could detect a hint of goaty flavour from the cream.

James caught her eye across the flames. He inclined his head questioningly. She smiled, but quickly lowered her eyes. She felt as though Luisa and Marielena surely must know what they'd been up to, and knew she would have to try her utmost not to stare at James or touch him when they were in the company of the others.

103

Chapter 11

James and Josephine slipped away together after breakfast the following morning. As James climbed the headland ahead of her Josephine admired his muscular, suntanned physique. She felt a little thrill at the knowledge that he was now her lover. She felt very grown-up.

'How's your sunburn?' she called ahead to him. She could see a patch of red where his trousers had slipped down a little.

James turned back and grinned. His grey eyes twinkled with amusement. 'My arse is hot and sore. How's yours?'

'The same,' she replied, dropping her eyes modestly. She wasn't about to tell him that her breasts were like hot, red globes.

'There's a little cave up ahead that's hidden from view. I don't think the others know about it. You can show me your sunburn when we get there.'

'Why the sudden interest in my sunburn?' said Josephine flirtatiously.

'I know how to take your mind off it,' he said, winking lewdly as he turned and strode ahead.

Josephine paused to catch her breath. She stared out across the bright blue water. Today the island was a place of beauty, a place she never wanted to leave. She included every rock, leaf and grain of sand in her new-found benevolence. Looking higher up the slope she saw James disappear behind a large rock.

'Wait for me!' she called, hurrying after him.

Keeping her eyes on the place where she had seen him last, Josephine struggled up the steep slope, over and around the boulders. Finally she caught sight of his tanned legs sticking out from behind a large rock. She scrambled the last few feet and flopped down beside him, wincing as her sunburned bottom met the uneven rocky surface.

'Penny for your thoughts,' she said, staring adoringly into his fascinating grey eyes.

His face softened. 'I was just thinking what a lucky fellow I am. I'm in love with the prettiest, naughtiest girl in the whole world.'

Josephine blushed and lowered her eyes. 'I didn't mean to be naughty. Still, I'm glad you love me even though I'm a fallen woman.'

'Forget all that fallen woman nonsense, will you? We're only doing what comes natural. We can do that out here. But it wouldn't be a good idea for the others to find out. I don't want to cause embarrassment, least of all to you. But if we're discreet, we can keep doing what we like …' His voice trailed away as he slipped his hand under her skirt.

Within moments they were naked together in the tiny cave, cushioned by their discarded clothes.

James winced as he entered Josephine.

'What's wrong?' she whispered.

'I reckon even me old John Thomas got sunburned yesterday.'

'Oh, you mean your …' she giggled.

'Yeh, it's a bit sore, but I think I can still manage to do the job at least once,' he said with a grin.

Much as she revelled in his attentions, Josephine knew she wouldn't mind if they didn't make love so much today. The soreness of her bottom grinding on the hard floor and her tender breasts being crushed against James's chest detracted from the pleasure.

'I do love you,' she said quietly as they lay spent on the floor of the cave.

James grinned broadly and hugged her. 'And I love you, my Empress Josephine.'

'One thing puzzles me, though. When I first arrived you didn't seem to like me. You always had something sarcastic to say about my aristocratic family and you pointed out my faults. What changed your mind?'

'I wanted you from the moment I first saw you. I was just trying to fight it, but it was no use. I was like a fish caught in a net.'

Josephine sighed happily, revelling in the new direction her life had taken.

***

Robyn was finding it difficult to concentrate on the intricacies of the financial database, so she turned her attention instead to the menu for dinner on Saturday night. Colin had said yes! She would have liked to serve a feast of Pacific Rim cuisine, her favourite, but doubted whether she could find the required ingredients in Eastleigh's supermarkets particularly at this time of year. And anyway her cooking skills were decidedly lacking. So she decided to go French instead. Home made soup and crusty bread, followed by boeuf bourguignon (which was really just stew), pommes duchesse and lots of red wine. Possibly tarte tatin for afters, which was simply posh apple pie. From her experience men didn't like fussy food. That should fill Colin's belly, she thought, if not his heart. Not that she particularly wanted to fatten him up. She just wanted him. And she knew that whatever she cooked would be fine with Lori. The rotten cow could eat and eat and still never gain an ounce. She didn't believe for a minute the story about Lori having been plump before she went off to Uni.

A mysterious postcard arrived on Saturday morning. It showed a giant cactus, so she could only assume it was from Maggie. It was addressed to Robyn Trescowe, but there was no message.

Robyn spent all of Saturday afternoon cooking and cleaning. By six p.m. she had to admit that the dining room looked pretty fabulous. The red candles on the lovingly polished table really did the trick.

Robyn took a glass of wine up to the bathroom, lit a scented candle and took a leisurely bath. She'd already ironed the sexy black dress she'd bought earlier in the week. However when she wriggled into it she was distraught to find she simply couldn't force the zip any higher than the middle of her back. Damn! She put it down to her skin being warm and clammy from the bath. Surely she hadn't gained that much weight in just a few days?

Suddenly inspired, Robyn draped her green pashmina around her shoulders, covering the expanse of open zip. Perhaps Lori could help with the zip a bit later.

The doorbell rang at half past seven. Lori and Colin bundled through the door, rosy-cheeked from the cold.

'Wow!' said Lori. 'Look at you, all dressed up. I'm wearing my jeans as we walked here. Seemed a good idea to leave the car at home if we're having a few drinks.'

'Looks like a possibility,' said Robyn, accepting a carrier bag of assorted bottles from Colin. She took Colin's suede jacket and hung it on a hook by the door. Its gloriously masculine scent sent her hormones racing.

'Umm, dinner smells good,' said Colin, sniffing the air.

'Thanks,' said Robyn with a grin. 'Can I get you both a drink?'

They settled in the sitting room. Robyn had been exploring Maggie's CD collection in her absence and had developed a liking for an American band called Steely Dan. Their complicated rhythms murmured in the background.

Robyn checked the boeuf bourguignon and potatoes. Cooked to perfection! She switched the oven off, leaving the main course on hold. She ladled her French onion soup into a warmed tureen and carried it through to the dining room.

'Would you like to be seated?' she called.

At home she probably would have just chucked a few prawns on the barbie, but Robyn found she was enjoying playing hostess to a proper grown-up dinner party.

'Great soup,' said Colin, ripping off another chunk of bread and wiping his empty bowl.

Robyn topped up their glasses with red wine.

'I'm glad I'm not driving,' said Lori with a giggle, already sounding a bit the worse for wear.

'A toast to absent family and friends,' said Robyn, thinking of everyone back at home. Hastily calculating the time difference she thought they'd probably all still be fast asleep.

The main course also went down well, with clean plates all round.

At the end of the meal Colin leaned backwards in his chair and folded his hands across his stomach. 'That was fantastic, Robyn. How did you know apple pie was my all-time favourite?'

Robyn felt her cheeks flush. 'Just a lucky guess, I suppose. Coffee?'

'Please,' said Colin, suppressing a belch.

Lori shook her head. 'I think I'll stick with this,' she said, helping herself to another glass of wine. 'It's a succulent drop. Is this one of yours or one of Colin's?'

'Gee, I've lost track.'

'Doesn't really matter.'

The two girls dissolved into drunken giggles.

'Actually, I feel pretty shmashed,' slurred Lori as she rose unsteadily to her feet. 'Okay if I have a little lie down?'

Robyn helped her friend upstairs to her bedroom.

'I'll be all right as soon as the wallpaper stops spinning,' mumbled Lori as she sank onto the bed.

When Robyn returned downstairs she found Colin had moved back to the sitting room and put an Eric Clapton CD into the player. *Old Love* throbbed gently from the speakers.

'Lori'll be down soon,' said Robyn, feeling unexpectedly shy now that she and Colin were alone. 'I'll get that coffee.'

Dealing with the kettle and cafetiere, Robyn realised that she felt almost sober again.

The sitting room lights were definitely more dim when she returned with the coffee. Colin had switched off the overhead light and turned on the standard lamp. He was sprawled on the sofa, thumbing through a book about Australia.

He looked up with a smile that could have melted the ice cap at both poles. 'Is it really like this?' he asked, tilting the page so she could see the picture.

She sat down next to him and squinted at the caption. 'The Glasshouse Mountains, Queensland. Yup, that's just what they look like. I remember going there on a school trip. They're volcanic in origin, I believe, that's why they're such a weird shape.'

Colin kept his eyes fixed on hers. 'Did you know your zip is undone all down your back?'

Robyn gasped. She couldn't remember where or when she'd lost her pashmina.

'Would you like me to zip you up?'

His hands on her back made her insides feel like molten lava. Fortunately he managed to close the zip without too much effort. Remarkable, thought Robyn, considering the dinner I've just eaten.

When she turned round Colin moved his hands up to her shoulders, and drew her in for an earth-stopping kiss. Eric Clapton sang on alone. Robyn was suddenly in orbit. She hadn't dared dream that things would go quite so well. Only when they were tumbling on the carpet in a state of undress did she spare a thought for her friend upstairs.

'What if Lori ...?'

'She'll probably sleep all night,' said Colin, running his fingers sensuously up her spine. 'She's never been very good with drink, passes out cold if she has too much. Still, she doesn't do that very often. My luck that she chose tonight and gave us a chance to get to know each other better. You ... are ... gorgeous!'

Robyn's brain reeled. This was just too much to take in all at once.

The following morning Robyn felt a bit disorientated when she awoke. Gradually the events of the night before fell into place. She focused on the condom wrappings discarded on the carpet. Her left arm was quite numb, trapped under Colin's chest. They had retreated in the wee hours to the single bed in the spare room, Robyn having first checked on Lori and left a large glass of water on the bedside table.

Colin shifted slightly and opened his eyes. 'Hello, gorgeous.'

She felt his groin surge enthusiastically. The man was insatiable!

Robyn woke some time later from her post-coital snooze. Her movement in the small bed caused Colin to stir.

'What?' he mumbled sleepily.

'I heard a noise. Might have been Lori,' explained Robyn, swinging her legs around and scanning the floor for items of her clothing.

Colin sent out a warm, octopus-like arm and drew her back to him. 'She usually sleeps pretty late after she's had a skinful.'

'What's the time?'

Colin squinted at his watch. 'Around ten to nine. Lori won't wake for ages, believe me.'

Robyn lowered her eyes. 'Um, should we tell her that we spent the night together? Would it be better if you pretended you'd slept on the couch?'

Colin grinned, and his dimples dimpled disarmingly. 'Feeling guilty?'

'Of course not! Gee, I'm no prude.'

'Not so you'd notice,' said Colin, sliding his hand down the rounded curve of her stomach.

'Later, sexy,' she said, disentangling herself from his clutches and reaching for her clothes.

Lori emerged just as Robyn was pouring boiling water into the cafetiere. She looked dreadful. Pale, with dark circles under her eyes. She clutched the kitchen bench.

'God, whatever possessed me to drink so much?'

'We've all done it,' sympathised Robyn.

'Well you feel a lot better than I look, er … you know what I mean,' said Lori feebly, subsiding into a kitchen chair.

'I'd give you the coffee intravenously but I can't find where Maggie keeps the drip.'

Lori offered a wan smile. 'Too early for jokes. Just coffee, please.'

After a few mouthfuls of the strong brew she spoke again. 'Anyway, thanks for a lovely dinner. You went to a lot of trouble. At least I didn't chuck it all up afterwards. So. You and Colin. How's tricks?'

Robyn busied herself with laying bacon on the grill pan. She could feel an annoying flush creeping up her cheeks. She searched desperately for something to say.

'What happened after I passed out?'

'The room stopped spinning?' suggested Robyn evasively.

'Methinks you scored. Yes, from the look in your eye, I definitely think you've scored.'

The kitchen door opened and Colin breezed in, looking as though he'd just been for a morning run. Robyn thought that if he'd looked any more healthy he would have burst. She was relieved to be preoccupied with bacon sandwich preparations.

'Morning, ladies!' he said, pulling up a chair and sitting astride it backwards.

'Morning yourself,' mumbled Lori weakly, stirring more sugar into her coffee as she smirked at Colin.

Colin ignored any possible hint about horizontal activities between himself and Robyn.

'Feeling a bit sorry for ourselves, are we?'

'I've got a head like a dead bear's bum. Or whatever the expression is,' groaned Lori.

'The best cure for a hangover is a bacon sandwich, and here comes one now. Looks great, Robyn. That's two great meals cooked by you within twenty-four hours. I might just have to move in here.'

Robyn couldn't think of anything to say, clever or otherwise. All she could do was blush.

Lori filled the awkward silence. 'I've already told her that you have a habit of eating all the peanut butter.'

'I thought that's what it was for,' he said, noisily squirting brown sauce into his sandwich.

Robyn thought Lori was looking a shade paler. 'Alka seltzer?' she suggested.

'Sounds like a good idea. Followed by more coffee. Hold the bacon sandwich for now.'

Chapter 12

By November Josephine knew she was going to have difficulty getting through the winter on Hogshead Island. In the summer it had been easy to pretend that everything would be fine, particularly after she and James began courting. But reality was by this time hitting home. Her love for James, her close friendship with Lucy and her affection for most of her companions wasn't going to make up for the lack of creature comforts and the intense boredom when bad weather enforced lengthy periods cooped up in the cave.

The island seemed to be constantly buffeted by storms. It was usually too cold for lovemaking in the few private places she and James frequented, so they were mostly making do with meaningful glances and walks along the shore.

Josephine found the cave cramped and smelly, and the shortening days oppressive. Mildred the goat was allowed to sleep in the cave when the weather was bad, adding another dimension to the unpleasant fug.

Josephine would often wake at she knew not what hour, almost overcome with claustrophobia. She longed for daylight to show at the mouth of the cave. Sometimes she had to get up in the dark, no matter what the weather, in her desperation for fresh air.

Months of bleak days and long, cold nights stretched ahead.

Luisa encouraged Josephine to join in with preparations for Christmas.

'You have a fine touch with the needle,' she said, examining Josephine's handiwork. 'I will have to find you some more thread.'

Luisa had painstakingly unravelled a couple of jumpers that were too badly holed even for the boys to wear. She had washed the wool and wound it tightly onto small pieces of wood to take out the kinks and make it reusable. Josephine and Mari were embroidering Christmas trees onto small pieces of cloth that they would use to decorate the walls of their cave.

Josephine thought longingly of Christmas at home in London: the huge tree in the hall hung with sugar canes, the dining room decorated with *Maman's* collection of golden glass ornaments from France, the presents, the warmth of the fire … Her eyes filled with tears which she tried to ignore until they trickled down her cheeks.

'What's the matter?' asked James, ever attentive.

'I was thinking of home.'

Josephine stabbed her blunt needle determinedly into the grubby piece of cloth. James lowered his eyes, sighed and stared gloomily at the piece of wood he was carving.

When he had gone to work on the Roquebrun farm he'd had to deal with the sorrow of losing his own family. Perhaps it was worse for posh folk unaccustomed to life's hardships. Maybe there was more to miss. He was trying to be patient, but Josephine's moods certainly detracted from their relationship at times. He hoped she wouldn't become a bad influence on the others' morale; Mari was a moody lass at the best of times. He supposed he should be thankful that Lucy and Luisa were more even-tempered, likewise the boys.

***

Robyn took a long, hot shower after Colin and Lori left. Once dressed, she tackled the remaining dishes to the sounds of the Spice Girls, singing along in a less-than-tuneful voice.

As he left Colin had said that he'd phone her in a couple of days. That was enough to make any girl want to sing. She booted up her laptop and logged on, pleased to see a message from her father.

Hello, m'girl. Good news. The drugs they've given me have reduced the growth in my oesophagus and I'm feeling quite a bit easier. Plenty of life left in the old dog yet. Your mother is fine, nagging me into the ground. Hope your work is going well. Pleased to hear about your visit to Morvah and Emily, and I hope you'll be going again soon. At least now I've established email contact with them, thanks to you. I can't quite get to grips with Morwenna having a daughter. Still think of her as a little girl. Mind you, I still think of you as a little girl too. Steve and Giulietta and Joey are well, and send their love. As do Rose and I.

Robyn was just about to start typing a reply when a new message popped up. It was from Nick. She immediately felt guilty; nearly three weeks had passed since she sent him her last progress report on Paul Sinclair's activities. And that had been pretty sketchy and meagre.

Robyn, I need to ask you a favour.

This was Nick through and through, thought Robyn. No polite chit-chat, just straight in, boots and all.

Would you mind staying an additional month? I know your father is ill and you would miss Christmas with your family, but I'd be very grateful if you could stay a bit longer. That will be it. I promise it won't turn into a never-ending stay in the UK. If you don't come up with anything on our friend Sinclair by the end of January we'll have to find some other way of smoking him out. Let me know by return whether you agree to stay on.

Robyn sighed and shook her head despairingly. Nick Robinson was the absolute limit! But Dad was doing all right at the moment. And what about Colin? Kisses under the mistletoe at Christmas, and the prospect of Millennium Eve together ...

No problem, she emailed straight back. *Sorry I haven't been in touch, but nothing to tell. I keep going through everything I can get my hands on, but no irregularities apparent. However I'll keep my nose to the grindstone.*

Another message popped up. Robyn smiled. Gee, Sunday night in Sydney must be boring if everyone was staying in and sending her emails. This time it was from Delia. Robyn had expected that contact with Dee would be intermittent as she had no computer.

Daer Robbie, typed Delia in her usual hit-and-miss fashion. *Suprise! It's me! I'm ruond at Cassandra millingtons house. You kno, the thetare producer. Anyway, graet news. Iave got the part of Melissa in her new play wich startsat the opera ouse in 5 weeks so I better get my skates on, eh, learn some lines. THE LEAD ROLE!!! Well done little me is wot I say. Any snow yet??? Ha! I phoned your perants last weekand I know they aer incontact with you so you will kno that your dad is doin well. Iam lookin after Rober, hesens his love and so do I Deedls XXX*

Robyn emailed back:

Deedles darling, gee, well done! The lead role! You didn't tell me what the play is called. I'm sure you'll learn your lines in time for opening night. I hope the play runs for a while because guess what? Nick wants me to stay on here until the end of January. I don't really mind as Dad seems to be making a good recovery. And I've met someone! His name is Colin, gorgeous looking, an architect. It's not all fun and games here though, I do actually do some work from time to time and I've been down to Cornwall once to visit the rellies. Interesting. Going again next weekend. Thanks for keeping in touch with Ma and Pa, love you lots, Robyn XXX p.s. No snow yet. What about Mad Terry's party?

Contact with Delia brought Casey to mind. She sent him a quick email headed 'Sacrifices in the Line of Duty', one of their ongoing jokes. Grinning as she typed salacious details of Saturday night's dinner party, she suddenly realised Casey's new office companion might open his emails. So she tamed it down a bit. Remembering that Casey fancied the new bloke, she enquired whether his new colleague liked cricket. Casey would get it.

Robyn also emailed her flatmate Jenna that she'd be a month later returning, and that she'd transfer another month's rent into the bank account.

Communications dealt with, Robyn pondered what to do with the rest of the day. She looked longingly at the telephone, willing Colin to ring and murmur husky endearments. Better to be out and about than sitting by the phone, she thought. The sky was showing enough blue at least to make a posing pouch for a sailor, so she decided to drive to Portsmouth and see if she could get a ferry to the Isle of Wight. It was supposed to be a pleasant place to visit even in the off season.

***

Josephine got through the winter somehow, but by March 1926 she was quite poorly. Her skin looked drab and stretched tautly over her cheekbones. She had become far too thin, finding little interest in food. Her lovely hair had lost its shine, likewise her eyes.

Luisa beckoned James to one side after breakfast one morning.

'We must do something about that poor girl,' she whispered.

James nodded.

'You know what I'm thinking, I'm sure,' intoned Luisa with a meaningful glance.

James averted his eyes. 'I thought we agreed she must stay here.'

'If we do not get her back to her family I'm afraid she will die.'

'We'll have to see,' said James, turning his attention to untangling the fishing net.

'I know you love her, James. But sometimes we have to set our loved ones free.'

It looked like a suitable day for trawling the shallows, and they could certainly do with a change from shellfish and seaweed.

Their goat had made it through the winter, but the remainder of the meat from her deceased offspring had gone bad. Once they disposed of it the smell in the cave became slightly more bearable for Josephine, but having a live animal in with them during the worst of the weather was at times more than she could stand despite her fondness for Mildred.

James looked across to where Mildred was munching under the windswept trees. Goodness only knew what she found to eat, but it seemed to keep her happy. The future of the goat preyed on his mind, pushing aside the greater problem of Josephine. They would need to make a voyage to the mainland shortly and somehow get hold of a male goat. If they couldn't mate Mildred and produce live offspring this year the poor old thing would have to be slaughtered, and he didn't relish that task. None of them would want to do it; they had all become fond of their yellow-eyed friend.

Simon and Roberto had hauled the net out into the shallows and were dragging it in broad sweeps through the leaden water that was thankfully calm after several days of heavy storms.

Thomas, Solomon and Lucy were foraging along the high water mark. At breakfast they had suggested that the storms might have washed ashore something useful as had happened sometimes in the past.

A sudden shout from the water brought James to attention. Where was Simon? James was on his feet and half way down the beach before Simon's head bobbed back into view.

Roberto got to him first, and shouted for help. As he waded out to the boys, James glanced back to see the others assembled at the water's edge. Mari waded toward them, hampered by her long skirts. There was a lot of blood in the water. Simon didn't seem to be moving. Was he dead?

But then he let out a shudder of breath. Between them Roberto and James hauled him into the shallows.

'Tiburon! Tiburon!' repeated Roberto, his eyes glazed with fear as they dragged Simon towards the beach.

Mari wallowed towards them and rattled off a question in Spanish. She and Roberto engaged in an animated exchange. Meanwhile he and James finally managed to haul Simon up onto the sand.

'What about the net?' shouted Solomon.

James turned back, and was knee-deep in water once more before Mari noticed what he was doing.

'Don't go back out there!' she yelled. 'There's a shark!'

James paused, but the thought of how long it had taken him to repair the net drove him onwards.

The net found him, rather than the reverse. He almost shot out of the water with alarm when something touched his foot, but it was only the net. He ducked below the surface, grabbed it in both hands and ran like a man possessed. He dragged it up the beach and ran to the group assembled around Simon, who was by this time coughing up water.

Luisa patted his back and murmured encouragement in a mixture of English and Spanish. Josephine had wrapped her shawl around Simon's chest and arms, but his white legs stuck out, cold and bare, one of them bleeding into the sand.

'How is he?' panted James.

'He will be all right,' replied Luisa. 'Maybe I will need to put a stitch in the wound, but if we can keep it clean it will mend in time. He was very lucky.'

Roberto and James carried Simon carefully between them to the cave. They turned, hearing a shout from the beach.

Little Thomas was crouched beside the net. 'Six fishes!' he called. 'One of them is quite big.'

'Come here, Thomas,' called Luisa, holding out her hand. 'We'll come back in a little while to collect the fish.'

James left the others once they had made Simon comfortable inside the cave. He had no desire to be there when Luisa attempted to stitch the jagged gash in his leg. He set off down the beach towards the net. Sure enough, there were fish. At least the excursion had not gone totally wrong. And the largest fish was a small shark, possibly the one that had bitten Simon. Its dark eyes were full of menace and its tail still twitched.

James ran back to the cave to get a sharp stick to kill the shark, to stab it through the eye into its brain. Only then would it be safe to remove it from the net, for its teeth were as sharp as razors. He paid no heed to the gathering in the cave, dashing straight in and out again.

Josephine hurried to catch up with him as he ran back to the net. She arrived out of breath just after he had dispatched the shark, and gasped in horror at the sight of him withdrawing the bloodied stick from the creature's eye socket.

'Shark meat for dinner tonight!' said James with a grin. 'It will make a tasty meal.'

'Ugh. Such an ugly thing,' said Josephine with a shudder.

'Lovely white meat. A finer flavour than cod. Some fresh fish will help make you well, Empress.'

Josephine lowered her eyes. 'I know I look awful. Lucy and I are going to wash our hair today, and as many of the clothes as we can manage. At least we don't have to ration the water so much at the moment, but we're very short of soap. Do you know when you'll be making the next trip to the mainland?'

James could not bear to look at the love of his life, so he stared out to sea.

'If the calm weather keeps up we should be able to go some time in the next week.'

Since they were alone, Josephine moved closer and slipped her arms around him. They held each other close. James felt a lump rise in his throat, and it was a few minutes before he could trust his voice.

'You're so thin, my darling. I could play a tune on your ribs.'

It was a feeble attempt at humour.

'What tune would you play?'

James forced himself to look into Josephine's face. Close to, her eyes looked bright enough. It was only when he held her at arm's length that the dark shadows were more apparent.

'Umm, I dunno,' he murmured. 'Come round behind these rocks and I'll think of something.'

Josephine obliged with a girlish giggle. The winter was almost over, and she hoped life was going to improve.

Within a couple of days Simon was back on his feet, limping but cheerful enough. The shark would not have been large enough to kill him, but its teeth had certainly torn a nasty hole in his shin. Thanks to Luisa's potions the wound did not become infected, and was already showing signs of healing.

The days continued bright and fair, and the shore party plotted their forthcoming voyage. This time Mari, James and Solomon were to row to the mainland.

Mari and Luisa were busy writing a shopping list. They were short of many things after the winter months.

James walked across to where Josephine was standing beside Mildred. She was staring out to sea, absent-mindedly scratching between the goat's horns.

'If I squat down next to Mildred will you scratch my head too?'

Josephine's attention drifted back to reality. She smiled affectionately at James. She loved the silly things he said.

'Getting ready for your trip?' she asked.

To James it was apparent that she was putting up a brave front. He nodded.

'I want to talk to you. Come for a walk?'

She fell into step beside him, and they made their way towards the water's edge. As they turned towards the headland, the great expanse of empty beach stretched before them.

'What did you want to talk about?' asked Josephine, breaking the silence.

'It's a bit difficult for me to put into words. You know I love you, right?'

'Yes, of course.'

'If I said you could go back to your family, would you want to go?'

His heart sank at her reaction. Her eyes opened wide and sparkled in the sunshine. Her cheeks turned pink. It was as though someone had breathed new life into her.

'Do you mean it? Do you really mean it?' said Josephine, running ahead and turning to walk backwards, dancing animatedly before him on feet as light as clouds.

He nodded. 'Luisa and I have been talking. You're still weak after that bout of influenza, and I'm concerned at how thin you've become. We think it's time for you to return to your family, if that's what you want.'

'But aren't you concerned that I might tell people where I've been these past months, and who I've been with?'

'We've thought of a way round the problem. It was obvious, really.'

Josephine was too excited to ask further questions.

'Oh, it will be so wonderful to go home! Of course at this time of year I expect only Mr and Mrs Cuthbert will be at Roskenner, but I'll be able to get myself cleaned up and then travel to London. Just imagine the surprise when Mother and Father hear that I'm alive after all this time! George will be thrilled too, I expect. I wonder whether Lucien was found? Oh, James! I wish I could take you with me.'

James looked horrified. 'Steady on, Empress! Don't forget, your mother is in with that French lot that got me into trouble.'

'Sorry, I'm not thinking straight. I'm too excited.'

'What would your parents think if they knew what you'd been doing with a man wanted for murder, the son of a common fisherman?'

'I know you're no murderer. And I know you're worth ten of any of those namby pamby idiots *Maman* would want me to marry.'

James knew Josephine truly loved him. But he also knew that the pull of home was stronger. It was breaking his heart, but he knew his Josephine had to go.

Chapter 13

The Isle of Wight was pretty dead in November. Robyn could believe that it probably heaved with tourists in the summer, but for now many of the shops and amusement arcades were closed. Not that she was at all interested in amusement arcades.

Having left the car at Portsmouth (the car ferry charge being something approaching highway robbery) she was restricted to wandering around Ryde, or catching buses that were few and far between. Still, it was a pleasant enough way to spend a Sunday afternoon, and Robyn found a lovely little café overlooking the harbour that served a state of the art cream tea. Never mind the calories, she though, as she experimented with whether it was best to put the jam on top of the cream on her scone or vice versa.

Once back on the mainland, Robyn made her way back to Eastleigh along a succession of minor roads. She revelled in the Englishness of the place names, how Soberton and Heath and Bishop's Waltham tripped satisfyingly off the tongue.

'Of course, I live in Bishop's Waltham,' she announced to a field of placid-faced cows in her best attempt at a plummy English accent. 'I have a sixteenth century cottage not far from the town centre, with roses around the door and a hedgehog living in my garden. Peter Rabbit comes to tea every Thursday afternoon.'

The cows chewed on, unimpressed. Robyn sighed. England was growing on her. She liked the way the rain blurred the field of vision on wet days, turning her world into an abstract of green and grey. And when the sun shone in a clear blue sky you couldn't help feeling that all was right with the universe. Careful, she thought. Too much waxing lyrical is bound to be bad for the brain.

Robyn skidded to a halt. What was that on the side of the road?

Backing up cautiously, she pulled in close to the edge and opened the car door. Taking care that no traffic was approaching on the narrow road she ran around to the other side of the car. As she had initially suspected, it was a black and ginger cat. Its head was hidden in the brambles. Thankfully there was no blood, but the animal appeared quite dead.

As Robyn rolled it into the bushes to avoid it being hit by other cars she heard a faint noise. There it was again. Then she saw the kitten. A little ball of ginger fluff concealed in the brambles. Its tiny mouth opened in a cry of protest.

Robyn reached carefully through the spiky tendrils and pulled the small, struggling animal out of its hiding place. It seemed unharmed.

'You poor littie thing,' she said, smoothing its damp, spiky fur. 'Your mummy has been hit by a car. Do you have any brothers or sisters?'

Robyn searched the bushes up and down the stretch of road but no other kittens were evident. She looked along the road but there were no houses nearby.

'Where did you come from?' she asked the small animal, which was nuzzling her arm. It was probably hungry.

She got back into the car and settled the kitten on her lap. A couple of miles down the road she came to a run-down looking petrol station. A young man in a greasy overall was tinkering under the bonnet of a car.

''Scuse me. I've just found this kitten a couple of miles back that way,' she said, indicating with a broad sweep of her arm. 'Its mother was dead on the side of the road. A black and ginger cat. Do you know anyone with a cat like that?'

The lad stared, open-mouthed. Robyn thought he looked a bit simple.

'You ain't from round 'ere,' he said.

'No, I'm not. Well, do you know anyone with a black and ginger cat?'

The lad thought a moment, shook his head, and resumed his tinkering.

Robyn placed the kitten carefully on the driver's seat while she rummaged in her handbag for a pen and paper.

'I'll leave you my phone number in case you hear of anyone whose cat got run over, in case they want their kitten back. I'll take it home with me.'

Robyn jumped back into her car and settled the kitten on her lap once more. Revving the engine and backing carefully out into the road, she addressed the tiny, warm bundle.

'Gee, I hope Maggie likes cats. 'Cos it looks as if we've got us a little kitty. I don't really think Brain of Britain is going to do much about finding out where you came from.'

For the remaining half hour of her journey Robyn talked to the kitten. She told it all about her father's illness, all about Waldron and Paul Sinclair,

about her night of passion with Colin (had it only been the night before?) …
everything she could think of. Meanwhile the kitten slept on in her lap.

'Gee, is my life that boring? Or are you completely tuckered out?'

Robyn pulled in by a farm gate to check that the little scrap of fur was still breathing.

'Not long now. And when we get home I'll give you some warm milk. Gee, that's a thought. I'd better get some proper cat food for you. And I guess I'd better give you a name. Any ideas, little one?'

The kitten slept on. Robyn looked back at the farm gate as she manoeuvred out onto the road. A makeshift sign hung off the gate, advertising rhubarb for sale.

'Hmmm, Rhubarb. That's not a bad name for a cat. Yes, it has character. Well, that's it, little fellow. Or girl. It will do for either. Rhubarb you are.'

Back in Eastleigh Robyn stopped at the mini market for supplies. She marvelled that these places always seemed to be run by Asians. As the Italians and Greeks in Sydney ran many of the little businesses that stayed open all hours, so did the Asians in England, sharing the work among all the generations of the family.

In the chiller cabinet she found a quarter portion of ready-cooked chicken that didn't appear to contain anything spicy, and from the shelves she took a couple of sachets of kitten food. She knew there was plenty of milk in the fridge at home. Rhubarb slept on, nestled into her coat on the passenger seat.

It was quite dark by the time Robyn negotiated the right turn into River Lane and crunched up the gravel drive of her lodgings. The house looked dark and forlorn. Thankfully Maggie was due back in just over a week. She hoped her landlady wouldn't mind too much about her newest lodger.

***

Luisa knew from looking at Josephine that James had spoken with her. Already she looked a little brighter than she had in recent months. She knew they were doing the right thing in letting her return to her family. She was relieved that James had agreed, despite the strong bond that seemed to have grown between himself and the newcomer. Luisa wondered whether, with Josephine gone, the relationship between James and Mari would return.

Her suggestion that Josephine should pretend she'd lost her memory, possibly as a result of a blow to the head while in the water, had fortunately met with James's approval. Simple, yet hopefully effective. Luisa had suggested to James that they should put Josephine to the test, questioning her thoroughly as though they were her family enquiring about her absence that now amounted to nearly nine months. Practice would make perfect, she hoped.

Yes, it was for the best that Josephine should return to her family, and Luisa could only hope that all would be well.

The trip to Poldhu Point was planned for the night of March 15th, when the tide would be running in their favour. Mari had fussed a little when she heard that Josephine would be joining them, but when she learned this would be the last she would see of that fancy little madam she stopped fretting about the reduced space for goods they could sell. If they didn't make enough money for supplies it would simply mean the next trip would be scheduled a bit sooner.

On the evening of March 14th they held a celebration to bid Josephine farewell. Luisa made a cake out of stack of pancakes, sandwiched together with jam.

Simon insisted they balance a candle on top. 'Like a birthday cake,' he suggested. 'She can blow the candle out.'

'But it's not her birthday,' said Thomas, puzzled by events.

'It doesn't matter, *pequenito*. It's a nice idea,' said Luisa.

'Can we give her presents?' asked Simon. 'I'd like to give Josephine my mouse what I carved out of wood.'

Luisa shook her head sadly. 'Josephine will have a long journey back to her family. It will be difficult for her to carry presents.'

Such an explanation was easier than trying to get the lad to understand that Josephine would have to pretend she'd never met them, that she hadn't spent the past months living on the island with them.

Josephine felt mixed emotions when it came to leaving the island. She knew she would miss James terribly, but she couldn't endure another winter like the last.

They asked her to make a speech before cutting her cake.

'I'll miss you all,' she said. And she meant it. She would even miss Mari, for she had never met anyone quite like her. A girl full of passion but with strong principles. Josephine wondered with a pang whether James would go back to Mari after she left. She envisaged a marriage ceremony being conducted on the beach, and in years to come, James and Mari surrounded by their children.

Josephine looked at them all in the firelight. Luisa's wise face, somewhat lined with the responsibility of caring and coping. Thomas's lovely brown face and his deep, dark eyes. Lucy's calm expression. Mari with her pouting lips and questioning eyebrows. Roberto's impossibly curly hair and dark, expressive eyes. Solomon's cheeky grin. Simon, seemingly always recovering from one scrape or another. And James ... Yes, she would miss them all.

As Luisa reminded Thomas that it was past his bedtime, James glanced at Josephine and inclined his head.

She slipped discreetly away from the gathering. James joined her a few minutes later. The night was still, clear and cold. Wordlessly they made their way along the beach and up the slope to their cave.

Josephine took comfort from the warmth of James's arm around her shoulders; her shawl was thin. Upon reaching the cave they sat quietly on the rocky ledge, staring out at the silvery trail of the moon across the sea.

'It's like a bridge,' said Josephine. 'I wish it was real, and that I could come back to visit you.'

'You'll soon forget me,' said James, tossing a pebble into the darkness. It rattled as it bounced away down the rocks. 'Your mother will soon match you up with a man with a pedigree as long as his arm and a ton of money.'

'I'll never forget you,' said Josephine, a tearful wobble in her voice. 'Am I doing the right thing in leaving? It's just that the winters here are so hard ...'

'You're a lady. You're not cut out for this rough life.'

'There have been plenty of good times. I love the freedom we have here. No corsets, no singing lessons, no elocution.'

'Nope. None of those things. Never worn a corset in my life.'

The couple laughed together, and fell into a tender embrace. Their kisses, at first slow and gentle, soon became passionate, and when they made love it was tinged with sadness. This would be their last time, thought Josephine as she felt tears run down the sides of her face and into her hair.

When they crept back into the cave all was silent except for Simon's intermittent snoring. James squeezed Josephine's hand, and she made her way over to her place beside Lucy. Lucy didn't even stir as she wriggled into her quilt. It was too difficult to search in the trunk for her nightdress so Josephine slept in her clothes. As she drifted off to sleep Josephine thought sadly about James. Leaving him was tearing a hole in her heart.

***

123

Colin appeared without warning just after seven on Monday evening. The doorbell rang and Robyn found him on the doorstep with a goofy smile on his face and a bunch of drooping Christmas roses in his hand.

'These are for you. May I come in?'

She felt a little put out at his assumption that she was available, but welcomed him in with what she hoped was good grace.

'I was just watching the holiday programme. All those lovely places in Europe that I'm not going to have time to visit before I go home.'

'You'll have to come back in the summer. Too cold at the moment for holidays, unless you're interested in skiing.'

'No chance,' said Robyn with a grimace. 'I tried it once on a school trip, spent most of the day sliding down mountains on my bum.'

'Yeah. Cold, wet, miserable sport. Not my thing at all.'

'Would you like a drink?'

'I thought you'd never ask. I fancy a glass of wine. And I fancy you too.'

Robyn laughed. What could a girl say to such blatant flattery?

As they kissed, Colin stiffened suddenly and reached behind him on the sofa, holding aloft a small, gingery bundle of fur that had narrowly escaped being squashed as he sat down.

'What's this?'

'Oh, that's Rhubarb. I found him yesterday. His mother got run over. Isn't he cute?'

'Got a fine set of claws. Ouch!'

'I hope Maggie likes cats. She'll be back in about a week.'

'Have you got a box or something to put this little fellow in for now? Roobarb, did you say? Didn't anyone tell you that Roobarb was the dog? Custard was the cat.'

'What do you mean?'

'You know. Roobarb and Custard. The cartoon.'

'Never heard of it.'

'Oh, I suppose it's all Skippy and stuff like that in Australia.'

'Probably. Anyway, I think Rhubarb is a good name for a ginger cat.'

'If you say so.'

'I'll put him in the kitchen. I've made him a bed out of a box. He seems to like it.'

'We don't want any Cattus Interruptus, if you know what I mean,' said Colin with a suggestive lift of his eyebrows.

Chapter 14

It was almost dark and growing quite cold by the time they set off. Josephine hugged everyone on the shore. Saying farewell to Luisa was like leaving a mother behind. The lump in her throat grew harder when she hugged Lucy. Even despite the secretive nature of her relationship with James she and Lucy had remained firm friends, and Josephine knew she would miss that friendship more than any of her school chums. She hadn't given them so much as a thought in months.

The thought of having to say a final farewell to James within the next twenty-four hours was starting to become horribly real. Josephine felt tormented by indecision, but she took her place amidships and bit her lip in an attempt to keep her churning emotions from spilling over.

The rowing boat sat low in the water, burdened almost beyond its limits. James pushed them out of the shallows and struggled to climb aboard without upsetting the boat.

'Let's just hope the weather stays calm,' muttered Mari. 'Otherwise that will be the end of us all.'

Mari crossed herself and cast her eyes dramatically heavenwards.

Josephine set her chin steadfastly into the cool evening breeze, determined not to let Mari get under her skin. After tonight she'd never again have to put up with her jibes and catty comments.

James had read the tides accurately and they made good progress, taking it in turn to row. Josephine insisted on doing her share, proud that she could row at least as strongly as Mari. She felt a very different girl from the one who had gone swimming from the beach off Marazion the previous summer. A girl with broken fingernails and callouses on her hands. A girl with a wild tangle of stiff, salty hair. A girl wearing a ragged dress and worn-out shoes that didn't fit. A girl who had survived near drowning, who had learned to cook with the most meagre rations and mend and make do with things her parents' servants would have consigned to the garbage. A girl who had learned the art of how to please a man. Yes, a very different girl indeed.

The night remained calm, and with the dawn came their first sighting of land.

Solomon gave a cry and pointed to the right. 'Land ahoy, me hearties!'

'Where?' said Josephine, staring uselessly in the direction Solomon had indicated. 'I don't see anything.'

'There. That grey mass. That's Poldhu Point.'

'Oh, I thought that was just low-lying cloud.'

'Take my word for it, that's land. Mother England. Terra firma. Call it what you want.'

Solomon relieved Mari of the oars. The currents were tricky, and at times they seemed to make little headway.

I swam through this and survived, thought Josephine with amazement.

Eventually the boat came to shore with a resounding crunch and jolt. Josephine felt almost ill with anticipation. Would everything go according to plan? Would she be able to find her way back to Roskenner House?

They pulled the boat up the beach and hid it in some scrubby bushes.

'You two go on to Helston,' instructed James.

Solomon held Josephine's hand between his, and beamed at her. 'Good luck! I 'ope you'll be happy once you're back with your folks.'

Mari's farewell surprised Josephine. The girl kissed her solemnly on both cheeks. 'Be lucky,' she murmured before turning her attention to gathering her wares for market.

James walked with Josephine as far as the main road. Josephine's heart hung heavy. She could tell that he was reluctant to let her out of his sight. They hesitated in the shelter of some trees, unnaturally shy at the moment of parting. Finally James plucked up the courage to say what he wanted.

'I love you, Empress. I won't forget you. And I've got a plan. I'll come over to Poldhu Point on the first of July every year, and I'll wait all day for you. Every year, mind. If the weather's bad I'll come as soon as I can, but I will come. I don't want to lose you, but I don't want to force you to leave your family. If you want to see me, even just to say hello and talk awhile, I'll be there. I won't force you to come away with me, back to the island. But if you do change your mind and want to come back, well ...'

'Oh, James! I don't want to leave you!' sobbed Josephine, flinging her arms around his neck. 'I love you so much! But I can't live in that cave any longer.'

'I know, I know,' he said softly, stroking her hair.

Josephine battled to bring her sobs under control.

'I'd better go,' she said, forcing a smile. 'If I don't go now, I'll ...'

'I mean it,' said James solemnly. 'I'll be there every year on the first of July.'

Josephine smiled. Somehow it made her feel better. She knew his intentions at that moment were sincere, but she didn't really believe him.

'I hope you manage to find a mate for Mildred,' she said.

'If not this trip, then maybe the next. What are we doing talking about goats at a time like this?'

She put her fingers to his lips. 'Hush. I must go now. Safe journey, my darling. Remember I love you.' Josephine felt her throat constrict painfully, and tears poured from her eyes. She broke away from his embrace and started off down the dusty track.

'I love you, Josephine. I always will,' called James from the shelter of the trees.

Josephine walked backwards, savouring her last glimpse of the man she loved. Then she turned resolutely in the direction of Porthleven, about an hour's walk along the coast according to James. And from there, quite a distance to Newlyn.

Every journey starts with the first step, and Josephine's first step was blinded by her tears.

***

Emily rang Robyn on Wednesday evening, fortunately before Colin's arrival. For Colin had already become a feature of each evening.

'Are you and your friend still coming to visit at the weekend, dear?' she asked eagerly.

'Of course!' replied Robyn, making a mental note to check that Lori was still coming.

'You'll be able to meet your Great Uncle William this time. He's joining us for Sunday dinner. He's looking forward to meeting you.'

'I'm glad. Lori and I will be with you as soon as possible on Saturday. Just depends on the traffic. I'll phone you on the way.'

'Take care, dear. 'Bye.'

Robyn rang Lori straight after and was relieved that she was still on for the weekend visit. Neither mentioned Colin.

After three nights of his company, Robyn decided the shine had gone off her initial attraction to Colin. Three nights of what? He would turn up just as she was cooking her dinner. On the first night he brought flowers, but they looked as though they'd been stolen from someone's garden. And since then, nothing.

He ate what she put in front of him and then bundled her off to bed for the rest of the evening. Didn't even offer to help with the dishes. To add insult to injury, he'd slapped her on the bottom the night before and told her she needed to lose weight. It was true, but it didn't need to be stated that bluntly.

Robyn had no time to herself, and she was irritated by Colin's presumption that she was free every night. Worst of all, little Rhubarb wasn't getting enough quality time. Robyn recalled what Lori had said about the rapid turnover of Colin's girlfriends. Maybe they had all felt smothered and used as she did, and the partings were not at his instigation as Lori had implied. Maybe that was what he'd been telling Lori.

Robyn didn't feel she could discuss Colin with Lori. It didn't seem right to diss the man to his flatmate and friend of many years.

Wednesday night turned out the same as Monday and Tuesday. Robyn decided to go somewhere by herself on Thursday night. After all, Colin didn't own her. But she didn't really want to go out. She wanted to stay in and watch The Fast Show on television. Just with Rhubarb. No Colin.

On her way home from work Robyn stopped at the mini market and bought herself a box of chocolates. Something to munch on while watching television.

Shortly after seven the doorbell rang. Colin, of course.

'Hello gorgeous. What's cooking?' he enquired, bowling in through the door and heading straight for the kitchen.

'Colin, we need to talk,' said Robyn determinedly.

'What about?' he asked, lifting the lid of the saucepan and inspecting its simmering contents. 'Is this sauce out of a bottle or did you make it yourself?'

'Colin, I don't want to talk about cooking. I want to talk about you and me.'

'Whoa, babe. Less than a week together and already you want to get into the heavy stuff. Slow down, eh?'

'I think it's you who needs to slow down, Colin. Gee, you're the limit! You turn up here every night, just assuming I'm not doing anything else. You haven't taken me out, haven't even offered to cook me a meal. It's not on, mate.'

She dramatically ripped a sheet of kitchen towel off the roll and stuffed it into his hand. 'As we say at home, you're wiped.'

Colin gaped like a freshly-caught fish. 'W-wiped? Me?'

'Yes, you. I think you've got a few things to learn about relationships. I'm sorry, Colin. You're not the man for me.'

Robyn crossed her arms and inclined her head towards the open door. 'Goodbye.'

Colin looked stunned. 'Just when I thought we were getting on so well ...'

He sloped off down the hall, out of the house, and got into his car without a backward glance.

Well done the Aussie girl! thought Robyn, putting an imaginary point on an imaginary scoreboard. Plenty of time for a leisurely spaghetti dinner and an evening of telly and chocolates with her little pal Rhubarb. Exactly what she would tell Lori was tomorrow's problem, definitely not worth losing sleep over.

Rhubarb seemed to understand. He rubbed his little chin against Robyn's leg, and she reached down to scratch behind his ears. He closed his eyes blissfully and purred loudly.

'What about some salmon tonight, mate? Fresh, not the tinned stuff.'

Rhubarb seemed to grin from ear to ear. Who needed a man when you had a cat, she thought as she chopped a small portion off a salmon fillet and slipped it under the grill.

Before hitting the sheets that night Robyn logged on and rattled off a quick message to Delia.

Subject: Wombat Alert.

Hiya Dee. Yes, I've found a man who deserves the Wombat of the Year Award. The scales have fallen from my eyes. He has revealed himself in his true colours, and in record time. Yes, I'm talking about Colin. The guy I was mad for last week. I dumped him tonight after five days of passion. Gee, that's got to be the shortest romance on record. Now I'm going to put on my flannelette nightie and fuzzy old socks and climb into bed alone (except for my little cat Rhubarb). That's it ... NO MORE MEN (until the next one comes along). Hope you're doing better than me. Love, Robyn xx

***

A brief shower of rain wetted Josephine's hair and turned it into dark ringlets as she trudged resolutely towards Penzance. She imagined how her sudden appearance from nowhere would affect Mr and Mrs Cuthbert, the family retainers who lived in and maintained Roskenner House. Mrs Cuthbert would probably get in a terrible flap, fussing about and force-feeding her with broth to build her up. Mr Cuthbert was taciturn almost to the point of surliness, unlikely to react much.

The first houses on the outskirts of Marazion came into view. And there, just off the coast, stood St Michael's Mount. Knowing that one could see from Roskenner House the landmark island with its stately home silhouetted against the sky made home seem that much closer.

Shortly after, she walked past the grand St Clair residence. She felt no inclination to call in on Monsieur and Madame, particularly now that she knew what Madame had forced James to do.

Josephine looked across at the stretch of beach where everyone no doubt believed she had drowned. What about Lucien? It felt rather strange to come back from the dead, and no doubt the day would become stranger before it was done.

Before long Josephine passed Penzance docks and was well on her way into Newlyn. In the distance she could see the line of trees marking the driveway of Roskenner House. Her heart nearly stopped: a man rode past on a bicycle and turned in at the gate. He looked very much like Mr Cuthbert.

Then she arrived at the gate and looked ahead down the drive towards the substantial stone house. It seemed almost as big as Hogshead Island, where she had shared a cave smaller than the Roskenner kitchen with eight total strangers and a goat. She made a vow to try and stop thinking about the island in case she let something slip.

It would seem very strange to sleep all alone in her bedroom, she knew.

As Josephine strode down the driveway in her worn-out shoes and rounded the side of the house she saw Mr Cuthbert's bicycle propped against the wall. The kitchen door was open. She almost felt as though she should knock, but before she had a chance to do anything Mrs Cuthbert appeared in the doorway with a basket of washing.

'Get off with you, beggar woman!' she growled.

'Mrs Cuthbert, it's me, Josephine Trethewey …'

'My word, so it is! We all thought you was dead. Now where you a-been these past months, Miss Josephine? You're in a right old state!'

This was the moment of truth, or rather, untruth. Josephine summoned every scrap of her courage, and everything she had learned in drama class about immersing oneself in a role.

'I'm not really sure where I've been, Mrs Cuthbert. The truth is, I don't really know what happened. I seem to have lost my memory. I've been living on a farm a long way from here, helping out to earn my keep. I don't know how I got there. Then lately I started remembering things, like who I really am and where I'm from. So I came back.'

It sounded terribly lame. Would Mrs Cuthbert swallow the story?

Mr Cuthbert appeared from within the house. It appeared he had heard the story.

'Goodness sakes, Emmie! Bring Miss Josephine in, get her a strong cup o' tea. I'll fetch her ladyship.'

Cuthbert pulled up a chair and motioned for Josephine to sit while his wife busied herself with the teapot.

'It's a miracle, Miss Josephine! We'd all given you up for dead. Oh dear, maybe you don't remember what happened ...'

'Is my mother here?' interrupted Josephine.

Mrs Cuthbert nodded. 'She didn't travel back to Lunnon with His Lordship last September. Oh, won't she have a surprise when she sees you!' Mrs Cuthbert's eyes brimmed with tears at the thought of the reunion between mother and daughter.

'Of course, there's still your little brother ...' Mrs Cuthbert shot a glance at Josephine.

'What about my brother?' Josephine realised she had to tread carefully. 'I don't remember ...'

'Oh, you poor lamb. You don't remember a thing, do you? You got two younger brothers, leastways you did. George and Lucien. Your mother took the three of you along to visit them St Clair people over Marazion one day last summer and you young 'uns went swimming. And only one came back. George. You and little Lucien got swept out to sea and was drowned. They never found no bodies. We thought you'd got ate up by the fishes.'

'Gosh! I don't remember any of that.'

The kitchen door burst open and Caroline Trethewey swept into the kitchen. She caught her daughter up in a crushing embrace. Josephine didn't think her mother would ever let go, but eventually her grasp loosened and she held Josephine at arm's length.

'Josephine! *Mon Dieu!* I can't believe it's you. What a miracle! You are alive! But you look simply dreadful! Where have you been?'

Josephine repeated the sketchy story about the farm. The more she told it, the more she believed it.

'But we must visit these people and thank them for taking care of you,' said Caroline earnestly.

This was something James and Luisa had not foreseen. Panicking, Josephine changed the subject. 'Mrs Cuthbert just told me about Lucien. I'm so sorry ...'

A glance at her mother's pale face told Josephine that Caroline had taken the loss of Lucien very badly indeed. She looked ill at the mention of his name.

'There was nothing more you could have done, Josephine. The currents were very strong. I thought I had lost you both, and now ...' Caroline brightened visibly. 'Wait till I tell your father and George! They simply won't believe it! I must telephone them right away.'

Mrs Cuthbert interrupted with a bowl of broth for Josephine. 'Can I get you anything, Your Ladyship?'

'No, thank you. Josephine, just look at the state of your hair! And your skin! Was there no bath at the farmhouse?'

'Farm workers don't have the opportunity to wash very often,' said Josephine, working hard at her fantasy life on the farm. 'And the work is very hard on the hands,' she said, holding forth her calloused fingers and grimy nails for inspection.

'Ugh! We must get you up to my bathroom right away. I expect we'll have to cut your hair to get rid of all the tangles. Never mind, you can have one of those fashionable shingle cuts.'

Josephine felt very tired. She was still weak from her winter of illness, and she had been walking for hours. She knew it was going to be very hard work trying to keep the truth from slipping out, and wondered whether she had made a dreadful mistake in coming back.

Chapter 15

Father dearest ... was that a bit over the top? Robyn was feeling quite drunk and emotional after three glasses of wine. It was nearly midnight, pitch black outside except for pinpoints of unidentifiable light. Unidentifiable but definitely not stars. Probably something dreary like the train factory. Robyn swigged once more from her glass and settled to the task of emailing her father. She had already sent messages to Casey and Delia. Displacement activity in avoidance of the main task.

I am so very sad to hear that you have had a bad reaction to the chemotherapy ...

Robyn was glad in a way that she was thousands of miles away. Part of her wanted to jump on the next plane to Sydney, but the sensible part knew that if her father could see her puffy red eyes he would know just how gut-wrenchingly wretched she felt. And that would not do him any good whatsoever.

She felt betrayed by all his upbeat emails promising a full recovery after the chemotherapy and the operation. And talk of his plans for his fiftieth birthday next year, and finishing the computer he was building from scratch ... Robyn's tears plopped onto the keyboard.

Dad was being brave, but reading between the lines of his last message she knew he was shaken to the core. He had said they would still be able to operate without the full course of chemo, but Robyn was beginning to have doubts. The night before, straight after receiving her father's message, Robyn had sent an hysterical email to Steve. He had replied almost instantly with soothing words, but he warned her to prepare for the worst. Dad probably wouldn't die, but best to be prepared anyway.

Robyn blew her nose on a squishy tissue and blinked back another wave of tears.

It is good news that you can still have the operation. At least that will take away the growth and make you more comfortable. I'm thinking of you and Mum all the time. I love you both very much. You just have to say the word and I'll be on the next flight home.

Robyn hardly slept that night. She hauled herself out of bed at seven a.m. Unheard-of for a Saturday morning, but she was due to pick up Lori at half past so that they could make an early start on their drive to Cornwall. Robyn looked in the mirror and winced. No amount of cold water or under-eye concealer was going to make her eyes look any better, so she didn't even bother trying.

At least she felt a bit more human after a hot shower and a piece of toast, but a nagging ache in her head told the tale of too much wine the night before. She flung a few bits and pieces into a duffel bag, grabbed the box of food and things for Rhubarb she'd prepared the night before, and went in search of her sunglasses. At least they'd cover her tell-tale eyes. Darn it, they'd probably still look a mess by the time she got to Cornwall. Usually when she had a good cry it took twenty-four hours for her eyes to sort themselves out. On principle Robyn hated all women who could cry gracefully and not look a bleary, snotty mess afterwards.

Thankfully Rhubarb went willingly into his travelling basket. He was too young to leave with extra food for the weekend. More likely he would devour the lot at once, sick it all up and then starve.

Robyn didn't have to go round the back and ring the doorbell. Lori was already there by the front gate. At least that meant she wouldn't run the risk of bumping into Colin.

'Morning,' chirped Lori. 'Are we travelling incognito? Thelma and Louise? Should I put my shades on also? And a head scarf?'

Robyn let her glasses slip to the end of her nose.

'Oh, I see …'

'Dad can't continue with the chemo,' said Robyn, taking a deep breath in the hope of circumventing further tears. 'Please don't say a word or I'll start crying again and look even worse. I just hope I look a bit more respectable by the time we get to the rellies. As it is, I don't know whether I'll be able to tell Morvah and Emily about Dad …'

'I think I'd better drive,' said Lori, undoing her seat belt and opening the passenger door.

'Gee, thanks. I got a bit tanked up last night, so I might be over the limit still,' said Robyn sheepishly.

'Understandable in the circumstances. So … what now?'

'With Dad?'

Lori nodded. Robyn told her about the planned operation and Steve's pessimism.

'When I get myself together a bit more I'll phone Mum. She must be feeling dreadful.'

'God, I'm so sorry, Robs …'

'I warned you! No sympathy or you'll set me off again. Do you want to drown? It won't take much for me to flood the car completely once I start blubbering.'

'Okay, calm down. Let's swap seats and get on our way. We can stop in a while for a nice strong cup of coffee. Or a large gin, if you'd prefer.'

'Yuk! Don't mention alcohol,' said Robyn with a hung-over grimace, slinking round to the passenger door. Within moments Lori had adjusted the driver's seat for her long legs and they were on their way.

***

Josephine admired her reflection in the triple mirror in her mother's bedroom. The severely shortened hairstyle quite suited her. The thickness of her hair was cut quite pleasingly into layers at the back, and the freshly-washed waves rippled to an abrupt end at the sides, accentuating the determined jut of her chin.

'At last, a bit more grown up!' she thought. 'If only James could see me now.'

She felt gloriously clean all over, right down to the tips of her fingers and toes. It would take time for her hands and feet to become soft once more, but at least they were clean. So were her clothes. It was so pleasant to revisit her wardrobe, to discover the joy of clothes that hadn't meant very much this time last year. Was it the advancing of womanhood that enhanced her joy in pretty things, the return from deprivation, or a combination of the two?

Thinking of womanhood, Josephine realised that she should tell her mother that she'd started her monthly bleeding. Smiling secretively to herself she knew however that she would never be able to confess that she'd lost her virginity. *Maman* would be astounded to know what her little girl had been up to in recent months. Josephine could never imagine *Maman* and Father doing the things she and James had done, but she knew they must have done so at least three times in order to have produced herself, George and Lucien.

Lady Caroline looked up approvingly at her daughter standing at the top of the stairs. Reflected in her eyes Josephine could see her relief that the grubby urchin had been banished. She expected the clothes she had arrived in had already been burned by Mr Cuthbert.

'Dinner will be served shortly, darling.'

Josephine revelled in the spaciousness of Roskenner House and the knowledge that she was about to eat a meal that she hadn't helped prepare. It was such a relief not to have to forage for food or mend clothes. It was simply wonderful to be back at Roskenner.

'Have you telephoned Father yet?'

'Not yet. Perhaps we could do that together after we've eaten. What do you think? What a wonderful surprise it will be!'

'I expect George is away at school. May I telephone him?'

'Of course, my darling.'

Josephine made her way carefully into the dining room. It seemed strange to be wearing shoes and stockings once more, and she had to remember to walk like a lady. In fact, it was strange to be walking up and down stairs after the rocky paths of the island. And the house seemed truly vast after the confines of the cave.

Josephine turned left into the dining room, but her mother caught her attention.

'Not in there, darling. Much too formal for just the two of us. I've been taking my meals in the breakfast room. It has such a nice view of the terraces.'

Josephine turned in the opposite direction and followed her mother's slender form along the cavernous hallway.

Once they were seated at the table Caroline cast admiring eyes over her daughter's hair.

'I must say I didn't do a bad job. It really suits you, darling. Perhaps I should get mine cut in the same style. It's all the rage in Paris.'

'What about London?'

Caroline cast her eyes down and fussed unnecessarily with her napkin. 'I wouldn't know. I haven't been back there since … I only know about the Paris fashions from my magazines.'

Mrs Cuthbert entered with a trolley. She deftly arranged crockery and cutlery before Lady Kenner and her daughter, and ladled soup from a tureen. There was a plate of fresh bread and pats of golden Cornish butter to accompany the soup. Josephine felt a rush of salivatory anticipation. Her mother probably thought this was the simplest fare, but to Josephine it was heaven!

She had to remember to eat with small, ladylike bites instead of stuffing a whole slice in her mouth and chewing with gusto.

'Could we possibly go into Penzance tomorrow?' asked Josephine. 'I'd like to visit that sweet shop.'

'Darling! What an oddity you are! Well, I suppose you do need fattening up a bit, but you must promise to take care of your teeth. Sugar does rot them so. I'll ask Cuthbert to get the Rolls out of the garage. He'll enjoy that.'

'So will I,' said Josephine. After her long walk from Poldhu Point the thought of a smooth ride was most welcome, particularly if it included a trip to the sweet shop. She could taste the caramel already, even though it brought bittersweet memories of James.

The garden was a paradise of spring flowers and soft greens. Josephine could hardly keep her eyes from the windows while they ate their second course of roast chicken and vegetables. She watched an old tabby cat slink off the wall, most put out that its nap had been disturbed by a shower of rain.

After dinner they retired to the drawing room. Caroline picked up the telephone receiver and dialled their London residence.

'Charles, Caroline here,' she said, stating the obvious. 'I have the most amazing news. Guess who is here? Josephine!'

Josephine could hear her father's bark of disbelief from where she sat. A joyous conversation ensued between her parents, and then her mother beckoned her over so she could speak to her father.

'Yes, Papa. It's me,' said Josephine. Then she had to relate the tale of her sojourn on the farm.

Having rung off, Caroline then dialled the number of George's school and asked for him to be brought to the telephone.

She handed the receiver to her daughter. Josephine was relieved that the conversation was less awkward than that with her father. 'Yes, George, it's true. It really is me. No, I don't remember much about where I've been ...'

She wished she could tell him the truth about her adventures.

The physical and emotional demands of returning from the dead took their toll on Josephine, and she retired to bed soon after. Ah, the bliss of sinking into a soft, clean bed, in a bedroom that smelled freshly of lavender.

The following morning after breakfast Cuthbert brought the Rolls Royce around to the front of the house. Caroline insisted that Josephine fetch her navy cloak from the cloakroom.

'We don't want you catching cold, dear,' she admonished.

Josephine was torn between feeling stifled by her mother's fussing and cosseted by her attentions. She rationalised that it was only fair to allow her mother to flap about like a mother hen; after all, for the past nine months she'd thought she'd lost two of her children.

Penzance was humming with activity. Josephine had never before appreciated the pleasures of shopping, but once she had overcome her anxiety at the bustle and noise of the streets she found herself enjoying the experience.

Caroline had her own agenda. Before Josephine was allowed anywhere near the sweet shop she had to endure the purchase of a new outfit. This involved being measured, and poked and pushed into the appropriate underpinnings before the dress of her mother's choice could be slipped over her head. And what a dress! Far more grown-up than anything she'd ever owned before. It was a slinky item in shining blue, a figure-flattering shift dress that came to an abrupt halt at the knee. Rather like the way her hair came to an abrupt halt before reaching her shoulders. Very fashionable, delivered just a few days earlier from a top London designer. Josephine temporarily forgot her desire for sweets.

'It's simply beautiful!' she gasped, turning this way and that.

'It suits you very well, darling.'

Josephine noticed that her mother's eyes had filled with tears, and was deeply touched. She had a wicked thought: it was rather nice now that *Maman* was not constantly distracted by Lucien. She wondered whether George had been fussed over and indulged in the months he'd spent as his mother's only remaining child.

The sales assistant had to make three trips to carry all their purchases out to the car: the dress, more underwear, stockings, shoes, a frivolous hat, and a new coat in the latest style.

At last they rounded the corner of the side street where Mrs Trescothick, vendor of sweetmeats, plied her trade. The smell of the place was intoxicating beyond description. Josephine could have quite happily bought everything on display, right down to the comfits that she'd never really liked. However she restrained herself and asked for a modest quarter of caramels.

Further restraint was called for after they left the shop. Josephine could have quite easily eaten all her sweets as they walked back to the car, but she knew her mother would be horrified if she stooped so low as to eat in the street.

As they turned back along the High Street a gentleman came out of the tobacconist's without watching where he was going and bumped clumsily into Josephine.

'My sincere apologies,' he said, removing his hat and bowing his head respectfully.

'Georges!' exclaimed Lady Caroline. 'For a moment I did not recognise you.'

'Nor I you,' replied the man.

'May I present my daughter? Josephine, this is Monsieur Roquebrun. Surely you must remember him?'

Josephine was struck dumb. Faced with the man who had been responsible for James being on the run from the law, she wanted to slap his face. Or worse. But she nodded politely and murmured something vague.

'Madame, surely you are not old enough to have such a grown-up daughter!' simpered the man.

Josephine feigned interest in the window of a bookshop while her mother fawned sickeningly at his flattery. Her thoughts were with James, wondering what he was doing. She wished she could tell him that she had met Monsieur Roquebrun.

Eventually her mother decided they should be on their way. After walking a short distance Josephine spied Mr Cuthbert and their car waiting in the next side street.

As they settled themselves and their purchases Caroline took Josephine to task.

'Really, darling. I did think you were rather off-hand with Monsieur Roquebrun.'

'I'm sorry, *Maman*. My feet are hurting. I didn't mean to be rude, but I couldn't bear to stand much longer.'

'A lady must learn to keep her composure regardless of physical discomfort,' admonished Caroline.

Josephine wished for a moment that she was back on the island, running barefoot in the sand with James.

Back in her bedroom, Josephine put away her new clothes, meanwhile dipping into her bag of caramels. Before she had a chance to appreciate them fully they were all gone, and all that remained was a faint, sweet aroma in the paper bag.

***

A strong cup of coffee and two paracetamol in a roadside café helped restore Robyn's equilibrium. Diet be damned, she had a jam doughnut as well. Licking her sugary fingers she caught a glance from Lori.

'I know. But I can hardly diet this weekend, can I? Aunt Emily is a great cook and it would be just plain rude not to do her meals justice. Oh, it's all right for you, Miss Skinny Britches.'

'I can't help being a beanpole. Honest.'

'I expect it runs in your family. Speaking of families, I'm looking forward to meeting my Great Uncle William. I'm hoping he'll be able to fill me in on some of the missing bits of the family tree. Honestly, all I seem to do is detective work these days. Searching out relatives, keeping tabs on Paul Sinclair … oops! Can we forget I said that?'

'We most certainly can not!' said Lori, open-mouthed with shock. 'What do you mean, keeping tabs on Paul?'

'Oh dear. Promise you won't tell a soul. I'm not really doing a time and motion study. My boss sent me over here to check Paul out. The top brass think he's on the fiddle, pocketing company money.'

'You've got to be joking!'

'Well, I must say I haven't found any evidence yet. I'm beginning to think I'm on a wild goose chase. Anyway, whatever happens I'm going home at the end of January. Nick understands I want to get home to see my Dad …'

Robyn felt a surge of emotion that threatened tears. The fact that her father was probably going to die was beginning to sink in.

Lori didn't appear to notice Robyn's distress. 'Just what evidence do they have that Paul's misappropriated funds?' she asked defensively, twisting a paper napkin in her fingers.

'Gee, I don't know. They don't tell little people like me things like that. I just get the job of trying to catch him out.'

'This is bizarre! I'd no idea …'

Robyn consulted her watch. 'Lori, if you don't mind we'd better get going again. Cornwall is still a long way away.'

Chapter 16

They were quite a crowd at the Trescowe home that night. Robyn was glad she had come despite the bad news about her father. So far she had managed to avoid an in-depth discussion of his illness. That, she knew, would be a true test of her tear ducts.

She felt warm and familyish, a feeling she hadn't until now realised she was missing so badly. Meals on the terrace at her parents' home were very much like the gatherings in the conservatory at her aunt and uncle's home.

Little Rhubarb was tucked away safely in the room where she and Lori were to sleep that night. Robyn was relieved that he was turning out to be a good traveller, having settled happily in his basket for the long car journey. Olivia had made a great fuss of him, and Robyn hoped she understood that the little kitty now had to stay in the bedroom for a rest. The last thing Robyn wanted was to lose Rhubarb in the wilds of Cornwall.

Robyn was amazed at the resemblance between her father, Morvah and Great Uncle William. All three had the same eyes and chin. Uncle William was pretty perky for seventy-one, and had clear recollection of incidents during the time she and her family had spent in England. But after a couple of drinks he began to expand at length on his exploits in France during the Second World War. This included a cringe-makingly lurid recollection of an encounter with a French farm girl at harvest time. Young Olivia had wanted to know what 'rogering' meant. Morwenna glared at William but with some quick thinking managed to satisfy her daughter's curiosity, telling her that it meant giving someone a thorough telling off.

'You must have been very young to go off fighting for your country,' said Robyn, eager to divert the conversation away from his sex life.

'Oh, we all lied about our ages. I was thirteen but I told them I was eighteen. They wanted as many men as possible and didn't always ask for proof of age.'

However it was proving difficult to get Uncle William onto the subject of the Trescowe family history. Robyn felt tired, and Lori also appeared to be struggling to keep awake.

Emily beckoned Robyn to one side. 'Why don't you both slip away to bed, dear? Your friend looks as tired as you do. Don't worry, Uncle William will still be here in the morning. Morvah's had far too much to drink to be able to drive him home.'

'Gee, where do you find room for everyone to sleep?'

Emily smiled. 'This is nothing, dear. Wait till Christmas. That's when we're well and truly bursting at the seams!'

Lori was grateful to be hauled off to get some shut-eye. 'I didn't want to appear rude, but I am quite literally dropping,' she said through a mouthful of toothpaste. Their room had its own handbasin, which was helpful.

Rhubarb was wide awake, busily investigating the contents of the waste paper basket. Robyn hauled him out and chastised him, but it was difficult to be serious with such a cute little fellow.

'You're right, they're a lovely family,' said Lori as she ran a brush through her hair.

'Yeah, they're pretty special, aren't they? I just hope I can get Uncle William on his own in the morning to ask him about his ancestors.'

***

It transpired that Josephine and her mother would return to London in a day or two, and George would arrive at their London home on Saturday. It wouldn't take him long to travel by train from his school in Berkshire.

'How would you feel about a private tutor to finish off your education, Josephine?' asked Lady Caroline.

Josephine was taken by surprise. She hadn't given any thought as yet to how she would spend her days.

'I suppose that would be a good idea.'

'I'm glad you agree, *cherie*. It's far too late to try and get you into the Academy. Unless you'd prefer a finishing school in Switzerland?'

'No, thank you. I don't really want to go away again.'

'And I don't want you going away either, just after we've found you again,' said her mother, giving her a hug. 'As well as some lessons, we must shortly begin making arrangements for your Season.'

'I suppose that will mean staying permanently in London.'

Lady Caroline nodded absently as she stared into the distance across the garden. She adjusted the comb holding her hair in place.

'Yes, I think it's time we went back to London. We can return here after your Season is finished.'

'Have you been here all the time since …?'

'Yes, *cherie*,' said Caroline with a tight little smile. 'Maybe in my heart I hoped that both of you would come back to me, but I don't expect more than one miracle in my lifetime. It's time to return to London and pick up the threads, join the world once more. Don't you agree?'

'Yes, *Maman*,' said Josephine dutifully. But she wasn't altogether sure that she was ready for the big city. Not just yet. She still had some adjusting to do. To go from cave-dweller to debutante practically overnight would prove quite a transition.

Josephine took a last walk around the gardens of Roskenner House on the morning of their departure. Behind the orangerie she came across something new: a headstone in the lawn with a rose bush planted in front of it. Moving closer, she saw Lucien's name was inscribed on the stone. His body had not been found, but at least there was a permanent reminder of his short life.

Then she noticed a bare patch next to Lucien's headstone, and her heart constricted with shock. No doubt this had been where her own headstone had stood for the past nine months. She was thankful that someone had seen fit to remove it; to see one's own grave would be a most unpleasant experience.

****

Despite the amount of wine he had consumed the night before, Great Uncle William was on good form at breakfast. He was working out tactical strategies for battle with the toast rack, sauce bottle and anything else he could lay his hands on.

'Can I be the enemy?' piped up Olivia, stretching forward from her high chair to reach the butter dish. 'I like playing with you, Great William,' she said with a winning smile.

William Rostrevor winked at the little girl and pushed the butter dish, jam pot and salt shaker in her direction. 'Those are your tanks, m'girl. Let battle commence!'

At that point William upset the milk jug with his elbow. He fished out a grimy handkerchief and made feeble attempts to mop up the damage, but the milk had engulfed the toast and was advancing towards the edge of the table.

'Emily, I need back-up from a fresh regiment,' he called.

Emily came in from the kitchen with a plate of bacon. 'What are you doing, you old rogue?'

'Wasn't us. Spot of enemy action,' he said, winking at Olivia.

'Pity those enemies of yours don't carry a cloth.'

Emily hurried back to the kitchen and returned with a sponge to stem the flow of milk.

William got up from his chair in order to give Emily rooom to mop up. Robyn shot a conspiratorial glance at Lori, who was having difficulty keeping a straight face.

Robyn stood up and picked up her great-uncle's mug of tea. 'Come in the conservatory, Unc, while Emily sorts out the mess.'

He did as he was told. Emily placated Olivia with the promise that Uncle would be back shortly to continue their game.

'So,' said Robyn, facing her uncle across the coffee table. 'You remember my Dad, Joseph Trescowe.'

'Ah yes, Maud's boy. Went off to Australia, right?'

'That's right. He's interested in the family history. He's been looking for information but he's stuck. None of the Rostrevors he's found seem to be related to him. Did the family originate from Cornwall?'

It was as though a shutter had come down behind the elderly man's eyes. 'Oh, I don't know much about all that. I think they were from round Truro, but I don't really know. They're long dead.'

Robyn's heart sank. Why was he being so evasive?

'So you don't know anything about your ancestors?' she asked point blank.

'No.'

'That's a pity. Dad will be disappointed. You know he's got cancer? He got all excited when I was sent over here to work because he wanted me to try and find out about them. Now I expect he'll die without knowing anything more ...'

Robyn immediately wanted to take back her words. She hadn't intended to play the drama queen, but desperate measures were called for and she was sure Uncle William was holding out.

'Emily told me he's in the hospital,' said William. 'Don't worry, girl. The doctors can do all sorts of wonderful things these days. Marvellous, really, when you consider how medicine has come on since the war ...'

You and your bloody war, thought Robyn.

***

London proved every bit as horrendous as Josephine had expected. The sheer noise after the peace of Cornwall was almost more than she could bear. From the moment they stepped off the train at Paddington Station her ears were assaulted by shrill whistles, the hiss and thunder of steam escaping from numerous trains, people shouting ... Nobody walked, they all bustled. Taxi cabs hooted and jostled with other traffic, and Josephine pitied the few horses forced to share the roads with the tide of motorised traffic.

It was at least quiet once they passed the portals of the family residence in Wilton Crescent. However the house seemed dark and oppressive compared with Roskenner.

Josephine went with trepidation to visit her father in his study. He had been quite abrupt on the telephone, and had seemed almost cross that she had returned from the dead.

Charles Trethewey looked up from his paperwork, and a rare smile lit up his face. He rose to his feet, strode around his desk and engulfed his daughter in a strong embrace.

Josephine was quite taken aback. Tears pricked her eyes and she took a deep breath in order to stem their progress.

'Welcome home, Josephine! What a miracle! Sit down and tell me all about it. I'll ring for tea. What on earth is the time?'

'It's nearly half past four, Father,' she said, settling in a firm leather chair. She was dying to slip off her shoes as they were pinching her feet.

In answer to his summons there was a knock at the door. It was one of the maids, who stared open-mouthed at Josephine but quickly recovered her composure.

'Tea, please, Miss,' requested Lord Kenner.

The maid bobbed a quick curtsey and left the room.

Charles placed a heavy hand on Josephine's shoulder. 'Let me look at you.'

She was astounded. His eyes were shining with tears. He feigned a sneeze, drew out a large, white handkerchief and turned his back briefly.

'I beg your pardon. Now, where were we? Your mother said you had been found by some farm people. Is this true?'

'Yes, Father,' said Josephine. Lying was coming more easily with practice. 'I don't remember very much, but they took me in and I worked for them in return for my keep.'

'How astounding! We must thank these people for their kindness.'

'I don't remember where the farm is. My memory has been affected. I think I must have hit my head while I was in the water. The last thing I remember from the day ... the day I nearly drowned ... is being swept out to sea, then things become quite unclear. Just faces and voices for a long time, then my life on the farm. A room in one of the outbuildings, meals in the kitchen. The farmer's name was John and his wife was Mary, but I can't remember their surname. Not sure I ever knew it. I don't remember much of the journey back to Roskenner. It was very tiring, I walked all the way.'

'Most peculiar.'

Josephine did not dare look at her father. She sat with her eyes lowered, twisting her hands in her lap.

'We must get Doctor Frobisher to have a look at you tomorrow, make sure you haven't come to any permanent harm.'

Josephine felt a shiver of fear, but knew it was pointless to try and resist. If she could just keep up the pretence a little while longer, surely the interest in her whereabouts would abate and life could go on as normal. She just had to keep her head.

'Yes, thank you Father,' she heard herself saying. At all costs she must not give away any clue about James and the other island people. How she missed him!

Wisely she changed the subject, asking her father about George.

'He had a nasty bout of influenza in the winter, but apart from that he's been quite well. Great shock to him to lose both you and Lucien. He blamed himself, of course, but we reassured him that he did his best. Eventually he bucked up his ideas. Going back to school seemed to help.'

'Of course. I know how much he enjoys school.'

'Ah, so you do remember some things.'

Josephine knew she was going to have to watch her step around her father. He didn't seem at all convinced that she was telling the truth. Or was that just her guilty conscience?

'I don't seem to have any trouble remembering the past,' she explained. 'It's the events of recent months that are very confused. I was surprised to learn just how long I'd been missing.'

Her father's expression softened. 'Ah, but how you've grown up! I like your hair cut shorter.'

'*Maman* had to cut it. It was a bit of a mess.'

'Understandable if you'd been shovelling hay and cleaning out pig pens, or whatever one does on a farm.'

'Yes, and milking cows, and lots of scrubbing and sweeping.' Josephine felt more confident, knowing this was in part true. She had learned to milk Mildred, and had done plenty of scrubbing and sweeping. What did it matter if these things hadn't happened on a farm?

Lord Kenner stood up and turned his back to the fire.

'Well, it's a shame that you can't remember the name and whereabouts of your farm. I would have liked to visit the family.'

'Oh, I thanked them very much before I left, Father.'

'Glad to hear you haven't forgotten your manners.'

A knock at the door heralded the arrival of the tea tray. As she departed, the little maid, Millie, much the same age as Josephine, curtseyed and murmured a greeting to Josephine.

'Ever so glad to see you back, Miss Josephine,' she murmured self-consciously, eyes lowered.

'Thank you, Millie,' said Josephine. Talking to the servants the way one did brought home to Josephine the vast gulf of society that she had leapt in the past few days. As she poured tea for her father she relished the solid, shiny feel of the ornate silver teapot and the fineness of the china. Getting used to her old life once again was strange in many ways, but there were some things that were comfortingly familiar.

Josephine was relishing the last mouthful of buttery teacake when the study door burst open and George hobbled into view, a broad grin on his face.

'Josephine! Great to see you!' he cried, hugging his sister.

She hugged him back. His blazer was damp and gave off a faint, familiar smell. A brother smell.

His voice was on the point of breaking, one moment low and the next cracked and squeaky. Or perhaps it was simply the emotion of the moment.

'Gosh! You do look grown up!' he said in awe, holding his sister at arm's length.

'It's the new hair style, I expect. And *Maman* got me a new dress,' she said, twirling for her brother's benefit. Her hair shone richly in the electric light.

'More expense!' chided her father. 'You women and your clothes!' he added with a conspiratorial wink at George.

Josephine and George sat down with their father. Lord Kenner rang for more tea, and Josephine once more dragged out her tissue of lies for the benefit of her brother.

Chapter 17

Robyn and Lori slept well despite Rhubarb's nocturnal racketing. Robyn had a vague memory of the kitten batting at her nose in the wee hours, but when she woke shortly after nine she found him under the covers, curled up next to her stomach. She was immediately concerned that she could have rolled on him in the night.

'Don't worry,' said Lori, who was already sitting up in her bed. 'I'm sure he'd move if he felt threatened. You'd move if a mountain was about to fall on you.'

Robyn hurled a pillow at her friend. 'Thanks a bunch! Gee, I may have gained a pound or two but I don't look like a mountain yet, do I?'

'I was speaking in relative terms. Let's go and see whether anyone else is up and about yet.'

Aunt Emily was stationed beside the cooker, monitoring the progress of a raft of bacon under the grill.

''Morning, girls. Toast's on the table, tea's in the pot.'

'Are we the first up?' asked Robyn.

'Goodness no, dear. Morvah, Colum and William have gone for a walk that will probably take them to some pub or other. They'll be back by lunchtime. Morwenna is still in bed, but Olivia is awake and playing quietly in their room.'

'Gee, is all that bacon for us?' said Robyn, suddenly finding her mouth watering.

'If you don't want it all I can put some out for the foxes. They like a bit of bacon.'

'Terrible waste of bacon,' said Robyn, her mouth full and her hand reaching for another rasher.

They passed the remainder of the morning helping Emily prepare their Sunday dinner.

Just before half past twelve, Great Uncle William's granddaughter, Moira, arrived. She looked at least ten years older than herself, Robyn thought. She was married to an auctioneer and mother to two young children who had gone to a well-known amusement park for a day out with friends.

Moira plonked herself down on a kitchen chair with a sigh, and dumped her expensive-looking leather handbag on the table. Untidy blonde hair framed her face, which wore a weary, rather petulant expression.

'Tea, dear?' enquired Emily, after introducing Robyn and Lori.

'Got anything stronger, Em? I could murder a stiff G and T.'

Emily left the room, returning with a bottle of gin and a clutch of glasses. 'G and T's all round, eh, girls?' she said with an impish grin. 'We'll all get a bit squiffy by the time the others return.'

'I mustn't get too pissed,' said Moira. 'I've got to pick the kids up from Marcia's at seven. I hope you don't mind me dropping in like this, but I just fancied some time away from house and kids. Grandad told me he was staying with you for the weekend. Sorry, I seem to be interrupting your preparations for dinner.'

'Not at all, dear. You're welcome to join us. There's plenty to go round. Your grandfather's gone off with Morvah and Colum to the pub. They'll be back soon I expect.'

Moira took a long swig of her drink. 'I'd love to stay for dinner, thanks Em. How is the old codger?'

'William? He's fine. Seems to be getting on all right by himself.'

'Wish I could say the same,' said Moira with a sigh. 'Richard's away all the time, going here and there to auctions, and the kids are driving me round the twist. I was glad to see the back of them this morning.'

'It'll get easier when they're a bit older, dear,' soothed Emily.

'I certainly hope so,' said Moira, helping herself to more gin. 'At present I feel like I'm halfway up the road to the loony bin.'

Emily was explaining that almost every mother feels like that at some stage when the men returned from their walk, full of high spirits and hungry as a pack of dogs. Robyn was glad to see them as Moira was dominating the conversation. Robyn's first impression of the woman was of someone rather spoiled and overindulged who needed to get a grip.

Morvah and Colum fetched chairs from all over the house, and extended the dining table to accommodate the crowd.

Emily, Colum, Lori and Robyn formed a production line to get the food on the plates as quickly as possible.

'How do you do it, Auntie?' asked Robyn, full of admiration for her aunt's ability to feed such a crowd without getting in a flap.

'My secret is to cook twice as many potatoes as I think we'll need. We often end up with a few extra mouths to feed.'

'You're amazing!'

At that point Morwenna and Olivia appeared and helped carry the plates to the table.

After dinner Robyn offered to wash the dishes, and was surprised that Moira pitched in to help. At first they washed and dried in silence.

'He's a funny old thing, isn't he? I mean Grandfather,' said Moira eventually.

Robyn wondered how she could tactfully voice her disappointment in his lack of co-operation with her family tree research.

'He seems to have enjoyed the war,' she said drily.

'God, yes! You've heard of the Boer War, well he's the original War Bore. You could be talking about painting your toenails and he'd somehow bring the conversation around to the war.'

They laughed together.

'Maybe nothing else as big ever happened in his life,' suggested Robyn.

'Nothing else that he wants to talk about, perhaps. I know he puts a brave front on it, but I think deep down he's disappointed that Gerald was always too pink and frilly to join the forces, and that he won't be getting married and having children. You do know he's gay, don't you?'

'Who, Gerald or Grandfather?'

Moira collapsed against the bench in a fit of giggles. 'Oh, stop it! The thought of Grandfather taking it up the … Sorry, best not go there.'

'I tried to get William talking about his parents and grandparents etcetera but he shut up like a clam. Or rather, he dragged the conversation back to the bloody war. My father wants me to do some family research while I'm over here, so I was a bit disappointed that I didn't get anywhere with William.'

Moira swirled the last of the foam down the plughole and dried her hands.

'Ah, I think I know why. Gran told me some things shortly before she died. Apparently his parents weren't married. Very unusual for those times, and probably a source of embarrassment to him.'

'That's interesting. I wonder why they didn't marry?'

'I don't know. Maybe one or the other was still married to someone else. Ordinary farming folk didn't go in for divorces back then. Too much scandal and expense. So they just papered over the cracks and carried on as normal.'

'I see. Gee, I'd really like to find out more, but if he's that touchy about it …'

Moira smiled. 'I may be able to help you. Grandfather has a bit of a soft spot for me. I'll try to get some info out of him but I'll have to be a bit devious. I suppose you want the usual sort of stuff, names, dates, places of birth …'

'That would be fantastic!'

'No promises, mind, but I'll do my best.'

***

Later that evening George and Josephine had a chance to spend some time alone. Their parents had gone their separate ways for a couple of hours before dinner, so they stayed in the sitting room.

George struggled to his feet and put a few more lumps of coal on the fire.

'My calliper went a bit rusty after getting wet that day on the beach. I had to have it taken off and cleaned. Sorry, do you mind me talking about that day?'

'Oh, no. I don't remember very much in any case.'

'Must be weird.'

'I'm getting used to it now, but it was very frustrating at first.'

George sat beside his sister and took her hand. 'I'm awfully glad you came back to us. It was very lonely being an only child all that time. I bet *Maman* got the shock of her life when you turned up out of nowhere.'

'You could say that.'

'Well, I think we can now say without a doubt that Lucien won't be knocking on the door of Roskenner. Poor little Froggy.'

'I only hope it was quick. They say you just sort of drift off to sleep when you drown,' said Josephine, drawing on her memory of almost drowning without giving too much away.

In the warmth of closeness with her brother she toyed with the idea of breaking her silence. She suddenly felt desperate to share her experiences with someone who might understand.

Josephine's seventeenth birthday came upon her without warning. She realised only three days beforehand, and felt a bit miffed that neither George, *Maman* or Father had said anything.

On the appointed day, the twenty-fifth of May, she awoke in a bad humour, feeling neglected and unappreciated. But when she reached the breakfast room she was stunned to see the table decorated with flowers, the

151

room hung with balloons, and a table at the side laden with brightly wrapped gifts.

'Oh, *Maman!*' she whispered, close to tears. 'I thought you had all forgotten!'

Caroline Trethewey embraced her daughter and planted a kiss on her forehead. 'Forget your birthday, *cherie*? Why, or course not! We are so very glad to have you back with us.'

'Father wrote to the Prime Minister,' announced George, winking at his father. 'He asked whether your birthday could be declared a public holiday. But I suppose since it's so close to Whitsun we could hardly expect an extra holiday.'

'George!' You're here!' exclaimed Josephine, having just realised that her brother should have been at school.

'Large as life. Father sneaked me in last night under cover of darkness while you were away at the gathering of your witches' coven.'

'You're just jealous because you're too young to attend balls and parties.'

'Now then, you two,' said Charles Trethewey sternly. 'Are we going to eat this fine breakfast or leave it to go cold?'

'May I open my presents first, Father?'

'No, Josephine. Kedgeree first, presents after.'

Josephine dutifully took her place, delighted that her birthday hadn't been forgotten after all. She glowed with happiness. It was just wonderful being part of her family once more.

***

The drive back to Eastleigh passed quickly with Lori as a companion. Robyn felt obliged to touch briefly on the subject of Colin.

'I mean, to turn from passionate lover to lazy bludger in just a few days ...'

'No details, please!' protested Lori.

Robyn grinned. 'He's what we in Australia call a wombat.'

'Huh?'

'Eats roots and leaves. Think about it.'

'I still don't get it,' said Lori, looking blank.

'A root is what you'd call a shag or a screw.'

'Oh, I see. How quaint.'

'The point is, he kept coming round uninvited night after night. Never took me out for so much as a drink, but ate my food and drank whatever I

152

had in the fridge. Then hauled me off to bed. After just a few days I went off him big time, so I dropped him like a hot brick.'

'Well, you seem to be the first. Previously he's left a trail of broken hearts across the county.'

'Do you know that for a fact, or is it just what he's told you?'

Lori's eyes widened and a smile crept across her face. 'Surely not …? I won't say anything to him, but I'll see what I can find out. I see Claire Wenvoe in town occasionally, she had a bit of a fling with him last year.'

Then they discussed the possibility of Paul Sinclair being a bad guy instead of the civilised, cultured fellow Lori claimed he was.

'Just remember,' said Robyn, wagging a finger for emphasis. 'Not all thieves wear stripy t-shirts and masks over their eyes.'

'Okay, but please watch where you're going and keep both hands on the wheel,' said Lori nervously.

Before long they were passing familiar landmarks. Robyn felt altogether better after a weekend away, but returning to Eastleigh was a return to reality.

She dropped Lori off at the gates of her grand residence.

'Coming in for a cuppa, or do you want to avoid Colin?'

'What do you think? Anyway, it's getting late. Gotta get Rhubarb some food. He's the only man in my life from now on.'

'We are assuming Rhubarb is male,' said Lori.

'Oh, he shows all the signs. I'd be very surprised if he was a little girl cat.'

'What are you planning to do with him when you return to Australia?'

'Gee, I haven't really thought that far ahead yet. Want a cat?'

'I'll think about it. I'll have to discuss it with Colin.'

Robyn sighed. 'Everything seems to come back to Colin.'

'But probably not you,' said Lori, closing the passenger door.

'Definitely not. Anyway, thanks for coming with me. Sorry I was such a mess on Saturday morning. Was it only yesterday? I feel tons better now.'

'I'm glad. See you at work tomorrow.'

Robyn opened her mouth but Lori seemed to know what was coming. 'Don't worry,' she said. 'I won't tell a soul about your investigation of Paul.'

***

Josephine soon settled into a comfortable routine. Her days were a mixture of tuition with Monsieur Besnard, shopping, and preparations for her debut. In the hubbub of tea parties and talk of clothes she found she was thinking of James less and less. He was becoming a distant memory, almost like a lingering dream.

Josephine joined occasional weekend house parties. The families of some of the girls in her group of debutantes had substantial homes in Kent, Surrey and other Home Counties, and liked to entertain on a lavish scale.

Josephine was starting to be noticed by her friends' brothers and their friends. She was a natural beauty with little need for lipstick or powder. Her eyes shone with good health once more, and her skin was clear and fresh. Yet Josephine was dissatisfied with her looks, in particluar her plump stomach. She had been very thin upon arriving at Roskenner, and it was understandable that good living was putting back what hard living on the island had taken away. But it seemed unfair that it all went on her stomach.

Josephine vowed to cut out cream teas and puddings; she didn't want to end up looking like Rose Richardson. It was wonderful to have a wardrobe full of fashionable clothes and she didn't intend to burst out of them.

Josephine had just returned from an eventful weekend at the country home of Judith Herbert. People tended to whisper behind their hands somewhat because Mrs Herbert was a Jewess, but Mr Herbert's solid footing in the Bank of England counterbalanced the slur of alternative religion cast by his wife. In any case Josephine thought Mrs Herbert was delightful, very warm-hearted and more like a sister than a mother to Judith.

The Herberts had just had a swimming pool installed, a magnificent construction of marble surrounded by Roman columns and a vast patio. The weather had been flawless. It was early June and there was promise of a long, hot summer in the air.

The party had started on Saturday afternoon, and was still going strong when Josephine had retired exhausted to her bed shortly after two on Sunday morning. Her feet were throbbing their complaint against the ridiculous shoes she'd worn, and her head was fuzzy from too much champagne. She followed Judith's advice and drank a glass of water before retiring in the hope that she wouldn't suffer a hangover.

Still, it had been fun. She had felt very grown-up in her figure-skimming beaded gown, the latest fashion. No-one would have guessed at the corset beneath keeping her errant belly under control.

Josephine had to admit she felt attracted to Judith's brother Leo. He had looked very smart: his white suit showed off his bronzed skin, and with his slim moustache he looked like a motion picture idol. And he seemed taken with her. He'd danced with her more than any of the other girls.

Josephine drifted off into a haze of dreams, dancing away into the mist with Leo Herbert, transfixed by his dark, hypnotic eyes.

She awoke shortly after nine on Sunday morning to the sound of peals of laughter and splashing. Another glorious day, and from her window she could see that some of the guests were already in the pool. She dressed hurriedly in her new swimming costume and slipped on an elegant silk robe for modesty's sake, sliding her feet into matching sandals before scurrying downstairs and out into the brilliant morning.

It was a day to remember forever. After swimming and larking about in the blissfully warm water of the heated pool and plenty of time lazing and gossiping in the sun, the guests had retreated to their rooms to dress for lunch. Josephine sent aloft a prayer of thanks to her mother for insisting she take masses of clothes.

For luncheon Josephine chose a peach silk crepe dress that wrapped sensuously around her body and fell in soft folds half-way to her ankles. She admired the effect in the full-length mirror, checking that her stomach was held flat. Matching shoes set off the outfit to perfection.

She descended the staircase with the confidence of a young woman fully assured that she looked her best. The meal was served in the conservatory, a massive temple to indulgence filled with exotic plants. In the middle of the intricately tiled floor stood a vast table wrought in antique gold with a heavy glass top, laden with an opulent selecltion of tableware and fine china.

As soon as the guests were seated a fleet of waiters brought heated trolleys of food. They were served seven tiny but elegant courses, washed down with more fine champagne.

Josephine had to admit that Leo Herbert still looked very dashing by the light of day. Today he was wearing a cream suit with a matching shirt and bow tie, which would have looked ridiculous on anyone else but showed off his dark good looks to perfection. She admired the way his hair fell across his forehead, and longed to have the temerity to smooth it back into place.

Leo was deep in conversation with Amy Gilbert, and Josephine felt a pang of jealousy. However all was not lost; Leo sought Josephine out immediately after they rose from the table.

'Would you like to take a walk round the gardens?' he asked, bending his head so that his face came close to hers. She could smell the fresh tang of his shaving lotion.

'That would be very pleasant, Leo.'

He linked her hand through the crook of his elbow and patted it affectionately as he led her out of the conservatory.

They spent a pleasant hour walking in the sun and chatting about nothing in particular.

'You're a model of physical fitness, Josephine Trethewey,' said Leo with a lift of his eyebrows that suggested he was sizing he up for athletics of a more intimate nature. 'Many a girl would have begged to sit down by now.'

Josephine felt confused. Was this praise, or a criticism that she was less dainty and feminine than the other girls?'

'Oh, I could walk all day,' she replied. Convention be damned, she was who she was and she liked walking.

'I'm sure you could,' said Leo with a leer that implied he was really talking about her staying power between the sheets.

Then Josephine thought of James and felt guilty. Just a matter of weeks before she had vowed she would love James Penharrack forever, and now she was flirting with another man. She felt deeply ashamed of her fickle, shallow heart.

Chapter 18

Later that night Robyn rang her mother. She took a deep breath and put a smile on her face. People said that if you smiled on the phone your voice sounded happier.

'Hi Mum. How are you? Is Dad there?'

'Hello Robbie. No, he's still in hospital but he may be coming out tomorrow. He said he'd sent you an email about the chemotherapy.'

'Yes.'

Robyn kept her reply brief as she could feel her voice beginning to waver.

'Don't worry, love. They'll operate on the growth as soon as possible. At least the chemo has shrunk the tumour even though he couldn't finish the course.'

Determined to remain upbeat, Robyn changed the subject to her weekend with the family. After she rang off she felt glad she'd made her mother laugh over William's antics.

***

Josephine might have continued indefinitely with the leisurely life of a debutante, fickle or otherwise, at least until she found herself a husband. But this was not to be. One morning as she bathed she realised she couldn't remember when she'd last had her monthly period. She was sure there had been nothing since her return from the island. Then she started putting pieces of information together. Se had read articles on women's health in some of her mother's magazines. Absence of menstruation, gain in weight, tender breasts, queasiness sometimes in the mornings ... was she pregnant?

The likelihood of pregnancy came home to roost with a dramatic rush, causing her to feel quite dizzy. Josephine had to sit for a few minutes unil her head stopped spinning.

It must have happened that last time with James ...

The enormity of her situation took hold. What could she do? Get herself married off quickly to someone like Leo Herbert? No, that would take months to organise, by which time she would be enormous if not a mother already. In any case she had no intention of trying to deceive someone as charming as Leo into thinking he had made her pregnant, even though she rather fancied the idea of making love with him.

Another course of action would be to return to James and the island. But, by her calculations, the baby would be due some time in January, and it would be ridiculous to even think of giving birth in primitive conditions in the middle of winter with nothing more than an amateur herbalist to attend the delivery.

Then a thought occurred to Josephine. With her supposed loss of memory she could present herself to her parents, pregnant but unable to remember the act of conception. Jumped upon by some farm hand. Oh, the shame! They would be sure to go in search of the nonexistent farm. And send her to an asylum for the insane, lock her up and throw away the key. That was what happened to unwed mothers.

Josephine knew she had to come up with a plan, and quickly. In little more than six months she would have an infant to care for. Not a prospect she relished in the slightest. Life had just started to become enjoyable once more, and now it looked like the fun was over already.

***

Robyn was having trouble with her computer. She rang for Ed, the technical support guru of Waldron.

'I can't get it to boot up,' she explained. 'It goes so far, then shuts down again.'

Ed screwed up his mouth, deep in thought. 'Leave it with me. Can you find another computer to work on?'

'Okay,' said Robyn, looking around at her colleagues who were all beavering away at their keyboards. Then she realised Paul was out of the office for the day. Surely he wouldn't mind if she borrowed his computer for a couple of hours to get her reports typed. She could save them onto a memory stick and transfer them onto her computer once Ed had fixed it. She would have asked permission of Anthea, Paul's secretary, but she was away on holiday.

Robyn felt quite grand sitting at Paul's big desk. She swung around on his white leather chair, pretend-buzzed the intercom to ask for coffee. Then she switched on the computer and got down to work.

After about an hour she needed to go to the loo. Without thinking, she instructed the computer to save her document to the hard drive, naming it 'Interim Report'.

A response came back: 'File exists. Overwrite?' Robyn hit 'No' and saved her work onto the memory stick as she had originally intended. Curious, she opened the existing file named 'Interim Report'.

Within moments she realised what she was looking at. Her need for the loo suddenly became lower on her list of priorities.

***

Josephine's father offered to drop her at Paddington Station on his way to the office. It was a Friday morning, late in June, and the clear, blue sky promised a fine weekend to follow.

'We could get Carrington to teach you to drive, Josephine. How would you like that?' asked Charles Trethewey.

'That would be fun. Thank you, Father,' she replied, making a determined effort to conceal her preoccupation with other matters. 'Then perhaps I could have a car of my own?'

Her father chuckled. 'I don't see why not. But first you need to learn how to handle one of these monsters. We'll talk further when you return from your latest jaunt. Where are you off to?'

'Surrey, to visit one of my fellow debutantes.'

'You girls and your parties! Well, my girl. Enjoy yourself. Make hay while the sun shines. I must say you're looking very becoming this morning.'

Josephine flushed with pleasure at his compliment. She pecked him on the cheek and took up her valise.

'That's not much luggage for a weekend away,' he said. 'You normally take everything but the kitchen sink.'

'This is just a quiet weekend. Not much socialising. I have everything I need,' she said, patting the shiny leather. 'I must go, Father. My train leaves shortly.'

Josephine reached the station entrance and turned back to watch her father's car recede into the distance and merge into the traffic. Carrington at the wheel and he in the back seat. Only his bowler hat was visible over the parcel shelf.

Josephine made her way to the ticket office and bought a ticket for Camborne in Cornwall.

As Charles Trethewey settled himself at his desk he identified what was troubling his subconscious. Surely trains for Surrey left from Waterloo, not Paddington. He dismissed the thought from his mind, thinking he must have misheard Josephine's intended destination.

159

Robyn returned home at lunchtime. She had to get in touch with Nick urgently and confidentially.

She accelerated down River Lane and screeched into the driveway, narrowly missing the taxi that was depositing her long-lost landlady, Maggie.

'Hello, Maggie!' called Robyn as she rummaged in her bag for her keys. 'I'll talk to you in a minute, got a bit of a panic on.'

Maggie grinned and shook her head as she paid the taxi driver, gathered up her luggage and made a more leisurely entrance to her home.

Robyn was already on her laptop. 'Sorry, Maggie. It's an emergency. I need to contact my boss in Australia.'

'You can use the phone if you want,' said Maggie, dropping her backpack and other assorted bags on the floor. But Robyn was engrossed in typing an email.

I've found something! Paul had a file saved as a word processing document on his hard drive. Previously I only looked at the accounting package. I've copied this file onto a memory stick and I have it here at home. It's pretty serious stuff, he's got money stashed in various accounts. I'm sending it to you now as an attachment.

Nick replied immediately, even though it was late at night in Sydney.

Well done Robyn. You're definitely onto something, but leave it to me now. I'll be on the first available flight to London. See you in a couple of days, and keep that memory stick safe.

Robyn took a deep breath, nervous about what she had just set in motion. Meanwhile she had to pretend nothing unusual was happening.

She found Maggie in the kitchen with a mug of tea. 'Mmmmm, delicious! Those Americans know nothing about making tea.'

'Sorry I couldn't talk just now. Did you have a good trip?'

'Excellent. But is everything all right with you? You seemed a bit stressed just now.'

'Oh, just work stuff. All sorted now I've passed it on to my boss. How are you with cats, by the way?' she added, seeing Rhubarb's bowl on the floor.

'Why do you ask?'

'Um, I've sort of adopted a stray. A ginger kitten. I found his mother dead on the roadside. Would you mind very much if we kept him?'

'I don't see why not. Where is he?'

Robyn was a bit late returning to work after lunch. She bumped into Lori along the corridor.

'Been out for lunch?' said Lori.

'Just popped home. Maggie's back from her travels.'

'That's nice. Fancy a drink after work?'

'Another night, eh? I've already said I'll stay in with Maggie and look at her photos.'

Robyn was finding it difficult to contain the burden of her new-found knowledge. She knew she would have to avoid Lori until Nick arrived and took control of the situation. It felt like sitting on hot bricks.

'Are you all right?' said Lori.

'Yeah, fine. Just got a bit of a headache. Better get back to work.'

Robyn made her way back to her own desk. She couldn't risk being seen using Paul's computer again. And what if he returned and found her in there? She hoped no-one other than Ed had noticed. She felt guilty as hell, even though Paul was the one in the wrong. Hurry up, Nick, she thought, as she read the note from Ed saying he'd fixed her computer.

***

Josephine had plenty of time to think things through on the long train journey to Camborne. It was obvious, really, The best person with whom to discuss her predicament was the father of her child. After all, he had said he would wait for her at Poldhu Point on the first of July. He'd said he'd be happy just to talk, and that she mustn't feel obliged to return to the island.

Josephine planned to check into a hotel in Helston so that she wouldn't have to walk too far to Poldhu Point. She hoped she'd be able to muster up some form of transport to take her to Helston from the main line station at Camborne.

Aware that she had told her parents she would be away only for the weekend, she thought she could extend her absence by a few more days if necessary without arousing suspicion. She could always telephone them on Monday and give some excuse. Oh, how her life had changed in the past few days! To the outward observer no doubt she seemed as usual, but within Josephine's heart was turning over with anxiety. It was simply beastly being pregnant! Why, why, why did it have to happen to her?

***

Robyn had great difficulty sleeping that night. She sat up into the wee hours, surfing the net and visiting all sorts of ridiculous websites. Then, at last, an email came through from Nick.

Arrive Wednesday 1300 hours GMT. Should get to Waldron approx 1500. p.s. Not a word to anyone.

Brief and to the point as usual. Nick the shark was about to bite, and Paul Sinclair was swimming along unaware.

Robyn finally slept, so heavily that she woke late and had to scramble to make it to work by nine. Maggie must have been tired from her travels as she didn't surface during the brief time Robyn spent between bedroom and bathroom before leaving the house.

Robyn felt she could hardly face Paul Sinclair, but as fate had it, he was in one of his chatty moods and made her a cup of coffee. Robyn tried to keep her mind off his double-dealings. Glancing desperately around the office she caught sight of a poster on the wall and launched into a lunatic prattle.

'Gee, I really should make time for at least a day trip to France while I'm here. So near yet so far, you know. I wish I had time to explore more of Europe, but I'll probably only manage a bit of France.'

'It's a big country, plenty of variety,' said Paul, hovering unnervingly behind her. 'The ports of the north, Calais, Boulogne, Dieppe, are very different from the wine growing regions of Bergerac and Roussillon, and resorts on the Mediterranean coast such as Nice and St Tropez are different again. My ancestors were French, you know. From Aquitaine, in the west. My great uncle first visited England as a lad in the 1890s. He was a member of the minor nobility, wealthy enough not to need to work, but he dabbled in a bit of this and that. He liked England well enough to buy a house in Cornwall when he was older, and he and his wife spent their summers there. In the late 1920s he bought a bigger place, a mansion called Larkhollow Grange not far from St Ives. He left it to my father when he died, and that was where I grew up. I've got some photos at home, I must bring some in to show you.'

'My relatives in Cornwall are just farmers. Gee, don't get me wrong, their house is nice, but it's not a mansion.'

Robyn felt a bit more relaxed that they were talking about something totally unrelated to work. Paul finished his coffee and got up from the desk next to Robyn's.

'Sadly my family lost their money. My father went through a bad patch after the Second World War. The mansion was sold many years ago, I'm sorry to say.'

Further conversation was circumvented by the insistent ringing of the telephone on Paul's desk.

Robyn took a deep breath and did her best to concentrate on her work. But she couldn't help wondering how near this place was to where her relatives lived. And how weird it would be if Aunt Emily and Uncle Morvah had known Paul's parents, even Paul himself.

***

When Josephine left the train at Camborne there were men with horses and carts waiting in the station yard, plying their trade as taxi drivers. How different were these dusty conveyances from the smart taxi cabs of London! Thankfully she made it to Helston, a little jarred from the rough roads but at least without having been robbed or worse. She had sensibly covered her pretty dress with a plain coat in order to look less of a wealthy target for thieves.

The driver deposited her at the Ship Hotel, which had rooms available. She took an upstairs room with a pleasant view over the town.

Josephine felt glad to be away from London. Shopping and visiting one's friends were enjoyable pastimes, but there was something about the continual noise of the big city that made her feel oppressed, trapped. Back in Cornwall she felt much more at ease, better able to deal with her predicament in a calm and orderly fashion.

Josephine spent a comfortable night at the hotel, and woke to the sound of sea birds wheeling outside her window. It was the last day of June. She prayed James would keep his promise and row across from the island. Meanwhile, the promise of a sunny day stretched before her. No appointment with the hairdresser, no arrangement to meet the girls for afternoon tea. What bliss to have a whole day to oneself, to sit in the sunshine and read for hours on end, and to take a walk in whichever direction she chose.

***

Robyn felt unbearably restless while waiting for Nick to arrive. She fidgeted distractedly with anything that came to hand, and couldn't settle for more than a few minutes.

'What's up?' asked Lori as they sat over coffee in the staff room. 'Bad news from home? You've seemed very distracted the past couple of days.'

'Everything's okay I suppose. No news is good news,' she said vaguely.

'You would tell me if something was wrong, wouldn't you?'

"Course I would! Dad's bound to be in touch soon to let me know when they're going to operate. I suppose the waiting is wearing me down a bit.'

'You do look quite peaky. Why do you keep looking at your watch?'

'Gee, sorry. I hadn't realised I was. Well, I s'pose I'd better get back to my desk. Gotta keep crunching those numbers.'

Lori shot Robyn a penetrating look. 'You're not usually this diligent.'

'Maybe I'm hoping for a gold star,' she said, throwing her paper cup in the bin and leaving the room.

Lori shook her head despairingly and swallowed the last of her tea.

***

Josephine was awake before dawn on the morning of July 1st. She wanted to set out early on her walk to Poldhu Point. She washed and dressed hurriedly and left her room, locking the door behind her. She wore stout walking shoes and her coat, and if the wind blew cold she could take the scarf from around her shoulders and wrap it around her head and neck.

She slipped out of the side door of the hotel. The night before she had excused herself from breakfast, saying she would be attending an early church service.

Josephine smiled to herself as she walked down the street, wondering what church would hold a service quite this early. The morning was cool but fair, with the promise of sunshine once the breeze had chased the clouds away.

She grew more anxious as she walked. By the time she reached the last hill before the track dropped down to the sea she was convinced James wasn't coming. He had probably meant it when he swore his eternal love for her, but that had been a good three months ago. A lot could have happened in that time.

Sure enough, when she had her first glimpse of the expanse of beach that swept along to Poldhu Point there was no-one in sight. Was there any point in waiting?

Chapter 19

Nick Robinson's arrival was something of an anticlimax. In fact Robyn didn't even know he'd arrived until she saw two police officers making their way towards Paul Sinclair's office. When the door opened she caught a glimpse of Nick. How had he got in there without her seeing him? Had he scaled the outside wall of the building and done an SAS-type raid through the window, complete with balaclava and machine gun?

Then Robyn realised he must have arrived while she was in the loo. The important thing was that he was here. She didn't have to bear the sole responsibility of knowing about Paul Sinclair's misdeeds any longer.

Paul's office door opened once again, and Robyn decided the best place to be was back in the loo. She stooped low so she couldn't be seen over the partitions and made her way stealthily across the office.

***

A beach is a desolate place to spend the day alone, particularly if you suspect you are waiting for someone in vain. Josephine tried to will the passage of the hours, constantly consulting her wristwatch.

Her initial decision had been to wait until dusk, probably around ten o'clock that night.

However by early afternoon she was growing restless, not to mention desperately hungry. In her anxiety she had neglected to bring anything to eat or drink.

As the tide receded she noticed a small stream meandering across the beach, and followed it up the slope to where it bubbled up as a spring from beneath some rocks. She counted her blessings that it was fresh water, and slaked her thirst. She felt quite proud of her resourcefulness. The hardship she'd experienced on Hogshead Island had without doubt been character building. The old Josephine would never have considered drinking from a spring.

By four o'clock she was becoming increasingly hungry. Sadly there was no manna from heaven to help her in her hour of need. But then why should

God help a sinner who had lain with a man and become pregnant before marriage?

The tide was coming in again, gradually claiming the beach. The sun dropped lower in the western sky and took on a deep golden hue. Josephine watched it slipping towards the horizon. Then she noticed a tiny black speck on the rippling, glinting surface of the sea. Probably just a bird, she thought. But it came closer and grew larger. Finally she could see it was a rowing boat!

Hunger forgotten, Josephine paced anxiously up and down the firm, wet sand. Her footprints were a fractious trail in the smooth surface. There was just one person in the boat, rowing doggedly towards the shore. Could it be James?

She waved, and the rower waved back. When the boat was within a hundred yards she could see it was indeed James, and relief flooded through her body.

The boat breasted the gentle swell and came to rest in the shallows. James jumped out into knee-deep water holding onto a rope. He flung his arms around Josephine, who had waded out into the water to meet him.

'I can't believe you're here!' he said over and over, holding her close and burying his face in her hair.

Josephine felt tears trickling down her cheeks and began to sob. For hours she had been holding onto the slenderest fragment of hope that he would come.

They remained locked in an embrace for what seemed like ages. The sea birds cried their celebration of the reunion, and the sun met the horizon although time seemed to stand still.

Eventually Josephine and James turned their attention to matters practical. She helped him haul the small boat up the beach and hide it in the bracken.

'You must be hungry,' she said, feeling pangs from her own neglected stomach.

James nodded. 'I only brought water with me.'

'I even forgot water. I've been drinking from a stream. But I have some money,' she said, patting her pocket.

'There's a pub not far down the track,' he said, pointing south. 'We can get something to eat there. Sorry, Empress. I hope you don't mind paying.'

Josephine grinned and squeezed his skinny waist. There was nothing of him. 'I don't mind in the least. I can count your ribs, which means you need a good meal. Oh, I'm so glad to see you, James! I've been waiting all day!'

'Sorry. I would have caught the earlier tide but I didn't think for a minute you'd be here.'

Josephine matched James's stride as they marched along the path, his arm around her shoulders and hers around his waist. She noticed, despite his thinness, how strong and muscular he felt compared with Leo Herbert and the other boys she had recently danced with. She cast away such thoughts and turned her mind to the matter in hand. How was she going to tell James of her pregnancy? He was strangely silent; they'd hardly exchanged more than half a dozen sentences and she felt awkward and tongue-tied. Still, it was enough for the moment that his arm was around her shoulders. She hadn't realised how much she'd missed the feel of his body.

'You've cut your hair,' said James suddenly.

'Do you like it?'

'I prefer it long.'

Noticing her downcast face he added, 'Short or long hair you're still my beautiful Empress.'

Josephine smiled, thankful to feel the awkwardness between them easing.

Before long they saw the public house up ahead, not far from where their dirt track joined the road to Mullion Cove. But it was closed. Josephine's heart sank. She had the money ready in her hand, but where were they to buy food? She had grown soft since leaving the island, accustomed to meals that arrived on time without the need for any preparation on her part. To James it was probably just one of life's minor inconveniences, but to Josephine the lack of food was assuming monstrous proportions.

'Wait here,' he said, taking the coins from her hand and motioning for her to hide behind some bushes.

He rapped on the door of the inn, and after a pause Josephine heard the door creak open. She couldn't see through the bushes, nor could she hear more than a low murmur of voices. However after a few minutes she heard footsteps crunching on gravel. It was James.

'She gave me a bag of scraps for nothing. And I bought a bottle of ale,' he whispered, pressing the change into Josephine's hand.

They ran down to Mullion Cove, which was deserted in the cool, calm evening. Settled on the rocks overlooking the sea they fell to their meal. The bag contained broken pieces of pasty, a couple of stale cheese sandwiches and a crusty end of bread. It didn't matter to Josephine that she may have been eating other people's leftovers. She dabbed the last of the crumbs out of the bag with her finger, and James laughed.

'You look like an island girl once again, Empress.'

Josephine grinned and took a swig from the bottle. 'I like it when you call me Empress. I always did.'

'I always will,' he said, pulling her close. They kissed long and passionately.

With the ale warming a fire of courage in her belly, Josephine seized the moment. 'James, I have something to tell you. I'm pregnant.'

'You're what?' he gasped, grey eyes wide.

'Pregnant. With child. Expecting a baby. Your baby. It must have happened that last time ...'

James held her close, rocking her in his arms and chuckling softly. 'Looks like Mother Nature had her own plan for bringing you back to me,' he said softly, smoothing her hair. 'When's it due?'

'By my calculations, some time in January. James, what am I going to do?'

'You mean what are we going to do. It's obvious, isn't it? We're going to have a baby. I'm going to be a daddy, and you're going to be a mummy. Didn't they teach you anything in that posh school?'

'James, I can't go back to the island! I can't have my baby out there in a cave without a doctor or clean towels or proper hot water. I thought of telling my parents that I'd been taken advantage of by some farm worker but they'd probably put me in a home for young women of ill repute. Or worse. I also thought ...'

Josephine stopped abruptly. She could hardly tell James of her vague thoughts about marrying Leo Herbert. She looked at his face, profiled in the fading light.

'We'll make a fresh start,' he said. 'I'll change my name, and we can pretend we're married. Say we've come from Kent or someplace. If we go further east they're not likely to have heard about the murder of that girl in Penzance. Anyway it was years ago. I'll find work on a farm. We'll get ourselves a little house, and we'll be well set up by the time my son makes his appearance.'

It was a solution that had never occurred to Josephine. She had never dreamed that it would be possible for James to leave the island. She felt a great weight lift from her shoulders. She had been right in seeking out James, more right than she could ever have hoped. She knew that he would somehow make everything right, for she trusted him completely, more than she had ever trusted her parents.

But as they sat on the warm rocks contemplating a rosy future together they were not to know what the fates had in store for them.

Lori went into the Ladies after Robyn. She could run, but she couldn't hide indefinitely.

'Now I know why you've been acting strangely! You found something, didn't you. That's why the police are here.'

'Have they taken Paul away yet?'

'Yes, and your compatriot has gone with them. You can come out now.'

'The 'compatriot', as you call him in your charming English way, is my boss, Nick.'

'Nick the Shark? Come to think of it, he did have a toothy smile.'

'I wonder if he'll come back for me.'

'Why, are they going to put you in prison too? What have you been up to, Robs?'

Robyn glared at Lori. 'All I've done is expose the truth about Paul Sinclair. Is that suddenly a crime?'

'I'm sorry I doubted you. It just didn't seem possible to me that Paul was up to no good.'

A number of staff were gathered in the reception area talking nineteen to the dozen when Lori and Robyn walked through, fortunately unnoticed.

Lori had decided that Robyn needed a little retail therapy to calm her nerves, so she drove her to an out-of-town shopping mall. However Robyn was feeling too impatient for clothes shopping. She wanted to know what was going on at the police station.

After Lori had bought a top she dragged her friend into a café for coffee and doughnuts.

'There's no problem that can't be solved by my good old friend Dunkin',' said Robyn.

'Duncan? Who's Duncan?'

'No, Dunkin',' corrected Robyn. 'Dunkin' Donuts.' She pointed to the menu.

'Oh, I see.'

After they'd finished eating, Robyn checked her watch. 'I feel guilty, like I should be back there at the office. What if Nick is looking for me?'

'He has your mobile number, surely. And do you really want to face the baying mob? We were lucky to get out of there earlier before they saw you. By now they probably know all about Paul and suspect the Australian visitor has something to do with you. They'll be all over you for answers if you show your face this afternoon.'

At that moment Robyn's mobile rang. It was Nick.

'He's asked me out for dinner tonight. He's taking me to *Chez Henri*.'

Lori raised her eyebrows. 'Nothing but the best.'

'Help! What am I going to wear?'

Lori shrugged.

'I know, you're far too tall and thin for any of your nice dresses to fit me.'

Back at home Maggie came to the rescue. She lent Robyn a sparkly black top that went well with her best black trousers. Fortunately they still fitted. But only just.

'You seem to have gained a few pounds while I was away,' said Maggie bluntly as she fastened a button at the back of Robyn's neck. 'You're not pregnant, are you?'

'Gee, I don't think so,' replied Robyn, wishing she'd kept a proper track of her periods. She made a mental note to get a pregnancy testing kit in the morning. It would be great timing, on top of everything else going on at the moment, to find out she was pregnant by Colin, the one week wonder.

While showering, Robyn realised with a rush of joy that she'd most probably be able to go home now that Paul had been apprehended. She only hoped her father looked as well as he sounded from his emails. She planned to send him an email later, after discussing her return with Nick.

Nick arrived in a taxi just before eight. Before long they were driving down a tree-lined lane. Robyn could see what looked like a stately home around the next bend.

'I've read about this place on the net,' said Nick. 'Have you been here before?'

'No, but my friend says it has a very good reputation.'

'Tristan, the owner, inherited the mansion from his father. It needed a massive amount spent on it to stop it falling down round his ears. The family were as blue-blooded as they come, but had no money. Tristan fortunately had a top chef among his friends and he was looking for a new venture. The rest is history, and for the past couple of years *Chez Henri* has been rated one of the best restaurants in southern England. Two Michelin stars. I hope you appreciate that I had to pull some strings to get a booking at short notice.'

They were seated in a quiet alcove. After they'd ordered, Nick filled Robyn in on the afternoon's events.

'Sinclair confessed, completely spat the dummy. I won't need the memory stick. There was a lot more to it than the stuff you found. Well done though for getting the ball rolling.'

'I'd almost given up,' said Robyn modestly, meanwhile glowing from Nick's praise. 'I found the document completely by accident. What should I say when people at Waldron ask me about Paul?'

'Say nothing. Refer them to me. I'll deal with their questions. Now, can you stick it out here a bit longer? Five weeks at the most. I'll be staying on until the parent company puts someone in Paul's place. How's your father doing?'

'Waiting for an operation, but he seems quite upbeat.'

'The waiting is the worst. My mother had a skin cancer removed a couple of years ago so I have some idea what you're going through. I wouldn't blame you if you wanted to go home right away.'

'No, it's okay. I'll stay. Dad seems to be all right for the moment.'

Robyn couldn't deny she felt disappointed that Nick still wanted her to stay. But that was the trouble with praise. It left you wanting more, so she'd put her feelings to one side and agreed to remain in England. But she couldn't help feeling her loyalty was misplaced, and that she should be returning to Sydney.

***

James rowed back to the island on the next tide to tell the others of his reunion with Josephine and his impending departure.

Josephine meanwhile returned to the hotel in Helston to wait for him. She telephoned her mother to say there was no point in her returning home as she and her friend were leaving in a couple of days to attend another party. Fortunately her mother had seemed preoccupied and had not thought to query whether Josephine had suitable clothing.

Meanwhile she waited anxiously for James, hardly able to believe her luck. Surely fate would intervene and scatter their plans to the four winds?

But no. James returned on the evening of the third day. He threw pebbles up at her window until she looked out.

Her relief at seeing him was immense, as though someone had untied a knot in her stomach. She crept downstairs and sneaked him up to her room.

'We'll have to be very quiet,' she cautioned.

'Let's hope the bed doesn't squeak,' he whispered.

James gently and lovingly undressed the woman he'd thought he'd never see again.

'It won't hurt the baby, will it?' she asked.

'I'll be gentle with you,' he replied, running his fingers up her naked thigh.

As they moved slowly and carefully together, Josephine felt tears spring into her eyes. How she had missed James! She was so glad they were together again.

As they lay sated in bed, James remembered something.

'Everyone on the island sends their love. And speaking of love, I forgot to tell you Roberto and Mari are courting, and so are Lucy and Simon.'

'How sweet! Maybe there'll be a double wedding on Hogshead Island,' said Josephine dreamily.

'Dunno where they're going to find a priest.'

'I expect they were surprised and upset when you told them you were leaving.'

James shrugged. 'Luisa knew how bad I was missing you. I've taught Simon how to navigate here and back with the rowboat. The youngsters are all growing up now. They'll manage.'

Later that evening Josephine wrote to her parents telling them she would not be returning to London. That she would be staying indefinitely with friends, but not giving an address. She wrote that she had no enthusiasm for continuing as a debutante, and hoped they would forgive her for not returning to be presented to the Queen.

Very early the following morning James crept down the back stairs and out of the hotel. While waiting for Josephine to gather her belongings he paid a man who drove a brewery van to post her letter when he reached Bath, hoping that would throw Josephine's family off the scent.

Josephine looked at her meagre possessions and wished she'd thought to bring more. But not for a moment had she suspected that she'd be running away to start a new life with James.

They trudged many miles that week and the next, hitching lifts on farm carts. Josephine had just a few pounds left in her purse, as she hadn't planned to be away more than a few days.

They chatted as they walked, bringing each other up to date on what had been happening in the months they had been apart.

'We managed to get another goat back onto the island,' said James. 'A boyfriend for Mildred, and she's in kid again. And we got some chickens on the next trip.'

'I hope you didn't steal them.'

'No, we bought them in the market, Miss Goody Goody. Getting a cage of chickens back on the boat was no fun, let me tell you! I swear they were seasick, but they all survived. Hen eggs are a luxury compared with what we've been used to, and some time soon we'll be eating proper chicken instead of seagull. Ah, but I'm forgetting. All that is in the past for me. You and me, Empress, will be dining on proper eggs and chicken in our own home before long, you mark my words!'

A few days later James found work on a farm near St Austell. Accommodation in a tiny cottage was part of the deal.

'I've told the farmer that we are Mr and Mrs Rostrevor, Jim and Josie,' he told her.

'I wish we could be properly married,' said Josephine wistfully.

'We'd need our birth certificates, and permission from our parents as we are not yet adults. So that's out of the question. However we can have ourselves a wedding ceremony,' he said with a lewd wink.

And so they did. On their first Saturday in their new home, James came home from the fields to find Josephine had turned their cottage into a bridal bower. She had scrubbed and polished, then decorated the house with flowers from the hedgerows stuffed into jam jars, milk jugs and whatever she could find. The table was laid for tea and decorated with more flowers. She put on the peach-coloured silk dress she'd worn on the day she'd left London.

Josephine took James's hand and led him out to the garden. She sat him down on a rickety wooden seat where the evening sun bathed them in a rosy glow. The air was filled with perfume from the roses rambling up the wall of their cottage.

She sat next to him and took his hand solemnly. 'I, Josephine Trethewey, do take thee, James Penharrack, hereafter to be known as James Rostrevor, to be my husband, in sickness and in health, for better or worse, until death us do part.'

James glanced around to make sure no-one was watching before replying. 'I, James Rostrevor, what was known as Penharrack, do take thee Josephine, to be my awful wedded wife, in sickness and worse, for better or health ... oh, dammit! You know what I mean.'

Josephine laughed. 'I don't think you're meant to curse when making your marriage vows, but I hope The Lord will understand. What God hath joined together, let no man cast asunder,' she added formally.

James grinned and grabbed a handful of rose petals off the nearest bush, sprinkling them over Josephine's head. Then he kissed his bride.

One kiss led to another, and they retreated to their bedroom. Josephine had been busy in there also, and containers of flowers filled every available nook and cranny. She had scattered rose petals over the faded cotton bedcover and hung a garland around the paraffin lamp.

'You're truly mine now,' said James as he laid Josephine gently on the bed.

'And you are mine,' she replied.

He entered her urgently without removing her dress or his shirt. She realised she hadn't given James the opportunity to wash or change his clothes after he'd finished work. Still, she didn't mind the strong smell of his sweat. She loved everything about him.

It was truly wonderful to have a bed of their own after two weeks spent sleeping rough. Thursday had been their first night in their new home, but they'd had to sleep on the kitchen floor as the bed had been broken by previous tenants. James fixed it the following morning before going to work. Josephine spent Friday washing and mending the dirty old sheets she found in the back of a cupboard, and made up pillows using ragged clothing left by former occupants that she had to wash and dry first. She also washed and mended the old cotton bedcover. Luckily everything dried quickly in the summer sunshine.

Josephine realised they would have to find money for blankets before winter. The list of things they needed seemed endless, but for the moment they had the basics for a meagre existence. The most important thing was that they were together once more.

The cottage felt like a proper home already. Their bedroom was a sanctuary, and their loving was more tender, relaxed and poignant with the wonder that between them they had already created a new life. James teased Josephine that it had better be a boy, but Josephine didn't mind what it was as long as the child was healthy.

Performing a marriage ritual, having a new life growing inside her, and living with James as man and wife made Josephine feel grown-up and important. She'd gone from debutante to farm worker's wife and mother-to-be within a matter of weeks. At this major turning point in her life she felt secure, happy to rest on her laurels and look forward to the future. Little did she know what lay ahead.

Chapter 20

Robyn was anxious about going back to Waldron after Paul's arrest, but surprisingly nobody said anything. Then Lori pointed out the memo from Nick on the noticeboard in the tea room announcing that Paul Sinclair had resigned due to 'difficulties in his family'.

Realising her periods had been absent since her arrival in England, Robyn purchased a pregnancy test on the way home from work. She awoke early the next morning and nipped into the bathroom.

After an anxious wait she heaved a sigh of relief. Not pregnant! Noticing her accent, the pharmacist had said that absence of menstruation might be due to the radical change of time zones.

So that meant she was just gaining weight from eating. And Christmas, with its promise of more of Aunt Emily's cooking, was definitely not the time to start a strict diet. Robyn resolved to cut back on the calories once the festive season was over.

Robyn rescued the testing kit and its box from the waste paper basket and slipped it into her handbag for disposal on the way to work. No point in alarming Maggie unnecessarily.

The telephone rang that evening as Robyn was passing through the hall. She reached around a bundle of African spears in a tall vase and picked up the receiver.

'Hello, Robyn? This is Moira Hanley. You may remember we met at the Trescowes' recently.'

'Oh, yes. Hi.'

'Robyn, I have something rather interesting for you. I had a chat with Mummy, and she went to visit Grandpa William. To cut a long story short, she's managed to get hold of his mother's diaries. I've only briefly skimmed through them, but it's interesting stuff. Lots of things I didn't know.'

'Wow! When can I see them?'

'Am I right in thinking you live somewhere near Southampton?'

'Yes, Eastleigh.'

'I could call by tomorrow morning. I'm going up to London for some Christmas shopping.'

'Gee, that would be great! Thanks, Moira. Only trouble is, I'll be at work and I don't know if Maggie, my landlady, is going to be here tomorrow morning. She's out at the moment otherwise I'd ask her.'

'Then may I deliver the diaries to you at work?'

'I don't see why not.'

Robyn gave Moira directions, and rang off. She hurried up to her room and rattled off a quick email to her father. Contact with her parents had been intermittent during the past couple of weeks, but she'd had a long chat with Steve earlier in the week. As she suspected, her father was in and out of hospital, having tests for one thing and another. His illness was certainly keeping him and Mum busy. Luckily Stella at the hairdressing salon was an understanding boss who didn't mind if Rose had to take time off. And her Dad was now on long-term sick leave from the timber yard. At least his treatment seemed to be going quite well.

Diaries. Things nobody else knew. Dad would be pleased. She tried to picture him pottering about the house or waiting among a sea of other patients at North Shore General Hospital. A lump rose in her throat. She was having trouble remembering what his face looked like, and her mother's also. She dug desperately in her drawer for the wallet of family photographs she'd brought to show the rellies, and burst into tears at the sight of the family, herself included, gathered together in happier times.

Robyn wondered whether her father had lost his hair or become really thin like lots of people seemed to do when they had treatment for cancer.

Still, four weeks from Saturday she'd be on that plane, bound for Sydney at hundreds of miles per hour.

Christmas was almost upon them. Robyn was quite looking forward to experiencing Christmas in winter. There hadn't been any snow in Eastleigh yet, but maybe a miracle would happen over the next few days. Lori said it didn't snow very often but when it did it was lovely.

Maggie wasn't a very Christmassy person, which was fine with Robyn who also didn't see the attraction of a house full of twinkling lights and tacky decorations. Robyn had, several weeks beforehand, packed up and dispatched a parcel of presents for her parents, Steve, Giulietta and little Joey. Delia and Casey would have to wait until her return. In any case, she hadn't yet found the right thing for either of them. For that she would probably need to take a trip to London. It would be a good opportunity to meet cousin Gerald while she was there.

Robyn had left the rest of her gift buying until the last minute, and planned to visit the shopping mall after work in the hope that inspiration would strike. She needed to find gifts for Lori and Maggie, and there was also the question of what to take to the Trescowe family. She was invited to join them for Christmas dinner, and planned to join the exodus on the roads on Friday afternoon as Waldron was closing at lunchtime.

She knew the week's holiday would be a busy time as this year there was the turn of the Millennium as well as Christmas to contend with. Lori had talked enthusiastically of a massive party at Southampton's main football stadium, but Robyn was also tempted to stay on with Emily and Morvah to see in the new century more quietly. Robyn wished she wasn't so indecisive. So many things seemed to require an opinion or an answer. But not tonight.

***

The months passed, and Josephine's stomach swelled. She and James settled into the routine of farm life. James went off in the mornings when it was barely light, returning when it was almost dark. The days seemed long, the work was hard, and the wages were meagre, but he never complained.

'It's your birthday tomorrow,' said Josephine one day in September. 'What would you like to do?'

James rolled his eyes in anticipation. 'First of all I'd like to take the day off work and go for a meal at that chop house in St Austell. Followed with a tour of some of the town's finest public houses.'

Josephine looked shocked.

'You should see your face, Empress! I'm only joking. I'll be going to work as usual, and coming home to you in the evening is enough of a treat.'

'I'll cook you something nice for dinner. Maybe even some chops.'

'Just so long as I can have you for afters,' he teased, kissing her on the neck.

Josephine smiled. She hoped she'd have time to buy some food in the village. The farmer's wife had high hopes for her two sons, and when she heard somehow that Josephine was an educated woman she hired her for an hour after school each day to tutor the boys in English and Mathematics. Josephine didn't particularly enjoy the task as the boys, aged five and eleven, were insolent and unruly. She felt hardly able to control them, let alone keep them separately occupied with lessons at the appropriate level. Though the eleven year old, Nathaniel, was not at all bright or interested in

177

study, his mother insisted that he was a smart boy and should have a chance to make the most of himself.

The younger boy, Frederick, seemed to show more aptitude for learning. However at five years of age he hadn't even started school and it was difficult to get him to sit still for any length of time. He was fascinated by Josephine's swollen belly.

'Is there really a baby in there?' he would ask.

'Yes, Freddie,' she would reply. 'Now don't keep changing the subject. How many apples am I holding?'

Josephine found the lessons tiring, but the extra money came in handy. They now had soft, warm blankets for their bed, and new sheets and a heavy quilt. At the Friday market in St Austell she bought fabric to make new curtains for several rooms, and had already made a pretty yellow quilt cover for the baby's nursery.

'Very fancy,' said Mrs Trescowe when Josephine showed her. 'Where did you learn to do such fine embroidery?'

'My mother taught me,' replied Josephine.

'And where does she live?'

'Further east. In Dorset,' said Josephine with a level stare.

'I didn't think you and your 'usband was from round 'ere.'

Josephine changed the subject. She didn't want to start making up further lies that might catch her out. She knew she'd have to be careful. She didn't know whether her parents had made any attempt to find her. She hoped the man James paid had mailed her letter from Bath, and that her parents' attention had been diverted from Cornwall, her obvious choice of destination. She felt guilty about leaving so suddenly, particularly for deserting George. But her life with James was more important, particularly now that the baby was nearly with them.

Josephine justified her decision to run away with James by telling herself that her parents had busy lives and wouldn't really miss her. George was undoubtedly Father's favourite, and George was growing up now and hopefully wouldn't miss his sister too much. She and *Maman* had grown closer since her return from the dead, but she still believed she was second best to darling Lucien, made more special by his untimely death.

It could have been argued that the life of the fugitives was a lonely one, but Josephine and James were content in each other's company. After all, they had little enough time together considering the long hours James worked. Josephine was glad James wasn't the type of man to spend his evenings in the public house out on the main road like many of the farm

178

workers. He seemed as eager as she was to live frugally and put aside whatever money they could. It saddened her to think that he would be looking over his shoulder for the rest of his life, never really able to relax in the company of others. But on the other hand, that meant she had him all to herself.

***

Several days after Maggie's return from America, Robyn returned from work to hear her in the kitchen talking to someone.

'What about some fish, young man?'

Having reached the kitchen door, Robyn could see the recipient of the fish was none other than Rhubarb.

Maggie looked up with a smile. 'He certainly likes fish, doesn't he!'

'He's going to be a very fat cat if you keep giving him treats every day, Maggie.'

'Ah, a little bit of what he fancies won't do him any harm. You're a gorgeous boy, aren't you! Rhubarb is just the most perfect name for him, Rob.'

Maggie was starting to dote on the kitten as though he was her baby. Ah, but maybe that was a problem solved.

'Maggie,' said Robyn.

'You're using that voice you always use when you're going to ask a favour.'

'Gee, am I that transparent? I was going to ask you if you'd have Rhubarb when I return to Australia.'

Maggie held the kitten protectively in her arms. 'Just you try giving him to anyone else!' she said fiercely. 'Of course I'll have him, you didn't need to ask.'

'I never intended to get a cat, but I couldn't leave him on the side of the road. But what will you do if you want to go away for weeks on end, like another trip to America?'

'I'll cross that bridge when I come to it. You never know, I might just settle down. Me and my cat.'

Rhubarb closed his eyes, safe in Maggie's arms, with a blissful expression on his face.

'You won't mind looking after him over Christmas then, while I go off to the rellies?'

'That's fine with us, isn't it, Rhubarb? What would you like for your Christmas dinner, young man?'

With her feline arrangements sorted Robyn turned her attention to wrapping the presents she'd bought.

***

Maud Amelia Rostrevor entered the world screaming and kicking on the fourth of January 1927. It was a bitterly cold day, and Josephine wouldn't have blamed her small scrap of a daughter for wanting to stay in the warmth of her womb.

Josephine was attended by Mary Sedgehill, the wife of another farm worker. Josephine had been anxious about Mary snooping around their home, but knew that declining her assistance would seem odd, particularly at a first birth. Mary had the dubious honour of acting as midwife to all the farm women, including Mrs Trescowe, who surprisingly hadn't gone to the hospital like many other women of means. But no, Mary had birthed both Nathaniel and Frederick Trescowe at home.

Maud's birth had been a gruesome, agonising business, but Josephine refused to dwell on it. After all, it had produced a perfect little girl. Josephine had decided months ago that if she had a daughter she would be called Maud, after the ship whose life preserver had carried her to the island and to James. Luckily James agreed.

They hadn't been able to agree on a name for a son; James liked Arthur, whereas Josephine thought it a shame to call a baby by an old man's name. She preferred Sebastian, which he thought pompous. So it was a good thing all round that the baby was a girl.

After Maud was born, James suggested Amelia, his mother's name, for their daughter's middle name. Josephine agreed wholeheartedly.

James was totally besotted with his daughter. When he came home from his labours in the fields he would head straight for her cot, which was kept at the foot of their bed. The nursery was as yet unused. James was capable of spending a great length of time sitting at the end of their bed gazing at the perfect little girl, admiring her delicate eyelashes, button nose, perfect little mouth and wisps of fine hair, already with a reddish tinge.

'She's a beauty and no mistake,' he said proudly to whoever would listen. So much so that Josephine began to feel a bit jealous. Until, of course, she had James to herself in the dark of night while their daughter slept. Only then was she able to rationalise and separate the love of a man for his daughter from his passion for and friendship with his woman.

When Maud was just four months old Josephine found she was with child once again. She was not sorry. She enjoyed her settled family life even

180

though she was not yet eighteen. And her second child had been conceived properly in their bed, not on some rocky outcrop under the stars.

***

Arriving at Waldron the next morning Robyn paused at the Reception desk.

'Julie, I'm expecting a visitor. Her name's Mrs Hanley. Can you call me when she arrives please?' she asked.

Julie looked bleary this morning, and Robyn supposed she'd been doing some pre-Christmas partying the night before.

Robyn didn't get very far, for Moira Hanley pushed her way through the plate glass doors as she was waiting for the lift. Moira was carrying a large, brown-paper-wrapped parcel.

'Hello, Moira. Gee, is that the diaries? I didn't think there'd be that many.'

'Yes. Your great-grandmother started with one small notebook, and then bought another and another. Later on her daughter took up the task. That's Maud, your father's mother. She preferred to use hard-covered books. So there you have it. The family history,' said Moira, handing over the parcel. 'Enjoy. I must get going. London awaits, and the motorway traffic is horrendous already.'

'Sure you can't stay for a coffee?'

'Thanks, but no. Have a happy Christmas, and I hope the diaries are helpful.'

The temptation proved too great for Robyn. By the time she reached her desk she had the paper undone and then started sorting the books into date order. As Moira said, her great-grandmother had written in whatever cheap little books she could find, whereas her daughter's diaries showed style and forethought. She lined them up neatly, spanning the years 1918 to 1951. Written by Josephine until 1941, then, after a short gap, the task taken over by Maud. But there also seemed to be a gap of a few months in 1949, and Robyn wondered what might have happened for Maud to stop writing for a while.

Luckily Robyn had little work to do, and she supposed her small amount of data input could wait until she'd had a tiny peek at the diaries.

Lori walked in at lunchtime to find Robyn deep in some old notebook.

'Aren't you coming to lunch? I've been waiting for you.'

'Huh? Oh, sorry. Gee, is that the time?'

'What on earth are you reading?'

'These are my great-grandmother's diaries. Moira dropped them off this morning.'

'Nick not about then?'

'No, not in today. Gone ... somewhere,' said Robyn vaguely.

'Are you coming to the pub with the rest of us?'

'Um, I suppose so,' said Robyn, searching for her bag and putting on her unfavourite black coat. She cast a reluctant glance at the diaries and stuffed them into her desk drawers. They weren't the sort of thing she wanted to leave lying around.

Robyn didn't bother with an evening meal that night as she'd had a substantial plate of scampi and chips at lunchtime. With barely a greeting for Maggie she headed to her room with the diaries, which she had stuffed awkwardly back into their paper wrapping.

Rhubarb came up to join her and settled at her side on the bed, rolling over to have his pale ginger tummy tickled. He fell asleep with his paws in the air, still waiting for her attention. But Robyn was transported back to the past ...

Moira's great-grandmother had started her first diary in November 1918 aged nine.

I plan to keep a diary as my teacher says we are all living, breathing components of history. So here goes. The Great War has ended. Everyone is rejoicing, and I would like to write for posterity how happy we all are. No-one in our family has died in the war, for which I give thanks to God. But there are girls in my class at school whose fathers and brothers are dead. I hope there will never again be another war.

Josephine Trethewey didn't write in her diary every day, only when she had something of interest to record.

I don't see any point in recording mundane details of lessons at school, she wrote aged ten.

Two books covered Josephine's life from ages nine to sixteen, then there was a gap of a few months. The next book was written in retrospect in 1926, and the enormity of the events it covered kept Robyn awake practically the whole night. Just after midnight she reached the part where Josephine Trethewey set up home with James Penharrack under the assumed name of Rostrevor. And suddenly the penny dropped! Of course! That was why her father had had so much difficulty tracing the Rostrevor family. Josephine and James were living under a made-up name, therefore they weren't related to anyone else named Rostrevor.

Robyn plugged her laptop into the mains with tired, fumbling fingers and sent an email to her father.

Dad! I've got it! Or rather I've got them. My great-grandmother's diaries. Moira gave them to me today. Great-grandmother Josephine's maiden name was Trethewey. And guess what? Her father was a Lord. Lord Kenner. And her mother came from a titled French family. Bet you'd never have guessed in a million years we were that posh! But wait for it, here's the missing link. Josephine Trethewey never married, but she lived with a man named James Penharrack who was wanted by the police for murder (he didn't do it). They moved away and lived under the assumed name of Rostrevor. So that's why you couldn't make any connection with the other Rostrevors you found. The full story is much more complicated and fascinating than you'd ever believe. I'll get the diaries copied and send them to you by air mail. Hope you are doing okay. Lots of love to you and Mum. P.S. I'll phone you for Christmas.

The next bit of excitement came when Robyn read: *Here we are at Trescowe Farm.*

Trescowe, she thought. Gee, that's our name. Maybe this farmer was a relation. But she didn't remember anyone with a farm from her time in England as a child. It wasn't Emily and Morvah, as she remembered they'd lived in a village back then. She remembered her grandmother having a big garden, but it was in a suburban street somewhere. She scribbled a quick reminder to ask her father.

Robyn thought she was hallucinating a little later when she started reading about a cat named Rhubarb.

James found a kitten all on its own in the rhubarb patch, and as we need some help keeping the mouse population under control we've decided to keep it. We do have terrible trouble with mice. James thinks he is a tom cat, and as he was found in the rhubarb patch we've decided that will be his name. Maud is now crawling, she gets into all sorts of mischief. Yesterday I thought I'd lost her. I only turned my back for a moment, but that was all it took for her to scuttle out of the door. I searched high and low, and eventually found her and the little cat playing in the rhubarb patch. They were hiding under the canopy of big, green leaves. They were both covered in mud, and it took me forever to get both of them and Maud's clothes clean. I suppose I should be thankful that at least Rhubarb doesn't wear clothes.

Robyn's heart was full, and so were her eyes. Tears spilled onto her own Rhubarb's fur. What a remarkable coincidence! Surely the arrival of a cat named Rhubarb in her own life had to be somehow pre-destined.

As she settled down to sleep another thought occurred to Robyn. She remembered the vivid dream she'd had just before leaving Australia, about almost drowning and getting washed up on a beach. The hairs on the back of her neck bristled. It was almost as though Josephine had made contact from beyond the grave, somehow sensing that Robyn would soon be arriving in England. Spooky, possums!

Chapter 21

The telephone rang at precisely six on the morning of Christmas Eve. Robyn awoke to Maggie's hand on her shoulder, shaking her into consciousness. She felt cramped and cold as she'd fallen asleep on the desk in her bedroom.

'Your father is on the phone, Robyn,' urged Maggie.

Robyn staggered downstairs on stiff legs. ''Morning, Dad. How are you?'

'All the better for hearing your news, m'girl. What a turn up for the books! Tell me more.'

'It's pretty fantastic, Dad. Your grandmother met James on an island off the coast of Cornwall. She got washed out to sea off the beach at Marazion, near Penzance. Her younger brother drowned, but she managed to float all the way to this island where a bunch of people were living rough. Can't quite remember why. Anyway, James was one of them. Then she went back to her family in London, but she became pregnant. No, she was already pregnant when she left the island but she didn't know. Gee, the baby she had must have been your mother!'

'This is simply incredible!'

'Just you wait till you read it all, Dad. I'll get the diaries copied somehow and send them to you. It's great to hear your voice. I've been worried 'cos you haven't emailed lately. Is everything okay?'

'Oh, I'm doing as well as can be expected. Sorry I haven't been in touch, but I've been spending a lot of time at the hospital.'

'How's Mum?'

'She's fine. She's out at the moment getting me some of those yoghurt drinks she insists I must have. They taste like chalky water, but I drink them to keep her happy.'

'I was going to phone you tonight to wish you a Merry Christmas, but you've beaten me to it.'

'Yes, I was so thrilled when I got your email I had to ring as soon as possible. Well dear, I'd better go now. Have a good Christmas. Are you going down to Morvah and Emily?'

'Yes, Dad. I'm leaving this afternoon.'

'Take care, and give them my love.'

''Bye, Dad. You take care too. And Mum. Love you lots.'

'Love you lots too, Robyn.'

Robyn had a lump in her throat the size of a golf ball by the time she got back to her room. She felt guilty for not having heard the phone and causing Maggie to get out of her warm bed so early. But she was mostly overcome by a horrible feeling that she would never hear her father's voice again. Get a grip, she told herself sternly. You're being a drama queen, and that's Casey's domain. Of course Dad would be around for some time yet. She kicked herself for not asking about the operation. Then she remembered she'd forgotten to ask whether the Trescowes at the farm were any relation.

Half past six. She dared not get into bed, knowing if she slept now she'd never wake in time for work. So she crept downstairs and made a strong cup of coffee. Rhubarb followed her into the kitchen, loudly demanding his breakfast.

'Shush, you greedy thing. You'll wake Maggie,' she whispered, reaching for his food. Then she remembered the other cat named Rhubarb. Had she been dreaming?

Back in her room, Robyn booted up the laptop and sent her father a brief email asking about his operation, and whether there was any connection with some Trescowes living on a farm.

Then she sent an email to Delia and Casey.

Oh, you're going to love this! I've discovered that my great-great-grandparents were Lord and Lady Kenner, and that Lady Kenner was descended from French nobility. So you're going to have to bow and curtsey to me in future, you pair of peasants. Still love you though! XXX

With communications completed she delved back into the diaries, first checking that there had indeed been an earlier cat named Rhubarb. She also re-read the section about the birth of her grandmother.

Becoming a mother has somehow made me less anxious about our future, wrote Josephine. *You'd think it would make me more anxious, but with a small baby dependent on me day and night I have little time to fret about the police coming for James, my parents searching for me, or how we are going to manage on our meagre earnings.*

Robyn found it difficult to put herself in Josephine's place. Here she was, nearly twenty-two years of age, but feeling far less mature or responsible than it seemed Josephine had felt aged seventeen. Here was Josephine caring for a baby, pregnant with a second child, cleaning, cooking, going to

186

market, scrimping and saving, tutoring the farmer's sons ... And what did she do? Fiddle about with spreadsheets to fill her otherwise empty working day. Go out for a drink in the evening with Lori. No responsibilities or money worries. It was amazing how a woman's lot in life could have changed so much in seventy years. In Josephine's day there had been no computers, no mobile phones. Robyn wondered what Josephine would have made of a flight half way round the world in a jumbo jet.

That thought hung on the chill morning air, for Robyn realised that if she didn't run for the shower right away she'd be late for work. That led her to realise that in her sparse farm cottage Josephine would have had no hot water on tap, and no central heating.

With her wet hair snaking down her back Robyn tossed a few odds and ends in a bag for her journey to Cornwall, and grabbed her bag of presents. Beside that bag were Christmas gifts for Maggie, Rhubarb and Lori. Robyn glanced at her watch. Too bad, she'd just have to be late for work.

Maggie had just disappeared into the bathroom, but Robyn managed to interrupt her before any major ablutions had commenced.

'Sorry, Maggie. Gee, I know I'm a menace. And I'm sorry Dad got you out of bed so early.'

'Not bad news, I hope?'

'No, he just wanted to talk about the news of his family. The diaries, you know. Anyway, I've got a little Christmas present for you. And Rhubarb too.'

'Thank you, dear,' said Maggie, in danger of losing the towel she'd wrapped around herself. 'I've got something for you too, but I'll have to give it to you later. I haven't wrapped it yet.'

Robyn bit her tongue. She'd been about to say that she had planned to leave for Cornwall straight after work. But it wouldn't hurt to come back for a cup of tea first. 'Okay, I'll see you later. Have a good day,' she said, trotting downstairs.

The morning was bright and frosty. Robyn was pleased to see the sun again after a succession of heavy, grey days. The dormant front garden twinkled with sparkly frosting, and her breath formed a cloud as she scraped ice off Clio's windscreen. She wished it would snow. A white Christmas in England would be perfect.

Upon arriving at work, Robyn met Lori by chance at the coffee machine.

'Guess what! I've been reading my great-grandmother's diaries, and it turns out her parents were a Lord and Lady. So I'm not just a common little Aussie girl after all. How mad is that?'

'I knew you were special the moment I met you. So I got you a special Christmas present.'

'And I've got something for you,' said Robyn, thankful that she'd remembered the gift in her haste.

Robyn grabbed the little package out of her handbag before following Lori to her desk. Lori handed Robyn a box, beautifully wrapped in swirly crimson paper and tied with a green and gold ribbon. Robyn felt ashamed as she handed over her badly-wrapped offering.

As well as being a gift wrapping supremo Lori was clearly a champion gift unwrapper. Before Robyn had so much as unpicked the ribbon on her box Lori had stripped her gift of its paper.

'Oh, Robs! Thanks! It's just what I need.'

'Gee, you're just saying that.'

Robyn looked at the paperweight she'd given Lori and felt a bit mean. It had seemed a fun thing to buy at the time, but in the cold light of day it looked cheap.

'Mark is a bit of a fresh air fiend, even in winter,' said Lori, lowering her voice and pointing to the draughtsman working at the desk next to the open window. 'My papers are always blowing about, but not any more.'

Robyn carefully undid the paper on her gift and lifted the lid off the box. She couldn't make out what was inside. Something wooden.

'It's a traditional English musical instrument. I hope you like it.'

'Gee, I've never seen one of these before. How do you play it?'

'You hit it with the little drumstick. Here, I'll show you.'

'Thanks, Lori,' said Robyn, thinking it was a bit weird but well-meant. 'Now I'd better pretend to do some work. Nick's in this morning. Coming to the pub at lunchtime?'

'Sure. See you then.'

On the way back to her desk, juggling the gift box and a cup of coffee, Robyn was hailed by Nick.

'In here a minute,' he called.

She pushed open the door with her foot. Nick was standing behind his desk holding aloft yet another handsomely wrapped package.

'For me?' said Robyn, thinking she sounded scarily like Miss Piggy. Was this what weight gain did to you?

'For you,' said Nick. 'A token of my appreciation.'

Robyn blushed. 'Gee, Nick. You've caught me on the hop. I haven't got anything for you.'

'I didn't expect anything,' he said with a good-natured grin.

'Can I open it now?'

'Why not take it home and put it under your tree. You do have a Christmas tree I hope?'

'Of course,' lied Robyn. Maggie had put up a fertility tree carved by a woman from some obscure African tribe, but it wasn't decorated with tinsel or baubles and didn't look at all festive. Surely there was no harm in a little fib. She didn't want Nick to think that her Christmas in England was lacking in festivities, and anyway Emily and Morvah were sure to have a tree.

'What are you doing for Christmas, Nick?' she asked.

He consulted his wafer-thin gold watch. 'I'm off to Switzerland. Meeting some friends, we've hired a chalet for a week. Leaving in about half an hour. Got to allow extra time to get to Gatwick, the traffic's bound to be heavy.'

'Wow! Makes my Christmas with the rellies sound a bit lame.'

'I'm sure you'll have a wonderful time. I wish I had family here to spend Christmas with.'

Robyn wondered whether Nick had any family at all, but her pondering was cut short by the telephone. She withdrew from his office and hauled her bounty (and her now-cold cup of coffee) back to her desk.

All morning Robyn's thoughts kept straying back to the diaries, one of which she had in her handbag. Resisting temptation to start reading when she should have been working, she wandered over to the window and looked out at what was shaping up into a gloriously sunny winter's day. Robyn was fortunate that her office overlooked an expanse of fields. The grass was picturesquely green now that the early frost had melted, and a handful of plump sheep nibbled like mowing machines.

Robyn was glad she wasn't a sheep. She fancied something more substantial than grass for her lunch. It was a good thing she was going to the pub with Lori as there'd been no time for breakfast.

Robyn was startled from her wool-gathering by Nick.

'I'm off now,' he said, overcoat over one arm and an expensive-looking leather valise in the other hand. 'Have a great Christmas. No need to stay till lunchtime, Robyn. Why not make a head start on your journey?'

'Thanks, Nick. You have a good Christmas too. See you in the next Millennium.'

'Ah, yes, The Millennium. Hope you're not one of those who think the world is going to end.'

'No way! But if it does I'll make sure I'm partying hard to the last.'

'Well don't do anything I wouldn't do,' he said with a twinkle in his eye as he departed.

Robyn could see why Delia fancied Nick, but he wasn't her type at all. Too slick. She couldn't understand what a kooky oddball actress like Delia saw in someone so different from herself. A true case of attraction of opposites.

Robyn hoped Delia didn't think there was anything going on between herself and Nick. She'd emailed Delia after her night out with Nick, and had perhaps gone on a bit too much about what a great time she'd had, for Delia hadn't emailed back since.

Millennium Eve. A good excuse as any for the party to end all parties. Robyn imagined that Delia and Casey were looking forward to partying their little socks off. She wondered what revelry Jenna and Tony had planned, making a mental note to email Jenna. The people of Sydney loved a good celebration, and the harbour bridge lent itself spectacularly to fireworks. She imagined boat parties with champagne and all kinds of fun. However her father's illness dampened her enthusiasm for the festivities. Checking her emails she noted he hadn't yet replied to her questions.

Robyn found she couldn't care less whether she stayed in Cornwall for Millennium Eve or went to Southampton to spend it with Lori and her friends. For the first time she wished she could be at home with her own family, but it was too late to do anything about it.

Then she remembered she'd promised to get the diaries copied for her father. She'd meant to ask Nick if it would be all right to use the office photocopier.

Robyn dashed off a quick email to her father.

Dad, I'm sorry. I've missed my chance to get the diaries copied at work. I promise I'll do it as soon as I get back to work on January 3rd. Love you lots, Robyn (and love to Mum also) XX

Robyn decided to go back to Maggie's after her pub lunch with Lori. That would give her a chance to have a cuppa with Maggie and still make an earlyish start on the drive to Cornwall. Everyone was saying the roads would be packed today.

In the hubbub and fairy-lit splendour of the pub Robyn felt her first glimmer of enthusiasm for the festive season. And she hadn't had a single sip of alcohol! In one of the side rooms an inebriated party from some local company were noisily making complete idiots of themselves while wearing red and white Santa hats. The pub's Christmas decorations were so over-the-top that even Casey would have found them tacky.

190

Lori pushed her way from the bar with two splendid tropical creations. 'Non-alcoholic fruit punch, as you've got a long drive ahead,' she explained.

'Thanks. Well, Happy Christmas,' said Robyn, raising her glass.

It was impossible to hold a sensible conversation with the racket going on around them, so Robyn and Lori departed as soon as they'd eaten.

Robyn impulsively hugged her friend. 'Have a great Christmas!'

'I know you'll have a wonderful time with Emily and Morvah and the others. Have you decided whether you're staying or returning for Millennium Eve?'

Robyn wrinkled her nose. 'Gee, I can't make up my mind. Can I phone you?'

'Of course. The party at the football ground promises to be massive, but I don't want to pressure you.'

Back at home, Robyn found Maggie had gone out. She decided to wait, so she switched on the laptop to email Jenna. There was an email from Casey.

Merry Christmas, Lady Robyn. Sounds wrong, you're going to have to change your name to Lady Robinia. Much posher. Hope your stocking will be full and your cups running over. Oo-er! Daniel and I will be spending Christmas at Byron Bay. His mother has a house up there, but it will be just us two. I don't think I told you, he's moved in with me. Yes, we are officially a couple! In love! Anyway, enough of the mushy stuff. I phoned your parents a couple of weeks ago, had to ring a few times before I got through. Your Mum said they'd been spending a lot of time at the hospital. I went to visit also. Your Dad looks a bit thin but he's in good spirits. But you probably know this anyway, your Mum said you keep in touch regularly. By the way, although Daniel and I share a flat and a bed (hope that's not too much info) we no longer share an office. He changed jobs just before he moved in, we decided it was for the best. He's now working as PA to a theatre director. A girl called Jenny has taken over your job temporarily. All I can say is, come back soon! She's a complete disaster, loses everything. How's tricks with Nick? Hope his presence isn't cramping your style. Look forward to seeing you soon. Love from Casey and Daniel XXXX

As she read the last couple of lines Robyn heard a key in the door. With no time to rattle off a reply she made a mental note to email both Casey and Jenna later.

Robyn found Maggie in the kitchen pouring a saucer of milk for Rhubarb. He was winding enthusiastically around her ankles.

'Hi, Maggie. See, Rhubarb thinks you're his mum already.'

'Purely cupboard love. I'm glad you haven't left already. I didn't mean to be out so long but the traffic was heavy. Here's your present. Merry Christmas!'

Robyn opened the little box to find a pair of colourful enamelled earrings.

'Oh, Maggie! They're lovely! I'll put them on right away. Gee, they must have cost a fortune!'

'Not at all. I bought them in Mexico. Not that you don't deserve an expensive present, mind. You've been my best lodger ever. I'm going to miss you when you go. And so will Rhubarb.'

'Oh, Maggie. Let's not go down that road yet. You're stuck with me for a few more weeks. Gee, I've loved being here.'

'What's this?' said Maggie, noticing the Christmas-wrapped box on the kitchen table.

'Oh, that's my Christmas present from my Australian boss, Nick. I didn't get him anything, how embarrassing!'

Robyn undid the paper to reveal a hamper from Fortnum and Mason.

'That's a very expensive shop in London,' explained Maggie. 'Wow! Champagne, pate, stilton, port, brandy ...'

'That'll make a couple of decent late-night suppers. Feel free to help yourself while I'm away!'

After a cup of tea Robyn decided she'd better hit the road if she was ever going to make it to Cornwall that night. It was not yet three o'clock and night already seemed to be closing in. She replaced her plain silver earrings with Maggie's Mexican ones, gave Maggie and Rhubarb a big hug and set off on her journey.

Chapter 22

The wise folk of Eastleigh had been right. The traffic on the M3 on the afternoon of Christmas Eve flowed like ... well, something that didn't flow. A brick wall? Robyn found it difficult to focus her attention as she crawled along, sometimes down to ten miles per hour.

There was no need to make a snap decision when she saw the sign for motorway services. It took a good ten minutes to cover the distance to the exit. She had to park a long way from the building, and once inside it was like all hell had broken loose. The unruly masses waiting at the KFC counter were like an assembly of Genghis Khan's warriors, and Robyn hoped they hadn't left their horses anywhere near her car. She had managed the duration of her car hire without so much as a scrape, and hoped not to fall from grace in the remaining weeks.

Children with ketchup-smeared faces ran wild, pushing and shoving without any apparent parental restraint. Robyn imagined perhaps the kids had banded together, stolen a car, and decided to terrorise all the take-aways at the services. But perhaps not. She could hear a weary, whiny woman in the background telling Her Darren to 'stop it'.

It was enough to put Robyn off a chicken meal. Considering the snail-like pace of the harassed staff turning out the goods, the chicken had to be something of a salmonella lucky dip.

The café was no better. Packed tables were surrounded by people with trays circling like vultures looking for vacant seats. Eventually she found an automatic coffee machine surrounded by a litter of paper cups. Luckily the machine was still dispensing clean cups and although there was no milk, Robyn managed to extract a cup of something resembling coffee. Although for that price she could have bought a whole jar in a supermarket.

She headed back to the car, and decided to read some more of the diaries while waiting for her coffee to cool.

Our first Christmas as a family, wrote Josephine. *Maud is a strong little girl, and wilful with it. She doesn't understand about Christmas yet, of course, but she seems to know that something unusual is happening. We had*

193

great difficulty getting her to sleep last night. James and I are both tired today, but Maud is as lively as ever after very little sleep. The Trescowes gave us a turkey, which makes a fine treat. This is far better than last Christmas on the island, and better, in truth, than any festivities with my family. James and I have each other, and Maud, and our next child is due within two months. My parents, for all their wealth, seemed lacking in love for each other. I will never take for granted James's love for me, nor mine for him. It is far more precious than material wealth.

Robyn's eyes brimmed with tears. She felt like a confirmed old maid compared with her great-grandmother. Poor old Robyn, twenty-one and never been properly loved. Not the way James loved his Josephine. At the end of the twentieth century so many relationships seemed to be all sex and no love. Her last bedmate, Colin, bore testament to this. Robyn felt sad and empty. She hoped that one day she would have a great, true love. She hoped her parents had that special ingredient, that all-forsaking closeness. She had a feeling they did.

Robyn dabbed her eyes with a crumpled tissue from her coat pocket. Her coffee had steamed up the windscreen where it sat in wait on the dashboard, but it had cooled to a drinkable temperature. Coffee finished, she looked at her watch. It was time to get back on the road, but first she'd better put in a call to Morvah and Emily to report her progress.

A reassuring call to her relatives and a few more miles under her wheels cheered Robyn's spirits somewhat. She chided herself for being so silly. Okay, so she hadn't yet met her one true love, but plenty of people were also in the same situation. Or worse. Women married to men who used them as punching bags. Men married to women who nagged incessantly. She could almost hear her mother telling her to count her blessings.

Robyn tuned in to a comedy programme on the radio, and the remaining miles to the Trescowe home soon passed along with her fit of the blues.

She drove up the lane and stopped outside Primrose Cottage. All was quiet. It was pretty quiet in Eastleigh, but here in the rural acres of Cornwall sound registered in minus figures on the noise-ometer. She paused a moment to savour the peace of the cold, starlit night. All she could hear was the distant babble of voices inside the house; the dark, outdoor world was like a vacuum. Gathering up her bags, Robyn headed for the kitchen door.

Some time later with a brandy in her hand and its forerunner sending fingers of warmth down to her toes, Robyn felt more attuned to Christmas. Her stomach was full of Aunt Emily's excellent shepherd's pie. The smell of meat roasting in preparation for their Christmas dinner filled the house.

Olivia had gone off to bed, desperately excited but obedient in case Santa might suspect that she hadn't been a good girl.

Robyn had placed her badly-wrapped gifts under the tree with the others. Emily was still at work in the kitchen, having brushed off any offers of help.

'She's the same every year,' grumbled Morvah. 'Works herself into the ground preparing a meal that takes minutes to disappear. Won't let anyone help.'

'Ah, go on, Dad,' said Morwenna, patting him on the shoulder. 'You know you'd hate it if Mum stopped making a fuss of Christmas. She's the original Christmas fairy.'

Morvah snorted. 'Bit old to be a fairy. She wants to slow down.'

'Oh, she's as fit as a fiddle apart from her hip. Keeping going is what keeps her going, if you see what I mean. She loves having everyone here. Remember how put out she was the year Colum and I got married and I wanted you to come to us?' Morwenna turned to Robyn. 'I gave in in the end, just to keep Mum happy. But now that she's having problems with her hip I agree with Dad. I wish she'd take it easier.'

'Bloody National Health Service!' grumbled Morvah into his drink.

'Mind your language, Morvah,' said Emily from the doorway. 'Would anyone like a nice cup of tea?'

Robyn and Morwenna rose as one and forced Emily into a chair.

'For goodness' sake, Mother, SIT DOWN!' said Morwenna. 'I'll make you a cup of tea. Personally I'm going to stick with the brandy.'

'I'd just about finished out there anyway,' said Emily. 'I suppose a small brandy might be nice,' she said with an impish twinkle in her eyes.

Emily looked at her watch. 'Robyn, dear. Would you like to phone your parents? It will be Christmas morning already in Sydney.'

'Gee, you're right. Thanks. I won't talk for long.'

'Talk as long as you like, dear. I'd hate to think Christmas went by without you phoning them.'

Morvah passed the phone to Robyn, who dialled the number. Her mother answered quickly.

'Hello, Mum, it's Robyn. Merry Christmas!'

'Hello, love. How nice to hear from you!'

Robyn heard her mother cup her hand over the receiver and call for her husband. 'Your Dad's just coming,' she said to Robyn.

'How is he?'

'Not bad. Anyway, here he is.'

Robyn could tell her mother was putting on a brave face.

'Hello, Dad,' she said, forcing herself to sound cheerful. 'Merry Christmas! I wish I was there with you.'

Robyn wished she could take back her words, and hoped Emily and Morvah weren't offended.

'Hello, m'girl. Merry Christmas,' said her father. His breathing sounded laboured.

'What are you doing today?'

'Oh, nothing much. Steve should be here soon to pick us up, we're having lunch with them.'

'That's nice.'

Robyn felt inadequate. There were so many things she wanted to say, but the words dried in her throat. 'Here's Morvah, Dad. I think he'd like to say hello.'

Robyn could tell that Morvah was also at a loss for words, and he handed over to Emily. She chatted brightly for a minute or two before handing the phone to Morwenna, who quickly passed it back to Robyn. It was like some sort of bizarre party game: pass the telephone.

Then Robyn remembered her father hadn't replied to the questions in her last email.

'Sorry, m'girl. Must have forgotten. What was it you wanted to know?'

'When I was here as a little girl did we visit any relatives named Trescowe who lived on a farm? Not Morvah and Emily.'

'My childhood memories are rather vague,' he said, seeming to have missed the point of her question. 'I think I had some sort of illness, as I remember spending a lot of time in bed when other children were outside playing. Ask Morvah, maybe he remembers. Sorry, lass.'

'That's all right, Dad,' said Robyn, concerned that he sounded so vague.

She could do little more than wish her parents a Merry Christmas once again before severing the connection.

'Well, that was nice, wasn't it?' said Emily brightly. 'Now, where's that brandy you promised me?'

As Morvah poured his wife a drink Robyn asked him about the farm.

'I do remember going to visit our grandparents on a farm. Our father's parents. Goodness knows what their names were. We just called them Grandma and Grandpa. They had a pig named Cecil. I tried to ride him and he dumped me in the mud.'

'Dad said he was ill for a long time as a child. Do you remember?'

'Aye, I do, now you mention it. I was always getting told off for bothering him when he was meant to be resting. I've no idea what was wrong with him though.'

Christmas morning in Cornwall dawned cold and clear in meteorological terms, but for Robyn it dawned with a pounding head. Emily had gone to bed after one small, sensible brandy, but the rest of them had sat up into the wee hours sifting through childhood memories. Morvah had them in stitches with his stories. Later, soul-searching talk had drifted towards the prospect of Robyn's father not living much longer. In the harsh morning light Robyn struggled to remember everything that had been said. Her dreams had been an improbable tangle: missing her train to London to meet her father off the plane, and being unable to read the timetable to find the next train. Exhausting stuff that left her weary before the day had begun. She held her head and groaned at the prospect of Christmas Day, of having to eat and drink and be merry.

Looking in the mirror Robyn saw that one of her Mexican earings had dug a red mark into her cheek as she slept. She should have taken them off before going to bed.

Emily was in the kitchen when Robyn emerged showered and dressed.

'Good morning, dear. Merry Christmas. Would you like some eggs and bacon?'

Robyn's stomach lurched. 'Uh, no thanks, Em. I think I'll save my appetite for your lovely Christmas dinner.'

Emily pursed her lips. 'No-one seems very keen on breakfast this morning.'

'I'm sorry. Can I give you a hand with anything?'

'Perhaps you could do the sprouts.'

Robyn felt a bit better after several cups of coffee. The mindless, repetitive job of cutting the stalky bits and ragged leaves off the Brussels sprouts wasn't at all demanding on her woolly brain.

'Did I tell you Moira gave me some diaries to read? Written by Josephine, Dad and Morvah's grandmother, and later by their mother. There's some very interesting stuff in them.'

As they prepared the Christmas feast Robyn regaled her aunt with the details of her husband's family history.

A while later Colum, Morwenna and Olivia burst into the kitchen, having had a bracing walk.

'Merry Christmas, Auntie Robyn,' chirped Olivia. 'I got a tea set from Santa. What did you get?'

'I don't know, Olivia. I haven't opened my presents yet.'

Morwenna sank into a chair, shaking her head feebly. 'She's been non-stop since about six a.m. Got any paracetamol, Mum? My head's banging.'

'It's in the bathroom where it's always kept. Perhaps all that brandy wasn't such a good idea after all.'

Emily checked the quantity of sprouts in the saucepan. 'I think that's enough. The parsnips are next. Perhaps Colum can help you.'

Robyn relished the warmth of the kitchen, the hub of the Trescowe home.

Colum raised a questioning eyebrow as he took up a knife. 'How do you feel this morning?'

'Pretty average. You?'

'More like third rate. Even after that walk my head's still muzzy. Perhaps a couple of glasses of that Aussie red you brought will fix me up. And Morwenna.'

Robyn grinned, pleased that her contribution to the feast had met with approval. It had been a last-minute purchase in the supermarket.

'Bit early for a drink, don't you think, dear?' said Emily.

'I meant later with our dinner, Em,' explained Colum. 'Ten o'clock is a bit early even by my standards.'

By the time she and Colum had prepared the parsnips Robyn felt as though her brain was surfacing out of the fog.

By one o'clock they were all seated around a dining table crammed with every delight that Christmas fantasies are made of. A ham with its skin cross-hatched and studded with cloves. Personalised Christmas crackers. Little crystal dishes of home-made chocolate truffles. Holly and ivy patterned table napkins that only came out at Christmas. Red candles glowing in a silver candelabra.

Olivia's eyes shone as they took in the feast before her. 'I want sweeties!' she cried.

'You can have sweeties after you've eaten your dinner, dear,' explained Emily.

Morvah brought a partially carved turkey to the table on a massive platter. Everything had to be juggled about to make space for the turkey. Morwenna and Colum brought out steaming dishes of vegetables that had to go on the side table. Olivia forgot about the sweets with her dinner in front of her, and silence reigned as they all set about the task of emptying their plates.

Emily was relieved of dishwashing by Morvah and Colum. The ladies sat back with cups of tea and watched the Queen's speech. Robyn could feel the gravity of her full belly and the warmth of the room lulling her to sleep.

'How about a walk to work off all that dinner?' suggested Morwenna when the menfolk returned.

'When do we open our presents?' asked Robyn as they went in search of coats and boots.

Morvah chuckled. 'Not until tea time. You're as bad as Olivia, lass. She insisted on opening most of hers this morning.'

Robyn blushed. 'Sorry.'

'Never mind,' said Morvah. 'Santa Claus will come, all in good time.'

Their leisurely walk down the lane past fields of dozing cows took them to the crumbling ruins of a disused church. Robyn was secretly relieved that a ten mile hike wasn't on the agenda. Nevertheless the moderate exercise made a space in her stomach for cake and sandwiches on their return.

Emily had begged off the walk, pleading pain in her hip. But clearly the pain hadn't prevented her from laying the table with a wonderful spread.

The sky darkened to a mystical blue and the sun relinquished its short winter life, slipping below the horizon before four o'clock. Morvah pulled the curtains and suggested a game of Catch the Rat.

After a boisterous session of games, some of which were traditional Cornish pastimes Robyn had never heard of, it was finally declared by Morvah that the hour for present opening had arrived. Olivia was appointed Chief Present Giver, which meant she took each gift from her grandfather and brought it to the recipient. But after half a dozen presents she tired of the task and sat down to open more of her own.

'Here's another for you, Robyn,' said Emily. 'Came in the mail the other day.'

Robyn undid the package, mystified. Inside was a small book and a note from Moira Hanley.

Another diary, she wrote. *Sorry I overlooked it. Hope you're enjoying Josephine and Maud's story. I think this is the last of the diaries, but if any more come to light I'll let you know.*

Robyn took it to her room. She'd brought the rest of the diaries with her. Sure enough, this volume filled in the missing months of 1949.

By the time she returned they were wearily gathering up the worst of the paper rubbish. The opening titles of *Raiders of the Lost Ark* were rolling across the television screen accompanied by stirring music. The assembled company took their seats. Within half an hour Morvah was snoring loudly.

Olivia turned and glared at her grandfather. 'Can't you tell him to put a sock in it, Grandma?' she complained.

'Olivia, where did you get such an expression?' asked Emily.

'I heard you saying it, Grandma.'

'Out of the mouths of babes,' said Emily, momentarily embarrassed. 'Can you turn the volume up a bit please, Colum? Nothing stops Morvah once he starts his snoring.'

'We know,' said Morwenna and Colum in unison. Everyone laughed.

'We all went on a caravan holiday in France last year,' explained Colum.

'Dad snored every night,' added Morwenna. 'I don't know how Mum puts up with it. I'd divorce Colum if he made such a racket. How do you get any sleep, Mum?'

'Oh, I'm used to it,' said Emily stoically.

One film led to another, and Robyn drifted off to sleep. When she awoke she hoped she hadn't been snoring. Morwenna, Emily and Morvah were also asleep in their chairs, but Colum and Olivia were absent. Presumably Colum had taken his daughter up to her bed.

Robyn decided to call it a night, first taking her cup and plate to the kitchen and washing them. Everything was remarkably clean and orderly considering the scale of the day's culinary excesses.

Up in her little nook in the attic, Robyn slipped into her teddy bear pyjamas and comfy socks. She rolled into bed, but sleep eluded her. After a futile attempt at clearing her mind of all thoughts she gave up and reached for the diary in which she'd marked her place with a postcard from Tijuana.

Chapter 23

The story of Josephine's life unfolded as the hours slipped by. Robyn refused to allow sleep to overtake her. At one stage she caught herself dozing, but forced herself awake and picked up the diary from where it had fallen on the floor.

Josephine and James's second child arrived, and they called him William. Robyn felt intrigued. Was this Great Uncle William? Born in 1928. That would be about right.

With the generations properly spatialised in her mind, Robyn resumed reading.

I often think about Lucy and Luisa, and the others on the island. I wonder whether they are all out there still. James seems less inclined to dwell on the time he spent there, for he rarely refers to it.

We leave the Trescowe farm tomorrow. James has found better paid work on another farm. He will be working with cattle, and they say I can get work picking fruit in the summers. I will enjoy that, as long as proper arrangements can be made for care of the children. Maud is a headstrong girl, just past her third birthday. William is more placid. He has only just started walking properly at two, much slower than Maud. But the farm women say that is quite normal. There's certainly nothing wrong with his mind either, he's a clever little fellow. I'll miss this place and the friendship I've made with some of the women, but it's been difficult tutoring the Trescowe boys. Nathaniel seems unable to learn much, and although Frederick has an able mind he is easily distracted by his brother.

At the new farm James will earn considerably more money, and that will more than make up for the loss of my earnings from tutoring. You never know, perehaps somewhere along the way there will be other, better-behaved children in need of help with their school work.

Robyn finally fell asleep, dreaming of a time long gone when the life of a farmer had been satisfying and not the bureaucratic minefield within which Morvah and Emily existed. A time when people who worked the land ate what they grew and wanted for little else. A time before fast cars, designer clothing, pension plans and fancy furniture.

The following day the Trescowe family en masse ventured into Truro, the county capital. Morvah suggested Robyn might like to see the cathedral. Robyn thought it was a magnificent building, but was a little disappointed to find that the majority of it had been built comparatively recently.

There were very few shops open, but they managed to find one that sold ice cream, which was what Olivia wanted. It was while in the ice cream shop that Robyn noticed a sign advertising a photocopying service. She thought of the diaries and reached into her handbag, glad she'd thought to bring them in the hope of finding a copy shop in the city. Then she checked whether she had enough cash for a considerable number of copies at ten pence each.

'Would you mind if I caught up with you in a little while?' she asked Emily. 'I really want to get these copied to send to Dad. I said I'd do it before Christmas but I didn't get round to it.'

'What are they, lass?' asked Morvah.

'They're your grandmother Josephine Rostrevor's diaries. Moira lent me them, and I've been emailing information to Dad. They're helping us solve some of the puzzles about the family tree.'

'Ah yes, Emily was telling me about them earlier. Sounds interesting.'

Robyn checked her watch. 'Can I meet you at three o'clock back at the cathedral?'

'That's fine, dear,' said Emily. 'Now are you sure you won't get lost?'

As the cathedral loomed over the centre of the city it seemed hardly likely.

It took a while, but Robyn copied as many pages as she could afford. She paid the shopkeeper for her copies, a large envelope, and a writing pad. Pausing on a bench she penned a hasty note to her father, slipped it in the envelope with the copied pages and wrote her parents' address on the outside.

She stopped a woman who looked local and asked directions to the Post Office.

'Turn left, and take the second, no, the third turning on the left. You can't miss the red and white sign.'

Robyn found the Post Office, but it was closed.

'Aye, closed today,' said a man who had noticed her peering through the window.

'That's a shame,' said Robyn, stuffing the envelope in her handbag.

'Are you from Australia?' he asked. He then regaled her with details of his cousin who had emigrated in the sixties. Then he started on about the woman his cousin had married and the six sons they had.

'They live in Sydney. The Harrisons. Do you know them? Rodney and Linda, and the boys are John, Michael, Peter ...'

Robyn checked her watch. It was nearly three o'clock. 'I'm sorry, I have to meet someone,' she said, backing away.

The man's monologue continued. As she turned the corner the last Robyn heard of the slow, deliberate West Country accent was that the youngest son was studying medicine at Sydney University. Why did so many people think everyone in Australia knew each other?

As she hurried along the street she saw the Trescowes were already assembled outside the cathedral.

'I hope you haven't been waiting long,' she said, aware that they all looked frozen. The wind was bitterly cold.

'How about I treat us all to another cup of tea?' said Robyn, hoping she had enough money left.

'I want another ice cream!' said Olivia.

'Your little tummy will freeze solid if you eat any more ice cream,' chided Emily.

'Grampa said if I ate my Ready Brek it would protect me from the cold. See, it must be working. I don't even need my gloves.'

Robyn noticed that the child's gloves were stitched to the ends of her sleeves so that when she slipped them off they wouldn't get lost. Clever.

They found a café that was open and the adults warmed their hands on mugs of steaming tea. Robyn was surprised to feel as well as she did considering how little sleep she'd had and the hangover she'd had that morning. She raised her mug.

'Thank you all for a lovely Christmas. Cheers!'

The others, with the exception of Olivia who was blowing bubbles in her milkshake, raised their mugs in reply.

'We'll miss you when you go, love,' added Emily.

'Oh, you women!' grumbled Morvah. 'Always got to get sentimental.'

Emily and Robyn grinned sheepishly. Robyn could feel her eyes brimming once more.

That night Robyn took time out to email her father, telling him that she'd managed to copy some of the diaries and would mail them the following day from the nearest village. She felt her eyes growing heavy. It was time for bed.

While waiting for sleep to overtake her, Robyn realised that in less than a month she'd be back in Sydney. There was still so much she wanted to do before she left. She wanted to visit France, and visit Gerald in London. And she wanted to check out the place where records of births and deaths were kept while she was there. She cursed herself for having wasted so much time, for whole weekends in Eastleigh had slipped away doing nothing in particular. And she'd seen so little of England.

Robyn picked up her diary and drew up a list of the things she wanted to do before returning to Australia. Cramming everything in would take a will of iron, and she thought she'd probably need to sweet-talk Nick into giving her time off work.

So much for a good night's sleep, she though as she noticed it was gone midnight. Then she began agonising over how to tell Emily that she wouldn't be spending the rest of the week with them, much as she loved their company. Then she realised she'd have to find time to visit the Trescowes again before her departure. That would mean doing away with the weekend in France. She slipped out of bed, switched on the light and took up her diary once more to amend what she'd already written.

Robyn was warming to the idea of planning a return trip to England as soon as she'd saved enough. Maybe a working holiday. After all, other people did it. With thoughts of more time here with the family and visits to, say, the Lake District, and Scotland, and Wales, then on to France, Robyn finally drifted off to sleep.

Despite her late night Robyn was awake with the dawn. Deciding not to disturb the household by going downstairs she picked up the diaries once more. But she found they were becoming a little dull, with too much waffle about the joys of life on the new farm. She skipped ahead, skimming the pages for something more interesting than tending cows' udders and sewing children's clothes.

Robyn's eyes latched onto the name George.

James has news of my brother, George, wrote Josephine. *Farmer Smith is a garrulous man, and James admits he hardly listens half the time, but in a lengthy diatribe about saving one's pennies the farmer mentioned a young man named George Trethewey who works at the bank in Truro and has a sound head for financial advice. Surely there cannot be two people of that name! Hearing news of my brother has made me realise how much I've missed him. It's been nearly ten years since I last saw him.*

James is so understanding. He made a special trip into Truro on his morning off, went to the bank, and he says it's true. There is someone named George Trethewey there, and he wears a calliper on one leg. James has agreed that I may contact George. It's risky, of course, but we have been here for years now without discovery and I have a feeling that if George is working in a bank he may not be in Father's good graces. It's just a hunch, but instinct tells me that if all was well George would have gone into Father's business. Maybe Father is dead? Even so, if all was well George would surely be living in London.

Robyn read the next entry, dated a week later.

I have written a note for George and sealed it in an envelope marked 'Personal'. James is taking it to the bank this morning. If George wishes to see me I have asked him to write a message. I have told him that my 'friend' (James) will call back the following Tuesday to collect his reply. I haven't given anything away about where I am living or what I am doing.

Robyn skipped over the next entry about cake making, eager to hear more news of Josephine's brother. But something else caught her eye.

Sadly our cat, Rhubarb, has died. The children are very upset and are pestering us for another cat.

Robyn hoped it would be a long time before the Rhubarb of the twenty-first century went to meet his maker. Then she read more news of George.

It's so exciting! George is meeting me for tea in Cuffley's tomorrow! His note was very brief; he says nothing of his situation, only that he is pleased to hear from me after all these years and that somehow he hadn't given me up for dead.

Robyn read on.

It was so wonderful to see George today! My head is buzzing with his news. He looks well, and has filled out a little in adulthood. He is married to a woman named Lucy. They have had three children in less than three years of marriage, and they live in Truro. My instinct was correct. George and Father had a monstrous disagreement over George's choice of career, and he moved to Truro all on his own and started work as a bank clerk aged just sixteen. He worked hard and rose to assistant manager, only then allowing himself the luxury of a social life. Fortunately he met Lucy and they are happy together. He idolises his three boys, Edward, Albert and Hugh. He nas no news of our parents, having cut himself off completely from the family.

Instinct told me to trust George, so I told him everything about my life with James. He was simply astounded, having truly believed my tale of losing my memory. He questioned whether Lucien had indeed drowned, but I had to say I believe that to be the case.

He said that Maman *and Father accepted my second departure more readily. Shortly after,* Maman *went to Roskenner and Father remained in London. During his last couple of years at school George said they were living almost completely separate lives.*

This set me thinking about Maman *and Father. Over a period of a few years they lost all of their three children. It just shows you can never tell what life has in store. I resolve to make the most of every day and to treasure my children, and James.*

George's wife is eager to meet us, and we are invited to dinner on Saturday. I am looking forward to it, but James is extremely anxious. The children are excited at the prospect of meeting their cousins. I am so glad I took that first step of writing to George.

Robyn realised it was nearly nine o'clock, and wondered why she hadn't heard anyone moving about the house.

Upon reaching the bathroom she noticed tell-tale splashes of water on the floor indicating that some at least must have woken, but she had been so engrossed in the diaries she hadn't heard a thing.

Emily was on her own in the kitchen, sitting down with a cup of tea and a magazine.

'Good morning,' said Robyn, dropping a kiss on her aunt's forehead. 'What's this, you putting your feet up!'

Emily smiled. 'I do sometimes, but don't tell Morvah. What would you like for breakfast, dear?'

'Just toast, please. You stay right there. I'll make it. Where are the others?'

'Morvah is out with the sheep. Morwenna, Colum and Livvie have gone to the supermarket.'

'Gee, they must have been up early.'

'There's no such thing as late rising when you have a small daughter. What do you want to do today?'

Robyn decided to seize the moment. 'Actually, Em, I need to think about getting back to Eastleigh.'

'Not today, surely?'

'I really should go tomorrow. I'm running out of time! Do you realise, this time next month I'll be back in Australia. There are so many things I want to do before I go.'

'I hope you'll come back and visit us again before you fly away.'

'Of course. I could come for my last weekend.'

'Please do. I'll see if William can come over again for Sunday dinner. He's with Moira's mother for Christmas. And I hope you'll come back to England again before too many more years pass by.'

'Don't worry, Auntie dear, you haven't seen the last of me! I doubt I'll manage another freebie from my employers so it'll take me a while to save up. But I'd love to come back.'

'Back to the subject of today, how would you like to visit the seaside as it's a sunny day?'

Robyn laughed, thinking that only her crazy aunt would suggest a trip to the beach in winter. But she was right, it was a sunny day, a bit cold but not too windy. So why not?

Chapter 24

Robyn was on her way by half past eight the following morning. The roads were fairly quiet, and she made only one stop for coffee. As she sat in the drab café her thoughts were of the amazing beach Emily had taken them to the day before. Like a bite taken out of the cliffs, with white sand and brilliant blue water. They'd climbed up some steps cut into the cliff to see an open air theatre made from huge blocks of stone, set right into the edge of the cliff. Then when the tide went out broad expanses of white sand opened up and connected with the next bay. It was a funny little place, she couldn't remember its name. Something very Cornish. Just a cluster of houses and one small shop. Oh, and the Telegraph Museum. From that remote point on the Cornish coast the first undersea cable had been laid across the Atlantic Ocean to America, allowing telegraph messages to be sent between the two countries.

Robyn arrived in Eastleigh just before noon. Maggie's curly head appeared around the kitchen door as she bumped through the front door with her luggage.

'Hello!' called Maggie. 'I thought you were staying longer.'

Robyn shook her head. 'I'm starting to panic. Not long now before I return to Australia and there's so much I want to do.'

'Of course. What are you doing for Millennium Eve?'

'Gee, I don't know,' said Robyn, stretching her travel-weary shoulders. 'What are you doing, Maggie?'

'Going to a fancy dress party. You can come if you want.'

'Thanks, but I might go up to London. There's another cousin I'd like to meet.'

'Well if you change your mind there's always Mary's party. Plenty of things here to make another costume.'

'Thanks,' said Robyn, heading up to her room. There didn't seem to be much point in unpacking if she was off again so soon. Just replacing the dirty stuff with clean would do the job.

Robyn settled on her bed with one of Maggie's huge mugs of tea and the next volume of the diaries.

I went to the market in Truro today, wrote Josephine. Robyn smiled, pleased that she was familiar with at least one place her great-grandmother mentioned. She thought of Truro and tried to recall where the market was located.

I bought a length of cloth to make myself a new dress. I don't want to look like I've dressed from the rag bag when I meet George's wife on Saturday. I wish I'd allowed myself a little more time. I can see I'll be up into the wee hours stitching to get it finished. James at least has a decent shirt and jacket, and I've put a few stitches in his best trousers. The children have new clothes made for next summer that I can get out for the occasion.

I ran into Lily from Trescowe's farm. She had just finished her errands, so we dropped into the café by the market for a cup of tea. Lily is very outspoken. She had me in stitches. She thinks Mrs Trescowe is having a fling with one of the farm hands, young enough to be her son. It's probably just malicious gossip but Lily swears it's true. She says Florrie Trescowe is a woman with needs greater than her husband's, and she's been known to cast her eye about over the years. Lily says I was lucky she hadn't had the trousers off my James. Then I admitted I hadn't had the trousers off him for nearly a month. I can't think why I said it, it just slipped out. Lily was very understanding. She said it's just part of the way of married life. Sometimes you do, sometimes you don't. She said at least I hadn't let myself go since having the children, which was nice of her. We talked about whether James might be having an affair, but decided that he probably didn't meet any women during the course of his days. She said he's likely just tired out from hard work. It was good to talk with another woman, and I caught the bus home feeling much brighter. I suppose it's unrealistic to expect as much attention from your man when you've been together a number of years. We're just like any other old married couple, and I don't suppose many others in our situation are having regular passionate encounters. Ah well, as Lily says, that's life.

The next page was filled with the visit to George and Lucy Trethewey.

Luckily James was able to finish work a bit early, and I had the children scrubbed, dressed and admonished to behave. So after James had a quick wash and change of clothes we were out on the road waiting for the Truro bus. I must say I am quite pleased with my new dress. It was worth the effort. George and Lucy live in a comfortable house in a quiet area, not far from the bank where George works. George proudly introduced me to his wife and three sons. Lucy is small, with pale skin, dark hair and dark eyes. Like a little doll. She hardly seems strong enough to have produced three children in rapid succession. Edward is nearly three, Albert is one, and Hugh is just a few months old. The house gleams with cleanliness. I don't know how Lucy manages it. Maybe that's why she seems so frail.

George and Lucy made us very welcome. Their children had already had their meal and went off to bed like angels shortly after we arrived. Lucy served vegetable soup, roast beef and upside down pudding. William managed to spill his pudding down his shirt front, but apart from that the children were well behaved. In fact they were very good, probably because George and Lucy paid them so much attention. It has occurred to me that we will have to invite them to our humble abode, which I am rather dreading.

We chatted easily and looked at photographs of their recent visit to Lucy's aunt in Bude. Time just flew by. We only just managed to catch the last bus back to the farm. I could tell that James found it a chore to keep up with the polite chatter, but he bore it with good humour. Maud and William fell asleep on the way home. James said he liked George and Lucy, even if they are posh. I didn't dare tell him that our parents are far more grand. Hopefully there will never be any need for him to meet them. I wouldn't want to risk making him feel awkward and inferior, particularly as I could tell he felt like a fish out of water even with George and Lucy. What James will never understand is that he's twice the man my father is. Still, all that is in the past, and I can't say I miss them. I wonder even if Father is still alive being so much older than Maman. In any case, I have everything I want here with my own family, now enriched by having contact with George and Lucy.

Robyn realised she must have fallen asleep, for she awoke with the diary digging uncomfortably into her side and vague memories of a restless jumble of dreams.

After rising and splashing her face with cold water she felt better, and ventured downstairs.

'Sorry, dozed off,' she explained to Maggie, who was seated at the kitchen table with her sewing machine fashioning a strange-looking garment.

'I'm going to Mary's party as a gypsy,' she explained through a mouthful of pins.

Robyn thought that was about right for Maggie. People usually tended to dress as their alter ego where fancy dress was concerned. Robyn made them a mug of tea each and then remembered that she hadn't phoned Gerald. Back in her room she fished her mobile and address book out of her bag.

Within seconds a plummy voice answered.

'Hello, Gerald?' said Robyn.

'No, this is Martin. Who shall I say is calling?'

'Cousin Robyn from Australia. Gerald doesn't know me, but …'

She could hear Martin calling to Gerald, who had an equally formidable cut-glass accent.

'Ah, Robyn. Grandfather told me he'd met you. How are you enjoying your sojourn in Blighty?'

'Fine, thanks. I'm due to return to Sydney at the end of January, but I'd like to come up to London and meet you. Would it be all right if I called in tomorrow or the day after? I know a hotel I can stay in …'

Gerald cut her off. 'My dear girl, I will be most offended if you don't come and stay with us. We have plenty of room. Tell me, do you have plans to celebrate the Millennium? We're having a bit of a knees-up. Grandfather's joining us, and you'd be welcome also. It's fancy dress. Please say yes, that is unless you have other plans.'

'Gee, that's very good of you. But are you sure you've got room for me as well as your grandfather?'

'Of course. Now let me tell you how to find us …'

Robyn was glad she'd made contact. Gerald sounded nice, even if he was a bit posh. And his party appealed more than the other possibilities. The only trouble was finding a costume at short notice. She went in search of Maggie, who was trying on her finished outfit before the mirror in her bedroom.

'Looks great. Now all you need is a rose between your teeth.'

Maggie plucked a fabric flower from a vase and struck a dramatic pose.

'Perfect. Maggie, I'm going up to London tomorrow to stay with my cousin. He's invited me to his Millennium party and the theme is the turn of the last century. I haven't a clue what women used to wear back then.'

'And you think I might? Thanks, Rob. I'm not *that* old.'

Robyn could tell Maggie was only pretending offence. She opened her jam-packed wardrobe and started rummaging.

'Ah, this might do the trick,' said Maggie, hauling out a plastic dress bag. She unzipped the cover and held the dress up against Robyn so she could see the effect in the mirror. It was made of apricot satin, cut on the bias and dropping in soft folds almost to the floor.

'Gee, that's lovely! Are you sure you don't mind lending it to me? That is, if I can get into it. You're thinner than me.'

Maggie sized up Robyn's dimensions. 'It should fit you. It was my mother's, she was a bit bigger than me. I've still got half a dozen of her dresses, don't know why I keep them.'

Robyn pulled off her jumper and slipped the satin dress over her shoulders. Her jeans made it look a bit lumpy so she wriggled out of them. The dress was quite a close fit but at least it didn't bunch up on her hips.

'Hmmm, the colour suits you. Given a bit of a press it should pass muster. I've got some of Mummy's shoes. What size are you?'

Robyn had never thought it would be so easy. Within minutes she was kitted out for Gerald's party, complete with elbow-length gloves. Maggie wasn't sure how historically accurate the dress was, but Robyn thought it looked old-fashioned enough. In any case it was drop dead glamorous. All she needed to do was remember to pull in her podgy stomach and stand up straight. Or maybe invest in some gut-busting underwear. With her hair piled up on top of her head she was transformed.

Rhubarb emerged from his nap behind the curtains in Maggie's bedroom, stretched and batted a dead moth across the carpet.

'I'll take this off now before Rhubarb gets his claws into it,' said Robyn, slipping the dress off her shoulders.

The following morning Maggie and Rhubarb waved farewell to Robyn from the dining room window. It was raining again, but at least there didn't seem to be too much traffic heading for London. Robyn followed the A3 in through the suburbs, and after getting a little bit lost, found her way to Fulham. The street, a cul de sac, gave an impression of well-to-do residents with taste and style. The only problem was there was nowhere to park. Having reversed carefully past a solid row of BMWs, Jaguars and other marques with hefty price tags, Robyn finally found a space two streets away into which she could squeeze her modest vehicle. She hauled out her trusty overnight bag and the carrier containing her ball gown, carefully locked the car and made her way to number nine Langford Road. The front door was the colour of a ripe aubergine, and she timidly tapped the brass knocker.

Within seconds Robyn heard footsteps approaching. The door swung open revealing a slender man with a mop of shiny, dark hair, bright, intelligent eyes and a smile that showed off a set of dazzling white teeth. He was dressed in a black roll neck jumper and black trousers.

'Hi, I'm Robyn,' she said, feeling very much like a poor relation.

'Pleased to meet you. I'm Gerald,' he said, offering a well-manicured hand. 'Do come in.'

Another man appeared behind Gerald. 'Hello, I'm Martin. Let me take your bags.'

Robyn surrendered her luggage and followed the pair down the hall, which was tiled in a checkerboard of black and white. The walls were painted white, and the ceiling was black. An impressive coat of arms stood in a niche.

Martin disappeared upstairs with Robyn's luggage while Gerald ushered her into a cosy drawing room, again looking like something out of an interior design magazine.

'Do sit down,' said Gerald, indicating a comfy chair by the open fire. 'Can I get you a cup of tea?'

'Yes, please,' replied Robyn.

Martin returned while Gerald was absent. He was taller than Gerald, with neat fair hair and a closely cropped beard.

'I hope you found us without too much difficulty,' he said, seating himself in the chair on the other side of the fire.

'I had to stop once and check the map, but it was fine really. Gee, this is a lovely house!'

Martin smiled. Before he could reply Gerald returned.

'Traffic not too bad?' he enquired, putting the tea tray down on a small table.

'Busier than I'm used to, but I coped all right.'

'It will no doubt get worse over the next few days with the influx of visitors coming for the Millennium. I'm glad we're partying at home. Trafalgar Square and the Millennium Dome will be packed solid, and then there's the difficulty of getting around town. Milk? Sugar?'

'Just milk, please.'

'We've put you in the blue room. I'll take you up when you've finished your tea. Biscuit? I made them myself.'

Robyn succumbed to a biscuit. It would have been rude not to.

'When does your grandfather arrive?'

'Oh, he's here already. Having a nap in his room. He's getting on a bit, you know.'

'I met him while I was staying with Auntie Emily and Uncle Morvah. I also met your sister, Moira.'

'Moira and Richard will be coming to our party,' said Martin. 'Leaving the sprogs with someone, thank God. They're the most disobedient, spoiled children we've ever met.'

'Moira brought them once and it was a nightmare,' said Gerald. 'Grubby little hands all over everything, feet on the sofa, crumbs everywhere. And they're much worse in their own home. They scribble on the walls ...'

'Calm down, Gerald!' said Martin. 'We like everything just so, as you can probably tell. This house is not particularly child-friendly.'

'Children are over-rated,' said Robyn, and the two men laughed.

'I can see we're going to get along just fine,' said Gerald.

Robyn cast her eyes around the beautiful room, admiring the way everything matched and toned.

'Drink up, and we'll show you to your room. Give you the grand tour, if you like,' said Gerald.

'Thanks. You're very kind puttng me up at short notice.'

'The more the merrier. We have five bedrooms, and at a pinch we can accommodate someone in the study. The house doesn't look very big from the front, but it extends back quite a distance. And we have three storeys so that gives us a reasonable amount of space. When we're here on our own we rattle around like beans in a jar. We've thought of finding a smaller place in the country, but we've spent so much time getting everything as we want it ...' Gerald trailed off with an expressive shrug.

Robyn drained her teacup and took another biscuit. It was a long time since her last Mars Bar and she'd had no lunch. 'I'd love a look around the house,' she said.

The tour seemed to take in every nook and cranny, every ornament and dado rail. Robyn felt as though the sides of her stomach were flapping emptily against each other, and she was trying to disguise impolite gurgles and rumbles.

Then Gerald uttered a magical incantation: 'Lunch should be just about ready.'

Robyn had been thinking that somehow she'd have to make it through to the evening on two biscuits. Left in the blue room, she hoped she'd be able to find her way back to the kitchen. But as she came downstairs a savoury aroma led her in the right direction.

The kitchen was a vision in black and stainless steel, with a replica of the coat of arms on one wall.

'I hope you like tomato and red pepper soup,' said Martin. 'And I've made sundried tomato ciabatta. Shall we slum it and eat in the kitchen?'

'Sounds fine to me, and it smells amazing,' said Robyn, salivating already.

'I'll give Grampy a shout,' said Gerald, plucking the telephone from the wall.

Robyn marvelled that the house seemed to have every modern convenience known to man. An internal telephone system certainly saved a lot of running up and down stairs.

Although William Rostrevor had been a bit grouchy on being questioned about family history last time they'd met, he seemed pleased to see Robyn. When she addressed him as Mr Rostrevor he asked her to call him Grampy. 'Like everyone else does,' he said. 'Even this pair of uppity poofs.'

Robyn nearly choked on her first mouthful of bread, not daring to look at either of the uppity poofs.

Grampy dipped his bread in the soup. 'When's your gin-soaked sister arriving?'

'Not until tomorrow evening,' replied Gerald. 'And yes, she's bringing the Banker Wanker. Pardon my language, Robyn. Grampy is none too fond of Moira's husband.'

Robyn suppressed her giggles with another mouthful of bread. A girl could grow pleasantly plump in this house, she thought, helping herself to another slice and slathering it with butter.

'Overpaid fool!' muttered Grampy.

'Never mind, Grampy,' soothed Martin. 'That nice Mrs Protheroe-Thomas is coming, you like her.'

'Ah, yes. The Welsh Rarebit,' he said, brightening somewhat.

Martin choked on his soup. 'You're very naughty calling her that. She's the widow of a very highly respected conductor ... symphonies, Robyn, not buses. And she plays the violin exquisitely.'

'She definitely goosed me the last time we met,' added Grampy.

'Nonsense! It was an accident.'

'Well I wouldn't mind giving her one. She'll have to watch herself at midnight.'

'Grampy, behave!' gasped Gerald. 'We have a lady present.'

'She's Australian. They're all at it like rabbits,' he said with a lecherous grin.

'I'm sorry, Robyn,' said Gerald. 'He does it on purpose, I'm sure.'

Robyn shrugged. 'Gee, I'm not much of a goer. Can't even remember when I last went out with a man.'

The rest of the meal passed without incident. Afterwards Martin and Gerald excused themselves as they had some last-minute party arrangements to attend to. Grampy was soon snoring behind his newspaper in the drawing room, so Robyn returned to her room. It was painted a very dark indigo, with touches of gold that gleamed opulently in the feeble winter daylight. Time for another session with the diaries, she thought, wriggling under the midnight-blue quilt and taking up where she had left off.

War has been declared.

Robyn checked the date. 14th September 1939. Ah, that must have been the start of the Second World War. This was bound to be interesting.

I am most apprehensive that James will be called up, wrote Josephine. *He says that for the moment men from our farm are not going off to the war as the farms need to keep producing as much food as possible. As the weeks go by and men from the towns go off in their khaki uniforms I am somewhat reassured, for none of the men from the farm seem to be going. We hear on the radio news that imported foods are being restricted, and the more home grown produce we can generate the better we will be prepared as an island nation to withstand a siege if it comes to that. But they say it won't be like the Great War. Times have changed, and considering the advances in weaponry over the past 20 years those in the know feel that the skirmish can be brought under control in a matter of months. It is a relief to hear this. To have to say farewell to James, not to have his company for months on end, would be the hardest thing to bear. I do not know how other women can bear to be parted from their husbands. And the thought of losing one's husband to an early death in the field of battle ... too horrible to contemplate.*

Robyn skimmed ahead through pages of restrictions, rationing, gas masks and other interesting details. Josephine had appreciated that she was lucky to live in the country, for many of the cities were being bombed.

Shortly after, the time came for James to do his bit.

My worst fears are realised. Today James has gone into Truro to enlist in the army. We have had an influx of Land Girls on the farm, here to do the work of the men so they can go off to war. After James left I hid myself away and cried. I didn't want the children to see how upset I was. I fear I will never see my beloved man again.

The following day, a very different entry.

James was back by the end of the day. He failed the medical. It appears he has a heart condition. I am so relieved that he will not be going off to war, but he says he is being kept on a reserve list. I am most concerned about his health. He is to see the doctor tomorrow. It is astounding that someone who looks so healthy can be unwell. I suppose it is fortunate that his condition has been discovered before he suffered a heart attack.

With tablets to be taken daily, James's heart trouble stabilised. Several months later, another development.

Children from the cities are being evacuated to rural areas, and we are to present ourselves at the Town Hall in Truro on Tuesday to collect an evacuee, a girl from London. Maud and William are looking forward to having a companion. And I am very excited as I have been approached to work as a teacher's assistant now that the classes at the village school are having to expand to take in city children. I will be working with Miss Smith in the Junior Class. Perhaps I can train to become a fully-fledged teacher. Both Maud and William attend the school, and so will our evacuee, so we will be able to walk together to and from school, a distance of just over a mile. I will have two weeks to settle the newcomer, then off to school we will go!

Chapter 25

December thirty-first. The last day of the twentieth century. At first it seemed like any other day to Robyn. The grey sky hung damp and ponderous over London. The milkman clattered and whirred along the road in his electric cart just after seven a.m. But when Robyn reached the kitchen she discovered it was special milk. Millennium milk, according to the brightly decorated foil bottle tops.

'From Millennium cows,' said Gerald with a wink as he popped one of the tops and poured a dash of the celebratory fluid into his coffee.

'Busy day ahead, my little Robin-bird. I wonder if you'd mind popping to the supermarket for me? I need to be here to supervise the florist. Martin hasn't a *clue* when it comes to arranging flowers.'

'Sure, no problem. I'll just throw some clothes on.'

'Heavens, my dear. Not this very instant. Have some breakfast first. I'm sure the obliging Mr Waitrose won't have sold out of everything just yet.'

After showering and dressing Robyn made a quick calculation and decided it was probably a good time to put in a call to her parents.

Her mother answered straight away. 'Robbie dear. Lovely to hear your voice.'

Robyn thought she sounded tired.

'Hello Mum. How are you? And Dad?'

'We're fine. Steve and Jules and Joey are here. We're having a little party. I'll pass you over to your Dad.'

'Hello, m'girl. Happy New Millennium!'

'Hello Dad. Sounds like you're having a good time.' Since her parents were obviously trying to keep the conversation upbeat she thought she'd better play along.

'I'm playing a game with Joey. And I'm determined to stay up until midnight. We've got the TV on. The fireworks on the Harbour Bridge are going to be well worth watching. I'd like to be down there by the water, but your mother is right, I suppose. It would be too much for me.'

'How are you feeling? Any more news on when they'll operate?'

'No, dear. The doctors have got me on all sorts of pills. I get a bit tired but otherwise I'm okay. By the way, I received your parcel. Interesting stuff. Gives me a strange feeling reading my grandmother's handwriting, and her most intimate thoughts.'

'I'll send you the rest in a few days. I haven't got to the end myself yet.'

'I'll hand you over. Steve wants a quick word. Look forward to seeing you in a few weeks.'

'And I'm looking forward to seeing you too. Bye, Dad. Take care.'

Take care, thought Robyn. I'm picking up English sayings already. I bet everyone will think I sound like a total Pom when I get home.

Steve sounded a bit flustered when he picked up the phone. 'Sorry, Robs. Joey's a bit over-excited. Are you partying tonight?'

'Yeah, I'm in London staying with one of the cousins, Gerald. He's having a fancy dress party.'

'Have a great time. I'll pass you back to Mum. Jules and me and Joey send our love. See you soon.'

'Robbie? You be careful in London.'

'Yes, Mum. I'm safe here with Gerald. Grampy's here also.'

'Who's that?'

'Great Uncle William Rostrevor. Gerald is his grandson.'

'I remember William. I'd better go, Robbie. We'll be thinking of you when the clock strikes twelve. Looking forward to seeing you in a couple of weeks. Love you!'

Tears threatened, so Robyn went in search of distraction. Grabbing Gerald's list and her coat, bag and car keys she headed off to the supermarket.

The car park was full. After driving around in circles for some time she parked illegally several streets away. The scene inside the supermarket had to be seen to be believed. For a start, she had to queue for ten minutes to get in. And once inside she found some of the shelves were already stripped completely bare. The bakery had nothing more than a few crumbs; even the smell of bread was absent. Clearly a lot of people feared computer systems worldwide were about to crash and were stocking up in case the shops were unable to open again for a while.

It looked like a party was going on in the drinks aisle, and the shelves were rapidly emptying. A large man wearing flashing deely boppers was clumsily wheeling a heavy trolley containing countless bottles of Champagne. His female companion teetered behind him in a fur coat and high heels with another loaded trolley. A man in a pink rabbit suit was handing out leaflets – was he staff or a customer? He grabbed a pretty girl and kissed her, no mean feat through the rabbit head. The madness of the day was infectious. The queues at the checkouts snaked back down the aisles.

Luckily her hosts only needed a few bits and pieces. Robyn found butter, bacon and orange juice, but crème fraiche was out of the question.

She joined a queue and placed her basket on the floor, shuffling it forward with her feet as the line gradually crept towards the till. Her thoughts drifted back to Josephine's diary and food shortages during the war, wondering what Josephine would have made of today's excesses.

Robyn could tell the good-looking guy behind her was getting restless. She turned and smiled, hoping to strike up a conversation and while away the time.

'Jeez! The milk will be past its sell-by date by the time I get out of here,' grumbled Mr Caramel Eyes with yet another glance at the chunky Tag Heuer on his wrist.

Aha! A fellow Australian, thought Robyn. 'Yeah, and I'll probably miss my flight back to Sydney,' she quipped.

The caramel eyes focused on her. 'Here on holiday?'

Robyn shook her head. 'Work. I've been here for three months. What about you?'

'Mostly holiday, except when I'm crewing on my brother's yacht. We're moored in St Katharine's Dock. On the Thames, east of the Tower of London,' he added in response to her puzzled expression. 'Have you spent all your time in London?'

'No, I'm based in Eastleigh. That's in Hampshire, to the south. But at the moment I'm staying with my cousin in Fulham. Gee, living on a yacht must be fun!'

'We don't sleep on the yacht while we're moored. Greg has an apartment nearby. Hey, you'd better move up before some bastard decides to cut in on the queue!'

Robyn pushed her basket forward to close the gap. By the time she turned back, Caramel Eyes was tapping at the keypad of his mobile phone.

'Gee, that's a long number you're ringing,' she said, eager to keep the conversation going.

'Haven't you heard of texting?'

Robyn's compatriot seemed disinclined to talk further so she left him to play with his toy. She'd heard about text messaging but hadn't got round to trying it out.

Finally Robyn was through the checkout. As she lifted her bag of purchases she glanced back but Caramel Eyes was still preoccupied. Shame.

When she reached her car it was fortunately free of parking tickets. After a few minutes of driving she spotted a delicatessen with an empty parking space outside. Once inside she found a tub of crème fraiche, and noticed they also had orange juice, butter and bacon. She could have saved herself at least an hour and a half, but the prices in the deli were astronomical.

Back in Fulham she scoured the streets, hoping to find a space that was at least in the same postcode as her cousin. Successful at last, she returned to Gerald and Martin's where the atmosphere was one of ordered chaos. A small, harassed-looking florist was rushing from room to room with what looked like bundles of sticks, muttering under his breath about vases.

The kitchen looked like an explosion in a food factory. Robyn wedged her purchases into the overloaded fridge and retreated to her room.

She dutifully emailed Casey, Delia, Jenna and Tony with good wishes for Y2K. No word from Delia, so Robyn still had no idea whether her friend was annoyed about her dinner date with Nick.

Robyn dialled Lori's home number. Colin answered. 'Hi Colin,' she said as nonchalantly as possible. 'Is Lori there?'

With a curt acknowledgement he called for Lori.

'Hi there!' said Lori, sounding exceptionally cheerful.

'G'day. Sounds like you're in a good mood.'

'The prospect of a good night out, I suppose. Does this mean you'll be joining us?'

'Sorry. I'm in London staying with my cousin. He's having a bit of a do tonight. Should be okay, I suppose.'

'You don't sound too sure. In fact you sound a bit down.'

'Sorry. I just met this gorgeous bloke in the supermarket who was more interested in his mobile phone than talking to me. I'm going on a diet starting tomorrow. Gotta lose a stone before I go home.'

'You haven't gained *that* much weight, surely?'

'I dread to think. Haven't weighed myself since before Christmas. Anyway, enough about me. Have a great time tonight, and I'll see you back at work.'

'Happy New Year!' called Lori before hanging up.

Robyn felt guilty. She knew she should be downstairs offering to help, but she was more in the mood for curling up with a good book. A good diary. Flopping onto the bed, she took up where she'd left off.

24ᵗʰ November 1940

George called to visit us yesterday evening. He arrived in his new car, and the children were thrilled. He broke the news that Father and Maman *have been killed in the Blitz in London. They were at dinner with friends whose house scored a direct hit. It happened over a month ago. It feels very strange to think my parents have been dead all this time and I didn't know. But of course no-one knew how to contact George or myself. Eventually Father's solicitor traced George through some banking organisation. The solicitor also tried to contact our grandmother in Paris, but she has disappeared. No doubt due to this terrible war. So the upshot is that George is now Lord Kenner, and we stand to inherit quite a bit of money as well as Roskenner and the London house. The will apparently divides the estate equally between us. It hasn't quite sunk in yet. I feel numb and guilty that I didn't have an opportunity to say goodbye to them. How strange that* Maman, *who had been living at Roskenner, should be in London and at dinner with Father, when they had been more or less living separate lives. What an unfortunate twist of fate, and it's unlikely we will ever know why she was in London. Of course I will feel guilty taking their money. George feels, and I agree, that it will be best to sell everything: the two houses, the cars, the furniture ... it seems bizarre that two people had so much material wealth. George says he doesn't want to live at Roskenner, that he's not the slightest bit interested in the title of Lord Kenner. He's happy working in the bank and living in Truro with Lucy and the children, couldn't bear the thought of driving to and from Newlyn every day. I had a slight pang at the thought of selling the family home and our heritage, but George says one or both of us keeping it is just too complicated. Better to take the money and run. James and I will be able to buy a house of our own, possibly even a farm. It will be good not to be obligated to a landlord. It's always been nerve-wracking having a home tied to James's work, particularly since we found out about his heart trouble. But that at least has stabilised with medication. I expect it will take quite a few months for all the legal business to be done and everything to be sold, but we have plenty to look forward to.*

At the beginning of 1941 there was a new development.

James has been called up to serve with the Home Guard. Most of them are older men. James says he is glad to be able to do something at long last, as he has felt something of a fraud. He has been down to Falmouth Docks the past few nights, putting out fires after the bombing. Of course I worry every minute he is away, but this is far preferable than seeing him sent off to France. How I wish this miserable war would end!

The next entry, on 10th February 1941, described the family's new home.

222

We knew we wanted Penwithies Farm as soon as we saw it. It's a smallholding, nowhere near as large as any of the farms James has previously worked on, but it will be enough for us. We have an orchard, and I can't wait to see what fruit the trees will bear. When I wake in the morning and look out of the window I can't believe this place is all ours! We are applying for a Land Girl as James is off most days (and nights) with the Home Guard. But for the moment we are just about managing. The children are a tremendous help, and they love it here too. The house is delightful, and if it weren't for the restrictions of rationing we could furnish it as we please.

Robyn turned the page, but there was nothing more in the book. Puzzled, she picked up the next volume. It was written in a different hand. Ah, this must be where Maud took over.

21ˢᵗ May 1941

Since Father's death Mother has not felt like writing, so I feel it is my duty to continue.

Since Father's death? Robyn turned back to the previous book. Did she mean Charles Trethewey? But he was Josephine's father …

Robyn checked the inside cover of the new book: *The diary of Maud Amelia Rostrevor, Penwithies Farm, Trispen, near Truro, Cornwall, born 4ᵗʰ January 1927.*

Shocked, she realised James must have somehow died. How devastating for Josephine and the children! Robyn read on, expecting to learn that he had died serving his country.

We buried Father in the graveyard of St Athan's church. I do not know how we will carry on, but we must. Mother sits like a statue day after day, staring out of the window. She hasn't shed a single tear, not even at the funeral. I had to shout at her to get her to wash and dress for the funeral. This is most unlike Mother, who is always washed and dressed before William and I are out of our beds. But she has had a terrible shock. Everything was going so well. Mother and Father had not long since moved us to this lovely farm thanks to the money left us by the rich grandparents William and I never knew. And then Father was killed by one of our bulls, a tragic accident. They brought his broken body home and laid it on the kitchen table. Mother kept shaking his shoulders and shouting at him to wake up, but he was dead. My poor, dear Father.

Robyn felt tears well up in her eyes. What a tragic turn of events! Poor Maud, losing her father at just fourteen years of age. Not to mention having to cope with her mother going completely to pieces. Robyn read on through a blur of tears about James Rostrevor's funeral and the kindness of the local farming community. How through the weeks after his death Josephine had hardly moved from her chair. She read of Maud's efforts to keep the house clean and provide meals for the three of them. Of comforting William when his mother was unable to do so.

William is a brave boy, wrote Maud. *He has said little about his father dying, but he is doing everything he can to help me. He even sweeps the floor. We haven't been able to keep our evacuee, Miriam. I liked having another girl around the house but she's gone to live with Reverend Arden and his wife. And of course Mother has stopped helping at school. At least the Land Girl, Polly, is still here.*

Robyn began to think that the death of his father may have had something to do with William's reluctance to talk about his family. Perhaps it was still too painful.

The telephone on the bedside table rang at five to six.

'Tea's on the table,' chirped Martin.

'You guys are sooooo organised! I wasn't expecting anything to eat before the party.'

She suddenly regretted the packet of biscuits she'd scoffed while reading.

'It's only fish and chips.'

Martin's meal of 'only fish and chips' had been lovingly home-made, not purchased from a takeaway. After the meal Robyn returned upstairs to get ready for the party.

She showered, dried her hair and twisted it up into a French pleat. Then she slipped into the apricot satin dress, thinking it interesting how just a dress and shoes could transform her into something from the pages of a fashion magazine from decades gone by. The gloves also helped create the illusion. She turned this way and that in front of the mirror. The dress was a masterpiece of couture, with panels cut on the bias falling into lovely, soft folds. With her gut buster underneath holding in her paunch and keeping her ample behind under control she thought she looked quite presentable. Very much the descendant of a titled family!

With a slash of red lipstick and a liberal spraying of Chanel No. 5 Robyn looked and felt the part. She made her way downstairs, ready for whatever the turn of the new Millennium had in store.

Chapter 26

For a while it seemed as though the party would never get going.

Gerald and Martin had oohed and aahed over Robyn's outfit when she made her grand entrance. They were both smartly attired in black tie like a matching pair of up-market penguins. Grampy had made an effort and put on a dinner suit, complete with wing collar and white bow tie. He looked rather dapper.

The house gleamed from the attentions of the lady who 'did' for them, and the flowers were sumptuous. Robyn shuddered to think of the cost of such a quantity of lilies in winter.

In anticipation of guests, Gerald was hovering anxiously from room to room fiddling with the flowers. Martin was setting up the music: they had pre-recorded compilations which each ran for a couple of hours, doing away with the need for regular CD changes.

Grampy had settled himself in the kitchen and was watching TV, reports of millennium celebrations in parts of the world that had already passed the magical hour.

Gerald swept through the kitchen with an air freshener to disguise any lingering traces of the fishy pong from their tea.

'Calm down, son,' said Grampy, coughing. 'It smells like a tart's boudoir in here already.'

Time was ticking by and still no guests. Robyn settled in front of the TV with Grampy. Still Martin and Gerald fussed around, changing their bow ties and discussing whether the prawn crackers or the chilli cashews should be placed in the sitting room.

Then it all happened at once. The door knocker rapped constantly. A steady stream of brightly costumed guests milled in the front hall and spilled over into the rest of the downstairs rooms. Champagne corks popped like small arms fire. The house was filled with chatter and laughter underpinned with soft, sophisticated music.

Robyn hovered on the edges, envying Grampy his ability to mingle. Soon he was swapping stories with two elderly gents. She felt invisible in the throng of sophisticated guests, very much the country cousin in her second-hand frock.

She retreated to the kitchen, armed herself with a hefty gin and tonic, and hovered by the snacks, popping them into her mouth one after the other. It wasn't like a normal party. She was the only one in the kitchen apart from the waiters who had been hired for the evening. They chatted quietly among themselves as they polished glasses and popped trays of food in the oven.

Robyn struck up a conversation with one of the waitresses. Already getting the hang of regional accents, Robyn suspected she was from somewhere in the north of England.

'That's the trouble with nuts, isn't it?' said the girl, whose name was Coral. 'There's no such thing as eating one. And then you need another drink because of all the salt.'

Robyn grinned. 'Go on, have a handful,' she said, offering the dish.

'Thanks, love, but we're not allowed to eat on duty.'

'Gee, I'd never survive as a waitress. I can't stop eating for any length of time.'

'You're from Australia, right? Or New Zealand? Here on holiday?'

'Australia. I'm Gerald's cousin. I've been working in Hampshire for a couple of months. Office work. They don't mind if you have crisps or biscuits in your desk drawer. God, I've put on so much weight since I've been here! I don't stuff myself like this at home. Good thing I'm going back soon otherwise I'd get so fat they'd refuse to put me on the plane.'

'They don't do that, do they?' said Coral, her eyes widening in surprise.

'Only joking. But the weight I've put on is no joke. I'm going to have to live on lettuce for a year to get rid of it all.'

'I know what you mean. I only have to look at a biscuit and I put on a pound. I want to lose a stone before my holiday in May, so I'll be living on lettuce too. A right pair of rabbits we'll be!'

Coral generously imparted her top diet tips to Robyn, who had by this time moved on from the nuts to a tray of filo wrapped prawns fresh from the oven. She dipped another in chilli sauce and popped it whole into her mouth.

Gerald appeared in the doorway and wagged a finger at Robyn. 'Come on, my Robin-bird. Time to party. But wait a minute,' he said, reaching for a cloth and dabbing at a mark on her skirt which looked suspiciously like chilli sauce. 'Messy girl! There. I think you'll just about pass muster. Come with me and meet some people.'

Robyn grinned at Coral. 'Thanks for the info. See you later.'

Gerald grabbed Robyn by the wrist and dragged her into the sitting room. 'Roland, Esmeralda, this is my long-lost cousin Robyn from Australia. Now, where's that drinks waiter gone?'

Roland fixed Robyn with a beady stare. His tufty eyebrows seemed to have a life of their own, wriggling like dancing caterpillars. 'So. Visiting from the Antipodes?'

'From Sydney,' replied Robyn, trying not to stare at the caterpillars.

'Splendid place! Spent the summer there in '93. Or was it '92? Dashed if I can remember. Can you, Esmeralda?'

'Can I what, darling?' purred the tall, elegant lady, looking down her nose at Robyn as though she was a grubby mark on the carpet.

'Can you remember whether it was 1992 or 1993 when we last visited Sydney?'

'It was 1993.'

'Ah, yes. Carruthers lent us his place overlooking the harbour. Double Bay, I believe the area is called. I could have quite happily stayed there forever.'

'Gee, you were lucky. Double Bay is very, er, nice.' She'd been going to say expensive, but remembered it was bad manners to discuss what things cost.

'Which part of Sydney do you live in?' asked Esmeralda. Robyn decided she resembled Cruella de Vil with her pretentious cigarette holder and the grey wings of hair that swept over her ears.

'Newtown. Nowhere near the harbour.'

'Shame,' said Esmeralda. 'Stephanie! Darling!' she cried, turning her attention to another tall, skinny female who had just joined the group.

Lo and behold, Moira Hanley appeared in Stephanie's wake.

'Hello, Robyn,' she said. 'What a nice surprise to see you.'

'I decided to look Gerald up while visiting London, and he kindly invited me. Gee, you look lovely.'

'The dress belonged to my Grannie Annie, Grampy's wife. How are you getting on with the diaries?'

'They're fascinating. I've got as far as the Second World War. Is Josephine still alive?'

Moira shook her head and took a sip of her drink. 'Died years ago, aged around seventy. She never really recovered from losing James, and her daughter Maud dying young didn't help either.'

Robyn looked puzzled. 'I've just read about James dying, but what happened to Maud?'

'She died of cancer in her twenties. Not sure what year. Her two boys were very young. That would be your father and Morvah.'

'Strange. Dad's never mentioned anything about his mother dying. What about the others?'

'Maud's husband Frederick died years ago. I expect George, Josephine's brother, may be dead also. And his wife Lucy. No idea about their children though.'

Moira was distracted by a tall man making a bee-line for them. 'This is my husband, Richard,' she said. But when he turned to talk to someone else she whispered to Robyn. 'He's dead too, at least from the waist down. Is that a dreadful thing to say?'

Robyn giggled. 'You're not the only one without a sex life.'

'We should get together and go out on the pull one evening. But for now I'd better sweeten up the old toad, there's a diamond necklace in Mappin and Webb's window that I fancy.'

Moira turned her attention to her husband. Robyn was just about to drift away in search of another drink, when one of the men in the group with Richard Hanley caught her eye.

'Would you like to dance?' he asked in finest cut-glass tones. Robyn wondered whether Gerald and Martin knew anyone who wasn't posh.

'Okay,' she replied, throwing caution to the wind and allowing the man to steer her into the sitting room where several couples were waltzing sedately to elevator music.

Her dance partner was one of those rare men who can make a woman with three left feet feel as though she can dance. He was probably somewhere in his forties and looked a bit like Bryan Ferry.

'I've just returned from Sydney,' he informed her. 'My name's Giles. Giles Carruthers.'

'I'm Robyn Trescowe. From Sydney. Gee, are you the Carruthers with the place in Double Bay?'

He shook his head, puzzled. 'Must be some other Carruthers. I have just one house. In Surrey. I always say one house is enough for any man, as one can only be in one place at any given time.'

'Quite,' said Robyn, thinking the posh way of speaking must be catching. What would Mum and Dad think if she returned home sounding like Princess Anne?

'So what do you do, Robyn Trescowe?'

'I work for a firm of management consultants. Because I have dual nationality my boss sent me to England for a few months to sort out a problem with a client's subsidiary firm. I'm going home soon.'

'Lucky girl. You should arrive in time for the best of the summer. Think of us shivering here in England.'

'Don't you like living in England?'

'Of course, but there's no harm in wanting to spend time elsewhere. In any case I'm off on another little jaunt in May. Buenos Aires. Have you visited South America?'

'Not yet.'

'Make sure you see plenty of the world before some young man snaps you up, puts a ring on your finger and gives you a houseful of children to care for.'

'Are you married?'

Giles nodded with a hang-dog expression. 'That's my wife over there.'

The woman seemed a most unlikely match for Giles. She looked like mutton dressed as lamb in her frilly purple dress, and her overbleached blonde hair was coming adrift from its moorings as she and her partner danced a clumsy tango. The music had livened up in the interim.

'Pissed again, I'm afraid,' muttered Giles. 'Always gets completely rat-arsed at parties and makes a spectacle of herself trying to seduce anyone who takes her fancy. Claims she's bored at home now the children have grown up and flown the nest. Believe me, young Robyn. No amount of money can ensure happiness.'

Robyn was rather taken aback that Giles was confiding in a complete stranger. She felt a bit sorry for him.

'Gee, if anyone had asked me to guess which one was your wife I never would have picked her. Sorry, I didn't mean it to sound like that.'

'To tell the truth, I only married Camilla for her money. I used to work for her father. She pocketed his millions when he died. I suppose someone had to marry her. She's not a bad old stick really, as long as she keeps off the sauce. Would you like another drink?'

'Why not?'

'I'll be back in a minute.'

Robyn thought it a good opportunity to extricate herself from what could potentially become a tricky situation. Giles was getting a bit lecherous in drink, much like his wife. Pity they didn't lust after each other.

She slipped upstairs to the loo. A glance in the mirror confirmed that at least *her* hair was staying in place, and the sponged stain on her dress had dried leaving hardly a trace. She checked her teeth for stray bits of spinach (even though she didn't recall eating anything containing spinach) and took a sighting for the whereabouts of Giles before plunging back into the crowd. He was standing in the doorway of the sitting room, a glass of champagne in each hand, chatting with an elegant looking black man.

She ducked into the dining room. When all else fails, go in search of food, she thought. At that point Martin bustled in with two bottles of champagne.

'Charge your glasses, everyone!' he cried. 'Five minutes to midnight!'

Five minutes until the third millennium, thought Robyn a little wearily as she accepted another glass from Martin. She didn't feel particularly drunk, whereas many others looked the worse for wear.

Grampy appeared at Robyn's side on the stroke of midnight, and they clinked glasses.

'Happy New Year, young lady! I hope you've enjoyed your visit to England. Gerald tells me you're going home soon.'

'Yes, in a few weeks.'

Knowing what she now knew about Grampy's early life she avoided any mention of her enquiries about his ancestors.

Within seconds of the last chime of midnight Gerald and Martin organised a rowdy conga line, insisting their guests join in. With Martin in the lead, clutching a portable CD player from which a lively salsa tune blared, the party spilled out into the street. Martin hastily instructed a waiter to close the door after them, presumably in the hope of preventing intruders. Robyn thought it a sad indictment of their time that potential thieves could be waiting around in the hope of making off with the family jewels.

People from other houses ran out to join the conga as it wobbled on its way. They made it as far as the main road before the impromptu snake ran out of wriggles and fell apart.

'There you are, Robyn!' crowed Giles Carruthers triumphantly. 'Happy New Year!' he added, planting a smacker on her lips. 'Have some more champagne!'

'Thanks Giles, but I think I've had enough already,' she said, slipping deftly out of his grasp. If he had grown-up children that must mean he was around the same age as her father. Yuk!

Back inside the house, the hired help had replenished the supper table and were pouring more drinks. Robyn noted that Grampy had moved on to what looked like whisky, and hoped he wouldn't feel too sorry for himself in the morning. Throwing common sense to the four winds she accepted another glass of champagne and helped herself to a plateful of food. Oh dear, so much for the diet.

Chapter 27

Robyn felt surprisingly perky when she awoke just before eleven on the morning of January first. The house was silent, and there was only the faintest hum of traffic in the distance. She looked out of the bedroom window and saw a litter of champagne bottles, glasses and plates in the courtyard below. Smiling to herself, she went in search of her camera. This would be one for the album, she thought, sorry that she hadn't thought to capture for posterity any of the revelries of the night before. She wrestled with the window and leaned out to snap half a dozen shots from different angles.

After a welcome shower Robyn ventured downstairs. The kitchen was even worse than the courtyard. Martin was seated at the table looking palely dissipated, contemplating a glass of something cloudy.

'Morning, Martin!' she chirped. 'What about a nice fry-up to sort you out?'

'Oh, please ...' he protested, turning a shade paler.

'Gerald still in bed?'

Martin shook his head. 'Gone for a run. Don't know where he gets his stamina. I just want to die. My head feels like it could shatter at any moment.'

'Can I get you anything? Headache tablets?'

'This fizzy stuff should help. Did you enjoy yourself last night?'

'It was very nice, thanks,' said Robyn. It was just a small white lie. Martin and Gerald had gone to a lot of trouble to organise the party, and it wasn't their fault that she would have preferred to be in Sydney.

'What are your plans for today?' asked Martin with a grimace as he swallowed the last of his hangover cure.

'Um, no idea. Any suggestions?'

'You might like to do some shopping. The New Year sales will be starting today. High Street Kensington is a good bet for designer bargains.'

'Maybe I'll give that a try. Thanks. Are you sure I can't get you anything to eat? And help you clear up?'

'No, really. We have cleaners coming, they should be here soon.'

'Wow! That's the way to do it.'

'Send one's footman to wash one's champagne glasses. Pity the servants can't suffer my hangover for me.'

An hour later Robyn was making her way along Kensington High Street when she saw it. The coat of her dreams. She stood transfixed in front of the shop window. The coat was black, beautifully cut, with a froth of black furry stuff at the collar and cuffs. Without hesitating she went inside, and the sales assistant, by coincidence another Australian, got it out of the window. Robyn slipped it on.

'It really suits you,' said the assistant. 'The collar and cuffs are faux fur, and detachable. Soooo flattering!' she gushed.

Robyn could only agree. The coat was slim fitting but not too tight. Its elegant lines took pounds off her. Then she looked at the price tag. That would take a vast number of pounds off her also. Still, she had to have it.

Robyn kept the new coat on and took her old, moth-eaten one away in a smart carrier emblazoned with the store's logo. She'd hardly gone a block before she saw a woman sitting in a doorway wrapped in a sleeping bag. She thrust the bag into the bewildered woman's lap with best wishes for a happy new year before hurrying off down the street. She imagined the woman's disappointment at finding an old coat inside the fancy bag and didn't dare look back. At least she was recycling and saving the planet.

Then, in an exclusive department store, she saw something that looked like an ideal gift for Gerald and Martin: a bottle of Chinese gooseberry liqueur. Martin had mentioned that they liked inventing cocktails, and as far as she knew they didn't have any gooseberry liqueur.

Having blown enough money to keep her credit card in the red for the foreseeable future, Robyn decided to call it a day on the shopping front. She took the underground back to Fulham. As the train rocked along she tried to find ways to broach the subject of his mother's death with her father. Tricky.

The house looked much more orderly by the time she arrived. Gerald was returning their precious knick-knacks to their rightful places on the shelves.

'Ooh! Is that a new coat?' he enquired.

Robyn gave him a twirl.

'I didn't like to say anything, my Robin-bird, but the other one did absolutely nothing for you.'

'I know. I've been waiting to find the right one.'

Martin came in to add his approval.

'Where's Grampy?'

'I've just returned from dropping him at the station,' said Gerald. 'He's on his way home. He said to give you his best wishes.'

'I'm sorry I didn't get a chance to say goodbye. Still, I expect I'll see him at Emily and Morvah's. I'm going down in a couple of weeks to pay them a farewell visit.

'We should pop in and visit next time we're down that way,' said Gerald, standing back to admire his collection of glass Lalique goldfish. 'It's been simply years since I last saw them.'

'I've been doing some family research for my father, and Moira has lent me some old diaries,' said Robyn. She went on to outline what she'd discovered so far.

'My dear, that's simply amazing! I'll be giving Grampy a stern telling-off next time I see him for not filling me in on all the facts.'

'I get the feeling he's a bit touchy about it. I tried asking him some questions the first time I met him at Morvah and Emily's and he denied knowing anything. He might not want to dwell on things like his mother's death.'

'I see what you mean. Anyway, I'm stunned that we're descended not only from British titled folk but French also! I must look into a proper coat of arms to replace that rubbish one I painted. That will be such fun!'

After lunch Robyn felt as though the night before was beginning to catch up with her. She made her apologies and headed upstairs for a nap. But sleep proved elusive, so she dug out the diaries once more. She was by this time working her way through the second-last volume. Maud Rostrevor wrote less regularly than her mother.

11th July 1941

Mother, William and I have moved on from Penwithies farm to a nice house on the outskirts of Truro. It is such a luxury to be able to see a house we like and simply buy it outright, though I don't think Mother appreciates it as much as she should. To me the fact that we are comfortably off is some compensation for my father having died so young. I don't think Mother ever realised how much I hated to see her scrimping and saving, putting coins in different tins each week to cover the various expenses. I just wish my dear Father was still with us to enjoy the money.

233

Uncle George has explained that if we are careful with our money, investing it wisely, we will receive a decent rate of interest. Enough to live on. We have taken his advice, putting some in a savings account that we can access, and the rest in long-term investments. Mother should never need to work again. Not that she's capable of much. She is a shadow of her former self since Father died, able to do little more than light housework and a bit of cooking. I do as much as I can. I would gladly leave school, but Mother insists my education is important.

Several months elapsed before Maud's next entry.

24th October 1941

We are so lucky here, hardly touched by the terrible war. London and other cities have been so badly bombed. Our only difficulty is the rationing, but that is little hardship compared with those who have lost their loved ones and homes. It seems as though this war will never end. William hopes it continues at least until he's old enough to enlist. How typical of a boy! I tore him off a strip after he made that announcement at dinner, reminding him that it would be the last straw for his dear mother if he got himself killed. Hopefully that made him see sense.

It didn't, for William ran off to enlist shortly after, much to Maud's disgust.

Subsequent entries dealt with passing her exams at school, their acquisition of a dog, and mention of Frederick Trescowe, one of the boys Josephine had tutored at the Trescowe farm, starting work at the bank under Uncle George, who was by this time manager. The Rostrevor finances appeared to be holding up, and there was no mention of Maud seeking work after leaving school. She seemed to spend her days looking after the household and dabbling in watercolours.

I am so excited! wrote Maud in June 1943. *A tourist has bought some of my paintings! When he and his wife approached me on the river bank I hardly took them seriously, but now he has called at the house and paid the princely sum of two pounds each for three of my studies of the trees by the river. Nothing could make me happier. Except, of course, for my brother to return home safely.*

Robyn smiled. It was heart-warming to read about Maud gaining the confidence to exhibit her work in the Truro Summer Exhibition of 1944. She sold all six paintings on show, and Frederick Trescowe had invited her to tea.

In a diary entry dated 1st March 1945 Maud announced her engagement to Frederick. Ah, thought Robyn. This is where we became Trescowes, and Frederick's parents were of course the owners of the farm where James and Josephine had lived. Where Maud had been born. Mystery solved. Robyn took a break to email this information to her father.

Two months later Maud reported that the war had ended.

That means William will be coming home. What a relief! she wrote.

So here was Grampy returning from the war that he was still talking about more than fifty years later. Robyn wondered why Frederick hadn't fought for his country.

Further on, Maud wrote about her wedding preparations.

11th June 1946

It is so frustrating. I have plenty of money, but I cannot get hold of enough coupons to buy sufficient material to have a full-length wedding dress made, or to put on a decent spread at our reception. Still, I will do my best.

Two weeks later Maud described her wedding.

25th June 1946

Today was blissfully sunny, and the church looked a picture. Mrs Trescowe did us proud with the flower displays. Funny to think she is now my mother-in-law and that I too am now Mrs Trescowe. The marriage service passed like a dream. Everyone said my dress looked lovely even though it finished just below my knees. Mrs T came to the rescue once more with provisions from the farm, which helped greatly towards our reception at the church hall. Altogether perfect! I felt so glamorous in my going-away outfit, a stylish beige suit that was one of Mother's. From Harrod's, would you believe! Mother looked very smart in a blue suit and seemed happier and more animated today. Then Frederick and I drove off into the sunset in his smart new car. We are honeymooning in Ilfracombe. I can't say I enjoy Frederick's nocturnal activities in the bedroom, but I suppose if one wants babies one has to endure such things. I had no idea that men's bodies were so unattractive, or that they would be inclined to rut and grunt like animals. I can't imagine Mother and Father ever having done such things to create William and myself. They always seemed such a romantic couple. Perhaps Frederick is doing it wrong? I dare not ask Mother. Perhaps I can pluck up the courage to discuss it with my friend Cissie when we return home. That reminds me, I must be careful to find a safe hiding place as I wouldn't wish Frederick to find my diaries and read the nonsense I write, particularly about such personal matters.

Ah, but how my life is about to change! We are moving to a brand new house with new furniture. That's what I like most about Frederick I suppose, his good job and healthy bank balance. We will not be too far from Mother, and Frederick says he will teach me to drive and buy me a car of my own.

Robyn grinned. It was a bit cringe-making reading about her grandparents' sex life, but it was interesting to learn that Maud wasn't as sensual as Josephine had been. Maybe Maud *had* married the wrong man.

Robyn skimmed through a couple of pages about the new house and all the mod cons of the late 1940s, which amounted to little more than an electric washing machine and refrigerator 'like you see in the American films'. Maud also had high praise for her new vacuum cleaner. She even took the vacuum cleaner to her mother's once a week in her car so that she could give the carpets a thorough going over. It seemed that Josephine still did little more than stare into the distance and reminisce, but events occasionally prompted a reaction.

14th January 1949

Frederick came home last night and told us about a new client, a Mr Sinclair. Mother was with us for dinner. I suppose it's a bit naughty of Frederick to talk about the bank's business, but he knows I like to hear about what goes on. This Mr Sinclair is very wealthy, he's made a lot of money in stocks and shares. Then when Frederick mentioned that Sinclair's father was a Frenchman Mother dropped her soup spoon with a great clatter. She turned pale, and I thought she seemed about to faint. But she recovered quickly and ate the rest of her soup.

Later in the kitchen I asked her what was wrong, and she asked me if I knew that her mother was French. It seems odd talking about my mother's parents. I never met them due to some strange family feud, and they died at the beginning of the war.

Reading further, Robyn learned yet more about the Sinclair familly.

31st January 1949

At Mother's request I have made some discreet enquiries and found Hubert and Madeleine were not actually the parents of Robert Sinclair, client of the bank. He was their nephew.

Robyn remembered earlier reference to a Hubert and Madeleine in Josephine's diaries, and began to wonder whether there was a connection.

Hubert and Madeleine died childless and left their entire estate to Robert, the only son of Hubert's brother, Marcel. Robert, it appeared, went to great pains to disguise his French origins and changed his name from St Clair to

Sinclair. Frederick drew the man out in conversation, flattering him by saying no-one would know from his accent that he was anything other than an English gentleman. Sinclair said he spent hours with an elocution teacher to eradicate any traces of an accent.

Mr Sinclair has invited us to his home for dinner this coming Saturday, wrote Maud on December 7th, 1949. *I only hope my morning sickness doesn't last all day. Did I mention, dear diary, that I am expecting my first child? Due early next July. Frederick treats me as though I am made of delicate porcelain, and luckily I am spared the rigours of the bedroom for at least the duration of my pregnancy.*

Back to the subject of Robert Sinclair's family. Mother pointed me to the early parts of her diary. Ugh! To think that my father had relations with Robert Sinclair's Aunt Madeleine! Just imagine if that union had brought forth a child! And equally disturbing that my French grandmother Caroline was having an affair with Hubert. Such goings-on! Mother says she has often wondered whether her younger brother Lucien, who drowned, had been fathered by Hubert. But of course there is no way of knowing.

I told Mother I was disgusted to think that my father had an affair with a married woman, but strangely she doesn't seem in the least troubled. She says it happened before they met, and Madeleine forced him to make love to her with the threat that if he didn't she would ensure that he lost his job on the Roquebrun farm. She says we must remember all of Father's excellent qualities and dismiss from our minds those things that were not his fault.

Maud returned to her writing a few days later.

11th December 1949

It is a foul day, but Frederick has nevertheless gone for a walk so I am left in peace by the warmth of the fire to write my diary. Our diary. The joint effort of my mother and myself. Ever more linked by history and coincidence, it seems. It was interesting to meet Robert Sinclair last night. He and his wife live in a mansion near St Ives, surrounded by acres of parkland. They have put in a tremendous amount of work, or should I say, they have paid a tremendous amount of money for artisans to restore the house. I would have felt totally overwhelmed by them were it not for my insight into Robert's family. Elizabeth, his wife, is the daughter of a Lord, and Robert behaves as though he too were born into the aristocracy. No mention whatsoever of his French forebears. He did however make some reference to his Uncle Hubert having been a terrible womaniser, but nothing about his aunt, and nothing about their having been French. I will never, ever tell Frederick about my father and Madeleine, or my grandmother and Hubert. He would in all probability disown me, even though I am with child. Children do make a woman vulnerable, even in these modern times. At least I do not yet look pregnant, that delight is yet to come. I only hope I can get my figure back afterwards. Mother is still slim as a wand after two children, so I hope I will be similarly lucky.

Robyn read more ramblings about Frederick's importance at the bank, being considered Uncle George's right hand man. Then further mention of William. Robyn stood up a moment to stretch, hopping around the room until her numb left foot came back from the dead.

9ᵗʰ May 1950

William is to be married. He seems so happy. He was very much at a loose end for some time after the war, but these past few months he has turned his life around. He has started work as a postman, and has become engaged to a girl named Annie Trelawney. She is a farmer's daughter. My only problem is that my baby is due shortly after their wedding. I will look simply awful in the photographs! I'm enormous already, my stomach is like a barrel. I wonder whether I am expecting twins?

Robyn looked down at her own plump stomach. She stood sideways before the mirror, sticking her stomach out to its full extent. Gee, just like being six months pregnant, she thought. But there was no baby in there, just the memory of lots of cakes and take-aways.

Robyn resumed reading.

12ᵗʰ June 1950

Frederick tells me that Elizabeth and Robert Sinclair have just had a son. I am astounded, for she didn't even look the tiniest big pregnant when I last saw her. Perhaps the upper classes have minions to bear their children for them? They have named the child Paul, which is a proper, saintly name. I would quite like to call my child Paul if it is a boy, but that would look as though I was copying the Sinclairs. So I'll have to think of something else. Maybe it'll be a girl. Who knows? We'll have to wait a little longer to see.

Robyn looked at her watch. Six o'clock already. She'd been in her bedroom for hours. Gerald and Martin would think she was very hung-over and sleeping it off. It was time she showed her face to make amends, so she brushed her hair and went downstairs.

They were slumped in the sitting room in front of some dubious television programme.

'Hi, guys! What are you watching?'

'God knows,' said Martin. 'I'm so tired I could watch EastEnders without complaining.'

'How about I cook dinner tonight? I do a mean omelette.'

'I think I could just about manage to eat something,' said Martin. 'Are you sure you don't mind? We could always send out for an Indian.'

'Oo-er!' said Gerald in his campest voice. 'I didn't think you liked the chocolate-flavoured ones.'

Martin shot Gerald a withering glance. 'Don't take any notice of him, dear. Just shout if you can't find anything you need.'

Robyn went through to the kitchen, which was pristine once more. The fridge was stuffed to bursting with all sorts of exotic fare, and before long she had concocted a massive omelette which she divided between three plates and carried through to the sitting room.

They passed a pleasant evening watching some very low-brow television. After they'd eaten, Martin said he felt like he needed a hair of the dog.

'I know!' said Gerald. 'Cocktails! Fruity little things that slip down so easily you don't realise they're full of alcohol. We can try out that bottle you gave us.'

'I've got to drive back to Hampshire tomorrow,' warned Robyn.

'I'll make sure they're not too strong,' promised Gerald.

The two men ended up competing with each other to make the most extravagant concoctions. Robyn realised as she tried one cocktail after another that she was becoming quite drunk.

Chapter 28

When Robyn awoke the following morning she had no recollection of having gone upstairs to bed the night before. She didn't emerge from her room until early Sunday afternoon, and was definitely unfit to drive. She went for a walk by the Thames mid-afternoon to clear her head, then, once back in her bedroom, decided she really should telephone Emily.

It was Emily who picked up the phone.

'Hello, dear. Happy New Year!'

'Same to you, Emily. Good party?'

'We had a lovely time.'

As Emily chattered on about the silly games they'd played, Robyn wondered how to broach the possibility of Morvah's mother having died when he was a baby. But there was no tactful way of doing it.

'Moira and her husband were at Gerald's party, and I spent some time talking to her. Did you know Dad and Morvah's mother died when they were young?'

'No, dear. Are you sure?'

'Moira says she died of cancer when Morvah was a baby.'

'But that's ridiculous! Morvah's mother died in her late sixties. Surely you remember staying with her when you were little? Given the amount she drinks I wouldn't have too much faith in Moira's memory.'

'Gee, you're probably right, Emily. But I remember Dad saying he was puzzled why his mother's name was shown as Maud in official records when as far as he remembers she was called Nellie. I wonder whether Frederick remarried after Maud died. I think I need to check things out at that records office here in London. And I must finish reading the diaries.'

'Okay, dear. But for the moment I won't say anything to Morvah about his mother.'

Robyn went in search of the London telephone directory and dialled the number of the Public Records Office. She listened to a recorded message advising that it was no longer possible to visit the Public Records Office to obtain copies of certifiates. A telephone or internet service was available, but the office was closed until January 10th. Damn! Then she remembered her Dad mentioning the parish records in Cornwall. Hopefully they'd have what she needed.

Robyn spent another companionable evening with Martin and Gerald and an Indian takeaway.

'No cocktails tonight, please!' she pleaded. 'I really must go tomorrow.'

Robyn awoke on Monday morning feeling refreshed. She gathered her belongings and was on her way by ten o'clock.

'Come back and see us. Any time!' called Martin from the doorstep.

'Try to pop in before you fly out,' added Gerald.

'Thanks again, guys,' said Robyn, cramming her bag into the back seat. 'It's been great getting to know you.'

'Have a safe journey,' called Gerald as Robyn reversed anxiously around an expensive-looking Daimler. With a final wave she was off.

Back in Eastleigh, Robyn found the house empty except for Rhubarb asleep on the sofa. The cat barely opened an eye as he tolerated her affectionate greeting. His middle was warm and soft, and he was certainly putting on weight.

'Welcome to the pudding club, Rhubarb,' said Robyn. 'My diet started today, what about yours?'

She knew she would miss the little cat when she returned to Australia.

Robyn decided to telephone her parents, calculating it would be around nine p.m. in Sydney. If Dad was in and out of hospital he probably wasn't checking his emails regularly, because she hadn't heard from him in a while. She decided not to say anything about the Maud/Nellie conundrum until she had more information.

'Hello Robbie,' said Rose. 'Lovely to hear from you again. Did you enjoy your party?'

'Yes, Mum. How are you? And Dad?'

'Robbie, I've got a bit of bad news. The doctor told us today that they're not going to be able to operate. Your Dad's heart isn't strong enough. Robbie? Are you still there?'

Robyn forced herself to speak. 'Yes, Mum. Oh, I'm so sorry. How did he take it?'

'He hasn't said much, love. Between you and me I don't think he's going to last much longer. Maybe a month ...'

'Oh, Mum! You must be devastated.'

'You may think it strange, but I'm relieved in a way that he won't have to suffer too much longer. It's been very hard watching him deteriorate over the past few weeks.'

'Oh, Mum! I wish you'd said. I would have come home sooner.'

'No point, love. Nothing can make my Joe well again.' Rose drew in a great, sobbing gulp.

'I'll get onto the airline right away, change my flight. I can probably be back within a few days.'

'There's nothing you can do, love.'

'Maybe not, but I want to spend as much time as I can with Dad,' said Robyn, holding back the sobs in her voice. 'Have you told Steve?'

'I've just come back from visiting them. He said for me to ring him any time if I need to talk. And he'll be popping in every day.'

'You can ring me, too. You've got my mobile number if you can't get me at Maggie's. I'll let you know just as soon as I've sorted things out with the airline. I'll be home soon. Love you, Mum.'

'Love you too, Robbie. And Dad sends his love. 'Bye, darling.'

Robyn rang off in a daze. She couldn't cry. This wasn't real. She'd get back to Sydney and it would all be a mistake, an error in diagnosis. Mum and Dad and Steve and Jules and Joey would be there to meet her at the airport, and they'd go home and have lunch under the grape vines on the patio.

Maggie returned at that moment, sweeping into the house laden with bags from the supermarket. 'Hello Robyn! Happy New Year!' she called.

Robyn turned and the flood gates opened. She fell into Maggie's arms and sobbed. She wept uncontrollably until there was nothing left, until she was dehydrated and Maggie's shirt was soaked. Between sobs she brought Maggie up to date on the latest news from home.

Maggie sat Robyn at the kitchen table and made her a cup of tea, the British panacea for all ailments, she said. Robyn wished a few good cups of British tea could fix her father.

'So. Back home without delay,' said Maggie.

'Yeah. I'd better ring the airline.'

'You'll get through this, love.'

Robyn rang the airline, explained her situation, and the pleasant-voiced man at the other end of the phone changed her flight to the following Friday, departing at 1.00 p.m.

Robyn rang her mother, and they had a more cheerful conversation.

'I'll see you early on Sunday morning, Mum. I'll get a taxi from the airport.'

Maggie made another cup of tea and they settled in the sitting room.

'I'm still wading through the diaries,' Robyn explained. 'Maud, my grandmother, has taken over from her mother, Josephine. Josephine hasn't been the same since her husband died. Actually he's not her husband, they never married ...'

'It's already getting too complicated for me,' protested Maggie, munching on a biscuit.

'I'll shut up and read quietly,' said Robyn with a feeble smile.

'Just think, if you hadn't come to England and met your relatives none of this would have come out. Your Dad must be very pleased with your detective work.'

'I must get the rest of the diaries copied to take back to him. There are so many things I need to do before Friday. Waldron won't be open until Wednesday, so I'll have to find a photocopy shop. I must tell Nick I'm going home on Friday, I hope he won't mind. And I must get down to Cornwall again to check out some more stuff. Gee, if only I hadn't wasted yesterday!' Robyn's voice rose in despair. 'And there's no time to get together with everyone again ...'

'You can phone them all to say goodbye, they'll understand.'

'You're right, Maggie. I suppose that's better than nothing. And I must phone Lori too. Don't worry, I'll pay you for all these calls.'

'Don't worry about it, dear. I'll help you, and somehow we'll get you on that plane on Friday. Now don't start crying again.'

'I won't, I promise. I'll phone Lori first.'

Lori wanted to meet Robyn that evening. She said she had some news. Robyn agreed, despite not feeling much like going out. But she knew it might be her last chance to say goodbye to Lori.

Maggie was curled up in her armchair reading a magazine. Robyn still had four hours to kill before she had to get ready to go out, so she settled into the last diary with another cup of tea and some Jaffa Cakes. So much for the diet she'd started that morning.

Maud was on her high horse.

17th June 1950

Annie Trelawney is common, there's no other word for it. She is a vulgar, scheming little farm girl who has seduced my poor brother with her feminine wiles. I envisage losing touch with William after his marriage, which grieves me, but I have no desire to be united with that girl and her family.

We had the Sinclairs over for dinner on Saturday night. Elizabeth was charming as always, but Robert made some unnecessary comments about the size of our house compared with theirs. He may be rich, and Frederick no doubt wants to cultivate him as a friend, but I don't like the man. He got quite drunk and unpleasant. I don't suppose he falls out of public houses at closing time like Annie Trelawney's father, but he is like a pig in a trough in drink and I don't like him encouraging Frederick. Frederick was quite squiffy on Saturday night and was most put out when I wouldn't do my marital duty. At least Elizabeth didn't partake of alcohol, she said it's because she is breast feeding. But she left the baby with his nanny. I was quite surprised that someone so well-to-do would feed her baby at the breast, and I'm still not convinced that she has indeed given birth to that baby.

At least the men left us in peace when they went into the study for port and cigars. Frederick told me later that Robert was bragging about his Uncle Hubert again, saying he was rich enough to buy his way out of any scrapes with the law. In my opinion Robert Sinclair thinks he is also rich enough to give the police a back-hander, and Frederick needs to be careful not to get too deeply involved with him. Apparently the uncle killed a friend's servant, a girl who threatened to tell his wife that he'd made her pregnant. It seemed that Madame St Clair was the one with all the money, and Hubert didn't want to risk being slung out on his ear without a penny. He blamed the murder on one of the servants, but the lad managed to escape before the police got hold of him.

Robyn was intrigued. Hubert St Clair a murderer? Then it dawned on her that this may have been the murder that was blamed on James. Had Josephine ever known the truth?

She read on.

1ˢᵗ July 1950

William and Annie's wedding was surprisingly pleasant. William scrubbed up smartly, and Annie looked very sweet. I noticed she was drinking lemonade, and William says she doesn't touch alcohol because she's seen what it does to her father. Mrs Trelawney made all the food for the reception, which was held under the trees in the field behind their house. The weather was glorious. Unfortunately I felt very tired, and disgruntled that I looked like a hippopotamus. Pregnancy is so tedious! Mr Trelawney behaved himself. I think Annie may have had a word with him,

for I saw him raise only one glass of beer in a toast to the happy couple.
The rest of the time he seemed to be drinking water. It could have been neat
gin I suppose, but he seemed sober. William seems so happy. Perhaps I was
hasty in my judgement of his bride and her family.

Robyn felt a glow of happiness at reading a first-hand account of
Grampy's wedding day. She vaguely remembered Annie from the time
spent in England when she was young.

Robyn flipped through the rest of the diary. There wasn't much more of
Maud's tiny, neat writing to read. She contemplated giving Gerald a call to
say goodbye but decided to wait until she'd finished reading.

4th July 1950

My son is born, wrote Maud. *It was a painful experience and I am torn*
asunder, but we have a healthy boy. Frederick has agreed that we will call
him Joseph. I am thankful that I will be through the worst of the sleepless
nights before the cold and dark of winter. I must plan to have the remainder
of my children in the summer. We cannot stop at one, much as I dislike the
means of conception. I shall do my duty.

Robyn laughed, and Maggie looked up from her magazine.

'My grandmother didn't enjoy sex,' explained Robyn. 'Though I've just
read about my father's birth, and he has a brother so she must have done it
at least twice. Make that three times. She wrote about losing her virginity on
her wedding night.'

Maggie peered over her glasses. 'Those diaries of yours sound pretty X-
rated.'

'I suppose both Josephine and Maud must have kept their diaries locked
away in order to write so freely.'

'And now, in the liberated twenty-first century, you sit at home reading
about their sex lives.'

'Thanks, Maggie. I really needed to be reminded of my single status.
Though I'm pleased to inform you that I have lost my virginity.'

'Too much information!' protested Maggie.

Robyn resumed reading, determined to finish the last book before she
went out.

14th January 1951

Uncle George and his wife and their four children came to Joseph's
christening. I haven't seen much of Uncle since my marriage. Mother seems
disinclined to keep in contact, she still lives very much in the past with her
memories. Frederick finds Uncle quite an exacting boss, and therefore
doesn't choose to see him outside banking hours. He says the other staff

whisper behind their hands that he gets preferential treatment from George, but if anything the reverse is true.

Uncle George is very much a family man, he adores Lucy and the children and spends all his spare time with them. He doesn't get about so well these days with his gammy leg. I think he's worn a calliper practically all his life, poor man.

William and Annie are already expecting their first child, due to arrive next summer.

Robert and Elizabeth Sinclair gave our son a very extravagant christening present, a silver-plated cup, plate, fork and spoon. Frederick insisted on inviting them whereas I would have preferred to keep the occasion just for family. I felt awkward because we didn't give them anything when Paul was born, and we weren't invited to his christening. Paul is a plump little boy, with white blond hair unlike either of his parents. Perhaps it will darken with age. At least he behaved well, not like George's boy, Hugh, who put jelly down the back of his little sister's dress. From the way she screamed you'd think her brother had put a live eel down her back. Uncle George and Aunt Lucy don't discipline their children enough for my liking, but far be it for me to say anything. My little Joseph behaved well, and hardly murmured at all when the minister dabbed him with water. It is easier to love a well-behaved child, and I hope I will be as fortunate with my next. For I have a feeling I am pregnant once more.

That must have been Morvah on the way, thought Robyn. Then another thought began to form in her mind. St Clair … Sinclair … Paul. Was it too much of a coincidence that the fraudster she had exposed at Waldron might be related to Hubert St Clair? He would be the right age, she thought, remembering that the Paul Sinclair in the diaries had been born shortly before her father, and knowing that Paul Sinclair from Waldron was also around fifty now. He'd told her that his family had owned a vast estate somewhere near St Ives. If only she could remember the name he'd mentioned.

4th February 1951

I am indeed pregnant, and glad to be able to plead abstinence in the bedroom. I let slip to Mother that I don't welcome Frederick's attentions, and she thinks I'm prudish. I suppose her passionate nature comes from her French blood. I said that the French passion seems to have skipped a generation with me, but Mother says there's a man out there somewhere who could make me feel differently. I have no desire to go in search. It was nice though to have a light-hearted conversation with Mother for a change.

Mother went on to say that she and Father used to steal away to make love when they lived on their island. I told her she was disgusting to have given her body before marriage, and then she dropped the bombshell. She and Father were never married, they merely lived together as man and wife. I am appalled! I feel unable to walk down the street with my head held high. Mother has given me her early diaries to read in the hope that I will understand.

Robyn couldn't help thinking there was some justice in Maud discovering she was illegitimate, for she sounded stuck-up and quick to put others down. But at least she seemed to have been a dedicated mother.

4ʰ July 1951

Today is my darling Joseph's first birthday. We had a little party, just us three and Mother. Frederick bought him a fancy rocking horse that is far too big and frightened him somewhat at first, but he is a plucky child, and was soon rocking back and forth on his new toy. I feel less well in this pregnancy, and very tired. I will be glad when my nine months are up.

16ᵗʰ July 1951

Annie has given birth to a girl who they have named Catherine. I am envious that Annie looks so well, and is back on her feet so quickly after giving birth. She is not that much younger than me.

Then Robyn read about Morvah's arrival in the world on September 12ᵗʰ, 1951. She smiled at stories of his babyhood activities, and hoped she would remember to tease him about having peed in his mother's lap while sitting in church.

Then Maud's tale took a more serious turn. It seemed she had some problems after Morvah was born.

30ᵗʰ September 1951

I have been unwell in the stomach for some months. At first I put it down to my pregnancy, but now that the baby is born something seems to be wrong with my insides. I wasn't this bad after Joseph was born. The doctor is sending me to have some tests done. I do hope I will be able to have more children.

12ᵗʰ October 1951

Tomorrow I am to have an exploratory operation on my stomach, which is mysteriously swollen although Doctor Albright says I am definitely not pregnant. I am concerned that Frederick and Mother will struggle to look after the boys while I am in hospital.

21ˢᵗ October 1951

At last I am back at home. I have missed my children! I hope I never again have to endure such a long stay in hospital. The Matron is a fearsome woman. Doctor Albright said they removed a growth the size of a large potato from my stomach. I must take things slowly, for it will take time for the wound to heal. I am not able to do any housework, so Frederick has organised a live-in housekeeper, a widow named Eleanor Prendergast. She is occupying the spare bedroom and seems very capable. I am fortunate to have a husband who earns a decent wage and can afford such a luxury.

25th October 1951

I fear that I will never again know good health. I am now bedridden and feel very weak. The days come and go, as do my husband and darling sons. Mrs Prendergast takes good care of the boys, and is an excellent cook and housekeeper. Frederick has bought single beds for us, and I am more comfortable in my own space and glad not to keep him awake so much when I am restless. Frederick says little, but I can tell from the way he looks at me that he is most concerned for my well-being. William and Annie visit every now and then and bring little Catherine, who is adorable. Mother visits several times a week. She sits with me for hours on end, ready to chat when I have the strength, otherwise working on her embroidery. She has made a beautiful cloth for my tea tray embroidered with irises in pale lilac, my favourite flowers. Her work is exquisite. I wish I had the strength to take up my brushes and paint, but I feel no inspiration, only pain and weariness.

28th October 1951

Doctor Albright called again today and took Frederick aside for a chat after examining me. I heard Frederick see him to the door, then he came up to talk with me. I knew something was very much amiss because Frederick wouldn't look me in the eye. It's bad news, I'm afraid. Doctor Albright says it appears the cancer was too far advanced for the operation to have been successful, and that I will probably not survive more than a few weeks. Oh, my poor little boys! I will never see them grow into men. My poor mother, who has already lost her husband, will shortly lose her daughter. How will I tell her? I am so very afraid. I don't want to die.

Robyn's eyes filled with tears, and she rummaged in her sleeve for a tissue. Maggie looked up at the sound of Robyn blowing her nose.

'More tears?'

'Sorry. Gee, this is sad! My grandmother is dying of cancer.'

'Are you sure you should be reading that in your present state of mind?'

'It's okay. Anyway, I've nearly finished. I promise I won't cry too much.'

There was only one more entry, written in a shaky hand.

30th October 1951

I have decided I must give these diaries to Mother when she next calls. It is up to her whether she takes up her pen again. I have done my part in recording the history of our family since Father's death. Now it is my turn to die.

Robyn felt hollow as she closed the cover of the last notebook. Poor Dad and Morvah, motherless at an early age. Moira had been right after all. Poor Maud, whom she now felt she knew intimately though they had never met.

'That's it, all done,' said Robyn to Maggie. 'I've decided to pop down to Cornwall tomorrow. There are some things I need to check in the parish register of the church where Dad was christened. I'd better phone Emily.'

Emily must have been sitting on the phone as she answered immediately.

'Hi Emily. Bad news I'm afraid. Dad isn't expected to last more than a few weeks, so I'm flying home on Friday.'

'Oh, Robyn! I'm so sorry to hear that.'

'Do you remember me saying that I wanted to check whether my grandfather married twice? The office in London doesn't open until January 10th, so I'm hoping the church where Dad was christened will have the information I need. I've decided to drive down to Cornwall tomorrow. Any chance you could come with me to the church?'

'Of course, dear. I won't tell Morvah. Anyway, he's got a busy day tomorrow so I'll be able to slip away quite early. Text me on my mobile when you're nearby and I'll come to meet you.'

'Thanks, Em. I'm a bit of a novice at this detective work. Two heads will be better than one. See you tomorrow.'

'Gee, is that the time?' gasped Robyn, catching sight of the clock as she put down the phone. 'I'm supposed to be meeting Lori in fifteen minutes!'

Robyn hurried upstairs, dropped the final diary on her bed and grabbed her new coat before rushing off to meet her friend.

Chapter 29

Robyn pushed her way through the battered doors of the Blind Vicar, spotting Lori at a table by the fire at the far end of the pub.

'Hi! Sorry I'm a bit late,' she said, plonking herself down on the bench next to her friend who had already got the drinks in.

Robyn took a large swig of her Bacardi and Coke and peered at Lori over the rim of her glass. 'You look like the cat that got the cream. What's up?'

Lori grinned. 'I'm in love.'

'That was fast work. Let me guess, New Year's Eve?'

'Right first time. His name's Wade, he's American but lives in Southampton. He's 28 and works for the Forestry Commission.'

'A lumberjack?'

'Not really. Anyway, I thought they were Canadian. He mostly goes around checking plantations, I think. He's going to take me with him on Saturday. He's *soooo* good looking! And his accent is divine!'

'Did you meet him at the party?'

'Yes. He was all by himself, has only been in England for a few weeks. Oh, Robyn! We danced and danced, we've got the same taste in music. And even before the night was over I knew I was in love. He kissed me at midnight, just a bit of a peck. Then the band played a slow number after Auld Lang Syne and we got down to some serious snogging. Makes my toes tingle just thinking about it!'

'Have you done anything more than snog yet?'

Lori blushed. 'We went back to his flat and spent the whole day in bed. I went home on Saturday night, but I stayed with him last night. He says he loves me and wants me to move in with him.'

'Fast worker.'

'Oh, I'm not going to move in immediately. I've said we should get to know each other better first, but I know already. He's The One. I'm introducing him to Mum and Dad on Sunday, we're having dinner with them.

'Wow. It's all happening for you.'

'How was your visit with Gerald and your Millennium Eve?'

'Gerald and Martin are great, loads of fun. But the party was a bit dull. All their friends seem to be very posh and kind of old. All they talked about was the stock market, their cars, their houses, their wine cellars. Bor-ing! Still, I got to know Great Uncle William a bit better, he was staying with them too. I only came back this morning, got completely wrecked on cocktails and lost a day! But I'm not back for long. I'm flying home on Friday. Dad's taken a turn for the worse.'

'Friday!' said Lori, her eyes wide. 'Oh, Robs! What happened?'

'The doctor says they can't operate as his heart is too weak. So now it's just a matter of time. A few weeks perhaps ... sorry. I don't mean to keep crying.'

'Have a tissue. I'd cry too if I was in your shoes. Have you told Nick?'

Robyn shook her head. 'I must ring him. And I must let Waldron know, but I can't do that until they open on Wednesday.'

'Everybody will understand. Are you flying from Heathrow? Can I come and see you off?'

'Gee, that would be nice. Will you be able to get the day off work?'

'I'd like to see them stop me!' said Lori forcefully.

'I'll give Gerald and Martin a call, see if they want to come too. You'll like them, they're sort of like Frasier Crane and his brother. You know, that show on TV.'

'Would you mind if I asked Wade along too? I'd love you to meet him.'

'Yeah, bring him along. Gee, you're so lucky. I wish I had a strong man to lean on right now. Still, I suppose he'd get fed up with me crying all the time.'

'One of these days the right man will come along. Someone who won't mind if you cry all over them. By the way, I think you were right about Colin. I saw Claire the other day and she said she finished with him because he was tight-fisted. So now, thanks to you and Claire, I'll be taking what Colin says about his love life with a pinch of salt.'

Robyn grinned. 'By the way, I finished reading the diaries. Got pretty sad towards the end. My grandmother died when my Dad and Morvah were little. The woman I thought was my grandmother was probably my step-grandmother, but Dad and Morvah don't seem to know that their real mother died. Weird. I'm dashing off to Cornwall tomorrow to try and check the parish records. And I must get the diaries photocopied before I leave. Know anywhere?'

'Try the library.'

'I've got so much to do before Friday! I haven't bought any presents for the family yet.'

'The most important thing is that you get home to be with them. They won't be expecting anything else.'

'You're probably right.'

Robyn felt a bit better after her chat with Lori. As she opened the front door on her return she heard Maggie talking to someone.

'That must be her now,' she heard Maggie say. 'It's your brother on the phone, Rob,' she said, turning toward the door.

Robyn dropped her bag on the floor and ran to take the receiver from Maggie's outstretched hand. Was it more bad news?

'Steve?' she said anxiously.

'Hi, Robs. Boy, am I glad to hear you're coming home at the weekend. Mum rang me. You know all about Dad, do you?'

'Yeah, Mum told me.'

'She said he was pretty brave when the doctor told him. Of course he's worried about how Mum's going to cope when he's gone. I'm going to see him again this afternoon. I'll make sure he knows you're coming home, though I expect Mum's told him already. He's got a direct line at the hospital if you want to ring him. Have you got a pen handy?'

Robyn took down the number and chatted with her brother a little longer before hanging up.

'Okay if I ring Gerald?' called Robyn to Maggie who was in the kitchen.

Maggie came in and handed Robyn a mug of cocoa. 'Just in case you have trouble sleeping. Ring whoever you want. I'm turning in now. And make sure you use the land line, it's much cheaper than your mobile.'

'Thanks, Maggie.'

Robyn was thankful to have Maggie around at such a time. Then she remembered she also had to ring Nick to tell him she was leaving on Friday.

'Of course, no problem,' he said. It sounded like he was in a pub. 'I'll tell the people at Waldron that you won't be back. Take whatever time you need when you get back to Sydney, just give HR a call to put them in the picture. I'll be back at the end of the month.'

Robyn thanked him, rang off, and drained her mug of cocoa before ringing Gerald.

'Hello, Robin-bird. You sound a bit down in the dumps.'

'It's Dad. He's not expected to last much longer. I'm ringing to let you know I'm flying home on Friday. I'd love it if you and Martin could come to the airport to see me off. Sorry about the lack of notice.'

'Oh dear. Of course we'll be there! Just give me the flight details.'

Heartened that at least there would be a few people to see her off, Robyn went up to her room. She opened up her laptop and emailed Delia.

Dad is worse so I'm flying home on Friday. I'll be in touch. That is, if you'll speak to me. I have a feeling I've upset you by going out for dinner with Nick. See you soon I hope. Love, Lady Robinia x

While she was emailing Casey a message popped up. It was Delia.

So sory to here about yr dad. Of corse Im not cross wit yu, silly ol posh tart! Have bin ver busy lerning my lines. Drector is a nitmare! See u soon. Lov and kises, Dee xx

Robyn eventually fell asleep with Rhubarb curled up at her side.

Robyn awoke at six on Tuesday morning to the sound of the alarm on her mobile. It was still very dark. Then she remembered why she had set the alarm so early: she was driving to Cornwall. She groaned aloud. She felt very tired, as though she'd only had about an hour's sleep.

Creeping around so as not to wake Maggie at such a ridiculous hour, she washed, dressed, drank a cup of coffee and gave Rhubarb his breakfast before slipping out of the house. Luckily Clio seemed to know her way to Cornwall.

When the sky lightened Robyn noticed the clouds were very thick and white. They were sitting low on the hills, but visibility for driving was thankfully okay. She was glad it wasn't raining.

She stopped for another coffee and doughnuts after a couple of hours. When she came out of the services Robyn was astounded to see fine, white flakes falling from the sky. Snow! Her first reaction was delight at finally seeing snow, then she became concerned about difficulty getting to Cornwall if it became too heavy. But she pressed on, even though the fields were soon dusted with white. Luckily she left the snow behind somewhere through Devon.

Robyn stopped just past Truro and sent Emily a text. Emily replied instantly that she would be there within half an hour. It was almost ten o'clock.

Robyn was pleased to see Emily's car approaching just after twenty past ten.

'Good morning, dear!' she called out of her car window. 'Follow me. It's not far to Penryn, and I know where to find the parish church. I've rung the minister and he'll be there to meet us.'

'Emily, you're fantastic!' sighed Robyn, a knot of tension loosening in her stomach. She was so glad she hadn't attempted her mission alone.

Penryn was a delightful village even on a winter's morning. True to his word, the minister was waiting for them at the church. Robyn explained her query, and he took them into a back room and switched on the microfiche.

'Gee, I was expecting to see a dusty old book,' said Robyn.

'We still have our books, but all our records have been photographed onto slides. It saves wear and tear on the books. Now, what year did you say?'

'1951. The name is Maud Trescowe. She probably died towards the end of the year.'

After a few minutes of searching, the minister struck gold.

'Died November 2nd, 1951. Now I will look ahead to see if there are any marriages in the name of Trescowe.'

And within minutes they had it. Frederick had married Eleanor Prendergast, the housekeeper, on May 4th, 1952.

'Gee, Dad would have been just two, and Morvah only around eight months old. No wonder they didn't remember Maud having died, and wouldn't have really known a mother other than Eleanor.'

'Eleanor, probably shortened to Nellie,' added Emily. 'We must go home and tell Morvah. And you must ring your father.'

'There's something else, Emily. Bit of a long shot. Someone I've met at work lived in Cornwall as a child, and I have a hunch his family was involved with the murder that James Penharrack was accused of. I need to find out about a mansion near St Ives that was sold, but I don't know its name and I don't know exactly when.'

'But you do know the name of the owner?'

'Sinclair, or St Clair. He said he spent his childhood there, and as he's around Dad's age that should give us something to work with.'

'I think we'd better pay a visit to the Land Registry Office in Truro. I know where it is.'

'Emily, is there any limit to your talents?'

To Robyn's amazement, before long they found that Larkhollow Grange had been sold by Robert and Elizabeth Sinclair in 1960.

'Larkhollow!' cried Robyn. 'I knew it had something to do with birds. Paul said his father had gone broke after the war, but it seems he managed to hang on for about fifteen years before he had to sell the family home.'

'Look here at the previous owners before Robert and Elizabeth. Hubert and Madeleine St Clair.'

'Robert was their nephew. Paul said his father inherited Larkhollow when they died. But Maud wasn't convinced that Paul was actually the son of Robert and Elizabeth, and she didn't remember them applying to adopt. She didn't think Elizabeth looked pregnant, and suddenly she had a baby. Gee, what if Paul had actually been one of Hubert's illegitimate children? Josephine had some idea that her brother Lucien had been fathered by Hubert. Apart from the fact that her mother was having an affair with Hubert, Lucien was blond like Hubert and looked nothing like their parents or herself or George. Hubert was a lot older by then, but probably still capable of ...'

'Randy old goat!' said Emily with a chuckle.

'Emily, the real reason my boss sent me over here was to investigate Paul Sinclair. I found stuff on his computer that proved he was embezzling money from the company. Remembering what he told me I began to suspect he was some distant relation of Hubert and Madeleine, but if he was actually Hubert's son that would make it even more of a weird coincidence. But how to prove it?'

'DNA testing would be the answer, but if Paul's father is dead that's going to be almost impossible. And in any case very expensive and probably not legal. But at least you can take comfort from knowing that Paul is in prison. Now, while we're here perhaps we could look up Roskenner House. Any idea when George sold it?'

'George and Josephine's parents were killed in the Blitz. What year was that?'

'1940, I think.'

Emily trawled through records from 1940, and soon found the sale.

'Here we are. Roskenner House, Newlyn. Sold on 14th June 1941 to a Mr Crispin Garstang.'

'Gee, I wish I had the nerve to go down there and knock on the door. See who's living there now.'

Emily checked her watch. 'I think we'd better head back home and tell Morvah about his mother. And you can ring your Dad. Besides, it's lunchtime. I don't know about you, but I'm getting quite peckish.'

'I didn't mean we should drive all the way to Newlyn now, Em. It'll have to wait until the next time I'm in England.'

Robyn did her best to swallow her frustration at leaving unfinished business, but there was simply no time left. And in any case it would take a certain amount of courage to turn up at the front door of a mansion. What if the current owners were stuck-up and horrible?

Chapter 30

Back at the farm Emily made a start on lunch preparations.

'Can you pop out to the lower field and tell Morvah to come in?' she asked, putting a pan of home made soup on to heat.

Robyn could see her uncle fixing some fencing in the distance. In her mind she turned over how she might tell him that the mother he remembered wasn't the one who had given birth to him. But that was up to Emily.

'Weren't you going to ring your Dad?' said Emily pointedly as they cleared the table after lunch.

'Thanks, Em,' said Robyn, knowing she had a difficult conversation ahead.

'Morvah, let's take our coffee out to the conservatory,' said Emily. 'I've got something to tell you.'

Joseph answered after a couple of rings.

'Robyn! Lovely to hear your voice, m'girl. What time is it at your end?'

'Just gone half past one in the afternoon, Dad. I hope I didn't wake you. Did Mum tell you I'm coming home on Friday?'

'Yes, she did. I'm glad. What day is it today?'

He sounded vague. Robyn felt her vocal cords constrict and tears spring to her eyes. She took a deep breath. 'It's Tuesday. I'm sorry I didn't send you any more of the diaries. I'll bring them with me. I was going to rush a copy off to you but I'll probably get there quicker. I've just finished reading the last book, and I've stumbled on a really weird coincidence. You know your grandfather James was on the run from the police, suspected of murdering a servant at the Roquebrun farm? Much later on in the diaries, Robert Sinclair, nephew of Hubert St Clair, is having dinner with Maud and Frederick and he gets a bit drunk and tells Frederick that Hubert murdered a friend's maid because she was pregnant by him and threatening to tell his wife, Madeleine. Robert said Roquebrun managed to convince the police that a farm hand had committed the murder. It's too much of a coincidence. I think he meant James had taken the rap for what Hubert had done.'

'I see what you mean, m'girl.'

'And there's more. The real reason Nick sent me over here was to try and catch one of the senior executives who was embezzling from Waldron, where I've been working.'

'My daughter the international spy! I'd no idea!'

'Nor did I until after I arrived. It took some doing, but I found his duplicate records and the police took him away shortly before Christmas. It will be a while before the case comes up for trial, but meanwhile he's in prison. Anyway, I got talking to the embezzler, Paul Sinclair, some weeks before it all came out. He was interested that I had relatives in Cornwall because he was born there. To cut a long story short, I'm convinced he was adopted as a newborn baby by Robert Sinclair. And there's a possibility his real father was Hubert. How weird is that?'

'Amazing. It's as though you've had your revenge on the St Clair family on behalf of your great-grandfather. Sounds like the lot of them were rotten to the core.'

'Yeah, and I hadn't figured out who Paul was at the time. And there's more. The next bit is kind of disgusting, so forgive me. Madeleine St Clair, Hubert's wife, seduced James when he delivered a parcel from the farm to her house. She made him visit the house several times after to have sex with her. He confessed to Josephine and she wrote about it in her diary. Josephine also had a feeling that her mother was having an affair with Hubert, and that Hubert may have been Lucien's father.'

'How bizarre.'

'There's something else. I don't quite know how to tell you.'

'After that lot I don't think anything else can shock me. Fire away, m'girl.'

'You remember you couldn't understand why your mother's name was listed as Maud on your birth certificate, whereas she was known as Nellie. Well, I've found out why. Your mother, Maud, died a few months after your first birthday, shortly after she had Morvah. Your father married Nellie a few months later. Her name was Eleanor Prendergast, she was a widow who came to live in as a housekeeper and look after you and Morvah when your mother became ill.'

There was a silence of a few seconds, then Joseph spoke.

'Does Morvah know?'

'Emily's telling him right now. I sort of figured it out when I got near the end of the diaries, but Emily and I went this morning to the church where you were christened. The minister was very nice, he let us look through the records.'

'Why on earth our parents never told us I will never understand. Still, it's all water under the bridge now. My darling girl, you've done a first-rate job.'

'I haven't done much more than read the diaries. And if Moira hadn't called in on Emily and Morvah while I was there I never would have got hold of them. Grampy, that's your Uncle William, denied knowing anything about the family history when I asked him. Yet it was he who had the diaries, and I suppose he's read them. It was a bit weird while we were both staying with Gerald over the New Year. I was reading all this stuff but I didn't feel I could discuss it with him. I told Gerald some stuff, but asked him not to say anything to Grampy as he seems a bit touchy about it.'

'I suppose denial is William's way of dealing with unhappy memories.'

'That's what I reckon. He mostly talks about what a good time he had during the war. Dad, I'm looking through the diaries and I can't remember which ones I've sent you. How far have you read?'

'The ones I have finish shortly after my mother was born.'

'Right. I'll look through them now and fill you in briefly on the rest.'

'This call will be costing you a fortune, m'girl.'

'I'm at Emily and Morvah's place. Don't worry, I'll make sure I give them some money. Now, I've found the bit where your mother was born …'

'I have some memories of Granny Josephine. We never knew Grandfather James, but I remember visiting other relatives in Truro.'

'That would have been your Great Uncle George, Josephine's brother. He wore a calliper on one leg.'

'Yes, it's coming back to me now. He was a nice man, used to give me boiled sweets.'

Time sped by while Robyn brought her father up to date on the remaining diaries. When she eventually hung up it was with a sense of satisfaction and relief. Now it was simply a matter of getting on that plane back to Sydney.

Robyn found Morvah and Emily sitting quietly in the conservatory.

'Good bit of detective work,' said Morvah gruffly. 'How did Joseph take the news?'

'He was a bit shocked. So you had no idea either?'

Morvah shook his head. 'If my Dad was still alive I'd knock his block off.'

'I suppose he felt embarrassed about marrying again so quickly. It's getting dark already,' said Emily, changing the subject. 'Why don't you stay the night, Robyn? I've got a nice casserole in the oven.'

Robyn didn't need much persuading. She spent a cosy evening enjoying a hearty meal and watching television with her aunt and uncle.

'I'll turn in if you don't mind,' she said shortly after ten o'clock.

'I'm glad you didn't leave earlier, dear. It's snowing.'

'Gee, I hope I don't get snowed in. Not that I don't enjoy being here, but there are loads of things I need to do before I leave on Friday.'

'We don't often get snowed in,' reassured Emily. 'Sleep well, dear.'

It was only to be expected that sleep would elude Robyn that night. There were too many thoughts running through her head like speeding cars. She went over every word of her conversation with her father, relieved that she'd managed to solve the mystery of his mother's name. She wondered whether cancer was hereditary. She revelled in her father's delight at finally getting some answers about their complicated family history. She wished she'd had time to do more, but that was a good excuse for a return visit.

But would there really be any point once her father was gone? Somehow she had to prepare for his imminent death. Just a matter of weeks ... It was far easier to live under the illusion that somehow he would get up from his bed and everything would be back to normal. But no, he would most likely be in hospital, hooked up to whatever paraphernalia they had to keep him alive. He would probably be doped up with drugs, barely able to acknowledge her return. She knew she had been lucky to catch him on a comparatively good day for their lengthy conversation.

What to say to Mum once they were alone together? What could you say to a woman who was about to lose her husband, her life companion, the father of her children? Much as Robyn wanted to meet a man and settle down, she was beginning to think life would be much easier if she remained single. So much heartache would be spared.

It was little comfort to know that other people all across the world were going through the agony of losing their loved ones. Husbands and fathers, wives, mothers, sons and daughters, dying in wars, road accidents, and from hideous diseases.

To lighten her mood Robyn got her laptop out of its bag and sent an email to Delia and Casey.

Advance warning: I've gained a little weight while I've been away. Correction – a lot of weight. Pounds and pounds of disgusting blubber. The rellies are all great cooks and, as you know, I have no willpower. I won't be

able to show my face (or my body) on the beach for the rest of the summer,
and I'll have to go on the diet to end all diets to shift this lot. Sadly my
boobs are still disappointingly small. Life is never fair. Please be kind to
me, don't laugh. Love from your fat friend, Lady Robinia xx

Robyn awakened the following morning to total silence. When she looked
out of the window she saw the world had turned white overnight. The fields
were blanketed with snow, and it was difficult to tell where they sky ended
and the earth began.

She pulled on a jumper over the nightie Emily had lent her and hurried
downstairs. Emily and Morvah were already in the kitchen.

'Wow! I thought you said you didn't get snowed in here?' she said,
wriggling her toes on the cold floor.

'This doesn't count as snowed in,' replied Morvah. 'Snowed in is when
the cars are completely buried, and when we can't get out of the front door.'

Looking out of the front door, Robyn saw that Clio was wearing a fluffy
white hat but was otherwise visible.

'Gee, I'd better ring Maggie. Find out what it's like in Eastleigh,' said
Robyn, heading upstairs for her mobile.

Maggie answered quickly. 'Just a scattering of snow here, Rob. I think it
was worse in Devon and Cornwall. Check the weather report on TV before
you start driving though.'

Morvah went one better. He tuned in to a local radio station and got the
farmers' weather report for Cornwall, Devon, Dorset and Hampshire.

'You should be all right, lass,' he reassured her.

'I'll cook you a good breakfast, dear,' added Emily. 'And you must take
some food, a flask of hot drink, a blanket and a shovel with you. And make
sure your mobile is fully charged.'

After showering Robyn presented herself at the breakfast table and put
away a plateful of bacon and eggs and a couple of slices of toast and home
made marmalade. Having borrowed wellington boots in addition to the rest
of the equipment suggested for driving in hazardous weather, she felt ready
to face the world.

'If it gets too bad, lass, give me a call and I'll come and get you in the
Land Rover,' called Morvah as Robyn set off cautiously.

It was a strange experience driving down the snowy lane. Robyn imagined
a sheep on ice skates would feel much the same. Everything happened in
slow motion, and she had to be very careful not to brake or steer suddenly.
However the main road was completely clear. It looked as though some sort

of machine had been through already, scooping the snow off the road and depositing it in a muddy hump at each side of the road.

When she stopped for a coffee she put in a call to Morvah and Emily to say everything was fine.

'We'll see you at the airport on Friday, lass,' said Morvah.

Robyn kept to a modest speed, concerned about the dreaded black ice that everyone went on about. Invisible stuff that you didn't know about until your car had skidded off the road. Eventually she reached the outskirts of Eastleigh and heaved a sigh of relief.

'Here I am!' she called to Maggie as she closed the front door behind her. 'That was quite an experience!'

'Glad you made it in one piece, Rob,' said Maggie, looking up from the bowl she was stirring. Packets of flour and dried fruit littered the kitchen table.

'Gee, driving on snow is weird. But once I got on the main road I had a clear run. However there was quite a lot of traffic.'

'Probably people out shopping, panic buying in case they get snowed in. Crazy. I've left my glasses upstairs, Rob. What quantity of apricots should I be adding to my cake?'

Robyn consulted the recipe. 'Umm, a hundred grams.'

Robyn had one of those lightbulb moments. She had been racking her brain for something to give Maggie as a farewell gift, and suddenly she had it.

'That looks about right,' said Maggie, plonking a handful of apricots on the chopping board and attacking them with a small knife. 'Have you had lunch?'

'No. Have you?'

'I thought I'd wait until you returned. Then I got sidetracked making this cake. Now I could eat a horse. I'll just get this in the oven then we can eat.'

'Maggie, how come you eat so well and don't gain weight?'

'Just lucky, I suppose. Although I do lead a more active life than the average pensioner I suppose. Anyway, did you find what you wanted in the parish records?'

As they tucked into sandwiches that Robyn made hastily while Maggie was adding the last ingredients to her cake mix, Robyn filled Maggie in on the latest developments. The sky was growing dark again by the time they'd cleared up after lunch. Another day almost over, thought Robyn with a pang of alarm.

'I don't know how I'm going to get ready to leave by Friday. There just seems to be so much I have to do!' she wailed.

Maggie rummaged in a kitchen drawer and produced a notepad and a pen.

'Write it all down, then number the tasks in order of priority.'

After a cup of strong coffee and some concentrated brain activity Robyn concocted her list. She decided her first task should be to phone Gerald and Martin. She gave Gerald a precis of the last of the diaries and the repercussions they had caused.

'Oh my, to think Grampy's been sitting on that lot for years. Still, as you say, best to let sleeping dogs lie. We'll be sorry to see you go, Robin-bird, but we'll be there at the airport on Friday morning.'

'That would be great, but what if it snows again?'

'Finito de fretto, my dear. We only had a few flakes here in London. Your plane will be flying, and we'll be there to see you off.'

Robyn realised her farewell was starting to turn into a party. Much better to go off in style than just slink through the airport unnoticed.

Suddenly Robyn's mobile rang. It was Lori.

'I'm phoning to invite you to dinner tonight. Sorry for short notice. Can you make it?'

'That sounds good. I think I've got a window in my Filofax.'

'I'd really like you to meet Wade properly, so I thought dinner at his place would be ideal. I'll give you his address. Have you got a street map of Southampton?'

'Yeah, I bought a book of local maps.'

'See you around seven, then?'

'Just hope it doesn't snow again tonight. I had to stay with Emily and Morvah last night. Snow looks great, but it's a bit of a nuisance.'

'Welcome to the real world, Robs. See you later, alligator.'

Robyn smiled as she ended the call. She knew she would miss Lori's easy friendship when she returned home. Looking at her watch, she saw it was a quarter to four already. She wanted to get a little something for Lori as well as a bottle of wine for dinner.

After a quick change of clothes Robyn jumped in her car and sped off to Southampton, thankful to find a car park in the city centre without difficulty. She'd abandoned the idea of buying presents to take home, but wanted gifts to thank the people who had made her stay in England so enjoyable. But what to buy?

First she ventured into a large bookshop.

'Do you have any Australian cook books?' she enquired.

The snooty assistant looked at Robyn as though she'd asked for a kilo of sausages.

'I wasn't aware that there was such a thing, but I'll check on the computer.'

After several minutes of tapping and tutting the assistant confirmed that there was no such thing as an Australian cook book. At least not in that shop. So Robyn went in search of other bookshops.

Time was ticking by. She trawled through several second-hand bookshops. In one she came across something Lori might like, a light-hearted books of magic spells which mostly seemed to deal with catching a man's attention, enhancing your womanliness and keeping said man entranced for the rest of his days. The book was fortunately in good condition so she snapped it up.

A book for Maggie required the sort of lateral thinking that was best done with the aid of tea and cake, but there was no time. In the next bookshop Robyn ventured into the travel section and luckily found something she thought Maggie would enjoy: *Australia by Motorbike*. And, surprisingly, something for Gerald and Martin. Now she was really on a roll!

Grampy was easier to buy for: a bottle of whisky. She bought wine for Emily and Morvah, and a bottle to take to dinner that night. The last gift however was proving the most difficult. What on earth to give Morwenna and Colum? Finally, despairing and footsore, Robyn gave in and bought a book token just as the shop was closing.

Six o'clock. Still a bit early to turn up for dinner, and Robyn didn't want to spoil her appetite by killing time in a café. So she made her way slowly back to the car, studying the shop windows in great detail. This proved to be a mistake, for with time on her hands she started thinking about her father. By the time she got to the car park Robyn felt more like heading back to Maggie's than meeting Lori's new man.

Chapter 31

Robyn gave herself a stern talking-to. Lori would be very disappointed if she pleaded a headache and backed out of the dinner invitation. Heaving a sigh, she consulted her map for directions to Wade's apartment. Then she hastily wrapped Lori's gift, regretting that she had no scissors to cut the paper. And she'd thought she was so clever remembering to buy tape!

Without too much difficulty Robyn found the park Lori had mentioned on the phone, and a few minutes later drew up outside the smart-looking block of flats. She pushed through the heavy glass doors and crossed the glossy tiles of the foyer. The lift opened obediently at her approach, and she selected the tenth floor from the illuminated panel.

Even the doorbell of apartment 1003 sounded refined. Within seconds Lori appeared at the door.

'Hello, Robs. Ooh, wine! Thanks. Come on in!' said Lori.

'I've also got you a little farewell gift, but don't open it yet.'

'Why on earth not?'

'You'll see. Now, where is he, this man of your dreams?'

'Right here,' said a deep voice from inside the apartment.

Robyn cringed with embarrassment.

'Robyn, I'd like you to meet Wade,' said Lori.

Robyn turned to meet an extended hand which she shook. A firm, manly hand. Her eyes travelled up Wade's denim-clad body to his bronzed face and twinkly blue eyes. Lori was right. He was a total hunk. Robyn drifted off into a brief fantasy, picturing Wade clad only in a pair of shorts, posing with a chainsaw for the Forestry Commission calendar.

'Pleased to meet'cha, Robyn,' he said in a voice that was peanut butter and caramel swirled together. Her mouth watered with a reaction fit for one of Pavlov's dogs.

'Howdy,' said Robyn, immediately wishing she hadn't. 'I mean, hello. Good to meet you too.'

Lori broke the awkward silence. 'Lovely coat! Did you buy it in London?'

'Yeah, thought it was time I pensioned off the old horse blanket,' said Robyn, shrugging out of her designer purchase. She realised she'd been wearing it when she'd met Lori for a drink the other night, but Lori had probably been too blinded by love to notice. 'Amazing how many shops were open on New Year's Day,' added Robyn.

'Poor folks having to get into work early and be nice to the customers all day despite their hangovers,' said Wade. 'Give me a forest any day.'

He ushered Robyn into the immaculate sitting room, a vision in chrome and white. 'Set yourself down, Robyn. What would you like to drink?'

'A glass of water, please. I'll risk one glass of wine with dinner, but I have to stay sober enough to drive home.'

'Still or sparkling water?'

'Oh, let's push the boat out. Sparkling, please.'

'I'll have the same please, Wade,' said Lori. 'I need to stay sober enough to cook.'

While Wade was in the kitchen Lori picked up her gift. 'Feels like a book. Can I open it yet?'

'Okay, but don't show Wade. He might think it's a bit weird. He's gorgeous, by the way.'

'Isn't he just!' said Lori, undoing the paper. 'Oh, Robs! It's beautiful! And you've written inside the cover. You're right, though. I'll put it in my bag for now. Don't want Wade to think we're a pair of scheming witches.'

'Lovely view,' said Robyn, sinking into a squishy white leather sofa by the plate glass windows. 'Stunning apartment too.'

'Here's your water,' said Wade as Lori disappeared into the kitchen.

'Thanks. Now I'm not much of an expert on American accents, but I'd say you were from the southern states.'

'That's right. Alabama. A little town called Twisted Tree, population around a hundred.'

'What brought you to England?' enquired Robyn, sipping her water and wishing it was wine.

'I'm teaching some English people a few things about forestry management. Lori already told me a bit about your stay in England. So you're flying home on Friday?'

'Yes.'

'Soup's ready,' said Lori, entering with two steaming bowls. 'Please be seated,' she said, indicating the dining table on the other side of the room.

Lori produced an excellent meal, and Robyn was amused to note a few Americanisms slipping into her speech already. Wade seemed totally

265

smitten with her, likewise she with him. Robyn felt glad that her friend had met someone so charming and sincere. If only her own Millennium Eve had been as productive, she thought for a moment, then realising the last thing she needed was a new relationship in view of her imminent departure.

As Wade poured her a second cup of coffee, Robyn suddenly noticed the time was approaching eleven p.m.

'Gee, I didn't mean to stay this late. I'd better drink up and get on my way.'

Robyn hugged Lori at the door and thanked them both for a lovely evening. Wade also moved in for a hug, and Robyn revelled for a moment in the perfection of his physique and the manly scent of his aftershave. Lori was a lucky, lucky girl.

'See you on Friday morning,' said Lori with a grin.

On the drive back to Eastleigh Robyn found herself wishing that her father had come to England with her. He would have loved spending time with Morvah and the rest of the family, reading the diaries first hand and unravelling for himself the tangled web of the past. She berated herself for not having thought to invite him. But then how would they have coped with his illness being so far from home? By the time she turned into Maggie's street she felt very down in the dumps. It was desperately unfair that her father had so little time left.

Maggie was still up watching TV. 'Enjoy your evening, dear?'

Robyn forced a smile. 'Yes, thanks. Lori's new man is gorgeous, and I've eaten far too much as usual. I think I need a nightcap to help me sleep.'

'What about a brandy?'

Maggie poured two generous measures.

'I've got something for you,' said Robyn, bringing forth the book she'd bought. 'Sorry I haven't wrapped it, but I hope it will inspire you to come and visit me in Australia. But you don't have to travel by motorbike if you don't want to.'

Maggie hugged Robyn. 'Thanks. You never know, the climate's probably great for biking. I've got a little something for you, too,' she added, opening a drawer of the sideboard.

It was a framed photograph of Rhubarb. Robyn felt a bit choked up at the thought that she would soon have to leave the little ginger cat behind. She and Maggie sat companionably for a while, drinking brandy and chatting about nothing in particular. Rhubarb joined them and settled cosily on Robyn's lap, kneading her thighs with his paws.

'You know what I think?' said Maggie as she took their empty glasses through to the kitchen.

'Surprise me.'

'I think we should go out for a slap-up meal tomorrow night. Just the two of us. My treat. I know the very place.'

'That's very kind of you, Maggie. I'll look forward to it.'

Robyn faced up to the inevitable on Thursday morning. She started the mammoth task of packing her belongings, seeing how much she could cram into the suitcase she'd arrived with. Not much, it turned out. So she had to decide what could be left behind. How had she accumulated so much clutter in such a short time?

Well, for a start she wouldn't need any winter clothes once she was back in Sydney. Once she'd put all the woolly stuff to one side the pile seemed a bit less daunting. She hadn't realised people had given her so many gifts while she'd been in England. These she couldn't bear to part with, so space somehow had to be made. The little drum Lori had given her for Christmas fortunately fitted inside one of her trainers. Most of the bulky gifts seeemed to be family photographs Emily had given her. These Robyn decided to remove from their frames, and that helped lighten the load.

Nearly ten o'clock already. Next on the agenda was returning the diaries to Moira, so she put in a call to check that Moira was at home.

Robyn's next task was to take copies of the rest of the diaries for Dad to read, and then buy a thank you gift for Moira.

After what seemed like an age at the photocopier in the local library she eventually arrived at Moira's just before twelve o'clock, having rung to apologise for the delay. As Robyn opened the gate and walked up the path she could hear what sounded like a battle taking place inside the house. Shouts, whoops and banging reverberated on the chill afternoon air. She hoped Moira's neighbours were hard of hearing.

Moira answered the door, looking rather harassed. 'Kids! Out in the garden, now!' she bellowed.

The boy and girl looked to be around ten years old. They picked up their weapons and made their way noisily through the house, dodging around furniture as they pretend-fired their guns.

Casting her eyes around the wreckage of toys in the room Robyn realised just what a difference a couple of children could make. Were Joey and Olivia this bad? Moira seemed at her wits' end; her hair was sticking up every which way and she had what looked like chocolate stains on the sleeve of her expensive-looking blouse.

'They're driving me crazy,' she said, shaking her head and rolling her yes. 'Teacher training today, so no school. You'd think the bloody teachers would be trained already, but at least once each term they have these stupid training days. Coffee?'

'That would be nice, as long as it's not too much trouble. I've brought you the diaries, and a little something to say thanks. I've only just finished reading them all. I spoke to Dad yesterday and filled him in on the rest of the story. He's very pleased to know why we aren't related to any other Rostrevors in the area, and all the other info has been fascinating.'

Robyn put the diaries on the kitchen table and handed Moira the bottle of wine she'd bought.

'Thanks. I may be forced to drink this before the day is out, but for now I'll try to make do with coffee.'

They sat in the comparative peace of the kitchen, with faint sounds of the children at war drifting in from the garden. Robyn was glad it was a big garden.

'Sadly Dad's not going to be around much longer,' said Robyn. 'The doctors have given him just a few weeks.'

'I'm sorry to hear that. Biscuit?'

Robyn didn't stay long. Well, long enough to wolf down four biscuits with her coffee. Although she was eternally grateful to Moira for the diaries she didn't feel a great rapport with her.

With the day fast disappearing Robyn decided to do some shopping in Ringwood. She'd passed the town on the way to Moira's and it seemed likely to have a decent shopping centre.

In an exclusive department store she bought a set of elegant wine glasses for Emily and Morvah, to accompany the bottle of wine she'd bought the day before. In the toy department she found some fairy wings that she hoped Olivia would like. Ticking off the items on her fingers as she walked back to the car, Robyn was relieved that she now had something for everyone.

Back in Eastleigh Robyn decided to call her mother. Fortunately Rose picked up after a couple of rings.

'Hello, Mum. How's things?'

'Much the same, love, although your Dad seemed a bit brighter today. He's really looking forward to seeing you. I must warn you, though, he's lost a lot of weight. They give him high-protein milkshakes but he can't take in much.'

'Oh, Mum ...'

'Steve and Jules will be there to meet you at the airport,' said her mother, changing the subject.

'It looks like I'm getting quite a send-off at this end. All the Trescowe mob are coming up from Cornwall, and Gerald and Martin will be there, and my friend Lori and her boyfriend Wade. I'll ring you again before I leave, Mum. Love you lots, and give my love to Dad.'

Robyn felt a small sense of relief as she hung up. Everything was starting to come together. Just one more sleep and she'd be on her way home.

Next job on the list was taking her surplus winter clothing to a charity shop. While in town she sampled a last slice of cake in her favourite tea shop. After all, she'd had no lunch and it was still early enough not to spoil her appetite for dinner.

Robyn borrowed a blouse from Maggie to wear for their night out. It was a colourful chiffon garment that went well with her black trousers, and disguised the rolls of fat around her middle. Maggie looked ethnically stylish in a flowing cotton dress.

'Here we are,' said Maggie as their taxi drew up outside a sprawling pub on the outskirts of town. 'This place has a very good reputation for seafood. You do like fish, don't you?'

'Of course. It's compulsory for Sydneysiders to devour prawns and scallops by the bucketload.'

They were seated in a quiet, dark alcove in the upstairs restaurant.

'Posh in here, isn't it?' commented Robyn, noting the array of shiny cutlery in front of her. 'No paper serviettes in this joint.'

They started with half a dozen oysters each.

'Mmm,' said Robyn. 'Just as good as anything I've had at home. Plump and succulent.'

'Just the way an oyster should be,' said Maggie, squeezing lemon on the last of hers.

'I'm going to treat us to some real Champagne,' announced Robyn. The restaurant was pricey, and she didn't want Maggie to pay for everything. Thankfully she'd thought to bring her credit card.

The waiter returned and made a great performance of opening the bottle and filling their glasses.

'When I do that I usually misjudge it and the bubbles overflow,' whispered Robyn as the waiter slipped back into the shadows. 'I suppose he's been to waiter school to learn how to do it properly. Years of experience don't seem to have made me any better at it.'

'Here are our main courses already,' said Maggie. 'Wow! Smell that garlic!'

Maggie had opted for garlic prawns, and Robyn had a trio of fish. She raised her glass in a toast.

'Thanks, Maggie. Not just for tonight, but for everything. You've been a great friend and I'm going to miss you.'

'I'll miss you too. And so will Rhubarb.'

'Gee, I'll miss him too, but I could never put him through the hassle of flying to Australia. I know he's better off with you. He has a garden to play in, whereas I live in a concrete jungle.'

'I'm sure it's not that bad.'

'I do love Sydney, but my flat isn't a great place for a cat. No room to swing one, for starters.'

'That's a daft saying, isn't it? Who would be so cruel as to swing a cat by its tail?'

Of course the pair managed to make room for dessert. Robyn tried lemon posset for the first time.

'So light!' she sighed blissfully. 'There can't be many calories, they must have all floated away.'

'Dream on, it's ninety-nine percent cream.'

Sated and mellow, they piled into their taxi and headed back to River Lane.

'Coffee? Brandy?' suggested Maggie.

'I'd explode. Thanks anyway, but I think I'll turn in while I'm feeling sleepy. Thanks again for a lovely night.'

Robyn settled down for her last night in Maggie's house. Her alarm was set for seven a.m. Soon she would be on her way. Before long she would be back home to spend whatever time was left with her poor, ailing father. Within minutes she was fast asleep.

Chapter 32

Robyn awoke before the alarm. She sat bolt upright, her heart hammering in her chest, convinced she'd overslept. A glance at her mobile phone reassured her that it was not yet half past six, and she settled back on her pillows with a sigh. Rhubarb opened one eye and closed it again before settling back to sleep at the foot of the bed.

'What I need is a nice cup of tea,' she informed the sleeping cat as she slipped out of bed and into her dressing gown and slippers.

Downstairs while waiting for the kettle to boil, Robyn heard the phone ringing. Who on earth could it be at this hour?

'Hello? Robbie, is that you?'

Robyn felt a warm rush of relief. 'Hello, Mum! That was good timing. I've just got out of bed. I was going to ring you shortly. Not long now and I'll be on that plane. How's Dad?'

Rose Trescowe sighed. 'Oh, Robbie. He's gone. Just a few minutes ago. He just … slipped away. At least I was with him at the end. So was Steve.'

'Mum! No!' gasped Robyn, tears welling in her eyes. What did she mean? Surely he was just in a coma.

'I'm sorry, Robbie. I was hoping he'd hang on until you returned. I kept telling him you were on your way. But he just … At least he's not suffering any more.'

'Oh, Mum …'

'Here's Steve.'

'Rob? You okay?'

'Tell me it's not true! He can't be dead, not yet …'

'Sorry, Rob. He was very weak, he couldn't hang on any longer. What time does your flight land?'

'I … I can't remember!' sobbed Robyn, suddenly panicked.

'Don't worry, I've got your flight number, I'll ring the airline. I'll be there to meet you. Hang in there, sis.'

Suddenly the connection was severed as her brother rang off. Robyn slumped against the wall, the phone still in her hand.

Maggie appeared at the top of the stairs.

'What's wrong, Rob?'

'It's Dad. He's … dead.'

Moving like an automaton, Robyn somehow managed to scrape herself and her luggage together. But her head was all over the place. How could she drive to the rental office at Heathrow and return the car?

'We can go in my car,' suggested Maggie.

Maggie rang the hire company and arranged to return Clio to the Southampton depot the following day.

'Maggie, I don't know what I'd do without you,' said Robyn with a watery smile.

Despite her distress Robyn managed to put some money in an envelope for Maggie along with a card, which she taped to a bottle of very good brandy that she'd had the foresight to buy earlier in the week. It was difficult to know how much to allow for all the phone calls she'd made to Australia. And there was also Maggie's petrol for today's trip to Heathrow, and transport back from Southampton tomorrow after returning the hire car. She hoped she'd erred on the side of generosity.

Robyn heaved her suitcase onto the back seat of Maggie's car. The things Morvah and Emily had lent her on Wednesday morning she put in a bag in the boot, and could only hope she or Maggie remembered to hand them over at the airport.

Robyn paused to say a silent farewell to the house. She had already said a private and tearful farewell to Rhubarb and given him a tin of salmon for his breakfast which he'd sniffed disinterestedly before settling back to sleep.

With Maggie at the wheel they soon left the urban sprawl of Eastleigh behind. Robyn looked out across the countryside as the early morning mist evaporated to show the promise of a clear, sunny day. England seemed determined to leave a picture of sunny skies in her mind to obliterate any memories of dismal grey days full of rain.

The journey to Heathrow passed in a blur. Robyn was unable to form coherent thoughts, let alone voice them. But she knew Maggie didn't expect anything much in the way of conversation.

Once inside the terminal and in possession of a trolley, Robyn and Maggie headed for the check-in desk. They were ahead of schedule, but Morvah and Emily were already there by the desk. Robyn introduced Maggie to her aunt and uncle.

'I've got a bag of things for you in the boot of my car,' said Maggie.

Morvah and Emily looked puzzled.

'The shovel, blanket, flask and wellingtons you lent Robyn the other day.'

'I'd better get myself checked in,' said Robyn, wondering how she was going to break the news of her father's death. Saying it would make it real.

With Robyn busy at the desk, Emily laid her hand on Maggie's arm and brought her head close to whisper. 'We had a phone call from Robyn's brother. Luckily he had my mobile number. Does she know about her father?'

Maggie nodded. 'Her mother rang earlier this morning. Very sad. I'm glad Steve rang you. Robyn's been agonising over how to tell you.'

'Poor lass,' said Morvah, shaking his head despondently.

'I'm sorry too for your loss,' said Maggie.

When Robyn returned she instantly knew.

Morvah nodded. 'Steve phoned us. Sorry, lass.'

Robyn shrugged and pulled an expression of resignation. 'At least he's not suffering any more.'

'Morwenna and Colum and the little 'un send their condolences, sorry they couldn't make it today,' said Morvah.

'And William too,' said Emily. 'He sends his love.'

Then Gerald and Martin arrived, followed closely by Lori and Wade. After the introductions had been made, Robyn took Lori to one side.

'I had a phone call this morning. Dad's just died.'

Lori held her friend close. 'Oh, Robyn! I'm so sorry.'

'Please don't make a fuss or I'll start crying again. Serious risk of a major flood alert.' Robyn managed a feeble smile to accompany her attempt at humour.

Lori gently released her friend, then Wade came forward with a gold-wrapped package.

'We got you a little something,' he said.

'Hope you like it,' added Lori awkwardly.

'Gee, thanks!' said Robyn, hugging them both and opening the box to find a beautiful necklace.

Within moments gifts were flying back and forth.

'I hope you don't mind taking the things I've got for Olivia and Morwenna and Colum and William,' said Robyn to Emily.

Gerald and Martin gave Robyn a tiara.

'It's compulsory attire considering your titled background,' said Gerald.

Within minutes Robyn acquired enough carrier bags to make her look like a bag lady. A very posh bag lady wearing a tiara and a necklace.

'Lucky I only had my handbag as hand luggage,' she whispered to Maggie as she stuffed the smaller carriers inside the largest so she ended up with just one.

Then Martin noticed Robyn's flight had been announced.

'Well, everyone, the time has come,' said Robyn, taking a deep breath to stem the quaver in her voice. 'Thank you all for your gifts, and I hope you like the things I've given you. It's been great getting to know you all, and I'll miss you ...'

The group became a mass of hugs and promises to stay in touch.

'Email me as soon as you can,' said Emily. 'I'm only sorry we can't be there at Joseph's funeral.'

Robyn noticed Morvah had taken Gerald to one side. He was no doubt explaining about her father.

'Robin-bird, I'm so sorry ...' said Gerald.

'Thanks, Gerald,' said Robyn with a tight smile. 'Well, goodbye everyone, and thanks once again. I'll start saving for a return visit, but in the meantime you'll all be very welcome if you want to come and visit us.'

'What, all of us at once?' quipped Martin.

Robyn picked up her hand luggage and set off with a cheery wave. People turned and stared.

She turned back for a last glance as she disappeared through the double doors, beyond which a travelator waited to carry her away down the long corridor. As she stepped onto it her mobile phone rang. She dropped the cumbersome carrier bag at her feet and fished her phone out of her handbag.

'Hi, sis,' said Steve. 'Where are you?'

'I'm just about to get on the plane. What's up?'

'Just checking on you.'

'I'm okay. How are you? And Mum?'

'Mum's asleep. We're at home now, and the doctor's given her a sedative. I don't think it's really hit me yet that Dad's gone.'

'Nor me. I don't think it'll sink in until I get home. Is Jules there with you?'

'Yes. She's with Joey in the kitchen. He doesn't really understand what's going on.'

'Poor kid. I'd better go now, here's my departure lounge.'

'I'll be there at the airport, Rob. I've got your arrival time. See you soon.'

'Thanks, Steve.'

Robyn switched her mobile off before returning it to her handbag. A man shot her a disapproving glare as he stepped over her hand luggage. As she picked it up she realised she was still wearing her tiara, so she took it off and tucked it into her handbag with a smile. People probably thought she was on a hen weekend, possibly the bride.

There was already a queue of parents with young children slowly making their way through the departure gate, followed by two ladies in wheelchairs.

Then it was Robyn's turn to pass through the gate, past the smiling faces of the airport staff. Strangers who didn't know that her father had just died. She found she could smile back at them and play the part of the jet-setter, looking smart in her new coat and stylish necklace.

Once on board Robyn let the tide of humanity carry her forward until she found her seat. Then, with her hand luggage stowed in the overhead locker, she sat back and took a deep breath. All around her people were chattering happily, setting out on their separate adventures.

Only when the plane made its mighty leap into the sky did Robyn begin to feel a sense of parting. The places and people, and the way of life that had become familiar over recent months, were now a thing of the past. They became smaller and less distinct, like the toytown landscape spread out below. Then the plane banked steeply and headed out across the ocean, leaving England behind.

Robyn took another deep breath and tried to clear her mind of dismal thoughts. At least the millennium bugs supposed to throw the world's computer systems into chaos didn't seem to have materialised. Disruption to her flight would have been too much to bear.

She noticed the couple on her left were holding hands. Newly-weds perhaps? And the little boy in the seat ahead, asleep already. Was he on his way to meet relatives in Australia, people he'd never seen before?

Robyn looked ahead at the screen in front of her, at the simplistic map showing a little aeroplane following a dotted line across Europe and Asia to Singapore, where those like herself onward bound for Australia would board their next flight. She willed the little plane to eat up the miles, to make a mighty leap and get this tiresome journey over and done with.

She whiled away some time replaying yet again her final conversation with her father, hoping she would never forget the sound of his voice.

Robyn resolved to return to England as soon as possible. There was so much more she wanted to research. How many chldren did William and Annie Rostrevor have? Was George Trethewey still alive aged eighty-nine? And what about his wife and children? If George had died, the eldest son would be the current Lord Kenner. And what had happened to all the money left to Josephine and George when their parents died? Next time she'd pluck up the courage to visit Roskenner House. She could introduce herself as a descendant of the former owner. There were probably a whole lot more relatives yet to be discovered. And perhaps she could continue her investigations in France, delving into Caroline de Crespigny's lineage, and the St Clair family …

Robyn knew that somehow she would pick up the threads and life would go on. They would all, Mum included, find ways to get through each day now that Dad was gone. All she had to do was hold to that thought and believe.

THE END

Thank you for reading *Beyond the Island*. I would be grateful if you could take a few minutes to return to Amazon or Lulu, give a rating for the novel and leave your comments.

My website is www.karennegriffin.yolasite.com and you can follow me on Twitter @KarenneG

Regards, Karenne Griffin.